# Handling Mr. Harper

Elle Nicoll

Rose Hope Publishing Ltd.

**<u>Author's Notes</u>**

Content Warnings—This book is intended for adult readers only and contains profanities, detailed sexual acts, reference to sexual assault, cheating (not main characters), and pregnancy.

This book takes place in the UK, with a cast of British characters.

But for continuity with the rest of the Men Series, it has been edited with mostly American English spelling conventions.

# Contents

*Drew's been waiting patiently for his turn... I thought it was time our obsessed 'daddy' got the girl,*
*enjoy ;)*

For author notes and CWs please turn back to copyright page.

# Chapter 1
# Drew

*Four Years Earlier*

"Um, it's a hard one... Okay, Cinderella."

"Great choice." My friend, Logan grins across the table at my date, Kelly. His eyes drop to the neckline of her low-cut dress as she giggles, making her large breasts bounce.

I roll my eyes. Subtlety is not Logan's strong point. I knew the minute we arrived that Kelly was more his type than mine. It wouldn't be the first time we've swapped mid-date.

"How about you, Sophie?" Logan turns his attention back to his actual date, who's sitting opposite me at the table of the Italian restaurant.

We like to double date. We've been each other's wingmen for as long as I can remember. Our mates, Tanner and Dax, sometimes mix it up and join us. Usually, it's me and Logan; a pairing with an unrivalled first date success record. Successful meaning something that involves beautiful women and them moaning our names before the night is over.

Sophie smiles politely, tucking a stray strand of caramel-colored hair behind her ear. She came straight from work to meet us, which explains her white blouse and gray pantsuit, and the way her hair is swept up in a classic style. She's quiet and focused, a direct contrast from Kelly-jiggly tits, who's spent the past ten minutes talking about the wedding of some reality TV star.

"Well..." Sophie rolls her lips before they settle into an accepting smile as she joins the game. She doesn't want to be here. It's obvious from the way she's subtly checked her watch five times since she arrived.

I notice the way her eyes narrow at the corners as she thinks. It's the first time I've had dinner with one of the country's top criminal prosecution attorneys. Ironic really, considering mine and Logan's colorful past. One that resulted in me spending six months in a juvenile detention center for grand theft auto as a teen.

"Yes, do share," I say, flashing a smile.

She takes a sip of her wine, eyeing me over the rim.

I lean back in my chair as I continue my assessment of her. Apart from the obvious—the curvy body and beautiful face with glossy, full lips that are both kiss-able and fuckable—she's unlike anyone I've met on a date before. She's filling in for Kelly's friend at the last minute. A fact she was keen to get across as soon as she arrived. Like the possibility of anything happening as a result of this night was completely out of the question. But she's not wearing a ring. And hasn't mentioned a boyfriend. So her attempt at closing herself off has done nothing but pique my interest in her. *How is she still single?*

"And they have to be a cartoon character?" Sophie asks Logan.

He nods, confirming the rules of the game.

"*Legally Blonde* is a film, so Elle Wood's doesn't count," I add, running a thumb over my bottom lip.

"Wow, original." She arches a brow at me, and the corners of her lips twitch.

"You mean, you don't have a furry canine hiding in your purse? Damn," I murmur, my eyes leisurely roaming over her face and coming back to her mouth.

This time, I get a small hum of amusement from her as she smirks. "No. Just the balls of my last date."

Logan guffaws, slapping the table before pointing at Sophie. "You're funny."

"Smart," I counter, holding Sophie's gaze. "Wit requires a person to be smart."

Sophie inclines her chin, accepting my compliment, before she lifts her glass of wine and takes a sip. "Who's your cartoon hero then, Mr. Harper? Seeing as we're sharing."

I pretend to think, although I know my answer. This is one of Logan's favorite party tricks, asking who their cartoon hero is. You can tell a lot from someone's answer. And that nugget of information helps oil the wheels of success for the remainder of the night. Kelly, choosing Cinderella, for example, is showing her desire to believe in fairytales. A few chivalrous gestures from Logan—re-filling her glass, standing from his seat should she visit the restroom—and soon he'll have her eating from his hand... or dick.

"Well, it has to be Mufasa," I declare.

Sophie's eyes drop from mine to her wine glass, her brows falling.

"Simba's dad from *The Lion King*," Logan adds, as if further explanation is needed.

"Oh, I love Disney!" Kelly shrills, giggling again. Logan's grin stretches wide as her tits threaten to break free from her dress. "And Mufasa is hot. You know, for a lion," she adds as Sophie glances at her in question.

"Mufasa..." Sophie repeats, the words coming out soft and breathy through her pillowy lips as she looks back at me.

"Yeah, because he's a powerful—"

"Leader." A hint of what sounds like boredom creeps into her tone as she looks at me like she has me figured out.

I hold her gaze, something pulling tight inside my chest. She stares back, unaffected.

Logan chimes in, "Actually, it's—"

I knock his leg with my knee beneath the table before he can finish his sentence.

"—dessert time. Would you look at that?" Logan deflects, lifting his menu up and turning it around, offering it to Kelly with a flourish. She giggles as she takes it, a blush creeping over her cheeks as she reads it, her eyes darting back up to Logan's and away again.

*Yep, eating out of his hand/dick.*

"Here." I offer a menu to Sophie, but before she takes it, a loud ringing comes from her purse. She pulls her phone out and looks at the screen.

"Please excuse me. I need to take this." Frowning, she stands from the table, striding out into the evening air. I watch her talk through the window, one hand on her hip, before she throws it up against her forehead, her fingertips pressing into her temples. She shakes her head and then ends the call, tipping her head back to the sky like she's frustrated. I turn my attention back to Logan and Kelly.

"It'll be work," Kelly says. "She never gets a day off. I'm always telling her she works too hard. She wants to help everyone, even the ones who can't pay her. I mean, who works for free? I told her she's burning herself out taking on all those pro-boner cases."

"Pro bono," I correct her, making eye contact with Sophie as she walks back through the restaurant's front door. I can't help but admire the way she carries herself—head held high, shoulders back, eyes on target. She isn't a woman who drifts along without a plan. She's confident. *Sexy.*

"I think pro-boner sounds better," Logan says, eliciting more giggles from Kelly. "I'm definitely more of a pro-boner man."

"Really?" Kelly flirts.

I ignore their hushed whispers as Sophie returns to the table. Instead of sitting, she bends to retrieve her purse, flashing us all a regretful but practiced smile.

"I'm sorry. It's work. I have to go. It was lovely meeting you both." She looks from me to Logan before focusing on Kelly with a serious look. "Text me when you get home. If I don't hear from you, you know what I'll do."

Kelly's eyes widen and she nods like an obedient puppy. What will Sophie do if she doesn't comply? *Call the police? The army? Send in a SWAT team?* I can't even be insulted that she thinks Kelly isn't safe with Logan and me. I'm too impressed with the way she delivers the command so effortlessly, like she gives no shits about whether she offends someone as long as she protects those she cares about. Confident and assertive. *A challenge.*

My dick twitches in my pants.

Sophie places some folded bills on the table.

"Dinner's on us," I argue, gesturing toward Logan.

"I prefer to pay my own way," she says curtly, closing her purse and turning to leave. "Nice to meet you."

"You too," Logan says.

"Bye, babe," Kelly trills.

"I'll help you get a cab," I say, standing up.

Sophie shakes her head. "No need."

But I'm already on my feet, gesturing for her to lead the way.

She looks at my outstretched arm before glancing back at Kelly, who's already giggling again at something Logan has said.

"He'll take care of her," I assure her.

Sophie smirks as another loud laugh erupts from the table, this time from Logan. "I'm sure he will."

I walk her outside and hail a cab, placing one hand on the roof and leaning over the open rear door as she slides into the backseat.

"Thank you for a nice evening," she says politely, the way I imagine she speaks in court. It isn't cold, but it conveys no emotion.

Heat flares in my groin at her polite dismissal. She isn't playing hard to get. She actually doesn't give a shit if she ever sees me again. And that headstrong attitude only makes me want to see her again more.

She reaches into her purse, pulling out her phone and bringing up her calendar. It's covered in blocked-out areas.

"Thank you for being a wonderful date," I say, injecting warmth into my voice as I smile.

She raises her eyes from her phone, the deep green of hers glittering as they meet mine. "I wasn't *your* date."

"But you could be next time," I counter with a playful grin.

One of her brows arches. "Good night." She reaches for the door handle and shuts the door as I hold my hands up in the air so they don't get stuck in it.

I signal the driver to wait and tap on her window. Her lips curl up slightly as she lowers the glass.

"How's Thursday for you?"

"In five years' time? Sure, I might be free." Her eyes drop over my shirt, and I inhale, puffing my chest out as her gaze lingers on the way I fill out the fabric. I knew all the extra bench presses would pay off.

"You're busy. I get it. I work a lot too. Next week then?" I rest my forearms on the window opening and lean a little closer to her. She doesn't flinch at my intrusion, but the pulse in her neck flutters beneath her skin.

"I live in Bath. The only reason I came to London today and got talked into tonight by Kelly was because I had to catch a client before they boarded a flight at Heathrow."

"Then I'll come to Bath." I shrug. "You can show me those famous spas, and I'll take you to dinner afterward." My smile widens at the thought. Sophie in a bikini on a date? It's perfect.

She sighs. "Look. It's nothing personal. But I'm not looking for a relationship."

"Perfect. Because I'm only asking you out on another date."

She opens her mouth to respond.

"A first date," I correct.

She closes her mouth and looks at me.

"Then we can talk about how many kids we'll have after." I wink at her.

"Right." She rolls her eyes, then smiles genuinely.

Her phone chimes again, but she ignores it.

"Next week then? In Bath. It's a date. A first date." I hold onto the door frame and step back from the cab.

"No, it isn't," she replies.

"What are your favorite flowers?" I ask before she can roll the window back up.

"Irises. Why?"

"Irises," I repeat. "I'll bring you some so that you can look at them the day after and remember what an amazing night you had, and how glad you are that you agreed to go on a date with me."

"I'm not going on a date with you."

"We'll see."

She looks at her lap, shaking her head. "Good night, Mr. Harper."

I tap twice on the roof of the cab. The window winds up, and I wave as the car drives away because I know she'll be watching through the back windshield. She has to be.

"Good night Ms. Havers." I grin as I pull my phone from my pocket and bring up my calendar for next week. I type *Date with Sophie* into Thursday, and above it, I add, *Buy irises*.

Not looking for a relationship? That's what she says now. But I'm the head of staff for a global construction and design company. I persuade people into new designs all the time, until they believe it was their idea all along.

Sophie Havers might think she doesn't have time to date.

But she hasn't been on a date with me yet.

# Chapter 2
# Sophie

"Roses? You don't like them."

I fasten my earring as my friend, Halliday, squints at the flowers, looking for a card.

"They're from Henry."

I breeze over to my hallway table and pull my lipstick from my clutch to apply in the mirror above.

Halliday agreed to go and see a political movie I've been wanting to make time to watch. It's not her type of film, so the trade-off is that I accompany her to a launch party next week for a rocket eco-engine that she's invested in. I've no idea why she's investing in rockets all of a sudden. But this is Halliday, and I've learned it's better to just let her get on with it.

"I can't believe you're wasting your time on Henry," she mutters, narrowing her eyes at the flowers as she strokes a petal. "His aura is concerning." She wrinkles her nose and pulls her hand back toward her body like they've offended her, brushing it against the black silk of her T-shirt. She tucks a lock of platinum hair behind her ear, then takes a deep breath and closes her eyes as if needing to cleanse herself of the offending flower's presence.

Halliday and I have been friends since meeting at a summer camp as kids. We used to sneak out of bed to stare at the stars together. She's always believed in a higher power. A vibration, she calls it. She'd talk about finding a way to match people based off their energy and spiritual alignment. And she has. At just twenty-eight she was named businesswoman to look out for in The Economist magazine after establishing her dating company, Cosmic Connections. And as differing as our outlooks on life are, I couldn't love her any harder.

She breathes out slowly and opens her eyes. She smiles at me, her face lighting up. "I pulled a card for you today. Magical things are coming."

"Like finishing up with this case and then going somewhere without signal for a while?" I ask as my phone chimes with another incoming email.

"Maybe. You deserve a vacation. The cards are never wrong, though. Something is about to happen."

"Maybe it can happen soon. Please, universe," I mutter, collecting my phone from my bag on the hallway floor and scrolling through the emails. They're all about the case I'm currently working on, but contain nothing I don't already know.

"It will happen when the time is right," she muses, gazing at the roses.

I deal with cold hard evidence and facts all day. I have no idea how she measures something she can't see. But it works for her. She loves her job and has partnered up swathes of influential people and celebrities, who are now gushing over her company and her extraordinary talent. The waitlist for people who want to work with her is over a year.

"But if it's a trip, then please, don't go with Henry," she adds.

"You don't even know him." I shake out my hair, attempting to get the long loose curls to play nice. "We've only been seeing each other for a couple of months. And you've met him once."

She scoffs. "Once was enough."

I don't know what she has against Henry. He's charming and intelligent and works hard. He doesn't crowd me and understands I have to work most evenings. He never bothers me to give him more of my time. But when I am free, he always makes the effort to see me. We've been managing to spend one night together a week, which is a miracle in itself with my schedule. If that isn't a sign from the universe that Henry is a positive addition to my life, then I don't know what is. I've not made it this far in a relationship in years.

"Henry works a lot, the same as me, which is perfect. Things with him are easy."

Halliday lifts her eyes from the roses to meet mine in the mirror's reflection. "Easy is hardly inspiring, Sophie. Easy sounds boring."

"Easy is simple. Uncomplicated," I counter.

"Easy isn't irises." She sighs, looking back at the roses with a frown.

"Oh my god." Huffing, I scoop up my clutch from the table and put my lipstick inside. "That was three years ago."

"You're counting then?"

"Don't be ridiculous," I say. But the truth is, I remember exactly when I got those irises delivered to me. And I vividly recall the card that accompanied them.

*It's been one year and we're sitting looking out over a lake as you feed the canine tidbits in your purse, the old balls of your past date long devoured. DH.*

Drew Harper.

A man who remembers your favorite flowers from a one-time date; not even with him. And then sends them to you on the one-year anniversary of the day you turned him down.

"Remind me why we don't like Iris man?" Halliday asks. "Was he ugly?"

I pause, before raking my fingers through my hair some more. "No. Why?"

"Did he smell bad?"

"No."

"Wear leather pants?"

"No." I laugh. "You know all this already."

She knows how Drew asked me on a date that night when I was in London four years ago. He turned up in Bath the following Thursday, just like he said he would. He walked right into my office and declared to the reception team he was there to take me to dinner. Cocky bastard. If he'd listened to me in the first place, he could have saved himself the journey. I was leaving work in a rush for the airport that night. I almost felt bad for him, all dressed up, his broad chest snug inside a crisp, white shirt. But I'd warned him. I wasn't looking for anything.

Halliday crosses her arms over her chest. "I'm just recapping."

I chuckle. "Right."

She likes to 'recap' this story frequently, convinced I missed some giant cosmic alignment by failing to accept the invitation of a date from a man I barely knew. She said she consulted her card decks about us and that apparently we pulled some interesting results. And although I'm happy for her that she's found her calling and that it brings her joy, I have no interest in learning about my cosmic vibrations.

Or Drew Harper's.

When I moved to London last year, she was convinced the universe was at work, bringing Drew and I closer together again. The promotion and hefty pay rise I got from being offered a job as a senior prosecutor with the Crown Prosecution Service were minor details in her mind.

"It's a shame he stopped sending them. Irises are so beautiful." She flicks her eyes back to the roses and glares at them.

"Will you stop?" I laugh. "They're not going to magically transform if you send enough hate their way."

She sighs, her shoulders dropping as she looks at me. "I want you to be happy."

"I am."

"With Henry?" She snorts as I place my phone into my clutch.

"I told you. Things with Henry are—"

"Boring. Yeah, I know. I'm just saying, I bet Iris man's vibration is insane."

"Well then, why don't *you* go on a date with him? Then you can question him and tap into him or however you do it."

"Do you still have his number?" She perks up, her eyes eager and alert.

I know that face. It's the one she gets every time she makes a new love match at work. Like the universe has just handed her another magic cookie on a gold platter.

"No," I say firmly before her idea can sprout and grow faster than Jack's beanstalk. "I deleted it ages ago. After I threatened him with a restraining order."

"Huge mistake," she grumbles as I pick up my keys.

She's never forgiven me for it. I didn't mean it exactly. It was more a friendly joke when Drew kept being persistent about taking me out. I was working on a huge case and had a shit day. So when he texted me again, I told him I might be forced to file for one if he wouldn't take no for an answer. I wouldn't have done it. I still remember his response.

> **Make sure whoever he is treats you like his queen. Be happy, Sophie Havers.**

And that was the last time I ever saw or spoke to Drew Harper. He'd have forgotten about me a long time ago. Men like Drew Harper don't waste time. I could have found a way to contact him if I'd wanted to. Especially after discovering my sister, Holly's, best friend, Rachel, is married to Tanner Grayson—the man who runs the company Drew works at. Another twist of fate that Halliday clutched on to, like it all meant something.

I open the front door and turn to her. "You've willed my flowers dead and questioned my life choices. Are you happy now? Can we go?" I ask with a smile.

"Fine. We can go. You can watch the film and I'll meditate or something."

I open my mouth to argue, but she grins at me playfully and links arms with me as we walk out the door.

# Chapter 3
# Sophie

"WHY DOES IT HAVE to be morning already?" Henry rolls off me and stretches his arms above his head, then wraps one around me, pulling me toward him. "We could have gone for round two."

I breathe deeply, letting my mind clear of everything to do with work as I rest my hand over the soft hair on his chest. His skin is warm beneath my palm, his heartrate still accelerated from the way he woke me up.

"I have a breakfast meeting," I say, by way of apology as I extract myself from his embrace and sit, holding the sheet against my breasts. "Do you want to shower first?"

He yawns, his light brown eyes meeting mine. "Sure." He swings out of my bed and saunters buck-naked into the bathroom, scratching the back of his head as he goes.

I wait until the door closes and the shower turns on before I fetch my robe from the back of the door.

Henry stayed over at my place again last night. I'd love to go to his place and see what it's like, but he lives out of the city, and it would take over an hour to travel there during rush hour. He said he doesn't mind leaving work early and coming to mine instead. And it makes sense because we get more time together this way.

I look at the bathroom door as the sound of him humming in the shower floats out. Halliday might not like him, and she's my only friend who has met him. But the amount of people I meet through work means I'd recognize someone with a 'bad aura'. I see them all the time. Sometimes, I read over a case and I know there's guilt, even if the evidence is lacking. Call it intuition or experience. But those times a case gives me that gut feeling, I find a way to get the evidence I need. Because there's always a slipup somewhere. A mistake. People make errors; it's in their genetic makeup.

They call me the 'Handler' at work because I've never lost a case. No matter how heinous the charge. No matter how complex the case, or how flimsy it seems at first glance, I can handle it.

I don't care who the defendant is, or how much money, power, or status they have. If they're guilty, I'll find a way to prove it. I never went into law to make friends. I went in to make a difference. Integrity is priceless to me. Dad was a highly respected judge before he retired. I need to make him proud.

I reach up for my robe on the hook. Henry's jacket is hanging on top of it, so I lift it off, but it drops to the floor. As I bend to retrieve it, something slips from the inner pocket. I pick the item up, its weight increasing in my fingers as I study it.

Nausea coils in my stomach, making it lurch. The object taunts me, its shape and the meaning of it so glaringly obvious. An unbroken bond. No beginning and no end.

A circle.

A ring.

I swallow the bile in my throat as I turn the gold band between my fingers and read the inscription.

*"V & H 27th May."*

The 27th is today.

My heart leaps into my mouth as the shower in the bathroom stops. I grab my robe from the hook and throw it on, knotting the belt tightly. Henry's jacket is a forgotten, crumpled heap on the floor as I turn around, the evidence of betrayal lying perfectly in my palm like an offering.

A sacrifice.

Except all that's been sacrificed today is my self-belief that I can spot a liar. People lie in court all the time. It's my job to notice it, expose it, and then use it to my advantage to win.

For the first time, my instincts were wrong. They've let me down. This time, I've lost.

*I'm so stupid. How did I miss this?*

The bathroom door swings open and Henry wanders out, a towel slung low on his hips as he towel dries his hair with another. He grins at me, but it freezes on his face as he spots my outstretched hand.

"This fell out of your pocket," I say calmy, holding the ring out to him.

His expression closes off in an instant, and he strides over to me and snatches it from my palm. The steamy, heated air from the bathroom comes with him, hitting me in the face and quickly turning to tiny droplets over my already scorching skin. I don't move. I don't breathe. I don't do anything that will give away the fact that I am trembling inside as a mix of betrayal and disappointment floods my veins.

"Why are you going through my stuff? Don't you trust me?"

"I thought I could." My voice is even, despite my pounding heart.

"Fuck's sake. I thought you were different." He looks at the ring in his hand and then closes his fingers around it, forming a fist.

The soft laughter lines around his eyes that I thought were attractive have been replaced with deep, etched grooves as he scowls.

He towels off his chest and abs roughly, his limp dick flailing around between his legs as he grabs his boxers and forces his feet into them. I never noticed how wrinkly and loose his balls are before. They slap against his inner thigh before he yanks his boxers up over his hips. I look at his face. His eyes have lost their twinkle, and he's staring at me with a hard, cold detachment.

I stare back.

He exhales with a deep groan, rubbing his hands down over his face. "I'm sorry, baby. I shouldn't have said it like that. It's not your fault." He drops his hands and holds them, palms facing up as he looks at me. His eyes have softened to the way he usually looks at me. The way that made me feel cared for. But I can't unsee who he is. I feel sick. Sick and used.

I press my fingers to my lips, warding off a rising swell of nausea as he keeps talking.

"I should have told you. We're separated. We have been for months. But things were going so well between you and me, and I didn't want to ruin it."

"You're married," I state.

"Separated," he snaps as he grabs his shirt from the back of a chair and drags it over his head.

"But not yet divorced."

"Separated," he repeats.

"Is that the only word you can say?"

"Jesus, Soph. Don't be a bitch." He glares at me.

"Me?" My calm exterior snaps, my blood pressure spiking as I point at him. "I'm not the one with a wedding ring in my pocket. I'm not the one waking up in someone else's bed on my wedding anniversary. How many years?"

"What?"

"How many years would you have been married today? It's your anniversary, after all."

"I'm not fucking doing this." He turns his back on me and strides out of the room.

I follow him into my living area and bark the question at him over and over again while he grabs his shoes and sits on the sofa, yanking them on.

"How long?" I hiss.

"We're separated. How many times do I have to tell you?"

"Right. Because separated men still wear their wedding bands, then take them off and put them in their pockets when they're seeing their girlfriends." My eyes drop to the glinting gold band that he's already slipped back onto his left hand, like a habit he can't break, and I snort. "I'm not stupid."

"You're acting like it."

"What was all this?" I throw my arms wide, the realization that I might be the mistress sinking in. "Sex on the side? Am I the only one or are there more?" The feeling of being used is quickly overtaken by dread. We stopped using condoms a couple of weeks ago. Things were going well and I'm getting the injection. It seemed like the next step.

*I was really trying at this whole relationship thing. Stupid.*

Henry finishes tying one shoe and moves to the other. He yanks on the lace too hard and it snaps. "Fuck's sake," he mutters. "Yes, you're the only fucking one." He looks up at me, his jaw tightening. "I want to be with you."

He abandons his shoe, leaving the stubby, broken lace loose and flapping as he stands. I can't help but liken it to the sight of his flaccid dick flopping about as he tried to pull his underwear on.

I raise my eyes to his, and it's obvious in the shift in his stance, the slight pause before he swallows, the way his eyes dart to the right before he can meet mine. *Guilt.* I've seen it a million times in the courtroom.

"You're not separated." I breathe out slowly, tipping my head back before bringing my eyes back to his face.

"We are." He reaches for my hand and laces his fingers through mine before lifting them to his lips.

I hold my breath as he kisses my knuckles with his warm lips.

"We're... going to be... soon," he whispers.

"Going to be?"

"It's been over between us for years. We're like friends more than anything else."

I blink as I stare at him.

"Come on, Soph. You know this is good. What we have here. You and me." He pulls me closer and slides his free arm around my waist, dropping his lips to my neck and kissing me beneath the ear. "We're *good* together," he whispers, his voice deepening.

"When was the last time you slept together?"

He pauses, and the brief hesitation is all it takes for my heart to fall to my feet.

"The truth, Henry."

He clears his throat, before he kisses my neck again. "All that matters is that I want you. And you want me."

"When?" I grind out.

He pauses again. "Last Saturday."

"It's Friday. That's six days," I say without giving away my shock. Another trick that I've learned through my job—never let them know if they've caught you off guard.

I try and step out from his hold, but he tightens his arm around my waist.

"It's not like that. Please," he urges, pressing his lips to my neck again and pulling me closer to him. "I want you, baby." He moves his lips to mine, pressing them to mine in a bruising kiss.

"Get off!" I place both hands on his chest and shove him backward, giving myself enough room to finally breathe properly.

"Don't be stupid. It's nothing. Don't ruin this."

*Stupid?* He's dismissing me like a silly girl. He's a gaslighting, chauvinistic pig. Possibly even a narcissist. How did I miss this?

He reaches for me, but I step back again, creating more distance between us, making his brow knit with annoyance.

"Come on. Let's forget about all this. You know I love you."

Those words leaving his lips break my final resolve. He's ruining everything they stand for as they pass his lying, cheating lips.

"You wouldn't know love if it came and bit your dick off! Does your wife know where you are? What you do behind her back?"

His eyes darken.

"Didn't think so." I storm over to retrieve his crumpled jacket. I launch the creased ball at his chest, and he catches it with one hand. "Get out."

"Soph."

"Out!"

He doesn't move. "I'll let you calm down. Then we can talk about this like adults."

"Now!" I yell, heat firing over the back of my neck as my skin prickles like a thousand tiny needles are pressing into it. "Get the hell out!"

He sniffs before walking past me slowly. He parts his lips to say something as he reaches the door, but maybe I look like I'm moments away from murdering him, because he opens the door without uttering another word.

"And don't call me," I hiss.

Even though I'm shaking inside, I don't allow him even the tiniest glimmer of weakness that he might use to manipulate me with.

"Forget everything about me. The way I'm going to make sure I forget you. You are a liar and a cheat. And we are done."

He stares back at me as I deliver my closing statement. Then he walks out the door and slams it so hard that the roses he gave me last week shake in the vase on the table.

I storm over and lock the door, blood rushing in my ears. Then I scoop up the vase and march into the kitchen. I open the trash can and tip the vase up, emptying its contents, water included, straight inside.

"Roses," I snarl as the lid slams down, hiding their blood red petals.

I don't even like roses.

# Chapter 4
# Drew

"How long ago did she turn you down? And you're still not over it. A decade?" Logan asks.

Tanner snorts into his glass.

"Fuck off."

"Four years," my sister, Maddy, says as she leans into Logan's side.

We're at the launch of Vex, Logan's new eco rocket engine design. The lucky bastard isn't only a master at engineering, but he also won my sister's heart along the way. Although, as far as I'm concerned, the two of them hold hands. Nothing more.

"Why don't you go and talk to her?" Maddy asks.

My eyes stay fixed on the golden-haired beauty across the room. She's wearing a long purple evening dress. One that hugs every feminine curve of her body. My mouth goes dry before I drain the rest of my whiskey.

"Apparently, she's dating someone," I say before tipping my empty glass toward Logan and motioning to the bar.

He shakes his head, looking around at all the investors that have come to the lavish party. "We need to speak to some people."

I nod, and Tanner joins me as we move toward the bar. I signal the bartender, and he replaces our glasses with two fresh ones.

"You know, maybe Maddy has a point," Tanner says, taking a sip as he follows my gaze back across the room.

Back to *her*.

I grunt, leaning one elbow on the bar, watching as she smiles at something her friend in the blue dress is saying. The two of them are in a deep discussion with our friend, Dax, and his girlfriend, Rose.

"All this staring at her." Tanner chuckles. "Why don't you just go and talk to her? You're not getting any younger."

"Says the guy who took over eighteen months to even tell his wife who he really was."

He grumbles, "Yeah, all right. Do as I say, not as I do."

He knows I'm joking. But it's still a fact. He met his wife, Rachel, randomly at the airport on his way to a meeting in New York. She helped him find his lost laptop and saved the company from losing a multimillion-dollar deal. Then he pined after her for eighteen months before finally asking her out. And the entire time, he never told her that he was the airport guy that she'd forgotten about.

I straighten in my seat as a man approaches their group and places his hand low on her back. *Too fucking low.* I fight to portray a relaxed demeanor, leaning one elbow on the bar. When in reality, my body's urging me to jump up from my seat and march over there to demand he back the fuck off.

Tanner's silent next to me as he watches her expertly steer the clinger away with a few words and a polite smile. I relax into my seat a little.

*Good girl.*

"Lawyer woman can handle herself," Tanner comments as the man slinks away, looking dejected. "I can see why you like her."

"Sophie," I mutter. "Her name's Sophie."

As if she can hear me, she looks straight up into my eyes. Her green eyes hold mine long enough for my heart to pump so hard that I have to swallow it down for fear it will jump out of my throat.

She breaks our gaze, and I crack my neck before taking a large swig of my drink, trying to concentrate on the warm trail that it blazes down to my stomach instead of the warmth that's there from seeing her again.

*She's more beautiful than I remember.*

Tanner slaps his hand onto my shoulder. "Four years and you still haven't forgotten about her. Take it from someone who knows... You never will, Buddy." He squeezes my tense muscle, looking at me with pity. "So do us all a favor and go and fucking talk to her. You look like a dog that's been kicked."

I grunt, gazing back to where Sophie is standing with her friend, who's one of Logan's investors. When he received Sophie's name on the guest list as a plus one, the bastard took great delight in telling me that the first woman who's ever knocked me back would be coming tonight. A woman my friends all know I couldn't stop thinking about.

The only woman who has ever held my interest. Maybe because of her wit, her drive, and her beauty. Or because of her smart mouth. I don't understand it. But I know that she's the only woman I've still thought about years after a date. Thought about enough to have an unwelcome fist of jealousy grip my stomach when Dax told me the name of the lawyer who helped him out last year when he got arrested. A fist that only tightened when Rose added that she'd heard she was no longer single.

*That* woman.

Sophie Havers.

"Will it get your ugly face off my case if I do?" I quip to Tanner.

"Absolutely," he lies smoothly.

His tired eyes light up as I stand from the stool. Lucky fucker has just had his third kid. He might look and feel like shit. But he's happy. I've known him long enough to tell. He never looked like this before Rachel. I'd be lying if I said I wasn't jealous. He knows I want all that. I'm the last one of our group who hasn't gotten someone special. And kids. Fuck, I want kids. Maybe that's not a normal thing for a thirty-five-year-old man to dream about. But I don't give a fuck what's normal. I want the wife. The sexy pregnancy belly. The tiny babies. The crazy kids racing around. I want it all. And I'm going to be the most devoted father there is.

I throw Tanner one last scowl, which he chuckles at, then take my time weaving across the room. I don't head straight for her. Instead, I move to the wall at the edge of the busy room. She's no longer talking to Dax and Rose. But her friend is still with her.

I sip my whiskey as the two of them talk. Her friend closes her eyes and tilts her head up as if she's listening to an imaginary sound while she twirls a crystal bracelet around on her wrist. When she opens her eyes, she searches around the room until she sees me. A wide smile overtakes her face, and she whispers something to Sophie before disappearing into the crowd.

Sophie's eyes lock onto mine and I roll my tongue over my bottom lip as she walks over to me purposefully, full of that same confidence I admired all those years ago.

"Mr. Harper."

*Fuck, the way she says that has blood rushing south inside my body.*

"Ms. Havers. It's been a long time."

She studies me, her eyes glassy and her cheeks flushed as she sips on her drink.

"It has. How are you?"

There it is. The polite, practiced, clipped tone. All it does is make me want to break through it and dig deeper. *First woman to ever turn me down.*

"Breaking my restraining order it would seem. What's the rule? Not to be within one kilometer of you?" I smirk.

She shrugs. "They vary. I'm surprised you adhered so well to it. Didn't have you down as being such a good boy."

My dick twitches in my pants.

"You know it was a joke?" Her voice softens.

"Was it?" I hold her emerald eyes. "You sounded pretty clear on what you wanted. You were too busy to date."

She looks away from me, small lines pinching around her eyes as she swallows, and a frown settles over her glossy lips.

"Does he deserve you?"

I might have only met her twice, but I know the small talk is just polite bullshit to her. I learned that much from our meeting. And also, I want to know. A self-torturing part of me wants to know about the man who made her change her stance on dating when I failed. He must be something special. Another lawyer, perhaps? A politician? A fucking prince?

"No." She smiles sadly. "No, he didn't."

And just like that, my self-torturing part does a lap of merry victory through my body before the realization of what she means takes it out like a baseball bat to the knees.

"What?" I grit, my hand clenching tight around my glass as it freezes mid-air on the way to my lips. "What did he do to y—"

Her lips thin. "It wasn't serious."

She takes another drink, her eyes returning to mine. I take a deep glug from my glass, mirroring her movements.

"I suspect he isn't much of a loss," I say, mesmerized by the way her pupils dilate under my gaze.

"What makes you say that?" Despite the glassiness the alcohol is causing, she holds eye contact without faltering. I can just imagine her interrogating someone on the witness stand. I bet she makes grown men piss themselves.

The idea only makes my dick fight for my attention in my pants even more.

"Your purse." I tip my head toward the tiny clutch she has in her other hand.

Her eyes narrow as I continue.

"It's small. And you carry the balls of your ex-dates around in it. So..." I take another drink, and her lips curl into the ghost of a smile.

"So I do. I told you that... four years ago."

"I have a good memory."

"Lucky for you that you weren't my date that night, then." Her eyes twinkle as she holds up the tiny purse and gives it a little shake.

"If I were, my balls wouldn't be in that," I say, holding her gaze.

She lowers her hand back to her side with an eye roll. "Let me guess. Because it's too small."

"No." I step closer to her. She tilts her head back to meet my eyes as I stand a head taller than her. "Because if you had gone on a date with me, then I wouldn't be your ex-date now."

"You wouldn't?" She arches a brow, her lips twisting in amusement.

"No." I suck my bottom lip, dampening it as I look at her. Her eyes drop to my mouth, following the movement.

"What would you be?" she breathes.

I sink my teeth into my bottom lip with a concealed groan. I take my time before I speak, enjoying her rapt attention.

"I'd be your husband."

Her lips part in a tiny gasp. One that reaches right inside my pants and curls itself around my aching dick, teasing it.

I step back, creating distance between us again.

"... and because it's too small." I smirk, bidding her a good evening, and then I walk away.

# Chapter 5
# Sophie

"You're really going for it, huh?" Halliday remarks as I sit next to her at the bar and raise my glass in the air in a toast.

"To Henry." I hiccup. "And getting his married, lying ass out of my life."

She clinks her glass with mine. "I'll drink to that."

I slurp my gin and then clank my glass down heavily on the dark wood bar, before wiping my lips with the back of my hand. "And to getting wasted."

Her brows pop, and she signals the bartender. "Can we have two waters, please?"

"Hey." I point at her accusingly, my stool wobbling beneath me. *It must have a loose leg.* "Are you saying you don't think I can..." I hiccup again. "... handle my drink?"

"No." She laughs, reaching out and steadying me.

I frown at the stool, realizing it's me wobbling it.

"I'm saying, I *know* you can't handle your drink." She rolls her eyes as I prepare to argue. "You've never been able to."

I snap my mouth shut, and she gives me a pointed look. I fixate on her face as she carries on talking. Such perfect eyebrows. They begin to blur as I blink.

"... Only times you've drank like this are when you scratched your dad's car when you were nineteen and didn't know how to tell him, and when your sister had that awful sex tape thing."

"Ssh." I bat my finger against my lip clumsily. "I don't want to talk about that shit."

She sighs. "You're worth so much more than him. You know that, right?"

"I know." I slump miserably over the bar, cradling my glass. I frown at the water in it and then search side to side. My gin is gone even though I hadn't finished it. "Ugh," I groan, pressing one hand against my forehead. "I'll be fine tomorrow. It's just... I woke up this morning and everything was fine. And now..." I drop my hand and shrug, my head spinning.

"It's not Henry, is it?" Halliday asks, knowing me so well.

I shake my head. "No... Yes... No... It's this case I'm working on. It's tough, and... this stuff with Henry... I always know." My voice pitches as I search Halliday's eyes for answers. "I always know. In my gut. If I missed Henry being married, what else have I missed? What if I don't win this time?" My voice drops as a lead weight settles in my stomach.

"Listen." She swivels on her stool so she's facing me head-on. "They don't call you 'Havers the Handler' for nothing. You've got this. You've always got this. There is nothing wrong with your intuition. The universe is working with you, I've told you this."

I snort, and her face softens as she reaches for my hand and squeezes it.

"You were just distracted. Sex and hormones can interfere with our vibration, making us confused, even if the partner is wrong for us. Orgasms... they can be intense, on more than just our physical body."

"I don't... I doubt that's what happened," I mutter as I think about my sex life with Henry. Sure, I came. But not every time. And only when I touched myself at the same time as we... I swallow the rising bile back down as I shake him from my thoughts.

"Or stress," Halliday says as she studies my face. "I keep telling you to take a break."

"Can't," I slur. "Not until after this case, anyway."

She smiles. "Well, once this case is over, you and me are going somewhere hot with cocktails. And we're going to have an amazing time."

"Cocktails sound good." I crane my neck to look down the bar at the bartender who's serving someone. "I could go for a cocktail."

"Nu-uh." She slides my water in front of me and taps the side of the glass.

"Ruin my fun, why don't you?" I scowl, which only makes her laugh.

"Saving you from a hangover tomorrow, don't you mean? Any more and you'll feel awful. Get this down you now and you have a fighting chance." She nudges the glass a little closer and I pick it up. "Good. Now, we're staying here tonight. Huge hotel bed, crisp sheets, a good sleep. You'll have forgotten all about Henry's limp dick by the morning and be back to your usual fighting form."

"Amen." I throw back the contents of the glass, screwing my face up in disappointment as I remember it's water.

"That's more like it." She smiles and then her attention is caught by something across the room. "Oh, I see Logan. I'll thank him for tonight, and then we can go up to our rooms. You'll be okay for a minute, right?"

I flail out a hand in an ungraceful wave. "Go. I'll be fine."

She narrows her eyes, unconvinced.

"Honestly, I'm great." I lift my glass to my lips, forgetting it's empty, then glare at it like it's the source of all my problems.

"Okay. I'll be quick." Halliday hurries off, and I tip my head back, admiring the ballroom of the hotel we're in. The architraves and archways around the room are beautiful, even if they are a little blurry, thanks to the six, no seven, gins I've drunk.

"The guys who run the company that did the re-model are here tonight."

"Sorry?" I drop my head back down, meeting the friendly bartender's eyes.

He tips his head, and I follow his eyeline across the bar, spotting Drew talking to a beautiful, curvy brunette in a green dress. She grins at something he says and then wraps her arms around his neck so she can reach up and whisper in his ear. I don't need to be closer to know that his cool blue eyes are probably glittering at her now as he laughs at whatever she just said. The way they do when he's amused. The way they did when he joked that he'd be my husband now if I hadn't turned him down.

*Husband.*

Ridiculous. He's handsome, intense, and overconfident. A lethal combination that I've seen many times. Usually in the defense attorney's asses before I whip them in court.

I allow my eyes to rake over his broad frame in his tuxedo from head to foot and back up again.

Yep, handsome, intense, and overconfident. I should look away.

I swallow as heat swirls in my core, and I continue to study him.

"You know them?" I ask.

"I know of them. Tanner Grayson owns it. But that guy, Drew Harper, he's the one who ran the entire project here. Did a fine job," the bartender continues.

"Yeah, pretty fine," I mumble as Drew and the curvy brunette head toward the exit. "Excuse me," I blurt, sliding off my stool and stumbling. *Stupid stiletto shoes.*

I weave my way through the busy ballroom and out through the ornate exit doors into the corridor that leads to the lobby. I scan up and down but don't see anyone.

"Drew." A giggle floats around the corner.

I follow the sound, unsure why I'm even here.

I round the corner as Drew helps the brunette into her coat and then kisses her on the cheek. My stomach twists as she reaches up and hugs him and his arms curl around her.

"Thanks, Buddy," Logan says to Drew as he appears beside me.

"Sophie? So glad you could make it with Halliday tonight. Have you had a good evening?"

"Yes. Thank you," I reply, my eyes flicking to Drew, who's now aware that I was here watching him and his date like a weirdo.

His brows lower over his blue eyes as he looks at me intently. I raise my chin, readying myself to turn back around and head back into the ballroom.

"Oh." The brunette with him grins as though my name means something to her. "Sophie?" Her eyes dart to Drew's face, but he's still watching me. "It's so nice to meet you. I'm Maddy."

"Nice to meet you too." I smile at her politely.

"You ready, Smiles?" Logan asks, walking up to Maddy and linking his hand with hers.

She gives me a small wave and then pats Drew on the chest. "Night, big brother. I'll call you tomorrow."

Drew murmurs a response, his eyes still fixed on mine.

"Bye, Sophie," she calls, walking away with Logan.

"Bye." I wave back, off-balance. I reach for the wall but am caught by a warm hand around my wrist and another tucking itself around my waist.

"You're drunk," Drew states as he supports me. His brows pull lower as he studies my face.

I breathe in his warm, delicious scent. It's like honey on smoked wood. But it can't detract from the look of irritation on his face.

"Who are you to say what I am? A cop?" I snap.

A scowl passes over his lips, before it fades away and he loosens his grip on me, steadying me, before letting go completely.

"Where's your friend?" he asks, glancing over my shoulder like he's expecting her to appear.

"Halliday's in the ballroom. Why?"

"How are you getting home tonight?" he asks, bracing a hand on my upper arm and guiding me to one side so I don't get bumped into as two businessmen in suits walk past, laughing loudly and swaying.

Looks like they enjoyed the free bar too.

"We're both staying here." I cross my arms over my chest. "Why?"

"I'll go and find her so she can take you to your room." His eyes darken, and he steps past me.

"Excuse me?" I spin, the movement making me wobble again. Who does he think he is? "I can find my own room, you know," I snap at his back. His black hair curls a little over the collar of his jacket, silky and shining underneath the lights.

"You all right there?" one of the businessmen who passed us pipes up. "We can help you find your room if you need?"

"We're heading up to ours now," his friend adds as he reaches out and stops the elevator door from closing so that I can join them.

I smile gratefully but don't move. I'm not stupid. Like I'd get into an elevator with two drunk men. "Oh. Thank you. But—"

"Fuck off," a deep voice barks as a strong arm encircles my waist and pulls me protectively against a solid, muscular side. "She's with me."

The businessman shrugs, muttering under his breath, and lets go of the elevator doors.

"Assholes." Drew glares as the doors slide shut. I tip my head back to gaze up at him. Even with my heels, he's taller.

His thick neck contracts on a swallow as he looks back toward the ballroom doors like he's trying to decide something.

"Come on." His hand wraps around my hip as he steers us toward the elevators and presses the call button. "I'll make sure you get to your room and then come and tell your friend."

"I don't need taking care of," I argue, still pressed against his side, because my heels are ridiculously high and making me unsteady on my feet.

"Believe me, Sophie. If I were taking care of you, you'd know about it."

His words send an unexpected shiver running through me. His face gives nothing away. No hint of amusement or emotion of any kind. Even though that sounded a lot like flirting.

His jaw tenses, and I look away with a huff. I don't care what's crawled up his ass to make him so moody suddenly.

We ride the rest of the way in silence, and he helps me along the corridor of my floor. I fumble in my purse for my keycard when we reach my door, tutting when I can't find it.

"Let me." Drew takes my purse and pulls the card straight out, pressing it to the sensor and opening the door, all in under two seconds.

"How did you—?" I stare at my purse, puzzled.

"It had slipped down behind your ex's balls."

His lips twitch as I meet his eyes. "Oh," I mumble.

I walk into the room, stepping out of my shoes, then frowning as I keep swaying and stumbling despite ridding myself of them. Maybe I did have a little too much to drink.

My shoulder bounces off one wall and a tiny yelp escapes my lips. I stagger on, my bed screaming out to me like a giant, fluffy cloud of comfort across the room.

There's a click behind me as the door closes, and then my feet leave the floor as I'm swept up and held against something solid.

"Easy there. Let's get you to bed." Drew's voice rumbles in his chest as I rest my spinning head against it.

He sets me gently on the bed and then starts to move back, a frown marring his handsome face. I don't know what makes me do it, but I grab the back of his neck and arch up from the bed, capturing his mouth in a desperate, fumbled kiss.

There's a sharp hiss as he sucks in a surprised breath, and I take it as further invitation to pull him closer, trying to kiss him again as I drop one hand to the waistband of his pants.

"Let's have sex," I purr. Although it comes out slurred and even I can tell it sounds more like *Shex. Let's have shex.* What a chat-up line.

I tear the zipper down at the back of my dress, shrugging it clumsily from my shoulders. Then I pull at his waistband again, huffing in frustration as he moves his head back and I can no longer reach his lips with mine.

"Mr. Harper," I whine, "do you still want me?" The room sways around me, but I ignore it, searching for his blue eyes instead. "Or am I wrong about that too?" I sigh hopelessly, finally finding cool blue and clinging on to it as the rest of the world around it blurs. "Did I get it all wrong?" I ask, losing myself in his intense gaze.

It's the last thing I see before I pass out.

# Chapter 6
# Sophie

THE ROOM IS DIMLY lit as I open my eyes and squint at the bedside clock. 7AM. I blink before letting my eyelids fall closed again. My head is surprisingly clear, considering I had more than I usually drink last night. I'm sure I wasn't that drunk. Although, my eyes pop wide and I glance down at the large white shirt I'm wearing.

A man's shirt.

"What the hell?" I throw the covers back, revealing the rest of my body. The shirt comes down over my hips and my legs are bare. My underwear is on beneath it, so that's something.

I rake a hand back through my nest of tangled hair, heat flaring across the back of my neck as a figure sitting in the armchair facing the foot of the bed clears their throat.

"Sleep well?"

"God!" I shriek and reach out to hit the switch beside the bed, expecting the bedside lamp to turn on. Instead, a gentle whir begins as the drapes slide open.

The sunlight creeps across the room in slow motion, illuminating him inch by inch, starting at his feet, up over his black suit pants, then higher, over a chest that's broad, defined, and smooth, like it's been sculpted from marble. Then finally, to his face. To that dark, shadowed jawline, dark hair with a curl to it, and those cool blue eyes.

Watching me.

I stare at him as he regards me calmly, leaning back against the chair, relaxed and comfortable.

"You've been here all night," I state.

He steeples his fingers in front of his face and presses them against his lips. "You'd had a lot to drink. I wasn't about to leave you." His eyes slide to the fresh orange juice and bottle of painkillers on the bedside table.

I give him a questioning look.

"I got them last night. After I assured your friend I'd brought you to your room safely and would keep an eye on you."

My usual retort at being handled like a child dies on the tip of my tongue as it's replaced with curiosity.

"Halliday knew you were coming back here?"

"She said my aura wasn't concerning." Amusement laces his tone.

"Figures," I mutter.

My best friend trusts an almost stranger due to a 'feeling'. A stranger who somehow undressed me. I stare at my clothing and then snap my eyes back up to his face. "I'm wearing your shirt."

"You threw your dress off and needed something to sleep in. I turned the lights off and didn't look," he says matter-of-factly.

"Oh. That makes it okay, then?" I snort.

He ignores me and pulls his shoes across the carpet toward him.

"What are you doing?"

He looks up at me from beneath thick, dark brows, and the curve of his muscular shoulders tighten as he pauses.

"You can't leave without your shirt." I shuffle on the bed as I accept the growing heat between my legs at the sight of him half naked in front of me for what it is.

Lust.

He takes his hand back from his shoes and sits back into the chair once more. "Then I'll stay while you shower."

"Fine." I glance at his chest again before I swing my legs out of the bed. The heat of his gaze burns into me as I reach for the pills and then put the bottle down without taking any. I'm lucky; I don't usually suffer with hangovers. Still, the thought that he got these especially for me last night brings warmth to my chest.

I drink the juice while he watches me in silence.

"Thank you." I place the empty glass down.

He lifts his chin in response.

I walk to the bathroom, my heartrate rocketing as I feel his eyes on my back with each step.

I step inside and close the door, heading straight for the sink and squeezing a generous amount of toothpaste onto my toothbrush before brushing my teeth. My makeup is smudged, and my hair needs a brush. But my eyes are surprisingly bright. Maybe because despite last night's events, I slept really well.

Last night... Ugh.

I unbutton Drew's shirt, peeling off the cotton that smells of smoked wood and honey, and hang it on the hook before taking off my underwear and having a quick shower. The thought of Drew sitting in my room is enough to make me hurry.

*"Let's have shex."* The memory's hazy, but it's still there.

I threw myself at another man on the day I found out my ex-boyfriend is married. And he turned me down.

And not just any man.

I threw myself at Drew Harper.

Embarrassment curls in my gut as I step out and dry off roughly, wrapping the towel around myself and marching out into the bedroom with the sinful smelling shirt in my hand.

"Thank you. I appreciate you being a gentleman." I hold the shirt out to Drew, who stands from the chair as I stride over. I look to one side, avoiding his eyes as I wait for him to take it. When he doesn't, I turn my head, my stomach flipping as my eyes lock on to the expanse of taut, tanned skin of his chest.

"What else would I be?" His deep voice floats over me as he takes his shirt from me and slides it on.

"Married," I mumble.

"What?"

"Nothing."

Henry will be waking up with his wife now. I wonder if he took her out for their anniversary last night. If he woke up and had sex with her this morning. The thought doesn't hurt. It makes me angry. I was so stupid. What else have I missed?

Drew leaves his shirt hanging open as he studies me. Goosebumps prick over my bare shoulders as I stand wrapped in a towel, inches from him.

"No one's worth that frown on your face, Sophie." He reaches up slowly and places two fingers beneath my chin, tilting it up. "You know what I thought when I first met you?"

"That woman's like Elle Woods."

He smirks, his eyes glittering. "I thought, wow. That woman's a force. One who can do anything she wants. You don't need some prick holding you back. You're a flame, Ms. Havers." His smirk softens to a beautiful smile as he looks at my lips. "A bright, burning flame. Beautiful."

My breath hitches and a bouquet of irises pops into my head.

He thinks I'm a flame.

Flames don't doubt themselves and their own judgment. Flames glow. Flames ignite. Flames take what they want and don't apologize. Because it's their fuel, it makes them brighter.

Right now, Drew's words and cool blue eyes locked onto mine are making me brighter.

To him, I'm a flame.

*Fuck it.*

"This time, kiss me back," I blurt.

Drew's forehead creases in confusion, but I don't give him time to ask me what I'm doing. I wrap my arms around his neck and pull his lips to mine. Only, unlike last night, this time, I'm not clumsy or fumbling, with alcohol running through my veins. This time, I'm focused and determined, with nothing but liquid fire heating my body, racing through me like a flame on a lit fuse. My heartrate picks up as I kiss him, pressing my toweled body against his. My skin tingles, wetness growing between my legs in response to the deep groan that's forced from him as he buries his hands in my hair and kisses me back hard. And fuck, can he kiss. He devours me like I'm the only thing that's ever tasted good to him.

Lust. Pure and simple.

"You sure about this?" His voice rumbles as he pauses to tug my lower lip between his teeth.

"Don't you want to?" I breathe against his lips.

He pulls back, looking into my eyes. But whatever he's searching for, he's not going to find it. There's nothing more to this than the simple need for distraction and reassurance that I'm still in control of something.

Fuck married exes. Fuck questioning my judgment. Fuck everything else. Just for now. Just for this.

"Don't you want me?" I repeat, running my fingernails through the hair at the back of his head.

His eyelids grow heavy as he leans into my touch, a sinful smile dusting his lips. "You know the answer to that."

"Do I?" I tug on his hair, and he curses.

"I wanted you four years ago," he groans, watching me for a reaction. "I wanted you last night. And I've wanted you every day in between. I never stopped wanting you, even when I didn't see you. Don't act like you don't fucking know that."

The intensity in his words steals the air from my lungs. I draw in a deep breath to ground myself. He drops his hands to his sides, curling them into tight fists like he's fighting to hold himself back.

"Then what are you waiting—?"

He grabs my chin, making me gasp.

"I can't fuck you and walk away after, Sophie. It doesn't work like that."

His eyes roam all over my face, taking their time to drink me in. His chest expands on a deep breath and his grip softens a little. Then he sighs, and it's weighted with regret.

He presses a soft kiss to my lips. "I fuck you and I get to keep you forever. What do you say to that?"

I stand stunned as he looks at me.

"And there's your answer." He kisses my forehead softly before letting me go.

He gives me a slow, soft smile, his eyes dimming, as he steps back and turns to grab his jacket from the back of the chair.

"Drew?"

He walks toward the door.

My chest tightens. He can't leave like this. Maybe Halliday's talk of signs from the universe has some truth to it. Because as he opens the door, panic grips me, like a cold stab to the gut. Something's telling me that if I let him walk out of that door now, I'll regret it.

"Drew?" I raise my voice.

As he turns back, I tug the towel free, and it drops to the floor into a heap around my feet. The cool air dances across my skin, heightening my senses. Or maybe it's the way he's watching me with an intensity that sets my heart beating so hard it pounds in my ears.

He lets go of the door handle and the door falls closed, clicking shut.

We stare at each other. His throat constricts as he swallows, his eyes sliding over my body, drinking it in. He rolls his bottom lip between his teeth as his eyes meet mine again, blazing with desire. The move is so sexy that I suck in a breath, anticipation making me hot from head to toe.

My fingers tingle the way they do in the courtroom when I know I've won my case. That intuition I have. That gut feeling when I know... When I just know.

"We'll talk about the terms later. Now, come back here." My nipples pebble into aching peaks at his darkened stare. "Now," I add, "I'm not going to ask twi—"

He strides over and grabs me under one thigh, hoisting me up with one arm so that my legs wrap around his waist. His other hand grips the back of my head, cushioning it, as he slams me up against the wall.

"Do *you* want *me*?" he growls against my lips, our breath tangling as we pant. "You asked me if I want you and I told you. Now you tell me, Sophie, can you handle what you'll get with me?"

He looks at me without blinking, the blue of his eyes piercing, as his lips hover inches from mine. His nostrils flare, and his scent envelops me until I taste smoked honey inside my mouth.

I dart my tongue out and lick the corner of my lips. *Can I handle him?* It's just arousal talking, him saying that if I let this happen, then we're bound to one another. But even though it's just talk, it still sounds hot as hell.

My pulse beats a steady rhythm between my legs as I gaze at him.

"Yes. I want you and everything that comes with it."

"Fuck," he hisses. "You don't know what hearing you say that does to me."

The unmistakable bulge of his erection presses into my ass cheeks. Just the feel of it there, and the knowledge that I'm making this strong, hulk of a man look like he's about to lose control is enough to make wet heat pool between my legs. I roll my hips, rubbing shamelessly against him, searching for friction. Slick wetness spreads over Drew's abs where his shirt is hanging open.

His attention moves from my lips down to where his skin is glistening, a thin layer of my arousal coating the defined muscles above the waistband of his pants.

My heart thuds as I wait for him to react.

He slowly slides one hand between our bodies, trailing it over the shiny patch on his skin, before he slips two fingers inside me, achingly slow.

My body accepts them greedily, and my eyes roll back in my head. I stifle a moan as he goes straight to my G-spot and teases it.

"This for me?" He swirls his fingers, and my body makes an obscene, wet and needy sound. He presses the heel of his hand flush against my clit and rubs.

"Oh my god, that feels..." I drag in a breath as I blink at his fingers disappearing inside me. The veins are bulging in his forearm as he flexes it, causing another swell of wetness to rush from me.

"I asked you a question. Is this for me?"

I moan shamelessly, unable to react in any other way.

I'm always in control. My life only functions with control. At work. At home.

I shudder as his fingers move inside me again, making my muscles flutter around them.

Here, it's blindingly obvious that Drew has the control. He's turning me inside out with pleasure. My wetness soaks his hand as I grip the collar of his shirt, completely naked, pinned between his solid body and the wall. I'm a trembling, needy mess, about to come any second. And he's done this to me within minutes.

"Drew," I utter, my body desperately trying to hold onto his fingers as he slides them out. He brings them to his lips and holds my eyes as he sucks them with a low growl of appreciation.

"Tastes like it's made especially for me, Sophie."

I gasp against his lips as his hand returns between my legs, and he pushes three fingers in, stretching me wide.

"Feels like it's made especially for me too," he grunts as my body sucks him back in again.

I shake around his fingers, trembling with the need to come. "Please, I'm close..."

His lips curl in approval, as though he's got me exactly where he wants me.

"You about to come on my fingers, Darling?" He swirls them again, his grip on my thigh tightening.

I nod, panting against his lips, and he drives his tongue inside my mouth and kisses me until I'm dizzy and breathless. His fingers still inside me, and I huff in frustration.

"So close, huh?" He chuckles, his eyes sweeping over my face before he runs the tip of his nose up the side of my face until his lips meet my ear.

"Tell me you're sorry," he rasps.

"W-what?" I say, teetering on the edge of an orgasm.

He glides his thumb around my clit at the same time as he sucks on my neck. I edge closer to release, but his fingers freeze inside me again.

I cry out and tip my head back, banging it gently on the wall in frustration.

His hand on my thigh flexes, his fingertips pressing into my skin as his cock digs into the underside of my ass. The only small mercy to this torture is that I'd bet anything that he's finding it hard to hold back too.

"Tell me you're sorry for making me wait," he grits in my ear, his breath sending goosebumps skittering up my spine.

"Drew," I breathe.

"You should have been soaking my fingers a long time ago."

I squeeze my eyes shut, ready to burst at the smallest movement.

"Say it," he growls, bringing his lips back to mine and kissing me with a featherlight touch, making my lips tingle.

He moves away before I can kiss him back properly. I whimper with unmet need. It's almost more arousing than the mouth claiming kiss he gave me moments ago.

"Say it and I'll let you come for me like you should have been doing for the past four years. You want to come, don't you, Sophie?"

He leans into me, kissing me properly, pulling back when I'm panting for air.

*Oh my god.*

He's insane. But I'm too close to care.

"I'm sorry," I gasp.

His lips lift into a smug smile. "Good girl."

I exhale in relief. But instead of giving me what I want, he pulls his fingers out of me again, and the sound of his zipper being pulled down fills my ears.

He pulls his cock free and the thick head of it slides easily over me as he claims my mouth again, holding me up with both hands cupping my ass.

"You've got me dripping for you," he groans as his pre-cum joins the wetness between my thighs. "You're so fucking sexy."

I writhe, reveling in the sensation of the broad head of his cock pressing against my clit. "We need to use a condom. But just... just..." I stumble on my words, seconds away from coming apart. "Just one..." I swallow, my thighs trembling around his waist as I circle myself over the slick head of his cock. "Just give me—"

"Give you this?" He rolls his hips so the thick tip pushes through my lips. "You want this cock?"

"Mm-hm... just..." I give up trying to form a coherent sentence. "Please," I beg.

"Fuccckkk." He pushes inside me, filling me, stretching me. His forehead drops to mine. "You feel this?"

"Yes," I choke out as the pressure builds in my core to the point of being unbearable.

He pushes deeper, my body struggling to accept his size. "You know what this is?" he growls.

"No." I'm so close to exploding that it's taking everything in me to speak.

He lifts his forehead from mine and looks into my eyes.

"It's fate."

"Fate?"

"Yeah. Me. You. You coming for me." He drives deeper, and I cry out. "This was always going to happen, Sophie. You just liked making me wait."

"I—"

His eyes blaze as he drives the final thick inches inside me. The second his balls kiss my skin, I explode into the strongest, most consuming orgasm I've ever had.

"Oh god!"

My vision blurs as I come in waves. I don't want to close my eyes. I want to witness this. I want to see how he reacts when he sees what he's done to me.

His pupils blow wide, and he sucks his bottom lip, groaning low in his chest. I can only describe the flare in his eyes as awe. Awe as his fingers dig into my flesh and he watches me come for him. *Because* of him.

My body trembles. Every second is worth fighting the urge that I had to clench my eyes shut and concentrate on my own pleasure.

Seeing him getting off on watching me is enough to make me peak again, and I come hard a second time. I claw at his shirt collar, my nails scraping skin.

"Drew."

He looks at me with enough power in his eyes to light up a city. "Fucking fire, Darling." He pulls out and slams back in with a deep hiss. "You look beautiful, coming around my cock. Moan my name again. Make up for lost time."

I whimper his name, happy to oblige as warmth blankets my body.

"Fuck, yeah," he grunts.

He slides out as the last pulse leaves my body, then bends to suck one of my nipples.

"Don't stop." I sink my hands into his hair as he switches sides.

"I have to or I'm going to come inside you."

I moan while he continues to lavish attention on my breasts. Everything he does feels amazing.

"Do you have any condoms?"

My cheeks heat as he looks up at me again. One of his brows lifts and he smiles.

"I do."

I tug his hair, pressing my nipple closer to his lips. "Go on then."

He grins wickedly and slowly licks me. "Go on what?"

He wants me to say it, and hell, I'm so horny that I don't care. I'll scream it out the window if I have to.

"Put it on. I want you inside me again."

"So fucking bossy," he says with a sinful smile, lowering me down so my feet touch the floor. "Get on the bed and wait for me."

I rush to do as he says, dropping onto the bed as he throws his shirt off and steps out of his pants. He reaches down into the pocket and stalks toward me, his eyes on mine as he rips the foil packet.

My core clenches as I take him in. Those broad shoulders and strong arms that held me up against the wall, his defined, thick torso that I writhed against. And his cock. It's veined, and wide... so big. I swallow as he stops at the side of the bed and rolls the condom onto it, giving it a quick tug once he's fully sheathed.

"You're staring." He smirks.

He kneels on the bed and leans over me. I arch up to kiss him, but he grips each of my thighs and parts my legs.

"Ready?" A thick brow arches.

"Yes," I breathe.

He thrusts into me, making me fly up the bed. He grips my hips, pulling me back down onto his cock and I cry out as he plants his hands either side of my head and starts fucking me like it's an Olympic sport and he's destined to win gold.

I don't know how the hell he's doing it, but I'm ready to come again.

His lips curl into a devilish smile, and he pauses long enough to press down onto his hands, all of the muscles rippling in his shoulders, as he bends and kisses me.

"You feel so fucking good," he whispers.

I chase his lips, not wanting the kiss to end as he pulls back. He repositions his arms beneath my thighs and lifts my ass from the mattress. Then he pounds into me.

All I can do is clamp onto him and take it.

I come again, digging my nails into the back of his hands. He flips me over, dragging me up to my knees and holding me in place with one hand on the back of my neck as he drives into me from behind with a guttural groan.

I'm being fucked to death by Drew Harper. And my only reaction is loud whimpers as my wetness runs down my inner thighs and my body makes wet slap-ping sounds against his.

"Oh my god," I gasp.

He pulls me up so that my back is flush against his hot chest. His teeth graze my earlobe. "You got one more for me before I fill this pretty pussy?"

All I'm capable of is a garbled whimper of agree-ment.

Chuckling, he sucks on my neck and massages my breasts in his palms. "Yeah, Darling. I think you do. I think you've got a lot more to give me." Then he moves us again, dropping down onto his back and pulling me over his hips to straddle him.

He holds the base of his cock with one hand and lifts me with the other, guiding me down onto him.

"You have control, Boss. Now show me what I've been missing."

My breath comes in whimpered pants as I ride him. His hands grip my hips the entire time as he widens his thighs and relaxes back, content to watch me above him. I grind down onto him hard until a familiar tightening builds low in my core.

"I'm going to—"

He reaches up, fisting my hair and pulling my lips down to his.

"Kiss me while you coat my cock in your cum."

*Fuck.*

I try. But my moans overtake me as I come again, so hard that my head spins.

He pants against my mouth, every muscle in his body tensing. "You feel so damn good. I'm going to fucking co—"

I fight to get my composure back and kiss him, stealing his words as he comes deep inside me. His cock swells and I cry into his mouth, matching his own curses and groans.

"Fuck, Sophie."

Warm, fuzzy bliss washes over me.

"Wow," I breathe.

His hand loosens in my hair and moves to cup the back of my neck as he moves slowly inside me, emptying the last of himself.

He pulls my forehead to his. "I'd have waited four centuries if I knew that's what this would be like."

I shift back to look at him. His eyes are buzzing with energy, and a serene smile graces his face.

"And if I'd known, I might have said yes the first time you asked me out."

He flexes his hand on the back on my neck, pulling my lips back to his. "Might?"

He kisses me, slow and deliberate, like a promise that this is only the start.

"Monday night. What are you doing?"

"Monday?" I muse as he kisses me again. "I don't have plans."

His lips spread into a cocky grin. "You do now. Your boyfriend's taking you out."

# Chapter 7
# Drew

"Has Penny booked your flight?" Tanner asks, frowning at the design prints on the boardrooms meeting table.

"She did." I lean back in my chair, flexing my shoulders as I stretch. A groan escapes me and I wince.

"Been hammering it in the gym?" Tanner drops his pen onto the paperwork and looks at me.

"Maybe." I tip my head. "Fine... yes."

He chuckles, pressing a finger and thumb into his tired eyes. His youngest, Ruby, has started teething and he told me he was up half the night walking around the house with her in his arms because it's the only way she would sleep.

I don't feel sorry for him. He's a lucky bastard and he knows it. But since Friday night, my usual jealousy doesn't gut punch me as hard as it usually would.

"You only do that when you're worried about work. Or when you're pumped about something. So which is it?" he asks. "Something tells me it isn't going to the New York office to close this deal."

"Ten out of ten." I reach over and clap him on the back with a wide grin.

"The lawyer?" His brows rise in question.

"Sophie," I confirm with a grin. It's been there ever since Saturday morning. It hasn't left my face since the moment she dropped that towel and told me she wanted me. And it grew even wider when we'd finished and she reached for the painkillers I bought and popped two like she knew she'd be needing them.

I wonder if she's aching as much as me now. If she's still feeling me.

The thought makes my grin stretch further.

"Sophie," Tanner repeats, pursing his lips. "About fucking time."

"Yeah. Took a while, but I told you years ago it'd happen. No going back now. That woman is *it* for me."

Tanner opens his mouth and then promptly shuts it, nodding instead as I fix him with a look that says, *"You can't talk."* We both know he was a goner for his wife, Rachel the moment he met her. Sometimes your gut tells you the first time you meet someone. And my gut was pretty damn clear four years ago. Sophie Havers was always meant for me. And I'll fight anyone who argues otherwise.

"I'll schedule the global call for Thursday, then? When you're back," he says, picking his pen up and marking something down.

"Sure."

Even the thought of one of our long-ass meetings with all the branch heads from around the world later this week can't bring me down today.

Because tonight I have a date.

And this time, she's *my* date.

"Drew!" The surprise in Sophie's voice is evident, even though I see her face from behind the giant bouquet of irises I'm holding.

"Hey, Darling." I hand her the bouquet and kiss her on the cheek, curling one hand around her hipbone and fighting back my groan at the feel of her again.

"Thank you. They're—"

"Your favorite. I remember."

"I'll get a vase." Smiling, she walks down the hall and into a large open-plan living room of her apartment. "Did you want a drink before we go?" She glances at me over her shoulder before she walks through a door into what I assume is the kitchen.

"No. I want my date," I say as the sound of a running tap mixes with her laugh.

When we first met, she was so serious and focused. But hearing her now, the lightness in her laugh, I intend to make it happen a whole lot more. It suits her.

And it swells my fucking heart.

"It's like that, is it?" She walks back into the room, passing me with the vase of flowers.

"Yeah, it's like that." My eyes drop over her black dress. It hugs every curve of her body, stopping below the knee. And then she has these sexy high heels on with ribbons tied into bows around her ankles.

*Fuck me.*

She places the vase onto the hallway table and looks into the mirror above it, catching my eye in the reflection.

"You look nice," she says, taking in my black suit and white shirt. It's not the one she wore that night, but I wore white again to remind her. She looks good wearing my clothes. She looks good wearing *me*.

"And you're sensational."

My compliment makes her blush. Of all the times she looked into my eyes as she came for me two days ago, and a compliment has her flushing.

Cute.

My flame might be hot enough to burn when she's in ball-busting lawyer mode. But I'm seeing a softer side to her. A glow that's the basis for everything else.

"Shall we?" I place my hand on her lower back and guide her to the door.

Sophie seems impressed when she sees that I've brought her to the London venue of the same restaurant where we had the double date with Logan and Kelly. If I could have ordered her the same meal tonight too, then I would have. But the menu has changed since then.

"Do you have much time to yourself in New York?" She cradles her glass of wine as she looks at me over the top of our finished desserts.

We've spent dinner talking about both work and Logan dating my sister, Maddy. Sophie was mesmerized by their story and how they managed to keep it a secret in the beginning. She made a comment about how people we know can hide anything if they want to, despite us thinking we would be able to tell if they lied. The way her eyes dimmed as she told me had me clenching my fists. I'd bet it's got something to do with the asshole ex she mentioned. If I ever meet the guy, he'd better pray for mercy.

"I usually fly straight back once the meetings are all done. Tan and I lived there for a year, so there are people I like to catch up with if I do stay longer."

"I remember you telling me that."

"You do remember that night, then? You remember breaking my heart?" I smirk.

She arches a brow. "I remember you trying to climb into my cab with me and then standing in the road and almost getting hit so you could wave."

I lean back in my seat and allow myself a leisurely sweep of appreciation of her. She looks incredible tonight. Her blonde hair is shorter than when we first met, but her lips are the same full, glossy temptation that they were that night.

"What?" She narrows her eyes as she takes a sip of her wine.

"You sure I waved?"

"Yes. You defin—" She turns her head to the side, hiding her mouth in her palm as she realizes what I'm doing.

"You were looking back." I reach over the table, taking her hand from her face and linking my fingers with hers.

"No." She tries to disguise her smile.

"Ms. Havers?" I lean closer.

"Yes, Mr. Harper?"

I grin when her eyes sparkle. We hold each other's gaze, something unspoken and magnetic in the air between. A few seconds pass with us just looking at one another.

"I was ready to murder those two guys by the elevators on Friday night," I confess, stroking her knuckles with my thumb.

"What?"

"They wanted..." I take a calming breath to douse the sudden flare of heat lancing through my veins. "I know what they wanted."

"They weren't going to do anything."

"But they wanted to." I fix my eyes on hers and she studies me, frowning. "They wanted to." I run my other hand around my jaw as I look at her knuckles and stroke them again. "I don't care what's happened in the last four years. I can't fucking care about it. Not if I want to stay sane, but..." I grit my teeth. "Seeing people look at you like that, it does things to me."

"Things?" Her lips part, and I have the urge to reach over the table and pull them to mine to feel them between my teeth.

"It makes me want to tear heads off," I growl.

"Oh."

She looks so serious. I've screwed it. Forget four years. She's going to think I'm a psycho, possessive asshole, and change her name so she never has to see me again.

I know I'm coming on strong, but fuck, I can't help it.

I'm done wasting time. If all the shit that's gone down with my friends and family the past few years has taught me one thing, it's that you don't take a good thing for granted. Because you could lose it all.

And Sophie Havers is my good thing.

She brings her eyes to mine, and I ready my defense. She might be one of the country's top lawyers, but I'm not going down without a fight.

I open my mouth, but she cuts me off.

"Thank you for a lovely evening."

Heat flares across the back of my neck. She's brushing me off.

"Sophie—"

"It's my turn to arrange the date next time."

"Next time?" My brows shoot up.

"Yes. Is that a problem?" She looks at me, and I blink.

"No, no problem." My dick springs to attention at her confident tone.

"Good." She finishes her wine. "Are you ready to take me home now?"

# Chapter 8
## Drew

"YOU BOOKED YOURSELF INTO The Songbird hotel? When it's only a couple of nights you sometimes—"

"Not anymore. We've talked about this." I sigh, frustrated.

"I see." Alicia scowls, sitting back into the seat of the car the New York office sent for me.

She smoothes her dark hair back into its tight bun even though there isn't a hair out of place. There never is. She's immaculate. Even first thing in the morning. I swear she gets up and puts makeup on, then climbs back into bed.

My phone chimes with a text, and I pull it out.

**Sophie: I hope you had a good flight. See you Friday.**

My thumb hovers over the call button for a split second before I hit it, bringing the phone to my ear.

"I can't wait, Ms. Havers," I say the moment she answers.

Her soft laugh floats down the phone. "Mr. Harper, I'm at work. The same as you. Stop distracting me."

The line goes dead, and my grin stretches to my ears. Lawyer Sophie is sexy *and* fun.

"Personal call?"

"My girlfriend." I slip my phone back into the inner pocket of my suit jacket.

"Oh?"

Alicia turns back to the window when I don't elaborate and watches as the Manhattan skyline comes into view.

The remainder of the drive is made in silence until we pull up in front of the office. She was supposed to be briefing me on our latest project, a refurb of the prestigious *Seasons* members only club in Manhattan. But it doesn't matter. I've seen the design portfolio and read the client brief. If I have any questions, I can discuss them when I meet with the owner, Sterling Beaufort.

Alicia bristles in her seat as our driver stops the car and exits, holding the rear door open for her.

She clears her throat. "You don't do girlfriends, Drew."

"I didn't," I state flatly, stepping out of the car behind her and buttoning the top button of my jacket up with one hand. "Until her."

I extend one arm, indicating for Alicia to go first. She looks up at me, and I hold her eyes, challenging her to say anything that'll give me a good reason to fire her. She's pushed the boundaries enough in the past for this to be her final chance. And I'm not justifying my relationship with Sophie to anyone.

I look at her pointedly, tired of her games.

She spins with a huff, walking into the building.

# Chapter 9
# Sophie

"I THOUGHT YOU APPROVED of him," I say to Halliday as I gather up some files from my desk.

"I do. But you've never been in serious relationships, and now you've jumped straight from one and into another," she says down the phone.

"It's just another date when he's back from New York tomorrow. Nothing serious." I check my watch. *Five minutes until my client arrives.*

"Is that how Drew sees it?"

"You don't need to worry. I like his company. He makes me forget about work. I feel like a part of myself that I thought was lost forever re-surfaces when I'm with him."

"He told you he'd be your husband now if you'd dated him," Halliday deadpans.

I shake my head with a smile. "He was joking."

"Hmm," Halliday hums.

I fight the urge to respond because I don't believe myself either. Drew is intense. And something about the look in his eyes as he made the husband comment—the dark, primal way they bored into mine—tells me he wasn't joking. At all.

"It's just one more date. We didn't even sleep together again."

He kissed me goodbye on the doorstep and left after our date, even though I invited him in. I thought there'd be more and was disappointed when there wasn't. I shake the thought away. Now isn't the time to get distracted.

"I've gotta go; my client's due any minute."

"Me too. I have a call with a match-making daughter," Halliday says.

"The one in New York?"

"Park Avenue Princess," Halliday sings in confirmation.

"Exciting. Good luck. I'll catch you later."

I walk from my office to the door at the end of the hallway and knock. I wait for her timid voice to call out before I enter.

Large, scared eyes meet mine as I step inside and close the door.

"Hi, Chelsea. How are you doing today?"

She chews on her bottom lip, fidgeting with the cuffs of her baggy sweatshirt as I walk over and take a seat on the sofa next to her. I place the files I'm carrying onto the low table next to a mug of fresh tea that I make sure we have waiting for her when she comes in.

We don't meet in my office. We use one of the comfort rooms instead. The fear in her eyes lessens a trace amount in a less formal environment.

But merely a trace.

"Did you practice some of those breathing exercises we spoke about?"

"Yeah." Her eyes dart to mine and then away again as she nods.

She's young. Barely eighteen. And has seen far more of the ugly dark side of the human race than anyone ever should. But feeling sorry for her isn't going to help her in court. I need to prepare her for what's coming. Make her walk out of the other side with the power to live her life the way she should be doing.

"Good. Keep doing them. They're a useful tool to have in your back pocket. One that's yours and yours alone, okay?"

She nods again, her eyes sliding to the top folder on the table. "Are those...?"

I smile gently. "We can take as much time as you need. But I need you to look and tell me if you recognize anything, okay?"

She pulls her sleeves down over her hands and wraps her arms around her middle.

I open the folder and take out the first photograph. It's of a long, dirty hallway, dimly lit by a single yellow bulb in the ceiling. Apartment doors line both walls.

Chelsea sucks in a breath, and I slide out the next photo. It's inside one of the apartments. The room is bare of furniture except a double bed without sheets in the center. The mattress is stained and dirty, and there are restraints hanging from the metal headboard.

She swallows thickly, her bottom lip trembling.

"I need you to say it out loud," I encourage in a soft voice.

"Y-yes." She sniffs, blinking rapidly. "That's where... that's where it happened."

"This is where you were kept?"

"Yes. It's where..." She drops her eyes to the floor, her throat bobbing. "It's where he took me after we met. And..."

I wait patiently for her to continue. She's told me this before. But she's going to have to tell it again in court. And this practice is going to help her. We've spoken about it, and she wants to do this.

"... and it's where..." She swallows again. "Where he and his friend took turns to have sex with me."

"Okay. You're doing great, Chelsea. Do you want to take a break?"

"No." She shakes her head. "I want to do this. Keep going."

I press the button on my key chain and the lights on my BMW flash in the dark staff parking lot.

"Soph? You haven't returned any of my calls."

I spin, my heartrate spiking in my chest.

"Henry? What the hell?" I look around the suppos- edly secure car park for any of my colleagues who might also be heading home, but it's empty. "How did you get in here?"

"You look good." His eyes sweep over my cream silk blouse and fitted skirt suit. Once, the attention from him felt good. Now it feels cheap and nasty.

"Why are you here? I thought I made myself clear." I click over the concrete in my heels, opening up the trunk of my car to place some case files in.

"It's over with my wife. I love you."

I pause, looking sideways at him. His hopeful, deceitful eyes shine in the low evening light, and I sigh as I turn away. I can't tell if he's telling the truth. I don't care what the truth is. But I care that I can't tell. He shook the core of my self-belief when he fooled me. I can't allow him back into my life to shake it again. My clients need me on top form. Not doubting myself.

I slam the trunk shut and spin to glare at him.

"You have a funny definition of love. This is where I work," I hiss. "You're out of line coming here."

"Soph." He reaches out and wraps his fingers around my wrist. "Please. You know I want you. I've not been able to stop thinking about you since that morning. It's been almost a week. How long are you going to punish me?"

I shake my hand free from his grasp. "Punish you? You think I'm doing this to teach you a lesson?" I stalk past him to the driver's door and wrench it open.

"Baby." Henry's behind me again as I turn to face him.

"Did you have a nice anniversary after you left my place? Did you go home and kiss your wife after leaving my bed?"

His brow wrinkles. Not from guilt, but from being caught. He doesn't need to confirm it for me to know it's true. But the relief from being able to read him and knowing he can't always fool me is quickly replaced by a sickness washing over me.

"Goodbye, Henry." I climb into the car.

"Don't be like this," he snaps. "What was I supposed to do? She would have been suspicious if I hadn't. And with her, it's just sex. Not like what we have."

I snort in disgust as I reach for the door handle.

"I thought of you the entire time, I swear." He looks at me, a pathetic pleading in his eyes. "I couldn't get hard until I pictured your face."

I stare at him. "What did I ever see in you?" I shriek. "Now move, unless you want to lose your tiny, cheating dick!"

He steps back, narrowly avoiding being hit by the door as I slam it. I start the engine and reverse quickly, then speed off.

Asshole. Who the hell does he think he is coming to my office like that? Waiting for me to finish work.

The Bluetooth chimes with an incoming call and I hit the answer button hard.

"What?" I snap, half expecting it to be Henry with some more pathetic excuses.

"Bad day?" The deep tone sounds amused. But then it morphs to concern when I don't respond. "Sophie, where are you?"

"In my car," I murmur, taking a deep, cleansing breath.

"I'm sending you a location."

"Why?"

"Because I want you to meet me there." His voice is gentle, and it sends relief spreading through my tense shoulders just from hearing it. The effect he has on me should be disarming, seeing as I barely know him. Except it isn't. Not in the slightest. It's like my body trusts him already.

My brow pinches in confusion. "You're in New York."

The smile in his voice is unmistakable. "*Was*. I came home early. Seems like I missed you."

"Drew." I bite my bottom lip, my chest swelling as piece by piece, the heaviness of the day starts to shed. One proper date with this man and he already has the power to make a hellish day seem like a mere inconvenience.

"Drive safe. And you can thank me with a kiss from those beautiful lips of yours when you get here."

"Sure." I roll my eyes with a small laugh, my glass of wine and bath forgotten already. "We'll see about that."

"No, Sophie. We'll kiss about that."

A location pops up on the car's screen and I end the call and smile for the rest of the drive.

"I've driven this way to work for almost a year, and I never knew this place existed," I say, licking the ice-cream off my spoon.

The location he sent me was for a dessert café. It's got a cute fifties retro vibe with baby pink booth seating, black and white checkered flooring, and a vintage juke box playing over by the long serving counter. It draws in quite a crowd too. Every booth is filled with a mix of students, families, and people in business wear, as well as those calling in for takeaways.

"That's because you work hard and don't play enough." He winks at me as he mirrors my movement, licking the mint choc chip from his spoon.

"How did you find this place?"

"Tanner."

"Your business partner?"

"Yeah. Guy has three kids. Ruby is just a baby, and then he's got two boys." His smile lights up his entire face.

"You come here with them?"

"Every couple of weeks. They always manage to negotiate extra toppings when I bring them. They'll be great in business when they're older." He chuckles, and his eyes leave mine as he scoops up more ice-cream.

He must bring the boys here by himself. I'm not sure why, but the discovery makes warmth spread through my chest. My sister Holly has two children. But she married an American actor and they live in LA. I don't get to see my two nieces much.

I fill my spoon again, studying Drew at the same time. He's still wearing his work suit. I suspect he's come straight from the airport to see me after getting off the plane, but I don't ask him, because a part of me would hate it if I'm wrong.

*What the hell am I getting myself into?*

"My thoughts exactly," he muses, his eyes dropping to my lips as I lick the ice cream from them, having spoken out loud without realizing. I'm more tired than I thought. Meeting with Chelsea, Henry turning up... it's been a long day.

"What?" I frown as he looks into my almost empty bowl.

"Rum and raisin?" He arches a brow in disgust, making me laugh.

"I like it," I argue back, digging out a big spoonful on purpose.

"Okay." He lifts his brows as I lick my spoon and narrow my eyes at him.

"You're passing judgment on my ice cream choice like some sort of flavor connoisseur and I bet you've never even tried it." I wave my spoon in his direction. "Where's the fairness in that. Judge and jury all in one, Mr. Harper?"

He drops his spoon in his bowl. "Give me a taste then." He rises from his seat and leans over the table, planting one palm on it as he moves closer. The days' worth of stubble is more visible along his angled jaw-line as he waits in front of me. The sight has me wetting my lips.

I lift my spoon into the small gap between us like an offering, but he smirks, exhaling cool, minty breath against my lips. "Not like that."

He presses his lips to mine and kisses me softly, chuckling, as my spoon drops and clatters loudly on the table. I ignore it, gripping onto his tie and pulling him closer so I can deepen the kiss. He kisses me back with more urgency, sliding his tongue between my lips and groaning as I run my other hand through the hair at the back of his neck.

He pulls back, ending it far too quickly.

"I told myself to take this slow," he mutters around a soft smile as he sits back in his seat and looks at me.

"And I said I'd pick our next date. But I didn't." My gaze darts around the cafe, then comes back to meet his. "Things change." I tip my head to one side. "But just so I know... slow?"

This is why he kissed me on the doorstep but never came in after our date. Is this how he dates? Throws the word husband and boyfriend around freely, but doesn't attempt to touch me after the first night? Makes it a game, hoping I'll be the one to chase him? I fight from rolling my eyes as disappointment gathers low in my gut. I don't have time for games.

Warm fingers graze my chin as he turns my head, bringing my gaze back to his. "You deserve to be dated. Properly."

I lean into his warm touch as his hand slides up around my cheek. A few words and I'm already lapping it up. How does he have this effect on me?

"What if I want both?" I muse, making no attempt to move away.

"Both?"

"Orgasms and dates."

A chuckle rumbles from his chest.

"Would you think less of me?" I ask.

His expression turns serious. "I could never think less of you, Sophie."

I bat down the butterflies threatening to take flight in my stomach. This never happened with Henry. I didn't think I had any butterflies. But I do. They were just hibernating. Waiting.

"As long as you promise you won't think less of me either."

My breath stalls as he pins me with the look I've seen on defendant's faces before it all becomes too much and they confess their sins.

"I've..." His eyes drop to my bowl, then slide back up to me, a smile stretching his lips. "I've tried rum and raisin before."

"I see." I try to look annoyed, but I know my lips are in danger of matching his smile.

"Never liked the taste until it was from your mouth, though."

I stare at him, my eyes dropping to his lower lip that he's got his perfect white teeth sinking into to hide his smirk.

"Drew?"

"Sophie?" The way he says my name in a deep gravelly voice, causes the butterflies to swarm again.

"Let's go."

We burst through my front door like horny teenagers, all hands, mouths, moans, and gasps.

"Fuck," Drew rasps against my lips as he slams me back against the wall, kissing me like it would cause him physical pain to stop. "I came straight from the airport. I haven't showered. I wasn't planning on—"

He groans as I palm his hard cock roughly through his suit pants.

"I don't care." I squeeze him, smiling against his neck as he curses. He smells like honey on smoked wood, like he always does. "You already made this day better. Don't stop now."

"Busy day, Ms. Woods?" He grins, lifting me into his arms.

I wrap my legs around his waist as he strides down the hallway, looking through each doorway until he finds my bedroom.

"Quit with the blonde lawyer jokes," I breathe against his neck, kissing up and down it.

He drops me onto my bed, climbing up over me. "You know I'm kidding. I think you're fucking incredible. And smarter than any man I've ever met."

He slides my skirt up my thighs and moves down the bed, settling himself between my thighs. His eyes flash as he looks up at me with his mouth inches from my lace panties. He's so close that the warmth of his breath is fanning over me, making my panties damp in anticipation.

His admission catches me off guard. I'm good at my job. But I've had to fight hard to get to where I am. I've seen so many male colleagues promoted before me. When they win a case, the press hail them a hero and dole out god complexes to the ones whose egos thrive on it. When I win, the press focus on my outfits, occasionally expanding the piece to include statistics on the number of women working in law. It's a tiny victory.

The feel of Drew's hungry mouth kissing me through the fabric brings me back to my senses and my back arches off the bed in response.

"More of that. God, you're good at that," I moan.

He chuckles as my hands dive into his hair and I pull him back against me.

"Better than any ice cream I've ever tasted," he groans, hooking my panties to one side with a finger and driving his tongue up inside me.

Pleasure thrums through me like an electric current, and I writhe.

"Did I say you could move?" Drew growls and pulls my panties down my legs, smiling as he scrunches the wet fabric in his fist before placing them down on the bed. He wraps both of his arms beneath my thighs and clasps my waist. I'm dragged back onto his mouth with a rough jerk.

He lets out an appreciative grunt as I quiver.

So we're back to Bossy Mr. Harper. I bite my lip, smiling around my moan as he fucks me leisurely with his tongue, running the tip of his nose over my swollen clit. I haven't worked him out. He can be playful. But then he's also intense, like now. More than I remember him being four years ago. It's like something has hardened him.

I cry out as he changes his attack on me and sucks on my clit, nipping it gently with his teeth before running circles over it with his tongue.

"Oh, fuck..."

"Say my name, Darling."

I tremble, on the crest of a huge orgasm. My thighs tighten, and I suck in air, desperately trying to maintain some kind of composure. But I can't. My lips part of their own accord, and the whimpers and moans coming from them echo around the room.

"My name," he growls again.

One of the hands grasping my waist slides around to the side of my ass cheek and my skin stings as he strikes it with his palm.

"I want to hear my name on your lips when you come, Sophie. Understand?"

"Oh God," I whimper.

He angles my hips from the bed, lifting me onto his mouth like I'm a meal made especially for him to devour.

Then he slaps my ass again. "Now."

The initial rush of pain is quickly replaced by warming pleasure as he smooths his hand over my struck skin, massaging it.

"Drew!"

I feel his smile against me as I come violently. He sucks it up, continuing to lick me, drawing out my orgasm for as long as he can. Every time I think he's about to let up, he groans and sinks into me again, until I'm coming a second time, and then a third. Until I'm a whimpering mess of quivering limbs and shaking muscles beneath him.

He waits for me to come down enough to form a coherent thought, and then he kisses me between the legs, looking up at me.

"You want to take a break?"

I shake my head far too quickly, making him laugh.

He climbs over me, his eyes full of desire and admiration before he kisses me. I have a flashback of that first time together, and I smile against his mouth.

"Good," he murmurs sexily. "Because I wasn't about to give you one."

He kisses me again, then grabs a condom and rolls it on, before sliding inside me with a confident thrust.

Fucked to death by Drew Harper.

What a way to go.

# Chapter 10
# Drew

"Your house is burning and you can only take one thing. Not a person, they're all safe. I mean an actual object." Sophie traces her fingers over my chest and around each groove of my abs as we lie in bed.

I ended up sleeping over, which meant waking up next to her like this. *Fucking perfect.*

"You sound like Logan with his hypothetical questions." I chuckle as I pull her into my side.

"Ah, like I could forget. Which cartoon character would I be?" she muses. "I remember you said Mufasa. Didn't have you down as a Disney fan. But I get it. The big strong leader."

I stiffen, but she doesn't notice.

"Fine. I'll go first." She bites her bottom lip and hums as she thinks. "I'd take the first book on law my dad bought me for my twelfth birthday."

"You would?" I lower my chin and smile at her. "You two close?"

Her eyes light up, and her nose wrinkles. "We are. So much it annoys my mum and sister sometimes. But he was a judge, and we have a love of law in common. We used to watch all the episodes of *Murder, She Wrote* and *Diagnosis: Murder* together when I was growing up. He's brilliant. He was always respected as a judge. Fair, but firm."

I stroke Sophie's bare shoulder with my thumb. "I'm happy for you that you have a great relationship with him."

She studies my frown. "What's your father like?"

I blow out a puff of air. When I don't elaborate, she settles her head back onto my chest and resumes stroking my chest.

"We're different," I say, finally, forcing my body not to tense up the way it usually does whenever my father is mentioned.

"You're not close, then?"

"You could say that." I roll my neck, cracking it. I'm not that good at stopping all the tension. I hate that talking about him affects me.

I sigh and pull her closer. She deserves to know.

"To my father, I'm nothing but a huge disappointment. An embarrassment."

Her hand stills on my chest.

"I got into some trouble when I was a teenager. Spent time in a juvenile detention center for car theft and joyriding. My father never forgave me for it. Our relationship wasn't that great before. But after that, it never recovered."

"I'm so sorry. Do you think you can work it out?" Sophie presses her lips against my throat, kissing me softly.

"It's too late for that. My father is a selfish man. Unless it benefits him, he doesn't want to know."

I don't want to get into just how selfish he is, and all the ways he treats my mother. I've hoped she would leave him for years.

"So you're a reformed bad boy, then?" She hums against the column of my throat as she kisses me again.

"It was one stupid decision, years ago." I dip my chin so I can meet her eyes. "I know you must deal with all kinds of stuff in your job. But you have nothing to worry about."

Her lips lift into a smile. "I know. You're a law-abiding citizen now."

"You run a check on me or something?" I smirk.

"Or something." She bites her bottom lip playfully. "I knew a bit about you before the double date."

"Four years ago?"

She shrugs. "Kelly and I were meeting two guys we knew virtually nothing about. I just asked my sister what she knew about you both. It was the smart thing to do."

"Ah, Tanner's wife's best friend. Small world," I muse.

"Uh-huh. Holly asked Rachel for all the ugly truths." She smirks.

"Smart," I muse, sliding my hand up from her shoulder so that I can stroke her hair. "You're definitely smart. In fact, you helped Dax out so well last year when he needed a lawyer that if I do decide to get on the wrong side of the law, I can hire you."

"I helped Dax because I was there. I don't work defense usually."

"Damn." I chuckle.

"Maybe I could just keep you in line instead."

I look into her glittering eyes, then down at her soft, full lips. "Fuck, yeah, you could."

She laughs softly, then sighs. "Thank you for sharing that. About your dad, your past. I appreciate your honesty."

I wind a strand of blonde hair around my finger, mesmerized by it. I'm a fucking goner for anything involving this woman.

"I'll tell you anything you want to know. Communication is important to me. I've seen too many couples with secrets. In the end, they eat them up. We aren't going to be like that."

She leans into my hand, her eyelids fluttering closed for a brief moment. "I like the sound of that." She glances past me to the bedside clock. "Ugh. But I do not like the thought of the traffic I'm going to get stuck in if I don't leave for work soon."

"Noted." I kiss her head and then throw the covers back, exposing our naked bodies. "After you."

"You want me to go first so you can watch me walk to the bathroom naked, don't you?"

"You say it like it's a bad thing."

She laughs and pushes at my chest as she sits up. "You've spent all night looking at my naked—Whoa." She clamps a hand over her mouth, her eyes squeezing shut.

I'm up like a shot, concern tightening my muscles as she opens her eyes and swallows thickly.

"You okay?"

"Yeah, I..." She swallows again and nods. "Just feel a little weird suddenly."

"Have a drink." I reach to the bedside table to get the bottle of water there, but she's on her feet, racing into the bathroom before I even turn back.

"Sophie?" I rush after her.

She's hunched over the toilet bowl, retching into it as I walk inside the bathroom.

"No." She holds up a hand toward me without lifting her head. "Out. This is not how this goes. We don't know each other well enough for this yet. I don't want you to see me getting sick."

"That's ridiculous." I grab a robe that's hanging on the back of the door and wrap it around her shoulders so that she's covered. She can't argue back because she's already retching again. "Darling," I murmur softly as I crouch beside her and gather her hair away from her face, holding it in one hand. "Do you think it was the rum and raisin ice-cream?"

She snorts. "Is there a joke coming about my flavor choice now?"

"Of course not." I smile as I rub her back.

She sighs and lifts her head. "You don't need to hold my hair."

"Why? You'd rather I let go and you get sick in it?"

She grabs some toilet tissue from the holder and wipes her lips. "No."

"Right then. Stop saying stupid shit and let me take care of you." I let go of her hair when I'm sure she isn't about to hurl again.

"Sophie." My eyes drop to her lips, and I must be a goner for this woman, because the fact she's just thrown up does nothing to stop the overwhelming urge I have to kiss her again. "We've got something good here. I want you. And I'm pretty sure you want me as well."

She tuts, but it turns into an amused smile.

"What's a bit of regurgitated rum and raisin between us? Besides..." I look into the bowl and frown. "Getting flushed is the best place for it."

She shakes her head with a silent laugh. "Couldn't resist, could you?"

I wink at her, and she rolls her eyes. It's adorable. Big lawyer boss woman has made way for vulnerable Sophie for a moment.

"You know. I think I've found a new turn on." I stroke my knuckles down her cheek.

"What's that?"

"When you let me take care of you."

We stare at each other. She searches my eyes, two small lines appearing between her brows like she's looking for the joke. But I'm not joking. Taking care of Sophie Havers is like Viagra to my dick.

I lean forward and kiss her forehead. "You can't handle it all yourself, Boss... Okay, you can," I muse, knowing she's more than capable. "But I promise it'll be more fun if you let me do it with you."

I stand up, and the effect she's having on my dick is plain to see, presented at almost perfect eye level for her.

Her eyes are on it as she talks, like she's addressing it, instead of me. "Your *fun* has had me feeling like I ran a marathon last night. Fifty times," she adds.

I chuckle and hold out a hand, helping her up when she takes it.

"You good now?" Concern fills my voice.

"Yeah, I'm good."

We shower and get dressed, and thirty minutes later, I'm kissing Sophie goodbye beside her car in her apartment's underground parking area.

"Does last night count as date number two, considering you arranged it when it was supposed to be my turn?" she asks.

"You can organize the third date. I hear third dates are the really fun ones." I raise my brows at her suggestively.

"Drew, I don't..." She studies my face as she chooses her next words. "You said about honesty and communication upstairs. And I appreciate that. Which is why you should know that I don't normally... I've never had sex before date five before. At least. It's usually a lot longer than that. And you and me... this." She gestures between us. "This isn't what I usually do. I don't want you to think—"

I kiss her again, pulling her body flush to mine.

"Numbers don't matter to me. I don't care what you've done before. All I care about is that now it's about you and me. And *only* you and me."

"I never date more than one person at a time. That's just... That's not me." She looks away like the idea repulses her.

"You said you want orgasms and dates." I bring her gaze back to mine with two fingers beneath her chin.

"I did say that." The warmth returns to her eyes as she blinks up at me.

"Then that's what you shall have. But..." I sink my teeth into my lower lip as I run my thumb across her parted lips.

"But?"

"There's something I want too." I push my thumb past her lips, far enough to dust over the tip of her tongue. "The first time, I let you have for free. Last night..." I groan as she licks the tip of my thumb. "I couldn't fucking resist you. *Again.* But now? If this happens a third time..." I take my thumb back as I look at her. "If this is going to happen a third time, then I want to hear you say it."

"Say what?"

"That we're a thing. You and me. I'm too old to fuck around. I want your relationship status changed on Facebook."

She laughs. "I don't have Facebook."

"You sure you're human?" I quirk a brow before I press a kiss to her lips. "I'm serious. This happens again and you're my girlfriend. And I'm going to make sure the whole world knows it." I slide my hands down the sides of her body and curl them around her waist. "So, what's it going to be, Ms. Havers? You and me?"

Her eyes narrow as a smile plays on her lips. "You're unlike any other man I've dated."

"I fucking hope so." I pause when she doesn't say anything. "That a bad thing?" I tighten my grip on her.

"No. It's just... You're not afraid of commitment. In fact, you're the opposite. It's like you know exactly what you want and—" She sucks in a sharp breath. "Please tell me you aren't married."

"What?"

"I... Never mind. It's too much to get into now. But my ex, I found out that he was. It's why we broke up." Her forehead furrows, and her eyes pinch. I hate that he's inside her head right now, making her doubt things. Doubt me. Doubt us.

I cup her face. "Is there a ring on my finger?"

"No."

"Is there a ring on yours?"

"No."

"Then I'm not fucking married, Sophie." I stare into her eyes. "You and me?"

Her next words have calmness washing over me.

"Yes. You and me."

I hang up my call to the florist, confirming my flowers were signed for at Sophie's office. I drop my phone onto the bench and look up into three smug-ass grins.

"Fuck off," I mutter.

"He's sending flowers to a woman." Dax whistles and adds another plate to the end of his weight bar.

"About time one will have him." Tanner smirks, looking in the mirror as he towels sweat off his face.

"She must like the way you hold hands, the way I won over Maddy."

I scowl at Logan and then fire a deadly shot into the punch bag of my home gym. I'm questioning my sanity about inviting them here to do a workout together this morning.

"Still too soon for sex jokes?" Logan flinches as I still the flailing punch bag that served as a substitute for his face.

"You're dating my little sister," I growl. "It's *always* too fucking soon for sex jokes. Besides"—I look him up and down—"your ego's writing cheques your body can't cash."

It's a lie; Logan's built like a quarterback. But saying it makes me feel better.

He raises an amused brow as Tanner and Dax burst into laughter.

"And you two assholes can shut up. You're both pussy whipped."

Tanner nods. "Yep, wouldn't change a thing."

I grumble as he high-fives Dax.

"We're happy for you, man." Dax walks over and slaps me on the shoulder with a tattoo-covered hand. "Being pussy whipped is a privilege."

"And fuck me, it has its perks." Logan grins, but it slides off his face as I glare at him and crack my knuckles, drawing a snicker from Tanner.

"We're just messing," Tanner says. "You deserve a woman crazy enough to take you on as a boyfriend. When are you seeing her again?"

I don't know. I was so fucking elated when she agreed to being an item this morning that I didn't secure the next date. Schoolboy error.

"Don't worry about it. I'm sure she'll call you. Now that you're her *boyfriend*." Tanner snickers as Dax chuckles and Logan makes a 'woo' sound, before hiding his smirk behind his fist and making sure he's out of my reach.

"Did I tell you you're a bunch of assholes," I mutter, swiping up my phone and bringing up Sophie's number as I stride out of the room.

"At least twice," Logan calls after me.

I can still hear them laughing as I walk down the hall and into the kitchen.

She answers on the second ring.

"Third date. It needs to be this week and—"

"Mr. Harper," she clips, cutting me off mid-growl. "We're about to begin a meeting. Would you like to be placed on speakerphone so you can say hello to the team?"

My dick stirs in my shorts as bossy Sophie makes an appearance. But I can detect the playfulness in her tone.

"Sure. Then I'll have witnesses if you try to brush me off." I lean back against the kitchen counter, calling her bluff.

There's a shuffling on the other end and then Sophie speaks again.

"Team, my boyfriend would like to say good morning to you all."

Well, shit. I didn't expect her to actually put me on speakerphone in a room full of lawyers. But my grin isn't because she's surprised me. It's down to one fact.

*Boyfriend. She called me her boyfriend.*

There are some murmured greetings. I can make out at least three different voices, two of which are male as I respond and say hello, not caring what they think about this call.

*She called me her boyfriend in front of her entire team.*

"I'll call you later," Sophie says in a quieter voice like she's picked the phone back up. "And how's tomorrow sound? I might have to work a little later, but if it's not too late for you, then—"

"Tomorrow," I confirm. I don't care what time as long as I see her. "Are you feeling okay?" I add.

"I'm fine. I don't know what this morning was about. Probably a lack of sleep."

I chuckle. Keeping Sophie up half the night is my new favorite pastime.

"Thank you for my flowers," she adds.

I beam like an idiot hearing the happiness in her voice. It's one bunch of flowers and she sounds like she was given a whole Tiffany jewelry store. Fuck, if they make her this happy, then her ex-boyfriend's must have been complete wastes of space.

*"It's why we broke up."* That's what she said. She found out that her latest ex was married.

My empty hand clenches into a fist as I swallow, forcing down the rising urge to hunt him down and then mount his head on my wall as a trophy.

But I need to forget about it. He's gone. She said it herself. *I'm* her boyfriend now.

And I'm going to make sure she never fucking regrets that decision.

# Chapter 11
# Sophie

I LOOK AT THE empty vase inside the kitchen cupboard of my office as I put away a clean mug. It's a shame flowers don't last forever because the irises Drew sent me two weeks ago were beautiful. They brightened my days having them on my desk. Even the days when Chelsea came in to work on her case and broke down in tears recalling what happened to her. The case is beginning to gather a lot of attention in the press now that the trial is approaching.

I roll my shoulders back with a sigh and then reach up to rub the back of my neck. It's been another long week. My phone chimes with an incoming text.

**Drew: Tomorrow can't come soon enough.**

I smile as I type out a reply.

Me: I know. I can't wait.

He gets back from New York tomorrow night, after another few days there going over plans for a big re-design project he's working on. He said Tanner would usually go for some of the meetings, but baby Ruby is waking up a lot at night, so he wants to be home to help his wife. There are still some devoted husbands out there.

I scroll past Drew's message to all the unanswered ones from Henry. They start off nice, asking how I am, trying to engage me into conversation. Then when I don't answer, they turn uglier, slinging accusations around, saying that I think I'm too good to even hear him out, and that I need to remember everything he did for me.

Make me doubt my own judgment. That's about all he did for me. And make me unfairly suspicious of all men who claim to be single. If Drew wasn't so intense and spending every spare moment he can at my place, or taking me out to dinner, then I might even doubt him. But I don't. And it helps that Holly is friends with Tanner's wife and swears that Drew hasn't ever come close to getting married. The last relationship he had ended years ago, before our double date with Logan and Kelly.

"You heading off soon?"

I look up from my phone as Jules, one of the admin team, pauses in the open kitchen doorway, her bag slung over her shoulder.

"Yeah, I am. Do you have anything nice planned for the weekend?"

"Decorating." She grins. "I managed to convince Owen that rose gold in the master bedroom is a good idea."

I laugh, recalling her telling me about her boyfriend's lack of agreement in the design choices for the new apartment they've just bought together.

"Well, enjoy. I hope you get it all done before he can change his mind again."

"I'll make sure he doesn't. I have ways to make him come around." She lifts her eyebrows and I shake my head with a smile.

"What about you? You going to take it easy?" Her expression turns into one of concern. She found me being sick this morning in the staff restrooms. It isn't the first time it's happened. But it's the first time someone at work has seen me.

"Oh, that? I'm fine now. Don't worry about me." I wave a hand, the tension re-building in my neck, calling out for me to rub it again.

Jules smiles, and I say goodbye as I drop my phone into my purse on the counter and put on my coat. I can't wait to get home and change out of my pencil skirt and blazer. My sweatpants are calling to me—loudly.

I scoop up my bag and walk toward the bank of elevators.

I just have a small detour to make first.

"What was so urgent that you couldn't tell me on the phone?" Halliday breezes in through my front door and deposits her coat onto a hook in the hallway before turning to face me.

"Oh." Her eyes roam my face, and she takes a careful step toward me. She purses her lips, studying me as she draws her hand up and down in front of her, motioning at me. "Your energy has shifted. It's giving off some weird vibes. Did something happen on your case? A big piece of evidence come in?"

"You're good." I lead us into the living room and wait for her to sit on the sofa before I drop down next to her.

"Why, thank you." She smiles.

"But it's not about the case."

"It's not about work? It's always work. That's all you do."

"I don't." I bristle.

"Okay, not so much now that Drew's on the scene. You actually go to other places than your apartment and your office. Is it your mum and dad? Is someone sick?" She reaches out and grabs my hand.

"No one's sick. Except me... Regularly." I exhale a deep breath. "I'm pregnant."

There's a pause before she laughs. Then she sees that I'm serious.

"You really are?" Her eyes widen.

"Yep," I whisper. It's the first time I've said the words out loud since those two pink lines appeared on the test I picked up on my way home from work.

"I don't know how I didn't figure it out sooner. I've been getting sick, and..." I take my hand from hers and push into my temples with my fingertips. "Shit. What am I going to do?"

"I mean, you should talk to Drew. Unless you need longer to think about it yourself first to let it sink in? You said he'll be back from New York tomorrow night, right?"

"Right." I swallow around the thick lump in my throat. It's been there for hours now. "Except... it's not his."

"It's not...?" Her brows drop low, and she sighs. "Henry?"

"Yeah."

"Fuck."

"Yeah, fuck," I agree. "I mean, it has to be. We stopped using anything because I was getting the injection. I was due another appointment the week we broke up, but I missed it because work was so busy. I meant to make a new one, but the marriage bombshell made me forget, and... and then I saw Drew again."

"And with Drew, you—?"

"Condoms. Every time."

"Oh." Halliday falls silent for a few minutes. "You know, they're not one hundred percent effective. Maybe he has super sperm. He looks virile, I mean..."

She blows out a breath. "Sorry, I was just thinking of all possibilities."

I snort. "We're talking about whether this baby would be better off having a father who I've been dating barely a month, or an ex who I found out is married."

"At least its mother isn't a walking red flag." She gives me a small smile and my tense shoulders soften as she wraps an arm around me. "You want kids."

"I do." I sigh. "I just never imagined it being like this." I blink back the tears that are threatening my eyes. "I thought I'd plan it with whoever I was with." I suck in a shaky breath. "I thought we'd have that excitement, you know? I thought I'd know for certain who the father was." My voice trembles, which in itself is so out of character I'm surprised Halliday doesn't react. But she only holds me closer, sharing the reassuring warmth of her body against mine as I shiver.

"You've got this." She rests her head against mine. "You're Havers the Handler. You don't earn a name like that in all your fancy lawyer circles and not be able to cope with this like a queen."

I sniff around a weak smile. "Thanks."

"And your trial will be over before the baby is due, won't it?"

I nod. That's one small silver lining to this entire situation. I'll not be letting anyone down by going on maternity leave.

"You'll be okay. I'll support whatever decisions you make," Halliday says. "Tell people when you're ready.

It's your call. Whatever you decide, I'll be here with you, okay? You won't be doing this alone."

She squeezes me, not acknowledging what we both know is likely to be true. Drew will be long gone if the baby isn't his. Maybe he'll still run, even if by some small chance it is his. And Henry? I swallow down the bile rising in my throat at the thought of telling him. He'll probably want to be involved. Maybe he'll even think I'll want to get back together again.

If he does, then he's deluded.

Halliday's right. I can do this.

It's like winning my cases.

Failure is not an option.

I need to talk to Drew when he's back. But before that, I need to make sure Henry doesn't get any ridiculous ideas of riding off into the sunset together for a fresh start. Because I couldn't think of anything more sickening to me.

I fight down the rising vomit, composing myself enough to glare at Henry.

"No!"

"If you're worried about the money, I'll pay. It can be done privately. I can even come with you."

"So you can make sure I get it done?" I scoff in disgust. "I'm not having an abortion."

He checks his watch, his jaw ticking. I never used to notice him do it when we were dating. He'd check his phone a lot. I thought he was keeping an eye out for work calls. Not making sure his wife wasn't wondering where he is.

"Need to be somewhere?" I snap.

"I'm sorry, Soph, I didn't mean it like that."

"I'm pretty sure there's only one way you can mean the words 'get it taken care of'. And it's not in the *knit some booties and start stroller shopping* kind of way."

I study him, contempt spreading through my veins. He looks the same as he always did. I thought the tailored suits and the strong jawline were masculine. Strong, manly, dependable. But the flash of panic beneath his eyes when I told him I was carrying his child told a different story. He's never looked weaker before. More rattled. Scared.

"How's the divorce coming along?" I fold my arms, steeling my gaze as he fidgets with his collar and glances around the coffee shop we're in.

This is not how I pictured my Saturday morning. I was going shopping for ingredients so I can cook dinner for Drew tonight. He's coming straight from the airport. Work's been so manic I still haven't managed to arrange our official third date. Although, we've been out plenty of times in the past two weeks, and he's stayed over at my house as much as he can. He wanted to show me his house tomorrow. I'm not sure we'll be spending tomorrow together at all now. He'll probably leave once he finds out about the baby.

"It's..." Henry's jaw ticks and he avoids meeting my eyes. "It's on hold."

"She still doesn't know you're an unfaithful pig, then?"

His gaze whips back to mine and his eyes darken. "Seems you didn't care when you were sleeping with me."

My courtroom poker face and composure kick in just in time to stop me from flying across the table and slapping him. I'm getting to see a whole new side of Henry since we broke up. And each time I ask myself what the hell I saw in him.

"I didn't know. You think I would have wanted a relationship with you if I had? You lied and let me think you were single."

"Come on, Soph." He smiles but there's no warmth or humor to it. "You think you'll meet a guy who doesn't have baggage?"

"There's baggage, and then there's being married and using me as your part-time mistress," I whisper. "I thought you were busy with work, and that's why we didn't see each other much. I didn't think you had a whole other life you were hiding. I was honest with you. I thought you were the same."

"I'm sorry," he says quietly, looking at me with a pleading look. "It's a shock, that's all." He reaches for my hand across the table, but I slide it away.

"I still love you, Soph. I want you back."

I stare at him, a million insults hurtling around inside my head as he sighs again and presses his thumb and finger into his eye sockets, causing the lines at their corners to deepen.

"You only love yourself, Henry. I didn't ask to see you this morning to tell you I wanted to get back together. Or to even talk about what happened between us. I just thought you had a right to know that the baby might be yours."

I reach beneath the table for my purse. It was a waste of time coming to talk to him and expecting an adult discussion.

"Might?" His eyes blow wide showing an unnatural amount of white around his pupils.

I drop my purse and straighten in my seat.

"Yes. There's a chance it might not be. And I intend to find out for certain as soon as I can get an appointment."

"You've been getting fucked by someone else?" His face contorts like he's just licked a shit.

"I love the way you so eloquently put it." I scowl. "Not that it's any of your business, but yes, I am in a relationship with someone."

His face reddens like steam is about to blow from his ears. It's petty, but I can't resist the next words that fall from my lips. Maybe I just need to say them while I still can. Because after I see Drew, it could all be over.

"I didn't sit around crying over you when you went home to your wife." I smile sweetly as his lips flap, fighting for a response. "And yes, in answer to your question, we do fuck. Hard and often."

I grab my purse and coat and stand.

"Now, following your request for me to have an abortion, which is denied, in case you needed that confirmation again, you'll now only be hearing from me in writing with regards to any legal necessities required for the baby. *My* baby. And don't worry." I cast him one final look. "I won't be needing your money. I won't be needing anything from you."

I walk out of the coffee shop with my head held high. Henry doesn't follow me. I don't expect him to. He isn't good at thinking on his feet. He'll have to work out his next steps, and then he'll probably wait me out after work again like he did before, bringing more lies and excuses with him. But it doesn't matter. I can see right through him now.

My choices will all be what's right for the baby from now on. And that includes managing Henry from a distance, even if he is the father.

# Chapter 12
## Sophie

I SIP ON MY iced water and wait.

At the exact time he told me he'd be here, there's a buzz at the front door. I turn down the oven temperature and go to the screen in the hallway. Drew's blue eyes penetrate through the camera from street level.

"Come on, Ms. Havers, I've just gotten off a six-and-a-half-hour flight, and I spent seven hours of it thinking about you."

"Your math is off."

"No. It isn't," he replies smoothly.

I press down the button. "I might have missed you a little too, Mr. Harper."

*Might.* The word makes me wince. You also *might* be the father of the baby growing inside me.

I blow out a breath and lean back against the wall after buzzing him in. I didn't expect my heart to be hammering so hard in my chest at the thought of telling him. I'm going to wait until after dinner. It's selfish, but I'd just like that time talking with him before everything changes.

Three loud bangs on my front door indicate he's on the other side.

"Drew." The door is barely open before he's sweeping me up and pressing me back against the wall. My legs wrap around his waist instinctively as he kisses me, his warm breath falling over my lips as he groans out the words in between kisses.

"Fuck, I've missed you."

"Fuck, you're more beautiful than when I left."

"Fuck, you feel incredible."

*Fuck. Fuck. Fuck* repeats inside my head, but for entirely different reasons.

"Drew," I murmur as he kisses me again, sliding his tongue inside my mouth and slowing down to really take his time.

"Yeah?"

I moan as his lips travel down my neck, and he groans as my body quivers in response. He pulls back to look at me when I don't say anything, and I'm met with vibrant blue.

"How was your flight?" I stall, stroking the back of his head.

His eyelids grow heavy, and he leans into my touch. The act makes me smile because I'm learning how he likes to be touched. Just like he's learning what gets me breathless with need for him.

"It was in a plane in the sky. I don't want to talk about my flight."

"What do you want to talk about?"

"Nothing. I want to take my girlfriend to bed and show her what three days apart does to me." His lips return to my neck and he presses his body closer, his erection pushing against the underside of my thigh.

"I cooked dinner for us," I whisper as he trails one hand up the side of my body and then slowly circles his thumb around my hardening nipple through my thin T-shirt.

"Fine," he mumbles. "After dinner, then. But grant me one touch first."

"You are touching," I breathe as I look at his thumb stroking my nipple. I bite back a moan at how he can make something so simple feel so good.

"I don't mean touch with this." He removes his hand, then curls his fingers around the hem of my top, managing to push it up and pull the cup of my bra down at the same time. "I mean with this."

His mouth wraps around my nipple, and a whimper forces its way from my lips and a surge of wetness soaks my panties.

"Sounds like you did miss me. Not fucking *might* have." He slaps my ass cheek through my jeans and smiles around my nipple before flicking his tongue over my puckered skin.

I stifle another moan as he sucks it again. They've been getting more and more sensitive this past week, and I swear if he keeps this up, I'll come without needing him to touch me anywhere else.

"Dinner will be ruined if we don't eat soon," I pant.

He chuckles, giving me one last suck. "You'll be ruined once I've finished with you later."

He places me back down on the ground on shaky legs.

I press a kiss to his lips, unable to resist, and then entwine my fingers with his and lead him into the kitchen where I've set up two places on the marble counter.

"You can open a bottle of wine if you like? There's some white in the fridge."

I slide my hand from his and grab an oven mitt to take the buttered chicken out of the oven.

"You don't want one?"

I glance over my shoulder to where he's looking at the single wine glass on the counter.

"No, I shouldn't." I turn back around and start plating up. I swear he'll know something's going on if he sees the heat in my cheeks.

"Then I won't, either." He walks up behind me, curling a hand around my hip and pressing his chest against my back as he reaches up into the cabinet above me to fetch a water glass.

My breath stalls as his body heat melts into mine. He barely has to do anything and my stomach is fluttering around like crazy.

"You sure you want dinner first?" He chuckles.

I swallow and continue serving. "I do. It'll give us time to talk. We need to talk."

"Okay." He steps back. "As long as you aren't breaking up with me." He laughs and fills his glass before taking a seat.

A strange noise escapes my throat and I hide it with a cough as I take our plates over and sit next to him. Drew doesn't know how wrong that sentence is. He'll probably be the one dumping me after this conversation.

"Tell me about New York," I deflect, prolonging the inevitable. "Who were you working with over there?"

Drew takes his first mouthful and then smiles at me, before pressing a kiss to my temple. "Boss can cook."

I smile down at my plate, pushing my food around. "Sometimes. When I get time after work, I like to make things from scratch. So New York?"

"We're working on a big contract for a chain of private members clubs. We've had some teething issues with staffing, but it's all getting sorted."

"What are your team like? Do you miss them? I know you lived there for a year." My barrage of questions is a mix of genuine interest and desperation to have something else to think about while we eat.

"I spend enough time with them when I fly over. Some more time than I'd like."

"Oh?"

He places his fork down and takes my hand. "Look, Sophie. I'll always be honest with you. So you should know that I have an ex there. We dated the year I was living in Manhattan. She still works for the company."

"You dated someone you work with?"

He huffs. "Yeah, stupid idea."

"When you lived over there?" My mind does the math. That was before we even met on that double date. "That was years ago."

He lifts his glass as his jaw ticks. "It was. Alicia needs reminding of that sometimes." He knocks back his water as unease curls in my gut.

"Was it serious?" I don't even know why I'm asking, yet the words are out before I can stop them.

"Not really. I moved in with her for a while. We broke up before I came back to London. There's been the odd time we've hooked up since, but not in a long time."

*They lived together?*

"I appreciate your honesty. I hope it's not awkward working with her."

"It's not for me," he says matter-of-factly. "You want to tell me about yours now? Seeing as we've landed in the dreaded ex conversation."

He smiles at me and the tension melts from my shoulders. He has this way of looking at me that makes me feel safe enough to open up and share anything. Like nothing I could ever say would make him think any different about me.

I pray that continues to be the case.

I abandon my dinner and rest my chin in my hand. "My ex and I were together a few months. It was casual. We saw each other when we could, around work. It was going okay until I found his wedding ring in his pocket."

Drew watches me carefully, his eyes darkening. "This is the guy you broke up with before Logan's launch party?"

"Henry," I confirm.

His jaw hardens, and I swear his teeth grind. "Asshole," he hisses.

"I ended it the moment I found out."

"Don't think any of it is your fault, Sophie. Guys like him do it all the time. Walk all over the women in their lives. They don't deserve to be spat on if they're on fire."

He takes a deep breath. "Sorry." He tries to smile but it doesn't reach his eyes. "I just hate that he treated you like that. And his wife. You both deserve better."

"Yes, we do," I agree, watching his sudden spike in temper cool down to a simmer.

"He hasn't bothered you since you broke up with him, has he? Guys like that want everything their way."

I look into his intense gaze. *Honest.* It's what we promised we should be. I take a slow, deliberate breath, steeling myself for what I have to do.

"He waited for me after work one night, wanting me back. And he's been texting me. But it's nothing I can't handle," I add as Drew clenches his hands on top of the counter until his knuckles turn white. "And... I met with him this morning. I had to talk to him."

"To tell him to leave you the fuck alone?" His brows pull together, and his lips settle into a grim line. "If he needs a hand understanding, I can help him out."

"Not exactly. I had to see him, Drew." I take another deep breath. "I had to tell him that he might... be the father of my baby."

"You're pregnant?" His eyes drop to my stomach, then back up, searching mine with an unreadable expression. "Sophie?"

I wipe my clammy palms on my pants. "I found out yesterday. I can't be far along. It would have been around the time he and I broke up. Right before—"

"Before we slept together that first time?" Drew's brows lift.

"Yes," I breathe. "Sometime then."

"Do you love him?" His gaze sears into me like a blue flame, making heat flash through my veins.

"What? No, of course not. I—"

He stands so fast his chair topples to the floor. My stomach drops, and the air leaves my lungs in a fast rush.

I screw my eyes shut, waiting for the sound of the front door slamming.

But it never comes.

"Sophie?" Large, warm hands wrap around my cheeks. "You're pregnant?" His voice cracks as he holds me still and searches my eyes.

I nod.

"Pregnant," he breathes. His face screws up as he repeats the word again like he can't believe it. And I understand because I'm having a hard time believing it too.

"Yes."

He blinks, thick, dark lashes fanning down over his cheeks. Then he crushes his lips to mine and kisses me.

Hard.

"Pregnant," he mutters against my lips like the word suddenly makes perfect sense.

"I took a test. It was positive."

He pulls back. "Can I see it?" His eyes widen. "I want to see it. Fuck, Sophie, do you have another? Can we take another one now? Together?" His frantic words tumble out fast before he kisses me again.

"I don't. But we can get one."

"We're having a baby." He presses his forehead against mine. "Fuck, we're having a baby." Then he starts kissing me again.

"Drew," I whisper between his determined kisses. "The chances of it being yours are—"

"Stop." He pauses, his lips barely leaving mine. "It's yours, isn't it?"

"Yes."

He kisses me again. "And you agreed, remember? From now on, it's you and me?"

I stifle a sob as warmth rushes my chest and my stomach jumps toward my throat. This was the last reaction I was expecting but the most incredible. He's... happy. I look into his glittering eyes. *Scratch that, he's ecstatic.*

"You and me," I echo, barely able to form the words around the emotional lump in my throat.

His gaze softens and he kisses me again slowly, one hand dropping to my stomach. "Then this baby is *ours*."

"Tell me if I'm being too rough."

Drew pulls my T-shirt up over my head and then drops his lips to my shoulder, kissing me gently.

"You're not. Don't stop," I murmur as he unhooks my bra and peels it off before dipping his head to take my nipple into his mouth.

Pleasure thrums through me and I arch off the bed, desperate to be closer to him. Dinner was forgotten after I told him about the baby. He never stopped kissing me as he carried me into the bedroom. And now I'm sitting up, resting back on my elbows at the edge of the bed and being kissed and worshipped all over by his magic mouth.

"Drew," I gasp as he pulls my jeans and panties off and settles between my legs. He sucks gently on my clit. One of his large hands flattens against my stomach, holding me down, his thumb stroking over my skin at the same time.

"Fuck, Sophie. You taste sweeter." His mouth moves lower and he licks me from my ass to my clit in one long languid stroke, groaning so deeply the vibration makes my toes tingle. Then he slides his tongue inside me leisurely as I squirm and reach down to curl my fingers into his hair.

"It must be the hormones. Amazing," he murmurs, more to himself, like he's in awe, before he closes his eyes and gets lost in eating me out at his own pace.

"Oh God." My thighs shake around his head and before I know it, I'm coming on his face, my hands tangling in his hair and pulling him closer.

He groans, lapping up the wetness that rushes from me as he jerks himself off slowly with his other hand. "Another," he groans softly.

"What?" I pant, still pulsating as his tongue moves to my clit.

"Give me another," he says, tracing circles with the perfect pressure over me. Again and again. "I want to taste you all night."

His eyes are closed like he's in his own private ecstasy as his grip on his cock tightens and precum leaks from the end in thick, glistening strands.

"You do?" I throw my head back, relishing the feel of his mouth on me, and before long, I'm succumbing to his demand and coming again.

"Fuck yeah, I do." He opens his eyes and grins at me as my orgasm rolls through my body, leaving me breathless. "You... Our baby inside you." His eyes drop to the hand placed protectively over my stomach. "It makes me feel pretty fucking feral."

I laugh as he kisses my swollen clit, before pulling me in and bringing my face to his. I can taste myself all over him as he slides his tongue past my lips, groaning.

"I have a thing... about pregnant..." He nips my bottom lip. "I have a thing about pregnancy. The belly, the bigger breasts, knowing there's life inside, growing... the whole fucking thing."

He gazes down at my stomach, splaying his fingers out over it until only peeks of my skin can be seen in between.

"It's incredible. And it makes me so fucking hard." He grabs his weeping cock and gives it a squeeze. A drop of precum drips from the tip onto my stomach and he rubs it into my skin using the head of his cock.

A guttural grunt leaves his chest. "Incredible."

"You have a thing about pregnant women? Have you... How have you... I mean...?"

"It's not how that sounded." His eyes leave my stomach and the pearlescent smear he's left behind. "It's not any pregnant woman. It's the idea of *my* woman being pregnant. And that's you, Sophie. I have a thing about *you* growing our baby inside you." He drags the head of his cock over it again. "It's fucking magic," he groans in awe.

"But you said you were worried you'd hurt me. Does that mean you don't want to—"

He grasps my chin, bringing his eyes to mine. They're burning with an intensity I feel all the way down to my toes.

"I want nothing more than to fuck you pregnant, Sophie. It's the thing of my dreams."

My lips part, my breath growing shallow at how hot he just made that sound. "I want that too. But I don't want you to worry about hurting me."

His eyes cloud over momentarily. "You promise you'll tell me if it's too much? Because I can't guarantee I'll be able to control myself."

"I will."

My pussy is already throbbing at the idea of having him inside me. It's been a long three days. And the relief from his reaction to my news is much greater than I expected, which only makes me realize how fast I'm falling for him.

He presses a kiss to my lips, his mouth transforming into a smile. "You better ride me then, Boss. Make sure I stay in line."

He throws himself onto his back on the bed and pulls me to straddle him. I grind my hips down, biting my lower lip as I slide over his cock, teasing us both.

"When was the last time you were tested?" I look at his thick cock getting covered in my arousal.

"I've never gone bare."

His words make me halt. "You haven't?"

He drags his gaze from my pussy up to my face. "Except with you, when you came on my cock for the first time." He grins. "Other than that, no, I didn't want to get someone pregnant accidentally."

"But you have a pregnancy fetish?"

"I have a *you* fetish. It's not just anyone pregnant that does it for me. Like I said, it has to be the right person."

"And that's me." I run my nails down over his abs, enjoying the way they tense at my touch.

"And that's you. Now get on my cock before I explode."

I lift myself, circling my hips so I glide around his tip as he holds the base still.

"Fuck," he groans as the head slips inside me.

"Well, seeing as I'm already pregnant..." I sink onto his bare cock, moaning as each inch stretches me until I'm so deliciously full of him that my breath catches in my throat. "We can do it like this, I guess."

"Damn, that's good." His eyes roll back in his head as he grips my hips.

I clench around him, enjoying the way his neck tenses and he curses as he fixes his eyes back onto mine.

"You're a tease." He digs his fingers into my flesh like he's about to plow into me and fuck me hard from beneath. Then he stops, sliding a hand over my stomach, stroking me there possessively. "I mean it, Sophie," he grits. "Start fucking yourself with my cock or I'm going to flip you over and pound into you so hard you see stars."

Arousal pools between my legs and my pulse beats around him nestled inside me.

"Sophie," he warns as I moan, teetering on the edge of another orgasm without even needing to move.

It's the way he fits inside me, paired with the husky gravel in his voice when he says such sinful things. Orgasming with Drew Harper is as certain as the sun rising.

"You're so big," I pant. "So perfect."

I slide up and down slowly, setting a steady rhythm.

"Lord, give me strength," he utters, throwing his head back and screwing his eyes closed. A vein bulges in his neck as he sucks in a sharp breath, making his nostrils flare.

"Fuck, Sophie," he growls, snapping his eyes open and staring right into mine. "I'm not going to last much longer. You've got yourself clamped down on my cock. And you're so wet. It's..." He thrusts, unable to resist. But it's not as hard as usual. I know he's holding back. "Fucking incredible."

"You can come with me if you like?" I give him a breathy smile.

His eyes widen. "You're going to again? Good girl." His face erupts into a smug grin. "Good fucking girl. Do it. Show me how well you milk my cock for me."

His eyes drop to his hand, which is still stretched over my stomach, and his grin curves higher. "I'm going to fill this pretty pussy as soon as you come, Sophie. I can feel you tightening around me. Let go. Go on."

Energy races through my body, setting it buzzing with electricity. Another rush of wetness coats us both, making us slick as Drew guides me up and down on him with one hand on my hip, his other never leaving my stomach.

"Go on," he urges.

The first wave hits me, and I cry out, my nails digging into his chest as I force myself down harder onto him, letting go. My body threatens to fold forward, but Drew holds me in place as he gazes up at me, his eyes glittering.

"Fucking beautiful," he murmurs. He sucks in a sharp breath, all the muscles in his upper body tensing. His eyes are intent on mine as hot streams explode deep inside me.

I didn't think it was possible to feel a man coming inside you. But I can. I can feel every pulse and surge as his cock swells and heat spreads through me.

"Drew," I gasp.

"Take it," he growls, the grip on my hip almost bruising as he empties himself with quick, sharp thrusts meeting my frantic ones. "Fucking take it. It's all for you."

I moan the rest of my orgasm out around him as he tenses one final time and then lets his head fall back against the pillow with a satisfied grunt.

I try to catch my breath as a bead of sweat rolls down between my breasts all the way to his hand on my stomach. It drips onto his thumb, and he looks at it with a sinful, happy smile on his face before he swipes it up and presses his thumb to his lips, darting his tongue out to lick the droplet off.

"I don't need to be gentle, then? Considering when I said fuck yourself with my cock, you really went for it."

I gasp before laughing, but he chuckles and takes my hands from his chest where I've left red crescent nail marks indented in his skin. He brings both of my wrists to his lips one by one and presses soft kisses to them.

"You don't need to be gentle. I'm pregnant, not sick."

His teeth sink into his full lower lip and he flexes inside me. "Say that again."

"I'm not sick." I raise my brows at him with a smirk as his palm connects with my ass, giving it a playful slap.

"You know what I mean."

"I'm pregnant," I breathe.

"Yeah, that."

"Pregnant," I tease.

He grasps my hips, circling me over his still hard cock.

"So, I can fuck you again without holding back?"

"What? Now?" He's not even gone soft. Doesn't he need time to recharge or something?

"Pregnant," he says to himself as his eyes drop to my stomach again, and I swear his cock thickens more inside me. "Get under me, Sophie." He flips me onto my back beneath him. Then he sinks inside me again with a deep thrust and presses a kiss to my lips as he smirks. "And hold the fuck on."

# Chapter 13
# Drew

"Wait." I take Sophie's latte from the counter and lift it to my lips, taking a sip before handing it to her. "Good, not too hot."

She eyes me questioningly as I wrap my arm around her and lead her out onto the street. It's the same look she gave me when I checked the shower temperature before letting her get in this morning. I've heard things about hot baths not being good for expecting mothers. I don't know if it's the same for showers but I'm not taking that risk.

"What do you want to do for the rest of the day?" I ask as I maneuver her across the front of my body so I'm positioned between her and the traffic.

"Go home and snuggle on the couch." She bites her lip and looks at me. "I'm sorry if that's boring. But these"—she tilts her cup—"are all decaf now. And I'm tired. Someone kept me up all night after getting back from his business trip."

I grin. "He sounds like a capable guy."

Her nose wrinkles as she laughs. The sound makes my heart swell.

*Pregnant.* My Sophie's pregnant. The woman I spent years obsessing over. The one who got away once. Only now she's back. And she's mine. *And she's pregnant.* I know some people might think it's fast when we tell them. But I don't give a flying fuck. As far as I'm concerned, this is the best thing to ever happen to me. I finally get to be what I crave—a great dad. She's making my dream come true and she doesn't even know it.

"Okay. Let's head back," I say as we meander up the street. "You can take a nap. I have my laptop in my car, I'll work while you sleep."

"Don't you need to go home? You haven't been back since you landed from New York."

"You trying to get rid of me, Ms. Havers?"

"No. But don't you need clean underwear to keep that insatiable dick contained?"

I pull her closer and chuckle. She's more laid back than I thought when I first met her. I still love feisty lawyer Sophie. But this side of her—the one who lets me look after her and buy her venti-sized decaf coffees and stroll around her neighborhood after a night of non-stop sex—this side, I love even more.

"She's almost the size of a blueberry. How wild is that?"

"Huh?" Sophie murmurs sleepily as I stroke her feet, which I have draped across my lap while we lounge on her couch.

"What are you talking about?" She yawns and looks at me from the cushion she's been sleeping on. "I thought you said you had work to do?" She looks at my discarded laptop on the floor by my feet.

"I did. But this is more interesting." I turn my phone screen toward her to show her the baby development app I downloaded while she was sleeping. "See? A blueberry." I turn the screen back around and look at it again before dropping my phone onto the seat cushion. I reach out and stroke her stomach, grinning the second my hand connects with it.

She places her hand over the top of mine and strokes it. "You said she?"

"We can't call it 'it'." I shrug. "And I always saw myself with a girl. Maybe because I'm close with Maddy, I don't know."

"I'd like to meet your sister again. Without thinking she's your date this time." Sophie smiles. "She must have thought I was so weird."

"She thinks you're perfect. Because that's what I've told her."

"No one's perfect."

"I am. You said I was big and perfect last night." I laugh as she jabs my thigh with her foot and then swings her feet out of my lap so she can sit up and stretch.

"I was talking about one part of you, not the whole package." Her eyes slide to mine, accompanied by a smirk.

I grab her in my arms and pull her to straddle me. "Fine I'll take it. Do you want that big perfect part of me again before you kick me out?"

She giggles as I growl against her neck.

"Because it wants you." I flex my dick against her and grab onto both of her ass cheeks, squeezing them as I pull her down and grind against her.

Two hours later, I'm standing in my parents' kitchen with a stupid grin and my hand wrapped around the pregnancy test in my pocket. Sophie took one in front of me with a little persuading. She got all nervous and cute, claiming she couldn't pee with an audience, so I turned around. But there's no way I was leaving that bathroom. My girl is pregnant, and I still can't fucking believe it.

"You're acting strange." Maddy narrows her eyes at me as she walks over to the fridge and grabs a bottle of juice.

Neither of us live here anymore. But when we do come back, she makes herself at home like she never left. I'm happy for her that she still can. But it's never been like that for me, even when I lived here.

She goes to the cupboard and gets a glass out before turning to our mother who's ironing.

"Doesn't he, Mum? He's... smiling."

"I smile," I cut in as the two of them laugh.

"You started again since you met Sophie, you mean?" Maddy sings.

"Don't tease your brother." Mum smiles at me. "It's nice to see she's having this effect on you. Do we get to meet her soon?"

I run my thumb over the stick in my pocket. "I think you should. Seeing as I'm going to marry her."

"Holy shit!" Maddy shrieks, her entire face morphing into an excited grin.

Mum ignores her curse and drops the iron down onto the board. "You've proposed?"

"Not yet, but I will." I grin at the two of them as they exchange excited glances. I haven't planned on asking Sophie yet. But I've no doubt the day will come. "There's a reason she's back in my life. I'm not letting her go a second time."

They know Sophie's the same girl from the double date with Logan. One of the pitfalls of growing up with two curious women, they have a way of finding out everything. Although, granted, I've been more than happy to share. I could talk about Sophie all fucking day.

"Have you got a ring yet?" Maddy squeals.

"Who needs a ring?" My father walks into the room, not making eye contact with anyone as he reads something on his phone.

"Drew does," Mum replies.

Dad's eyes snap up from his phone and lock with mine. My grin flattens into a firm line as I stare back at him. He sniffs, then frowns. "What the—? Fuck's sake!" He grabs the iron up from where Mum dropped it. There's a large black, burned patch on the shirt underneath. "I only bought this last week. How the hell did you manage to ruin it already?"

"I'm sorry." Mum's face crumples as she starts to fuss with the shirt.

I step forward, staring daggers at my father. "It was an accident. And it's only a shirt."

He watches Mum trying desperately to salvage something that's beyond saving before his eyes slide to mine.

"Leave it, Mum," I say as I hold Dad's gaze. "Maybe he should iron his own shirts from now on if he has a problem."

His eyes penetrate into mine, but he says nothing.

"Drew's got some news," Maddy interjects.

Dad turns to her and she's smiling brightly in an attempt to diffuse the tension that is almost always inevitable whenever my father and I are together.

"Has he?"

Dad's interest is forced. Nothing I do is good enough for him. That day the cops brought me home after they found me and Logan joyriding as teens was the day all his interest in my life ended, crushed like a bug under a newspaper. It doesn't matter that I helped grow a multi-billion-pound worldwide business with

Tanner, or that I've won the company more industry awards than any other company in our field has ever won. None of my achievements matter, because when I was sixteen, I embarrassed him by making a stupid, juvenile mistake. And he's never forgiven me for it.

"He's going to propose to his girlfriend," Maddy gushes.

"Stella? The one you've been dating two weeks?" Dad's head spins back toward me and he grimaces.

"Dad, a little support would be nice." Maddy scoffs.

"Over a month," I correct. I don't say anymore. I don't have to explain myself to him. He can't even get her name right. He's going to be a fucking stellar grandad.

He snorts. "Sounds like the basis for a long, happy marriage."

"Like you'd know what that looks like," I mutter so only he can hear.

He bristles.

"Time means nothing when you meet the one." Mum smiles, having abandoned the burned shirt into the trash. "Bring her for dinner so we can meet her. I'll book us a table for next weekend." She looks at Maddy, who nods, then at Dad, whose jaw is ticking as he types into his phone.

"Sure."

My eyes flick to Dad as my grip tightens on the test in my pocket. Whether he cares or not, he better show up or I'll be hauling his ass from whoever's bed he's in. Because Sophie and I have news to share. And he better paint a fake smile on his lying face and not ruin it for us. Or for Mum. I know she'll be thrilled for us and that she'll love Sophie. How could she not?

# Chapter 14
# Drew

"NICE PLACE," I TELL Sophie as we take a seat in the plush all-white waiting area. I'm glad she didn't want to wait for an ultrasound. I've been dreaming of this day.

She looks around the room, her gaze subtly moving over a well-known British model and her husband who are sitting talking quietly and holding hands on the other side.

"It's the best fertility and pre-natal care clinic in London. And they're discreet." Sophie's eyes drop to her purse in her lap, and she whispers, "That's not her husband."

"It's not?" I fight the urge to look over at the model I recognize again.

She smiles. "Thank you for coming with me. I know you're busy at work trying to manage the New York project."

"Like I'd miss being here." My eyes dart up to the open doorway where a couple are being shown toward the main entrance by a woman in a pristine white pant suit. "But you don't have to do this. This baby is ours, no matter what some piece of paper says."

"I know." Her eyes shine. "And you've no idea how much it means to hear you say that, Drew. But *I* need to know. I want to know if... I need to make legal arrangements if Henry is the biological father. Even though he doesn't want to be involved, I want to be prepared and have a plan if that should change."

I grit my teeth at the mention of the fucker who tried to talk Sophie into aborting our baby. If I ever get my hands on him...

"I can communicate what he needs to know to him. You don't need to ever think about him again if that's what you want."

"I can handle him."

"I know you can. But I don't trust him."

"Neither do I. But it might not matter. Maybe I won't have to deal with him, depending on the results."

She sighs and reaches up to rub her temples. I take her other hand inside my own and bring it to my lips.

"You're working too hard, Boss."

She smiles as I kiss her wrist. "You always say that."

"And you never listen."

She's been working so much this past week that I haven't seen her as much as I want to. But I don't need to go to New York again for a couple of weeks, so I fully intend on us spending the entire weekend together.

Even if she wants to nap on the sofa, I don't care. I just want to be under the same roof.

"My clients depend on me. This case I'm working on... I can't tell you much about it, but I'm going for maximum sentencing."

"And you'll get it because you're 'Havers the Handler.'"

She smiles. "I wish I'd never told you about that nickname."

"Why?" I kiss her wrist again and then trace circles over it. "Own it. I'm damn proud of you."

"Thank you," she whispers.

"Ms. Havers?"

We both look up at the female doctor in the white pant suit.

"I'm Dr. Grace. Call me Melinda. It's a pleasure to meet you."

Ten minutes later, Sophie is lying on an inclined medical bed while I balance on the edge of my seat, resting my elbows on my knees with my hands clasped together.

"Is the baby okay?" I ask in a rush.

"Drew. Give the doctor a chance." Sophie shakes her head with a soft laugh as Doctor Melinda squeezes lube onto a wand-type thing.

"Sorry." I lean back in the chair a little but immediately straighten up as the Doctor instructs Sophie to open her legs.

She places the wand beneath the surgical sheet covering Sophie's legs.

"Will that hurt the baby?" I bark.

"Drew." Sophie sighs.

Doctor Melinda ignores me and carries on being calm and professional. She must be used to angsty dads being in here. But she's putting a lubed-up wand in Sophie's vagina, for fuck's sake. Of course I'm going to be on edge.

I place my hands onto my knees and dig my fingertips into the wool of my suit pants.

The two women look over at the screen next to the bed.

"You said you were having the contraceptive injection?"

"Yes," Sophie answers. "But I missed my last appointment. I should have had it around eight weeks ago, but I didn't. Then I started to feel sick. I'm just guessing that I'm about seven weeks along because that's the last time without protection that I..." She glances at me and I nod encouragingly for her to continue. "It's the last time I had sex without anything," she finishes, looking back at the Doctor.

"Okay. The vaginal ultrasound allows us to see pregnancies much earlier, so we should be able to give you a good idea in just a moment."

"Could it be less than that?" Sophie's voice rises. "Is there a chance it could have happened sooner?"

"No, I'd say seven weeks since conception is accurate." The doctor smiles as she looks at the screen.

Sophie exhales and then glances at me again. The disappointment in her eyes makes my stomach drop.

"Hey." I pull my chair closer to the bed and take her hand. "You and me, remember? This is our baby, regardless of the dates."

She chews on her bottom lip, her eyes shining.

"Do you have twins in your family?" Doctor Melinda asks.

"No, why?" Sophie snaps her head back toward the screen where the doctor is pointing out two small masses.

"There are two babies."

She starts taking some measurements on the screen as Sophie looks at me with wide eyes.

"My grandmother was a twin," I say.

She blinks, water collecting along her lower lids. "She was?"

"She was." I brush a lock of blonde hair from her face.

Sophie turns to the doctor hopefully. "Does it usually pass down through families?"

"It can," Doctor Melinda replies, finishing up with her measurements, removing the wand, and handing Sophie some tissue to clean up with. "I understand you wanted a paternity test while you're here too. We can do that with a blood test. And a mouth swab from you, Mr. Harper. We have the most advanced lab in the country, so they'll be able to test without the need for a sample of amniotic fluid. The results should be back with me in around three days."

"Great, thank you." Sophie rests her head back against the bed and lets out a deep breath.

"Do you have any questions?" Doctor Melinda walks over to me and instructs me to open my mouth.

"No. I don't think so. Thank you so much," Sophie says.

"I do," I say once the swab is done.

"Sure. Fire away." Doctor Melinda smiles at me as she prepares to take Sophie's blood sample.

"Is there anything different we should know about having twins? Apart from there being two, I mean?" I grin and run a hand around the back of my neck. I'm still processing the fact that we aren't just having one baby, we're having two.

"Well, Sophie's pre-natal care will give you some extra information on your birthing choices with twins. But most twin mothers can carry on like they would with a single pregnancy. I'll give you some details on pre-natal vitamins you should start taking, and folic acid supplements I recommend."

"Thank you." I clear my throat. "But I mean, with regards to sex."

"Sex is okay," Doctor Melinda replies, unfazed as she draws Sophie's blood.

"Great... But I mean... energetic sex. We've been..." My eyes dart to Sophie's face but she's covered her eyes with one hand. "It gets quite..."

Doctor Melinda looks at me innocently.

"What if I'm hitting the babies?" I exhale in a rush. "I mean, they're not that high up in there, and I'm... Some positions we do... I don't want to hurt them."

Sophie groans as Doctor Melinda smiles at me.

"No need to worry. They're well cushioned. As they get bigger, you might find they move during sex. It's perfectly normal. It usually means you woke them up, that's all."

"So I can't hurt them with my—?"

"Mr. Harper, my husband is six foot six and we had no problems when I was pregnant with any of our three children."

"Really?" My brows hitch. "Six foot six?"

Doctor Melinda hums. "I'll leave you both to get ready. Come out when you're done. Take your time."

Sophie eyes me the second the door closes. "I can't believe you asked if your dick was going to hurt the babies."

"I had to be sure. The way we fuck, Sophie. It was a valid question."

She snorts and slides down from the bed to get dressed.

"The way you fuck, you mean? You don't even need to rest in-between anymore."

"I can't help it. It's the whole pregnancy thing. And now I know there're two babies inside you?" I lick my lips as my eyes travel over her belly. "Fuck, Sophie, you're so sexy. Come here." I reach out to her, but she steps back with a small gasp.

"No! I let you touch me in here and you'll have me bent over this bed in seconds."

"We could be quick?" I arch a brow at her teasingly. Although who am I kidding? If I thought she was up for it, I would pounce at the chance of filling her up right now. Especially now that her stomach is starting to swell just a tiny bit. It's hardly noticeable yet, but I see it.

"No way." She laughs, pulling up her skirt and smoothing it down over her hips.

"Tonight then? After work?" I reach for her again, managing to slide my arms around her waist and pull her in for a kiss.

She smiles against my mouth. "I'll come to your place. I have a meeting near you."

"Can't wait." I place my hand over her stomach and drop my eyes to it. "You two make sure Mama doesn't work too hard."

"Drew." Sophie's eyes shine as I look into them.

"Sorry," I murmur, kissing her softly. Then I talk to her stomach again. "I meant, you two make sure your hot, sexy mama doesn't work too hard."

Then I grab handfuls of her ass as I steal another kiss.

# Chapter 15
# Sophie

CHELSEA PLACES HER FINISHED mug of tea down on the table and runs her hands up and down her thighs. "I'm doing okay, aren't I?"

"You're doing better than okay." I smile at her reassuringly. "You've got this. Just keep your eyes on mine when you're on the stand, okay? I'll be right there with you."

"I know." She nods quickly, as she places one hand on the stomach area of her baggy sweatshirt.

"Chelsea?" I place my notebook on the table and turn to where she's sitting on the couch next to me. "I'm your lawyer and you can trust me. But I also have to be able to trust that you're being honest with me as well."

"I am. I swear. I've told you everything I can remember," she says, panic filling her voice.

"I mean about you." My eyes drop to her stomach, and she moves her hand away from her stomach as she notices me watching.

"My parents don't know," she breathes, her bottom lip shaking as she takes a cushion and places it on her lap, her fingers finding one corner of it to fidget with. "The father... They wouldn't understand..."

"Do you think it's one of the two men who forced you?"

Her lips flatten into a thin line. She looks away, not answering me.

"Okay. Have you spoken to your therapist about the baby?"

She nods but still won't meet my eyes. "I'm keeping it."

"Okay. What matters now is that we get you proper pre-natal care. I can arrange that for you. Is there someone you trust who can go with you?"

"Yes," she croaks. "I have someone."

"Good."

"Will this affect the case? I mean, will you have to tell everyone?" Her eyes widen in alarm as she finally looks at me again.

"We've got some time before the trial. I won't tell anyone unless they need to know. And right now, the only people who need to know with regards to the case are you and I, okay?"

"Okay," she says, her shoulders softening.

"But these things have a way of coming out, Chelsea. You aren't going to be able to hide it for long. You might want to think about telling your parents and anyone else you need for support sooner rather than later."

"How did you know?" she whispers.

The fear in her young eyes makes my throat burn.

"Your body language. Touching your stomach. The oversized sweatshirts that are getting larger." I smile gently at her. "And because I recognize the look in your eyes—when something you weren't expecting has happened and you're asking yourself if you're strong enough to deal with it."

"I'm more scared about this than the trial." A couple of fat tears fight their way free from her eyes. I've never seen her cry. Not once. Not even when she's been recounting what those men did to her.

"I know." I reach out and squeeze her arm. "But I can tell you now. You're a fighter. You're strong. And you've got this."

She nods, wiping the tears away with her sleeve. "Thank you. I bet doing your job, you get good at reading people, huh?"

I pass her a tissue, not admitting that I recognize the look in her eyes because it's the same one I saw in my bathroom mirror after taking the first pregnancy test. I swallow around the lump in my throat. No one would believe it, 'Havers the Handler', riled by something as tiny as a baby...*two* babies. But I have that gnawing sensation in my gut that I get when I know I'm missing something in a case. It's been there warning me ever since I found out I'm pregnant.

"I've got someone who knows and will help me. I'm scared, but you don't need to worry," Chelsea says, studying my pinched brow.

I school my features so that my emotions are no longer written all over my face. I never allow them to show at work. I can't. It's how I win my cases. No emotion. Only facts.

"Good." I give Chelsea a more practiced smile. "I'll see you at our next meeting, okay?"

"It's not like you to have dessert at lunch," Halliday quips as I spoon up a lump of ice-cream from my bowl.

"Craving, maybe. I don't know." I lick the spoon, my mind wandering to Chelsea. Is the father of her baby the man who tricked her into going to that grimy apartment with him? Or the second, unidentified friend he invited over after?

"You're thinking about your client again," Halliday says.

"I am." I place my spoon down.

We've come to a small Italian restaurant close to my office. Halliday is going to New York to work with her new client in a couple of days, so it's our only chance to catch up face-to-face until she gets back.

"I know you can't tell me. Client confidentiality and all that. But I've never seen you distracted like this."

I look down at the melted remnants in my bowl. "It's just made me think about the babies and finding out who the father is, that's all."

Halliday grabs my hand. "The results will be back soon. I'll be on the other end of the phone whenever you need me. Day or night, okay?"

I smile at her gratefully despite the lead weight in my stomach.

"It's going to be Henry, I know it. And I can't help feeling guilty that I wish it weren't." My mind flashes back to Chelsea. She might not even know the name of her baby's father. And as much as Henry is a liar and a cheat, he isn't a man who has sex with young women against their will. He isn't evil.

"I don't believe it." Halliday shakes her head, making her short platinum hair glimmer beneath the restaurant lights. "The energy says otherwise. There's a connection to Drew there. It's strong."

For once, I wish that I had as much faith as her in cosmic planes and signs from the universe. But I'm a girl of science. I had unprotected sex with Henry around the date the babies were conceived. Drew wore a condom. Even though we had sex multiple times the morning after the gala, he wore a condom each time. And none broke. It's as simple as that.

"Henry keeps texting me and calling me," I groan. "I've got seven voicemails from him I haven't listened to. And that's just today."

"Wow. Is he still claiming he wants to be involved?"

"Alongside more or less admitting that he isn't leaving his wife." I snort at the audacity of the man. It amazes me that I ever fell for him.

"I never liked him."

"You told me. Many times."

"He bought you roses when he knew your favorites are irises."

"I never told him that."

"No, I did." She rolls her eyes with an exasperated sigh. "Thought I'd help the guy along a little. But he thought he knew better. I hate men that think they know better just because they have a dick."

"I should never have dated a man who works in law like me. He's seen too many liars being a cop. It gave him the perfect learning opportunity. I never even suspected."

Halliday gives me a small smile. "That's because you have a good heart beneath that tough woman lawyer suit you wear. Seeing through criminals is one thing. That's your job, it's not who you are. When you're not at work, you want to see the good in people. It's a nice trait to have. Don't knock it."

"Thanks." I blow a breath out and lean back in my chair. "But it feels like a weakness. For a while, it made me question my judgment. I hate that he did that."

"Hey." She fixes me with a stern look. "You're in control of how this goes. You could tell him the babies aren't his, even if they are. Make sure he has no reason to keep hounding you."

"I can't do that."

"I know. And I wasn't suggesting you do. It's not you. You do things the right way. Truth and justice. It's what I love about you."

"Yeah, truth," I mutter just as my phone rings on the table with the number I've been waiting on.

I wince as the ache in my head intensifies.

"The clinic?" Halliday's brows arch.

I swallow, my throat thick as I pick it up and answer. "Sophie Havers."

"Sophie." Doctor Melinda's soothing tone floats down the phone. "I have your paternity test results back. Is now a good time?"

"Yes." Desperation creeps into my voice.

"Great. Well, each baby is developing in their own amniotic sac. And the test showed heteropaternal superfecundation. It's extremely rare."

Drew's face flashes into my mind.

"Something's wrong with them?" I choke out. *How am I going to tell him? He's so excited.*

I rub my stomach protectively as nausea swirls in my gut. I was so worried about who the father was, I never considered the babies might not be healthy... might not *survive*.

"No, nothing is wrong," Doctor Melinda assures. "They're both developing normally from what I could see at your ultrasound. Heteropaternal superfecundation is the term we use when twins in gestation together have different biological fathers."

The throbbing at the base of my skull is drowned out by blood rushing in my ears. "Different fathers? I don't understand."

"Your body released two eggs. Both were fertilized within the same forty-eight-hour period. One matched Mr. Harper's sample. And the other did not. You mentioned an ex-partner?"

"Y-yes."

"We'll need a sample from him to confirm, but I would be confident in saying that the other egg was fertilized by his sperm."

"Oh."

I stare at Halliday across the table.

"It's a lot to take in. I'm going to send you some information by email for you to read through. I'll call you to arrange a follow-up appointment. In the meantime, if you have any questions, please do call me."

"Okay." My heart races in my chest as I hang up.

"Well, whose are they?" Halliday asks the second the call disconnects.

"Drew's." I swallow.

"I knew it—"

"And Henry's."

Her eyes go like saucers. "What?"

I take a deep breath to try and bring my heartrate down.

"They're both the father. One baby each."

# Chapter 16
# Sophie

"WHAT'S WITH THE FACE?" Drew holds my chin, his piercing blue eyes trained on me. "Something's wrong. What is it?"

I wanted to wait until I at least got through his front door before I told him about Doctor Melinda's call earlier today, but he has this way of reading me that no one else does.

"Sophie?" he presses as I look back at him.

I've spent all afternoon in my office reading the information in the email she sent me and then Googling for more. I was driving myself crazy, so I left work early, which I never do, and called Drew to see if I could let myself into his house and wait for him. Only, this is Drew, Mr. Protective, so he cleared the rest of his meetings for the day and was here when I arrived.

"Doctor Melinda called."

"Are the babies okay?" His eyes drop to my stomach as he sweeps me into the house and pulls me close.

He pulls back and looks at my expression, then his face screws up. "Shit." Warm lips press to my forehead. "It's okay. We'll manage together. Whatever the babies need. Whatever you need. We'll find a way, okay?"

"They're both fine." I place my palms on his chest. His heart is hammering.

"Then what?" His dark brows pull low, and my heart constricts at how beautiful he is. One baby might look just like him.

"The paternity results came back."

Relief softens his face. "So the babies are okay?"

"Yes."

"Thank god." He tips his head back and his Adam's apple bobs. When he lowers it, his eyes are sparkling. "Come on, I'll get you a drink. You need to stay hydrated, Mama." He winks at me and takes my hand, leading me into his kitchen.

"Don't you want to know what she said?"

He takes a glass from his cupboard, fills it with iced water from his fridge and then holds it out to me.

"Drew?"

He arches a thick brow at me and motions to the full glass.

I tut and drink it quickly. He smiles as he takes it from me and places it on the black marble counter.

"You asked for the test. I don't need to know what the results are. I can't want you and our babies any more than I already do."

I look back at him, reading the calmness in his eyes, the relaxed slant of his shoulders, his even breathing.

He's serious. It really doesn't matter to him.

"That means more to me than you'll ever know. But I need to tell you. It's not simple, and I need your help to process it. *Please*, Drew."

"Hey." He moves closer and takes hold of my face. "I hate seeing you worry. Tell me." He strokes my cheeks as his eyes hold mine. "Tell me what she said."

"She said without a sample from Henry, she couldn't confirm, but that it's likely he is the father."

"Okay." Drew's gaze never wavers from mine, and his thumbs continue stroking my face. "How do you feel?"

"I wasn't finished."

"Sorry, Boss." He smiles softly and I roll my eyes at his nickname for me.

"She said Henry was likely the biological father of *one* of the babies. The other baby was a confirmed match to you."

Drew's beautiful face pinches in confusion. "Me?"

"One baby is yours, and the other is Henry's. Apparently, it's really rare," I add as he continues to stare at me.

"Mine? I got you pregnant?"

"Somehow. Probably when you were inside me without anything that first time we—"

He crushes his lips to mine. "I made you pregnant?"

"That's what I said." I can't help my lips lifting into a smile at the grin on his face after he kisses me.

"That first time together?" He searches my eyes.

I nod.

"I got you pregnant that first time we...?" He laughs and presses his forehead to mine. "You came so hard on me, Sophie. But I never thought... Wow," he breathes, his brilliant white teeth snagging his full lower lip. "I knew that first time inside you was special, but... Fuck..." He kisses me again. "I told you it was fate. The first time you and I...? And we made a baby? God..."

He kisses me again, groaning into my mouth as his erection presses against me.

"We're having two beautiful babies." He drops one hand from my face and rushes to unbuckle his belt. His other hand goes to my skirt, yanking it up around my waist with urgency. "Two babies," he groans, lifting me onto the kitchen counter.

"We are," I choke out, emotion making my throat swell.

"We sure are, Boss." He kisses me again through his grin and drags my panties to the side. Then he's inside me, filling me, panting against my mouth as I cry out and wetness rushes between us.

"You're fucking incredible."

He encircles my waist with one arm so that he can keep me in place at the edge of the counter and drive into me with hard, deep pumps. His other hand fists into my hair, arching my neck back so he can run his nose down the column of my throat.

"Incredible," he rasps. "Now, remind me how you sounded moaning my name when I got you pregnant."

# Chapter 17
# Sophie

"YOU GETTING NERVOUS ON me, Boss?" Drew grins as he holds out his hand for me to take from the passenger seat of his McLaren.

"No. I'm just not sure about telling them about the babies yet. What if they ask questions?"

"Sophie." He helps me out of the seat and pushes the door shut before sliding an arm around my waist as we walk. "If they ask questions, we'll answer them. Simple as that."

I look up at his profile. His dark hair is curling a little above the collar of his deep blue jacket, and he's got a day's worth of stubble shadowing his strong jaw. I bite my bottom lip as my core flutters.

"You eye-fucking me, Ms. Havers?" He smirks and looks down at me. "Because we can be late." He slides his hand down to my ass in my silk wrap dress and squeezes a handful of it. "I don't care if we miss entrees. I can feast on your tits instead."

I laugh, breaking up some of the underlying tension in my gut. Drew's adamant my breasts have gotten larger already. He insists on checking regularly... with his mouth.

But no matter how much he's been trying to make me laugh recently, he can't completely dissolve the feeling of dread I have over telling Henry about the twins. The last time I spoke with Henry, I told him that I was having one baby. *His.* I'm still preparing myself to tell him the whole story. Drew's adamant that he will deal with Henry for me and has been asking for his full name to track him down. But I'm embarrassed to admit that during the few months we were dating, he lied about that too and gave me a fake one. Probably to reduce the chance of me finding out he was married. I only found out after we broke up and there was no Henry Jones registered at his station.

I'm a top criminal prosecutor, and I missed all the signs.

"This looks lovely," I say as we approach the fairy lit awning outside the restaurant.

The nerves I had about meeting Drew's family dissipate as his warm hand squeezes my hip reassuringly. It's only his parents and Maddy and Logan coming. Even if we do have to explain about the paternity, if they're like Drew, then they'll be great about it.

We step inside and I look around the space. It's a huge restaurant and every table is filled. There's a warm buzz of conversations flowing and people laughing and clinking glasses.

"Looks like we beat Maddy and Logan. But I see my parents." Drew moves his hand to my lower back as the maître-d smiles at us. Drew indicates we can find our table by ourselves.

"Where?" I look around the crowded restaurant.

"There." He maneuvers me across the room, weaving through tables.

I let him guide me, distracted by the giant palm trees in pots and lush plants decorating the space. They break up the large room, making the tables tucked in behind them more intimate.

"Sophie. This is my mum and dad, Violet and Hank."

Drew brings us to a stop, and I paint on a friendly smile as I turn to greet them.

I freeze, my blood turning to ice in my veins.

"Oh, so lovely to finally meet you." A smiling woman stands from her seat and moves toward me.

I step back, bumping into a man seated behind me.

"Sorry," I mutter, my eyes glued to the owner of the gray eyes, who is sitting at the table staring back at me. "I just... need some air."

I turn and wrap my hand around the top of the chair I've just bumped into. The man seated there looks at me and huffs with annoyance as I use his chair to steady myself before I turn and bolt from the restaurant.

I fly through the front doors and out into the evening air, drawing in deep gasps of air that make my lungs burn. Every cell in my body is tingling as dread spreads through them like a virus. But this one has no cure.

"Sophie?" Drew's eyes are wild as he races out of the front door after me, his suit jacket flapping behind him. "You okay?"

I look up, but my attention is drawn past him to the man exiting the restaurant behind him, hot on his heels. Gray eyes meet mine as he strides toward us.

"We need a minute," Drew says over his shoulder, his eyes never leaving my face.

"What the fuck's going on?" The man pushes past Drew so he's directly in front of me and I swallow down bile at the sound of his voice.

"What the hell, Dad? Don't talk to her like that." With one firm push in the center of the chest, he's moved aside, and Drew is back in front of me again.

Everything stops around me, slammed to a halt by that one three letter word.

*Dad.*

"Sophie?" Drew wraps his hands around my shoulders and bends to be eye-level with me. "You're worrying me. What's wrong?"

Realization settles like broken glass in my gut as I look between the two men. There are some similarities there if I look hard enough. The strong jaw line, the broad shoulders. But Drew is taller, and his eyes are the most captivating blue. Not gray.

*No.*

I'm dangerously close to throwing up.

"He's your *father*?"

Drew's brows jerk together as he follows my gaze to Henry, standing behind him, the silver flecks in his hair lit up beneath the fairy lights.

"Soph," Henry snaps. "What the fuck are you doing here?" He tries to move closer, but Drew blocks him.

"Quit calling her Soph like you know her. And get out of her face. She doesn't feel well. What the hell's wrong with you?"

Drew turns back to me, his hands rubbing my upper arms. "I'll take you home."

"This is who you're with now? My *son*?" Henry spits out the last word like it's poison.

My heart stops as I stare into Drew's eyes.

I see the moment he understands what's going on. The moment his beautiful face breaks. His pupils blow wide as he searches my eyes, his breath coming in short, shallow rasps, while mine stalls altogether. It's the most gut-wrenching sight I've ever seen in my life, and I have to fight to keep my legs from buckling beneath me.

"Sophie?" The anguish in his gaze pleads silently with me to tell him that he's wrong.

But I can't.

"I... I had no idea." My voice cracks.

"This is ridiculous. You can't date my son!"

Henry grabs Drew's shoulder and spins him around to face him.

"You don't know what the hell you've done bringing her here," he yells in Drew's face.

"Me? Sounds like you're the one who has some fucking explaining to do." Drew's voice is quieter than Henry's, but the low hoarseness of it is a thousand times more menacing.

"Your mother's inside," Henry hisses, his eyes bulging.

"Don't pretend you give a flying fuck about my mother when you've so clearly been cheating on her. Again." Drew screws his face up and curses. "And with *Sophie.*" His voice hints at cracking before he levels it out.

He turns to me, and his gaze softens immediately. "Tell me it's not true."

I swear my heart tears right down the middle as I look into clear blue, into that final glimmer of hope that I'm about to extinguish.

"I wish I could," I choke. "I'm so sorry."

"The ex you told me about, the one who was married. It's him?" Drew jerks his head in Henry's direction.

But I don't need to say anything to confirm it. The cloying tension in the air swirling around the three of us and making it hard to breathe is evidence enough.

"Break up with him. *Now.*"

Drew's expression closes off in a flash, like a storm cloud passing in front of the sun.

"What?" he spits at his father.

"You heard me. This can never work. She's having my baby. Did she tell you that?" Henry steps closer, his eyes trained on me. The corners of them pinch as his gaze drops to my stomach, and he frowns.

"A baby you wanted me to abort," I say, finding my voice.

His top lip curls into a sneer. "You were mine first. And the evidence of that is inside you right now." He points at my stomach. "You can't date her, Son. Not when I had her first." His eyes meet mine again and glint with something that makes sourness coat my tongue. "And I had you more than a few times, didn't I, Soph?"

There's a roar and the air explodes around us as Drew slams his father against the wall.

"What the fuck did you say?"

Henry doesn't back down. Instead, he glares at Drew like he has a death wish.

"She's having my baby. She'll never be yours."

"She isn't anybody's property, you selfish prick."

Henry only snorts as Drew's fists tighten on his collar, cutting off his air supply and making his face turn red.

"So you think she's with you now?" he splutters. "A man with a criminal past? Wake up, Son. She's a fucking lawyer. You're not good enough for her."

Drew crowds him more, the muscles in his back tensing beneath his jacket as he glowers at him, their eyes like acid burning into one another. Then he pushes Henry to one side and steps back beside me.

"That's about the only fucking thing we agree on," Drew spits. "I'm not good enough. But I'm blessed that she wants to be with me. *With* me. Not owned by me. One's forced, one's a choice. And you're old enough to know the difference."

"She's having my baby." Henry jabs his finger into his crumpled shirt over his chest. "Mine. Not yours."

I lay a hand on Drew's bicep. It's solid and unyielding like he's about to run into battle.

"I think we should leave," I urge.

I need to be away from Henry to process this. We both do. No good will come from them looking like they're about to kill one another any second.

Drew ignores me, squaring up to Henry as his eyes flick down and back up his body. When they come back up, they're full of a silent challenge that makes nausea claw at my windpipe.

"Not like this," I beg.

But he isn't listening. He's locked on target and nothing else around him exists.

"That's where you're wrong, *Dad*," Drew spits. "She isn't just having your baby. She's having mine too."

Henry snarls, "Don't be stupi—"

"It's twins. She's having twins."

# Chapter 18
## Drew

"WHAT?" DAD'S EYES WIDEN.

"You heard me," I grit, enjoying watching the smarmy smugness being scraped from his face by my revelation. "Sophie's having twins, aren't you, Darling?" I glance at her, but she's silent, shaking her head at me.

"You had sex with my son? With my leftovers inside you? Did you even shower in between?"

For the second time tonight, I throw my father against the wall. His face contorts as I hold him with my forearm pinned across his windpipe. The idea of crushing it altogether is looking more appealing by the millisecond.

"Apologize."

He grimaces as I force my arm higher and raise a brow.

"That's the mother of my children you're talking to. Now fucking *apologize.*"

"What's going on? Drew?"

"Dad!"

Mum's and Maddy's voices cut through the air, breaking up our cozy Father/Son bonding, as a large hand lands on my shoulder.

"Let him go, Buddy. Let's talk about this someplace else."

I incline my head toward Logan as he jerks his jaw toward the restaurant's giant window next to us. We're the fucking evening's entertainment.

"As soon as he says sorry, I'll let him breathe," I hiss, fixing my eyes back onto my father's.

"Drew, please!" Mum cries.

The despair in her voice makes my jaw clench, and I release Dad in a rush. He bends over, grasping at his neck, coughing.

"You see your son, Violet? See his temper? He's always been trouble. If it isn't stealing cars, it's something else," he wheezes.

"I saw. And I *heard* too." Mum's voice slices through the air with a strength in it I haven't heard before. "I heard it all."

I snap my gaze to Sophie as all heads turn in her direction. She's moved further away and is standing on her own.

I take a step toward her, but she holds up a hand, making me stop.

"I'm so sorry." She looks at my mum, then Maddy, and finally Logan. Her eyes never move to me or my father. "I never knew about any of you, I swear. You shouldn't be finding out like this. I'm so sorry."

Her voice is even and calm, and I recognize the pulling back of her shoulders. It's what she does when she puts on her suits for work in the morning. When she's putting on her mask. Sophie Havers, the lawyer who has to remain emotionless to protect herself from the ugliness of people and what they do to one another.

But her eyes can't lie. Not to me.

She blinks a couple of times, pressing her lips together. Then she spins on her heels and strides away.

"Let her go," Dad barks. "Crazy bitch. Making up stories like that."

My fist clenches, and I prepare to swing. But his head is already flying to one side from the force of something as I spin back to face him.

"Go, check on Sophie," Mum says from her position in front of Dad. She's shaking and rubbing her palm, which is turning a bright shade of red, matching the mark on my father's face. "Go on," she repeats. "I want to speak to your father. Alone."

It takes me fifteen minutes to find Sophie. She isn't back at the car. She's pacing a street nearby, her blonde hair lit like a halo beneath each streetlight she walks beneath. Any other night and I'd have something to say to her about being here in the dark alone. But from the way she freezes and lifts her chin with a tortured scowl on her face as she sees me, I'm pretty sure she'll rip my head off if I even try to tell her anything other than what I know should be the first two words out of my mouth.

"I'm sorry," I say when I'm close enough for her to hear me.

She sniffs and drops her eyes to the ground, wrapping her arms around herself.

"I shouldn't have told him it's twins."

"No, you shouldn't." She swallows. Her dark lashes clump over her eyes as her cheeks glisten.

"Fuck, Sophie." My heart clenches, and I step toward her, but she shakes her head.

"But you saying sorry to me, Drew, it isn't right. Not when..." She looks past me like they might have followed me. But they haven't. Dad sloped off with Mum into their car, and Logan and Maddy followed after asking if I was sure I'd be okay. I told them the only person I was concerned about right now was Sophie. Then I ran after her.

"My father is your ex," I say, which brings her tear-filled eyes to mine.

Her throat trembles as she swallows.

"I had no idea."

"Is it over?" My gut twists painfully as I search her eyes.

Her mouth drops open. "You know it is! How can you ask me that? It was over before I met you. I never... Oh God." Her face creases up and she starts to cry. My strong-ass boss starts to cry. And nothing has ever made my soul feel like it's being ripped from my body before like this.

"Not with him." I grab her and wrap her in my arms before she can protest. "With *us*? Tell me there's a way through this for you, Sophie. Because I'll burn the whole world to find the path that still leads me to you. Every. Time."

"I was with your father." She buries her face into my chest as I stroke her hair. "How can you even bear to look at me?"

I press my nose against her blonde strands and inhale. "Because any life without you in it isn't a life for me. It's hell."

"I'm having his baby." Her voice is quiet and muffled against my chest. I have to strain to hear it. But her words make fire blaze through my veins. I'm running on adrenaline. And I know shit will hit the fan when it wears off. But right now, I have to concentrate on Sophie. This is a shock for her too. She needs me.

"Forget about him. Forget about anyone else and tell me what *you* want."

She sucks in a shaky breath. "I want to rewind two hours to where I was happy about having *our* babies together."

Her hand slides down the small gap between our bodies and she flattens it over her stomach. I place mine over the top.

"They're still our babies. They're still a fucking miracle. And I'll still be a father who fights for them until the last breath leaves my body. And that includes fighting for you, too."

I drop my forehead to hers.

"Do I wish your ex was anyone other than my worthless, cheating father? Yes, of course I fucking do. I can't even allow myself to think about you and him together. I'll unpack that shit later."

Sophie winces.

"But he's right. I don't deserve you. I allowed myself to be baited by him. It's what he does. It's what he will try and do. I know him. He won't make this easy for any of us if he isn't getting his own way. It's how he's always been." I close my eyes and let out a deep breath, lifting my lips to Sophie's forehead. "He'll destroy us if we let him. And the idea scares the shit out of me. We have to communicate, Sophie. Promise me that above all else, we'll talk to each other? We'll always come to each other first?"

"I promise."

Relief flows through my veins like warm honey. My father stripped me of the life I dreamed of when I was a teenager and he gave up on me. But he's not going to strip me of this. I will not end up like him, whatever it costs me.

"I'll trade my life to save yours. All three of you. And I'll love you so hard that you choose to stay with me, no matter how messed up this all gets, okay?"

She nods, leaning close to me.

"Because it will get fucking messy, Sophie."

"I know," she whispers. "They never said it would be easy, only that it would be worth it."

I smile at the saying, praying that she truly believes every single word of it as much as I do. Because she's going to need every ounce of that strength.

# Chapter 19
# Drew

"WHAT THE HELL WAS he thinking, going out alone to deal with this? Why didn't he call one of us?"

I can hear familiar voices in the distance. I know who it is. And I didn't call them because after what went down last night I just needed to blow off some steam.

Alone.

"Fucking hell. I found him!"

My head pounds like it's being beaten with a steel pipe as the voices come nearer.

"Jesus. I hope the other guy came off worse."

A hand grips my chin, angling my face up to inspect it. The movement makes the metallic taste in my mouth stronger until I can no longer resist the urge to swallow. I wince as my stomach receives a mouthful of my own blood.

"Two," I croak. "Two other guys."

"You got a fucking death wish? Idiot."

That's when I recognize the two voices. *Logan and Dax.*

They take an arm each, hauling me up off the concrete floor and supporting me around the waist as they sling my arms around each of their shoulders. My head lolls side to side.

"God, you stink." *Logan.*

"Get a good sleep on those trash bags?" *Dax.*

Light invades my eyes through my slitted lids, causing me to groan as they begin to walk me up what appears to be an alleyway full of giant trash containers.

"Where the hell are your shoes?" Logan asks.

I grunt and drop my head to look at my bare feet as hazy memories of the previous night come to me in broken flashes.

"The ugly one took them after I made his nose bleed and called him a cunt. Pretty sure he didn't like it."

"No shit, Sherlock. You might want to reconsider next time you pick a fight with two giant fuckers on your own." Dax chuckles.

"Hey. Gang's all here. Now we can party. I'm guessing you heard the news?" I say as I try to smile at Tanner when he appears in my line of sight with a grim expression.

My lip burns and something warm and sticky runs from it down my chin.

"He's still pissed," Tanner gripes, looking from Dax and then to Logan. "Let's get him in the car and take him home to sober up."

"I don't need a babysitter," I groan before promptly vomiting all over my bare feet as well as Logan's and Dax's shoes.

Logan retches, and Dax curses.

Tanner walks over and pats me on the cheek. "Course you don't, princess. But you got three. So wind your neck in."

I scowl at him. "How'd you fuckers find me?"

He looks into my one open eye. The other's swelled shut and now that I'm awake, it's throbbing like a bitch.

He blows out a breath. "Sophie."

"Sophie?" My voice wavers and I let out a pathetic whimper, followed by a belch.

"Throw up on my shoes again and I'll drop you. You're already replacing these ones," Logan grumbles.

But his and Dax's grips around my torso tighten as Tanner gives me a tight smile.

"She called us. She was worried you were going to go and murder your father and get your ass slung in jail," Tanner comments.

I open my mouth and turn to Dax but the look in his eyes kills the joke I was about to make.

"Didn't think you'd be stupid enough to come out and pick a fight with two cage fighters," Tanner mumbles.

I chuckle, but it makes my ribs feel like they're being snapped apart like a wishbone at a roast dinner. Those guys were huge. At least their fists were when they connected with my face.

"How'd you know that?" Logan asks Tanner.

"Guy inside said." Tanner tips his head toward the wall of the alley. "This bar's their usual hang out."

"At least you aren't punching me this time." Logan snorts.

"You sure picked well," Dax says, sounding impressed as he and Logan continue to walk me toward Tanner's waiting car.

*I sure did.*

Dax is the one most likely to understand that need for blood. He's been there himself. It's how he ended up in jail for three years before he met Rose.

I knew where I was headed the second I left Sophie's last night. I waited until she was asleep, and then I went in search of the only thing I knew would numb the pain.

Alcohol and punching. *And being punched.*

Each hit those fuckers delivered last night felt equal parts good and painful. Anything was better than the feeling tearing me up inside when I thought about my father's cheating hands all over Sophie.

And that look on my mother's face when she heard it all.

I had to come out and get the shit kicked out of me last night. Because if I'd been able to walk, then Sophie would have been right.

I would have killed my father.

And no matter how great of a lawyer she is, even she wouldn't have been able to get me off.

The only thing worse to me than the thought that she's having his baby is the thought that if I kill him,

I won't be there with her to have mine. *Both* of them. Because they are both mine, regardless of what a DNA test says. And I'll love them both the same no matter what.

Because whatever my asshole father does, that's all I've ever wanted.

To be a better father than him.

Logan and Dax maneuver me to Tanner's car where I'm unceremoniously shoved into the backseat with my legs hanging out.

"Those aren't going in." Tanner points to my vomit-covered feet.

"Don't you get like baby shit and puke in your car all the time?" Logan's brow creases as the three of them stare at me sprawled out on the backseat, arms crossed as they decide what to do with me.

"Ruby's in nappies. And she's still exclusively breastfed. Her puke doesn't reek like this."

"Sure doesn't," Logan agrees, covering his mouth as he retches again.

"Breastfed," I murmur. "Pregnancy breasts... Fucking magnificent."

My eyes must glaze over because Tanner leans into the car and something cold hits my face, making me splutter.

"Here." He hands me the sippy cup of water he's just sprayed me with. "Drink this."

I take the bright green plastic, holding it by the two matching handles as I take a deep gulp.

"Fuck me, that's good," I moan.

Tanner snorts and then I hear Logan protesting about something. The next minute something wet is encasing my foot.

I peel my shoulders up off the backseat, craning to see my feet. Logan's busy cleaning them with a baby wipe as Tanner shakes his head and Dax watches on with a smirk.

When he's done, he shoves my legs into the car.

"Good job, Dada," Tanner says as he climbs into the driver's seat and Logan joins him in the front.

"Shut it," Logan grumbles. "Anything to not have to sit in the back with little Ms. Vomit."

As if on cue, my stomach groans and Logan's eyes narrow warily.

Dax sinks into the seat next to me, hoisting me up into a sitting position and doing up my belt.

"Here." He thrusts a bright yellow bowl into my hands. "You need to hurl again, you do it in that."

I frown at the weird plastic ring in my hands. I thought it was a bowl, but the bottom is made up of a plastic bag.

Tanner's eyes meet mine in the rearview mirror. "It's a travel potty."

I stare at the thing, noticing the yellow cartoon duck on it. Then I peer inside it, praying—

"It's clean," Tanner clips. "Let's try and keep it that way."

Then he floors the accelerator.

Sophie's lips press into a firm line as her gaze skims over my black eye again.

The boys brought me back home, cleaned me up, and let me sleep the residual alcohol in my system off before she arrived. Logan drew the short straw for being the one to get me in the shower to wash the vomit and blood away. Fucker set it to freeze-your-balls-off-cold to start with, claiming it was an accident.

Probably payback for that punch I landed when I found out about him and Maddy. He's never stopped going on about it. How else was I supposed to react when I found one of my best friends whispering something about his cum that I wish I could forget in my little sister's ear?

But regardless, he's still one of my best friends and future brother-in-law. And despite my right hook, I'm still his. Because we chose it to stay that way.

"You should have gone to the hospital to get it checked," Sophie says, her fingers lightly dusting over the cheekbone beneath my swollen eye socket.

"It's nothing," I grunt.

She sighs and then her lips return to the firm line they've been in ever since she walked through my door and saw the state of me. I know she's finding this hard, seeing me like this. She's so used to fixing things, for getting justice for her clients. My beautiful boss lady hates feeling helpless if things get out of her control.

"I'm fine," I say in a gentler voice.

"You said honesty, Drew. Communication. You made me promise."

"I know." I look at her with my good eye and take her fingers between mine, interlacing them.

"You could have talked to me instead of..." Her eyes skim over my face before she looks away and swallows. "You're lucky nothing was broken."

*Only my heart seeing the women in my life all in pieces.*

"Cuts and bruises heal."

Her glassy eyes meet mine again.

"Sophie?" I pull her to me, ignoring the tightening in my chest as my pummeled ribs scream.

She tries to move away. "You need to really think about this. You and I... Everything is a thousand times more complicated now. I never want to hurt you, Drew. Or your family. But look where we already are. I don't know how to fix this. If you stay with me—"

"Don't finish that fucking sentence," I hiss.

I pull her over me so that she's straddling me on my couch.

"Don't you dare ever breathe a word like that again. You got it?" I fist the back of her hair and pull her face to mine so that our noses touch. "You and me are having these babies. Together. No matter what any other fucker says or does. Okay?"

"But—"

I silence her with a kiss, making my split lip sting like a motherfucker.

"Promise me. I can't lose you, Sophie. I can't lose any of you." My eyes drop to her stomach.

"I don't want to come between you and your family," she whispers. "I can't make this right. Your father—"

"You are my family." I place my bloodied knuckles over her clean, white T-shirt, stroking her stomach. "You are my everything. And my relationship with him has always been... Some things stay broken. It's life. You didn't ruin anything. And what he did to Mum is not your burden to carry, you hear me? He made his choices."

She nods, her green eyes clearing, making way for understanding. "This is what you really want? No matter how complicated it might get?"

"It's not just what I want. It's what I've been fucking dreaming of." I crush my lips to hers again, ignoring the taste of blood as the cut re-opens. "You and the babies are everything to me. Please don't leave me because of him."

*Don't give me any more reasons to hate him.*

She pulls back and searches my eyes. There's a vulnerability in hers. I know I'm the only one she lets see it. By staying with me, she has to accept that she can't fix everything. But we will handle whatever's thrown at us. *Together*.

"I don't want to leave you. I'd have to have no choice in order to ever do that." She swallows like the thought alone is crushing her windpipe. "I know it's not been long, but I want to be with you, Drew. More than anything."

Hearing her say those words is like a soothing balm radiating throughout my body.

"Show me," I breathe, my breath clawing at my chest as her brows draw together in hesitation and her gaze darts to my bruises again. "Show me you want me. I need to feel it."

Her pupils dilate at my words, and I know she understands.

*Show me that you need me. And only me. Show me that no one else before me meant anything to you.*

"I don't just want you." She kisses me softly. "I want all the same things you do. Our babies. Our family. The four of us together. Always."

Her words are like a prayer, reaching into my battered soul and caressing it with healing light.

"Then fucking show me," I murmur, moving my lips to the column of her neck, my words vibrating against her skin like a plea.

I groan as she helps me out of my t-shirt. The muscles in my arms seize up, making them tremble as I lift them above my head. Sophie's eyes fall to the emerging bruises all over my torso. There are more bruises than unmarked skin.

"You're too hurt. We can't." Her face crumples with guilt, slamming into her as hard as the punch to my gut at seeing the pain on her face.

My bruises might be visible. But she took a beating last night too.

"Don't you dare stop." I grip her chin and kiss her, willing her to get out of her head.

She needs this. *I* need this.

She pulls back, breathless, her eyes sliding down my body again. "I wish you hadn't gone out alone. Not after everything that happened."

"You didn't need to see me. Not like that." I stroke her hair back from her eyes as she blinks, regret swirling in her gaze. "It's not your fault. I needed it. But now that it's done, I'm good."

"You got it out of your system? No going back for round two later?" Her glassy eyes travel down my body again, taking in every cut and bruise.

"Yeah, Boss. I did. Now come here."

She shakes her head and my heart threatens to give out as she moves away from me. Her rejection hurts more than getting my eyeball knocked to the back of my skull by that giant ugly fucker last night.

"Sophie?" I reach for her, but she drops out of reach, kneeling on the floor between my legs.

"I can't do something that causes you pain. Please don't ask me to."

I swallow the lump of acid in my throat and give her a curt nod. If I need to heal before she'll touch me, I need to suck it up and handle it. I've no choice. Even if every minute of not having her touch me feels like the cruelest punishment.

"You need to stop me if anything starts to be painful, okay?"

"What do you—?"

She pulls the waistband of my sweatpants down and my dick springs free.

Thank fuck it's about the only part of my body that isn't bruised.

"Okay," I agree with the eagerness of a puppy that pisses itself at the sight of its owner. But it's a barefaced lie. I'll do no such thing. A freight train could plow through my living room and straight between my eyes and there's no way I'd tell Sophie to stop sucking my dick.

She looks up at me. Big emerald green eyes. Perfect pillowy lips.

"Open," I growl.

She does as I say, her silky little mouth the most beautiful sight as I grip the base of my seeping dick and tap it against her bottom lip, smearing precum all over it.

She lets out a breathy sigh that flows around the head of my dick and a deep groan leaves my chest as my balls twitch. Fuck me, I'm painfully hard, my balls aching with the need to come, and she hasn't even licked me yet.

I spread my hand over the back of her head and lift my hips a little so that I can feed her my cock. She accepts it willingly, her eyes holding mine as she takes a few inches, swirling her tongue around the head before dipping it into my weeping slit.

"Fuck, Darling," I curse as she swipes up a bead of precum, moaning like it's the best thing she's ever tasted.

My hand closes into a fist on the back of her head, scrunching up blonde strands.

"You want to be a good girl and make me feel better?" I grunt as she cups my loaded balls in one of her soft hands.

"Mm-hmm." Her voice vibrates as she places a kiss on my tip.

I tug her hair, arching her head back. Our eyes meet and we just stare at each other for a few seconds. The energy multiplies in the room until there's no room for guilt or hurt or regret.

There's only room for this. Us. And the undeniable pull there's been since that first day I laid eyes on her.

She was always going to be on her knees like this for me. Because one look at her that first night and I fell to mine.

"Say it," I demand.

Her pulse flutters in her neck and I rub my cock over her chin, smearing her skin with wetness.

"I want to make you feel better," she breathes.

My lips curl. I already feel a damn sight better and we've barely started.

"You want to swallow this cock?"

She nods as much as my grip on her hair will allow.

"Tell me," I growl, my hand swiveling at my base so I can tap my dick against her parted lips.

Her eyelids grow heavy with lust as she licks her lips, catching me with the tip of her tongue and making my balls tingle. "Yes."

"You want to drink down every drop of cum that you're going to milk out of it?"

"Yes," she repeats, her warm breath fanning over my dripping head.

I can't take it any longer. I'll fucking explode.

"It's all for you, Boss. Take it."

I slide my cock through her lips, using my fist in her hair to push her down onto it.

She moans in appreciation, relaxing her throat around me.

"Good girl. Now, suck."

# Chapter 20
## Sophie

"I GONNA GET YOU!" A toddler in a green fairy outfit, wielding a magic wand, screeches, as he chases a larger boy in a pirate costume through the kitchen.

They race past Logan, Maddy, Dax, Rose, and another couple I was introduced to earlier, Megan and Jaxon, who have brought a little girl with them, then almost barrel into Tanner's wife, Rachel. She holds the hot tray that she's just got out of the oven above their heads. "Take it in the other room, kids. Teddy, keep an eye on your brother!" she calls at their retreating backs before rolling her eyes. "They never stop. I swear the devil knocked me up some days."

"Did he fuck. Pure Grayson genes those are." Tanner grins, kissing her temple, and balancing baby Ruby on one hip.

Rachel snorts, but a small smile plays on her lips.

Warm lips graze my ear from behind, and a hand slides around my front, cradling my growing bump. "You okay, Mama?"

I incline my head toward Drew and grin. "Yeah. All good."

I thought it would be weird coming to Tanner and Rachel's house for Ruby's six-month birthday party, seeing as I don't know any of them that well. But they've all been amazingly welcoming. Especially Maddy, who I was dreading seeing after that night at the restaurant two weeks ago. But she sought me out the minute Drew and I arrived and pulled me into a hug telling me she doesn't blame me for any of it and that she's over the moon about the babies and being an auntie.

She didn't mentioned Henry, who I now know they all call Hank.

She also didn't mention their mum, Violet.

But I know that Maddy shredded all Henry's shirts after that night. Drew said Henry thought Violet did it until Maddy screamed at him that she wanted to cut his balls off for how he's been behaving. Apparently, she's barely spoken to him since.

Henry's still at the house, sleeping in the guest room. Drew sounded pretty disgusted by it all. Apparently he's cheated on their mum numerous times, and she always forgives him after a week or two. But I don't know if that'll happen this time. It won't if Drew and Maddy have a say in it.

I don't know how I feel about it all. But one small positive is that Henry hasn't attempted to contact me again after that awful night. It's only a matter of time. But I'm enjoying the reprieve while it lasts.

"Here. Get some practice in," Tanner says, seconds before dumping baby Ruby into my arms.

"Oh, sure." I smile at her rosy little cheeks as she gurgles happily, staring at me with giant eyes. She fists my hair and then pulls.

"Killer handshake there, Missy," Drew coos as he expertly releases her grip. "You'll drive a harder business deal than your dad."

Tanner grins over at us proudly as he helps Rachel with the food they're plating up. "That's my girl."

I smile back at Ruby now that my hair's been extracted, and she looks at me with her lips pursed. Then she grunts. A second later, a vibration against my arms accompanied by the wettest sounding fart fills the kitchen.

"Oh my god." I laugh. "That's such a big sound for such a litt—"

She grunts again, her little round face flushing as she fills her nappy without an ounce of self-consciousness. When she finishes, she grins at me, her two bottom teeth poking from her gums.

"You literally just pooped for England and had a fresh nappy," Tanner mutters as he walks over, holding his arms out.

"We got it." Drew plucks Ruby from my arms and holds her up in front of him, pretending to sniff her. "Eww, you really do take after your daddy, stinker."

Ruby gurgles in delight and kicks her legs.

"Be quick, food's almost ready," Rachel says as Drew holds Ruby in one arm and gestures for me to follow him from the room.

"Thought you might like a minute away from that lot," he says as we head upstairs and into Ruby's nursery.

"Are you kidding? They're all great. I can't believe they're so chilled about all of this."

I follow him over to the changing table he's laid Ruby on.

"They've seen it all. Believe me." He chuckles. "Our babies' story is nothing in comparison. You know Dax was almost murdered, right? Twice?"

Drew strips Ruby out of her romper like a pro, then undoes the poppers of the vest underneath. The thick veins in his corded forearms pop as he removes the soiled nappy and bags it without hesitation and then reaches for a pack of baby wipes.

"I worked on some of his case."

"I know. He said you were awesome. I wanted to reach out to you back then. But you know... restraining order." He pops a brow with a smirk.

"That was a joke." I laugh as he cleans Ruby up and then reaches for a clean nappy, flicking it open with one hand easily as he looks at me.

I don't know why that move is so sexy, but it is.

He slides the nappy under her and secures it around her tummy. My stomach clenches as I look up at his dark profile. His eyes are crinkling at the corners as he smiles at Ruby, talking to her and rubbing her feet.

"I wish you had. Then things could be different," I whisper.

Drew turns, his blue eyes capturing mine. "Don't."

He's having a much easier time coping with the fact I'm having his father's baby than I am. Sometimes, I think he's in denial. But he doesn't avoid the subject like I'd expect him to if that were the case.

"If anything had happened differently, then we wouldn't be about to have two of these." Drew grins at Ruby as he finishes dressing her and lifts her up into his arms. She places her hands on his face and he immediately kisses them, making her giggle.

"That's true," I murmur.

"I wouldn't change a thing." His eyes meet mine. "Not one damn thing. I've got everything I ever wanted right here."

His gaze drops to my small bump. Doctor Melinda said I might begin to show earlier because I'm having twins. To most people, I probably look bloated. But to Drew, I must look like a *Michelin* meal, because he can't stop trying to devour me.

We take a clean and happy Ruby back downstairs and everyone cheers as we walk in. Rachel comes to take her and announces it's food time, and Drew gets pulled aside by Tanner to look for a lighter for the cake candle.

"I never thought I'd see the day," Maddy says, following my gaze to where Drew and Tanner are frowning in front of a giant unicorn cake in a deep discussion about where the single candle should go.

"Oh?" I smile as Drew's about to put the candle in and Tanner bats his hand away and points at another spot.

"Yeah. My brother's always loved kids. I think he'd almost given up on having his own. Especially when he told me the woman of his dreams turned him down." She giggles. "You made him work for you. You've been good for him."

"He's the one who's good for me."

Tanner puts the candle in and it promptly falls over, deforming the unicorn's eye, and Drew bites his fist to hide his laugh.

"I mean it," Maddy continues. "He'd become such a damn grump. But now..." She smiles as she watches Drew fix the cake. "Now he's joking again. He's got stuff to look forward to. He's got you." She squeezes my arm. "He's a lucky guy and he knows it. Although I'm not sure how I feel about you making me the middle child. Aren't they the weird ones?" She laughs, nudging me.

Warmth expands my chest as I stand next to her. She could so easily hate me after what I've done to her family, but instead, she's telling me that her brother's lucky to have me.

I couldn't disagree more.

Drew's laughter cuts across the kitchen at something Tanner says, and I smile.

*I'm* the lucky one.

# Chapter 21
# Sophie

*GREAT.*

My stomach twists at the sight of the familiar form outside my building as I step out for lunch. It's too late to avoid him because his gray eyes are already zeroing in on me. They widen as they take in the expanding curve of my stomach in my pencil skirt.

"Soph?"

I walk over to him, not returning his smile. "It's been weeks, and this is how you want to do this?" I glance back at the doorman of our office building and then gesture down the street.

Henry falls into step beside me as I walk.

"I was going to call sooner."

I say nothing because I'm glad he didn't. His radio silence has been a blessing. Some days, I almost forget Drew and I aren't a regular, happy couple expecting their first babies together. Like when we sit on his couch at night, and he rubs my feet while reading from one of the pregnancy books he's bought. He could start his own library with them all.

"You should have told me if you wanted to talk. I'd have arranged something when I wasn't working. When Drew could be here."

"My son," Henry snaps, grabbing my wrist and pulling me to a stop in the middle of the street, "doesn't need to be here to talk about *our* baby."

I raise a brow as I look at his hand around my arm and he drops it immediately.

"*Babies*," I correct, my voice filled with a quiet warning. "I'm having two, remember?"

Henry chuckles as if I've said something funny.

"You don't know what you're doing with him. He won't look after you the way he should."

I bite back my snort.

"He's unreliable, reckless... selfish."

"Sounds a lot like how I'd describe a man who cheats on his wife and lies about it."

Henry's lips curve, the skin around his eyes wrinkling. "I always loved that bite of yours."

I sigh and check my watch. I only have thirty minutes before my meeting starts.

"Is there a point to this, Henry? Because unless you actually came here to talk like adults, then—"

"I'm getting you back. I'll do whatever it takes, Soph."

I shouldn't be shocked, but I am.

The hairs on the back of my neck rise and my skin bristles as I look at him, all respectable in his charcoal suit and black shirt. A suit that hides a man who can't even begin to truly understand the word 'respect'. Whatever spell he had me under to fool my instincts when we dated is gone now. Replaced by the uneasiness I get when I know something is about to blow wide in court.

*I'll do whatever it takes.*

Those words circle around my head in a never-ending, foreboding loop.

"We're never getting back together. Ever."

"You don't mean that." Henry deflects my words with an arrogant shrug of his shoulders.

"I think you'll find that when I say something, I mean it," I clip back. "But by all means, hold your breath while you wait to find out if you like."

His eyes glint. "I know why my son wants you. He's attracted to your strong will. He might think he's a match for you. But he isn't. *I* am. You know it's the truth, Soph. Tell me you wish it were my hands on you, not his."

I'd laugh if he was worth the energy. But hearing his low hum of appreciation as his eyes drop down to my growing cleavage, and the way he tucks one hand into his suit pants to adjust himself, tells me he actually believes he's been blessed with some sort of godly sexual prowess.

"You're delusional."

Drew made me come more that first time together than I ever did with Henry the entire time we dated. I could easily unleash some harsh facts that would kill the leery look in his eyes. But one of us needs to be the adult.

"You and I are over, Henry. If you want to have a mature discussion about this when Drew is here, then—"

"We're having a baby. We owe it to it to try and work this out," he snaps.

"*I'm* having *two* babies. Plural," I say, keeping my voice devoid of emotion despite the fact each time he says *baby*, I want to smack him in the mouth. "Does Violet know you're here?"

His eyes flit away from mine and his jaw hardens.

"Guess that's a no." I spin on my heels. Forget lunch, I'll make do with something in the office kitchen. Anything is better than wasting time getting nowhere with him.

"She's filing for divorce, Soph." His words hit my back, making me turn to face him.

I stare at him, unsure what he wants me to say.

*Good for her? I know a great divorce lawyer if she needs a recommendation? Drew's been telling her to do it for years?*

I settle with, "Okay."

"So there's nothing stopping us from being together." He rushes toward me and grabs my hands in his. "We can have a fresh start. You, me, and our baby."

*Baby.*

"Babies," I snap for the last fucking time, pulling free of his grasp. "What do you expect me to do with the other one?"

"Drew's always wanted his own. Give it to him."

I gasp, bile clawing at my throat. He really must have been acting when we were dating because there's no way I would ever entertain the stranger in front of me for a minute otherwise.

"Give it to him? Like loaning a sweater?"

His face screws up. "You know what I mean. Jesus, don't put words in my mouth."

"You literally said 'give it to him' like you were talking about an object and not a baby. I'm not putting words into your mouth."

His face reddens as he takes a step closer, an edge creeping into his voice as he jabs a finger against his temple. "He's getting to you. Filling your head with garbage. You know this makes sense. We both get what we want. Drew gets what he wants. We all walk away happy. Think what it'll do to him bringing up a child that isn't his. That's hard enough for any man. But one that's his father's? Come on, Soph. Don't do that to him. He might claim he's fine with it, but it'll ruin him in the end. You can fix all of this with the right decision."

*Fix all of this.*

Something sour swirls low in my stomach, but I pull my shoulders back, taking a deep breath. "Drew wants them both. And he's going to be the best dad."

Henry shakes his head. "When you see sense and you will, I'll be here for you."

I take one final look at him. No other words are needed except, "Goodbye, Henry."

I stride away before the anger bubbling inside me makes me shake in front of him. I don't want him to think he's gotten to me. Because nothing he says is right. Drew wants these babies more than anything. He's told me a million times. It won't ruin him.

I could never do anything that would ruin him.

And Henry's wrong. I can't fix this. There is no fixing this.

All I can do is what's best for the babies. And my gut tells me that that's being with Drew. My *heart* tells me that's being with Drew. I have to trust that they will both keep telling me the same thing.

# Chapter 22
# Sophie

MY PHONE RINGS JUST as Drew's balls kiss my skin.

"Leave it," he hisses, tightening his grip on my hips as he fills me from behind.

"Like I'd answer it when you're inside me," I moan as he circles, loosening me up.

A shiver runs down my spine. If he's taking his time warming me up slowly like this, then he's intending on going at it hard. I bite my lip with anticipation. He was reassured by Doctor Melinda at our follow-up ultrasound that sex is still okay. I knew he was going to ask again, so I wasn't even embarrassed this time. But since my stomach has started to grow more, I've noticed he's been holding back again.

"So sexy," he murmurs, leaning over me and sliding a hand around to cradle my bump.

His teeth graze my neck, causing butterflies to erupt in my stomach.

"Drew," I whimper, "please."

"Patience, Mama," he tuts, stroking my bump and sucking on my neck as his dick stays nestled and unmoving inside me.

The pregnancy hormones flooding my body are ready to murder him, because all I want is a hard pounding. I'm practically salivating any time I think of his dick. Which is a lot. I swear my body has been taken over by these babies.

My phone starts to ring again, but the sound is drowned out by my moan as he flexes inside me.

"Fuck, you're so wet."

I push back against him. He's right. It's coating my inner thighs. Yet, he's still not moving.

"Come on," I huff.

He chuckles. "You'll be the one coming on, Boss. Coming on my cock in a minute." He straightens and gives my ass a gentle slap.

I grind back onto him, desperately chasing friction.

"You feeling needy?" He chuckles again as he slaps my other ass cheek.

I bite my cheek, clenching around him.

His reaction is a strained grunt.

I smile into the pillow before turning my head to the side to look back at him. His expression is serious as he looks down at where he's buried inside me.

"Are you going to stare at it all day? Because I'll get my vibrator out if that's the case."

A smirk tugs at his lips. "Not this time. We'll save that for when I christen this beautiful ass." A groan of appreciation leaves his chest as he stretches my ass cheeks apart and strokes a thumb down over the puckered skin.

Then he pulls back and thrusts back into me, knocking the air from my lungs in a moan loud enough to sound like I'm already coming.

But I don't care.

*Finally.*

"More..." I beg.

He sets a steady pace, driving into me from behind, slamming me back onto him with a punishing grip on my hips.

*God, yes. It's exactly what I need.*

I relish every thrust, pleasure thrumming through me.

"I'm close," I cry as my phone starts to ring again.

Drew grunts, his pace slowing as my phone stops ringing and immediately starts again.

"Do you think there's an emergency?" I pant.

Holly flashes to my mind. Or Mum and Dad.

The ringing stops. Then starts again.

"See who it is," Drew says, pausing.

His hands stroke my hips as I reach to the night-stand. I look at the screen and curse, dropping my phone face down where it continues to buzz against the wood.

"Keep going," I urge.

"Who is it?" he grits, his fingers flexing against my skin and keeping me still as I try to work myself on his cock.

"Doesn't matter," I breathe, trying my earlier trick of clenching around him.

His dick twitches inside me but he still doesn't move. Instead, he slaps my ass.

"Who the fuck is it, Sophie?"

"Your dad," I confess.

Drew's silent behind me. Then the ringing starts again.

"Ignore it," I plead, squeezing my eyes shut and trying desperately to feed the ache between my legs by squirming inside Drew's grip.

There's a soft thud on the pillow next to me, and I open my eyes. My phone's lying there, the ringing stopped.

Drew starts to move inside me again.

*Thank god, he put it on silent.*

I moan happily as he pulls back and slams into me. Hard. I grip the sheets, dragging the fabric inside my clenched fists as he drives inside me again.

"Yesss!"

"Soph?"

Panic coils its way around my windpipe like a noose.

I turn toward my phone. Henry's name lights up on the screen, displaying a connected call of ten seconds... and counting.

*What the hell?*

I whip my gaze around to Drew. His eyes are dark, trained on mine with an intensity that has my breath faltering. His jaw tics as he slides out of me slowly, then rams back inside, forcing me up the bed.

"*Talk*," he mouths to me, before dragging me back down the bed and thrusting inside me again. My greedy body makes a vulgar wet sound as it accepts him.

"I can't." I widen my eyes at him. He's gone mad.

He grits his teeth in response, thrusting inside me again, his eyes fixed on mine as his lips move. "*Talk, Sophie.*"

"Soph, come on. Don't tell me you can't talk to me. You can't ignore this. You're having my baby, for god's sake."

Drew hisses before slamming into me with a brutal force.

"Babies," I choke out, my inner thighs trembling with need.

"Baby," Henry corrects. "I told you what to do with the other one. You can fix this."

"Fuck!" I cry out, falling forward as Drew slams into me again, barely hiding his growl. He looked ready to rip Henry's spine out when I told him about his suggestions for splitting the babies up.

"Quit being so dramatic. The sooner you tell him it's over between you, the easier this will be on everyone," Henry says like he's already grown impatient of the one-sided conversation he's having.

A strong hand wraps itself around the back of my neck, holding me in place as my thighs are pushed apart.

Then Drew drives deeper, making my eyes roll in my head.

"It will never be over with him," I pant. "It's him I want."

Drew groans, his thumb dusting over my neck tenderly as his cock thickens inside me. The feel of it has my arms shaking and the unrelenting pulsing in my clit ramps up to a whole new level until it's teetering between 'can't hold on another second' and 'I'm about to explode'.

My eyes dart back to Drew's. "Please," I breathe, dangerously close to coming.

I reach out for the phone to disconnect the call, but he slaps my ass, making me stop. I cry out in response, unable to hold it back as I shudder around him.

"Soph?"

"I can't." I blink back at Drew, but his gaze hardens as he thrusts into me again.

"Do it," he grunts. "Let him hear."

"Are you... Are you with my son right now?" Henry yells down the phone.

"I..."

Drew circles his cock inside me before pulling back and driving back inside.

"Soph?" Henry demands. "Answer the fucking question!"

Drew thrusts into me again, and I moan. "Y-yes."

"What the hell are you doing?" Henry hisses.

Drew drives into me again, making stars dance behind my eyelids. Sweat prickles along my hairline and my whole body shakes with the pressure of holding back.

"Tell him you're enjoying his upgrade," Drew growls as his fingers dig into my flesh.

There's a brief pause as I suck in a sharp breath.

"The fuck? Drew? Is that you?" Henry rages down the phone.

Drew ignores him, his eyes flashing as I look back at him. I can't look away. He looks like a dark god, all rippling muscles and dangerous intent on his sinful face as he fucks me with the kind of vigor that might cause me to pass out with the orgasm that's hurtling toward me.

"Soph? Are you being fucked by my *son* right now?"

My mouth falls open. I can't hold back any longer; it's physically impossible.

"I prefer the term soulmate," Drew grits out in a deep groan as his cock swells inside me. "And the father of her *babies*," he hisses.

He holds my eyes as he says each word. And the last one is the catalyst that sets off my orgasm.

"Oh God," I cry out, a mess of moans, whimpers and yelps of pleasure as my orgasm rips through my body, setting every muscle pulsing in waves.

My ears ring as blood rushes in my ears. The only reason my eyes stay focused is because they're pinned by crystal blue as Drew watches me come undone for him.

"What the hell is this?" A distant voice spits out a string of curses. But I can't pay attention to it. Not when Drew's eyes are holding me captive.

"Sophie's busy being worshipped right now. The way a woman deserves to be. She'll have to call you back."

His eyes glint, and he bites down on his bottom lip.

"Oh, and she's about to milk my cock for me."

Then he comes, the muscles in his thick neck contracting as he groans out his release.

"That's it, Mama," he praises as his heat inside me sends me cascading into another orgasm.

I don't hide my loud moan of his name. I can't. He's controlling my body like it was always meant for him. And him alone.

He continues pumping his hips, emptying everything he has inside me.

His lips pull into a devilish smirk as he glances at my phone and the disconnected screen.

"I don't think he'll be calling back."

# Chapter 23
# Sophie

I FINISH PLACING THE documents in Chelsea's case file as I sit at my desk with Halliday on speaker phone.

"New York has some perks, then?" I smile as she reels off all the stores she's been to.

"I got the babies something too. It's not all for Mummy," she says before sighing. "Seriously, though, I'm going to have spent all the money from this match before I've even earned it if things carry on like this."

"Is your client still not cooperating? Sterling, wasn't it?"

"Sterling Beaufort. And no," Halliday huffs. "The stubborn asshole is the most difficult client I've ever worked with. You'd think he *wants* to be single for the rest of his life." She snorts.

The exasperation in her tone makes me laugh.

"How old is this guy?"

"Old enough to think he's impenetrable."

I type *Sterling Beaufort* into Google and hit search. The screen fills with various images, all containing the same man. He's wearing a suit in most, a tuxedo in one, where he's standing on a red carpet with a stunning woman on his arm. But there's one image where he's standing onboard a yacht in shorts and a linen shirt.

In every image he's undeniably handsome.

I study the glistening flecks that accentuate the glint in his eyes in the yacht picture. "Wow, he's fifty! And that silver hair is sexy on him." I say as I read his age in the caption. He has the body of a man half that age by the looks of it. All broad muscular chest filling out his shirt.

"Gray, silver, whatever. He's a pain in my ass. But I won't give up."

"You haven't got a match yet, then?" I think about all the people Halliday has in her database who are looking for a partner. Surely, one of them is a match for Sterling.

"Not a suitable one," she grumbles.

"Suitable?" I frown. "I thought you said when the energy matches, it's never wrong. So if he's gotten a match, then what are you waiting for?"

"How's the case going?" She steers away from my question. "Is court prep going okay?"

I take a deep breath, ignoring her change of subject for the time being.

"It's getting more complicated. We've been getting word of potential plans for witness intimidation."

"Your client?"

"Nothing so far, thankfully. I've told her how important it is that she tells me about anyone who tries to discuss the case with her. But other tenants at the apartment block have now refused to speak about things they saw and heard. It might only be a matter of time before someone tries something, though. I have to protect her. The guy who tricked her into going with him, and his friend that hasn't been identified yet... They've both got to get put away for this."

"It's a good job she's got Havers the Handler on her side then, isn't it?"

I try to smile at Halliday's confidence. But that uneasiness in my gut is back. It's like the anticipation before a show starts. Only as the curtain starts to rise you realize that you're in the wrong theater, and what's behind the curtain isn't lights and singing, it's a dark, chilling nightmare.

I have to win this case.

"How long do you think it'll be until you're back?" I ask.

"Pfft." Halliday snorts. "Depends how long Mr. Awkward wants to play this game before he realizes that I'm not leaving until I've completed my mission."

"Well, Drew's over there again next week for work. Maybe you two could meet up if you have time."

"Sounds good. I can give him your gifts to bring back. But I want to be there when the babies open theirs."

I place my hand on my bump. "That's still months away. You'll definitely be back."

She blows out a breath heavy with irritation. "I know that. But someone needs to tell Sterling."

I shuffle in my seat. "I think—" My words die in my throat as wet warmth soaks into my panties. "Shit."

"You think shit?"

"I think..." I grab a tissue from a box on my desk and stuff my hand up my skirt, wiping it against the wet fabric.

The sight of red as I bring my hand back has my heart racing.

"I think I'm miscarrying," I cry.

"Sophie Havers, which room?" Drew's deep voice booms from the corridor outside moments before he bursts through the door of the hospital room.

He rushes over to me in his suit, his blue eyes frantic and glassy, as he cups my face between his hands, his chest heaving up and down like he sprinted the whole way here.

"You okay?" His eyes ping pong from one of mine to the other as he searches them.

His scent surrounds me like a soothing embrace. *Honey and smoked wood.*

"I am now." I place one of my hands over his as he exhales in a rush and then screws his eyes closed, kissing me on the lips.

"I left the second you called." He pulls back and his eyes pinch as he looks up and down the hospital bed

I'm sitting up in, and at the gown I'm wearing. "The bleeding?" It comes out as a haunted croak.

"It's stopped. It can happen without being a problem. But it's something we'll be keeping an eye on."

Drew whirls around to face Dr. Melinda, who's reading my chart at the foot of the bed. She was already at the hospital when I came in. So she's been with me since I arrived.

I take his hand in mine and press a kiss to his palm as he keeps his attention on the doctor.

"What caused it? Do you know?" he asks.

"Well, there's no sign of placenta abruption, which is a risk in pregnancies with multiples, so I'm happy with that. Sometimes there is no clear cause, although it can be brought on by stress."

Drew turns back to me, his eyes raking up and down my body again like he needs to check again for himself that I really am okay.

"And the babies? Are they both okay?"

"One's heartrate was elevated when Sophie first arrived. But they're both stable now."

"Are you sure?" he fires out, his eyes widening as his gaze lands on my stomach.

"Drew," I say, squeezing his hand. "They're okay."

He rubs his free hand across his mouth as he draws in a breath, looking at Dr. Melinda again. "These babies, Doctor... They mean everything..." He exhales in a rush. "Are you *sure*?"

"I can show you on the monitor." Dr Melinda smiles kindly as Drew falls into the chair next to the bed and grips my hand.

"Thank you," he breathes.

His forehead is drawn, creases etched across it as he watches her set up the monitor and get the ultrasound gel ready.

"We can do a straightforward ultrasound of the stomach now that the pregnancy is further along," she explains to Drew as she lowers the bed and instructs me to lie back, then lifts my gown and places gel onto my bump for the second time in the past hour.

I felt guilty seeing the babies on screen when I first arrived without Drew here. Everything else we've done has been together.

I stroke my thumb over his knuckles as he holds his breath, staring at the screen. The second the room fills with a rhythmic *thump-thump*, he breaks down, burying his face into his other hand.

Dr Melinda nods. "That's—"

"The heartbeat." He sniffs and looks up, a smile breaking his face in half. Then he turns to me, his eyes cloudy. "Our baby's heartbeat."

"Yes," I whisper, my eyes glued to him as he looks back at the screen.

"Can I hear both?" He clears his throat, regaining composure, before glancing at me and smiling in awe.

"Of course." Doctor Melinda moves the wand over my stomach until a similar *thump-thump* fills the room.

"It's faster?" He looks at her for reassurance.

"It is. But still within normal range. If you believe the tales, then a faster heartrate signifies a girl."

"A girl," he breathes, his brows pulling together as he stares at the screen. "Wow."

"If you'd like to know the sex of the babies, then I can tell you. It's a little early to see much on the monitor. But the DNA tests showed their sex at your first appointment with me. I can tell you about both babies if you want to know."

Dr. Melinda's eyes meet mine over the top of Drew's head. He's still glued to the two gray masses on the screen with their little pulsing patch in each center. *Our babies' hearts.* I know what she's saying. She can tell us right now the sex of both babies. And which one is Drew's. And which one is Henry's.

"We can find out their sex if you want to. I don't mind if you want a surprise, though," he says, looking at me quickly before his eyes return to the screen again. He pulls out his phone and starts recording the heartbeat.

I wait for him to finish recording.

"I think Dr. Melinda means that we can find out which baby matched you in the paternity test results," I say.

His brow creases. "Why would we need to know that?"

"I'll come back and check on you later." Dr Melinda wipes the gel from my stomach and adjusts the bed so I can sit up again. Then she leaves.

Drew watches her go, then turns back to me.

"They're our babies, Sophie. Both of them. You think I'll love one more than the other because of a number on a piece of paper when we've watched you grow them both inside you?" He shakes his head and curls both of his hands around mine. "If you need to know, then we can find out. But it won't make a damn bit of difference to me."

I blink back my tears. "I know it won't. You're amazing, you know that?"

He brushes my hair back from my eyes. "I'll take it. Beats you doling out restraining orders."

I laugh as a stray tear breaks free. He brushes it away with his thumb.

"You *are* amazing." I smile at him. "We can—"

The door to the room flies open.

"Soph?"

My heart stalls in my chest as Henry races to the other side of my bed. Drew stiffens immediately. This is the first time he's seen him since that night at the restaurant.

Henry's eyes scan over my face. "Is the baby okay?"

The muscles in my fingers twitch as I take a calming breath and count to three. I don't know whether he does it on purpose, but I don't want him to see that he's getting to me.

"The babies are fine," Drew snaps.

Henry's eyes zero in on Drew, briefly dropping to our entwined fingers before he gives a curt nod. "Good."

"How did you know I was here?" I take in his black suit and tie. He must have come from work.

Drew clears his throat. "I called him."

I whip my head to him, my voice pitching. "You called him?"

"You said with the blood that…" Drew looks at me, guilt making his eyes pinch before they slide over to his father. "I thought he should know if it was serious," he says, his voice low.

I rest my head back against the pillow and look between the two men who are staring daggers at one another.

"Why was there blood?" Henry asks. "Did the doctor know?"

"She said it can happen. Sometimes it's related to stress. But the babies are fine, and that's what matters." I rub at my temples.

"You've been overdoing it, working on that case, no doubt," Henry snaps. "Putting the baby at risk."

Drew's on his feet in a flash leaning over the bed, his eyes murderous as he stares Henry down.

"Sophie didn't put anyone at risk. This isn't her fault. If you want to start casting blame, why don't you take a look in the mirror. Who's the one who keeps calling her? Waiting for her at her office? You think she doesn't tell me about your pathetic attempts to beg her to take you back?"

Henry's nostrils flare as he leans over the bed as well until they're almost meeting nose to nose in the center.

"Says the man who's always flying off to New York and leaving her alone. At least I know what I want."

"*I* know what I want," Drew fires back. "I've known since I met her."

"Then why aren't you here in case she needs you, like I am?" Henry launches back.

"We're working on a big project. I only go when I have to," Drew grits.

"Sure you're not chasing that American pussy you had working for you? Dipping your nib in the company ink again." Henry snorts out a chuckle which is ripped from his throat as Drew grabs the front of his shirt and yanks him closer.

"Don't fucking start an argument that you'll lose. Because unlike some of us around here, I date one woman at a time."

The tension radiating off both men as they crowd the small space makes the back of my neck flush and my head grow light and fuzzy.

"Stop! Both of you," I snap.

Drew lets go of Henry immediately.

Henry throws Drew one last filthy look, rolling his neck and straightening his tie, before turning his attention to me.

"Surely there's a man at the firm who can take over your case, Soph. Lighten your workload."

My laugh has no humor in it as I press a hand to my forehead and close my eyes. "Sure. Maybe I could also get a man to do this pregnancy for me and then give birth to these babies."

"You've still got weeks until the trial," Henry says, completely missing the point. "You need to consider it."

"No." I drop my hand and give him a challenging look. "My clients need me. I'm fine."

I look at Drew for back-up, but he's busy glaring at Henry like he's mentally running through ways of skinning him alive.

The air is still thick with unresolved tension as a nurse comes in, smiling brightly.

"The doctor asked me to bring these in for you." She waves a long piece of paper in the air.

"Who's the father," she clucks happily as she approaches the bed, unaware she's just prevented a war from breaking out.

"I am," Henry says at the same time Drew says, "We both are."

The nurse's forehead wrinkles, and she smiles gratefully when Drew says, "You take care of those, Sophie."

I take the ultrasound images from her. Then she turns and darts out of the room as fast as she can.

"Even the medical professionals can't get their head around it." Henry snorts. "What hope do the rest of us have?"

"I'd say it's pretty simple," Drew says in a low voice, which makes it sound more menacing. "Sophie's having two babies. They're healthy. We're blessed. Anyone who says otherwise can come to me and I'll straighten it out for them." His hand reaches for mine on top of the sheets, and he links our fingers together.

He stares at Henry. "It'll be my pleasure to straighten it out for them," he repeats.

Silence engulfs the room as Henry wanders around, hands in his pockets as we wait for Dr. Melinda to come back and discharge me. Drew sits next to me, stroking my knuckles with his thumb, but the muscles in his shoulders are taut and his eyes keep tracking Henry's movements like he's worried that he's going to throw me over his shoulder and try to kidnap me.

I lean back in the bed and will time to speed up.

When the door opens again, we all snap our heads toward it as Maddy rushes in. But it's the lady behind her, straightening her purse strap on her shoulder as she holds her head high and walks in that has my attention.

"Thank goodness, you're okay." Maddy races forward and hugs me. "We came when we got Dad's text."

I look over at Henry as I hug her, but his eyes are fixed on Violet as she approaches the side of the bed where Drew's sitting.

"You didn't have to come all this way. But thank you," I say as Maddy perches herself on the edge of the bed.

"Mum drove us. We needed to see that you were all okay. Didn't we, Mum?" Maddy looks over at Violet whose face has paled as she looks at my growing bump beneath the hospital gown.

She clears her throat and presses her lips together before she speaks. "We did. You have to be on the safe side. Especially with twins. My mother was a twin, and they almost lost her sister before they were both born. Of course, modern medicine is a lot more advanced these days, but..." Her gaze falls on the ultrasound images in my lap. "Are those...?"

I swallow before saying, "They are."

Her eyes meet mine for the first time, and my breath catches. Hers are the same striking crystal blue as Drew's. And although there's a lot of hurt being guarded inside them, they're also kind. They're eyes that have seen life and understand that sometimes things can be both painful and beautiful at the same time.

I tentatively hold the images out toward her.

"Thank you." As she takes them her soft hands brush against mine. A small smile graces her lips as she takes her time to look at each one.

"It's too early to see from the ultrasound if they're boys or girls," I say, feeling a need to fill the silence as all eyes are on the two of us. "But the doctor said she can tell us, because she has the results from the blood..." The words wither in my throat, and I swallow around the aching lump in my throat.

"From the blood test. I understand," Violet says, passing me the photos. "Thank you for letting me see these."

She turns to Drew. "You need to look after her. She's carrying precious cargo, you understand?"

"You can count on it," Drew says, his voice weighted with emotion as Violet blinks quickly a few times and then gives me a small nod.

"Make sure he does, Sophie. I expect a good report next time."

I struggle to make my voice work as emotion swells in my chest. "Okay."

Violet looks at Maddy. "I'll be outside when you're ready to go home."

She walks out, and Henry follows her, calling her name.

"Can I hide in here with you guys until they're done?" Maddy grimaces as they leave.

"Sure," I say as Drew lifts my hand to his lips and kisses my knuckles absentmindedly as he stares into space. "I'd like that."

Maddy stays for another twenty minutes, talking about an article she's writing for the magazine she works at, and I'm grateful to her for filling the silence. Because since Violet and Henry left, Drew has been lost in thought, like a dark-haired brooding statue next to me.

It's not until after I've been discharged and we're walking out to the parking lot that he finally speaks.

"I'm sorry."

"What for?"

His jaw tenses as he leads me down a row of parked vehicles. "For that shitshow in there. I shouldn't have let him get to me. He's right. I'm causing you more stress because I can't keep my fucking head straight."

My heart falls in my chest. "You're not causing me any stress. I can't believe how well you're dealing with all this." I stop walking so he has to stop and look at me. "Drew, you don't need to be strong for me all the time. We said we'd always communicate, remember? It's okay if some days your head isn't straight. Because mine definitely isn't either. And Henry is—"

"A selfish asshole? Yeah, I've had years of it. I shouldn't even be surprised anymore at the levels he'll stoop to. But the way he speaks to you? Like he's a fucking king?" He sucks air in through his clenched teeth. "I'd rather be nailed to a cross by my nut-sack than have him treat you like that." He gathers both of my hands inside his. "You're in control, Sophie. We'll do this your way. I called him today because I was trying to be the bigger man. But if you want, then I can be the pettiest bastard that walked the earth instead."

"You are the bigger man, Drew."

His lips twitch, and I roll my eyes.

"The *better* man," I say before rising on my toes to kiss him. "And I appreciate everything you're doing."

"It should be more." He wraps his arms around me and holds me close. "I want to give you the whole damn world. All three of you."

I kiss him in the middle of the parking lot until his hands slide lower and grip my ass.

"Right now, I'll take my own couch," I mumble against his lips. "And getting out of my work clothes."

"I can manage that." He smiles and takes my hand. As we walk, he pulls a key fob from his jacket pocket. He clicks it and the lights on a nearby vehicle flash.

"Where's your car?"

He stops in front of the brand-new shiny Range Rover in a deep, metallic blue, and tips his head toward it. "You're looking at it."

"I thought you were obsessed with your McLaren." I stare at him. I swear he's had that car valeted three times since we started dating. It's always been immaculate inside and out.

"There's only one obsession I have, and that's you." He opens the passenger door so I can slide into the seat. "And we needed a car that will fit the child seats in easily. And a stroller. Yours is being delivered to your apartment."

He shuts the door before I have a chance to speak. My gaze lands on him the second he opens the driver's side door.

"What do you mean?"

"I got you a white one." He starts the engine, and it purrs to life.

"A white what?"

"Car. Same as this." He places his palm on the back of my headrest as he turns to look out the rear window to reverse. The muscles in his thick neck contract and I stare at his profile and the way his dark hair curls a little above his collar as he swings the car out of the parking space with ease.

"It has a reversing camera," I murmur as I allow my gaze to wander down over his broad chest that his shirt is stretched over.

"I prefer doing it the old-fashioned way." He puts it into drive and pulls away smoothly. "If you don't want white, we'll change it." He keeps his eyes ahead and places one hand on my leg.

"You didn't have to buy me a car."

"I don't do things because I have to. I do them because I want to." He squeezes my thigh.

"Okay, well... thank you."

Drew glances at me and then smirks as he sees my frown. "No one ever bought you anything before, Boss?"

"Nothing like a car. I've always bought my own things. The same as with my apartment. I bought it outright when I got senior prosecutor."

"Mmm, about that." His fingers flex against my skin before he slides his hand a little higher up my leg. "We should decide if one of us is moving into the other's place or whether we're buying a new place together."

His face is calm, dark brows relaxed over cool blue eyes, watching the road as he drives. He's thought all this through. I've been so pre-occupied with work that I'm just living week by week. But he's right. We're doing this together. And we promised to communicate with one another above all else. Of course we're going to live together once the babies are born. I just hadn't expected him to bring it up yet.

"Someplace new." I decide on the spot as I rest my temple against the headrest so I can watch the way his fuller bottom lip curls into a smile as I speak. "I like the idea of choosing somewhere together."

"Okay." He nods, his thumb skating over my thigh. "I'll set up some viewings for after we get back."

"Get back from where?"

We pull up to a red light and Drew turns, his eyes caressing my face as he gives me a soft smile.

"You heard the doctor. A weekend away to relax will do you good. Plus, we'll have time together before I head back to New York next week." His smile falters, turning into a firm line as concern knots his brow.

"You don't need to worry about me when you're gone. Your dad was talking crap."

His jaw tics as the lights change and we pull away. "He's right, though. I should be here. What if you have another incident?"

"Don't." I reach up and brush my fingertips along his jaw. He turns his head, capturing my palm with his lips and pressing a kiss to it. "You've got work and so have I. They need you over there, the way my clients need me. It'll be easier after the project and trial are finished."

"I know." He takes my hand and holds it, resting both against his thigh, a serious expression taking over his face that I desperately want to ease.

"So, this weekend break? It's not some kind of out-door activity weekend with workouts, is it? Because I think I'd have to pass." I gesture to my stomach.

Drew's eyes land on my bump and his teeth sink into his bottom lip before he gives me a half smile. "Oh, there'll be workouts, Mama. Team ones."

I turn and look out of the window as something in my stomach flutters.

"Sounds fun."

# Chapter 24
# Drew

I SLIDE MY HAND into my pocket, checking the contents are still there for the hundredth time. My heartrate picks up as Sophie leans against the wooden railing of our roof terrace. We've come away to a private cabin, owned by someone Tanner knows, and the moment we stepped through the rustic wooden doorway, I knew this was a good call. Sophie has grown more and more relaxed each minute we've been here. We christened the front room the minute we arrived. Ate. Christened the kitchen... twice. Now, it's dark and she's changed into a cream loungewear set. Her blonde hair is loose around her shoulders as she gazes up at the night sky.

She's breathtaking.

"This is so beautiful," she muses.

I walk up behind her, curling a hand around the railing on one side of her.

"It certainly is." I slide my other hand around her and rest it on the underside of her bump.

She sighs softly and leans back against my chest. "I can't get over how clear the sky is. You never see the stars like this in the city."

"Why don't you make a wish on one," I murmur against her neck as I kiss her smooth skin.

She places her hand over the top of mine on her stomach and inclines her neck so that I can kiss lower to the juncture where it meets her shoulder. I smile against her skin as I take the hint, relishing the way she shivers as my teeth lightly graze her.

"Okay, done," she says softly, turning inside my arms and snaking her arms up around my neck.

"Fast work, Boss." I smile. "Did you wish for my father to stop being as ass?"

She brings one hand forward and trails her fingertips along the stubble on my jaw, watching its path.

"No. I wished for something for my client. She needs the magic more than I do. I've got my own right here." Her fingers brush along my jaw and then slip down my chest, coming to rest over my heart.

"It's hard to believe you're related sometimes. You're nothing like him," she whispers. "You're such a good man, Drew."

I take her chin between my finger and thumb and angle her head back so that her eyes meet mine. "He wasn't always like this. He loved my mum the way she deserved once. When Maddy and I were kids, they were happy. We looked like any regular family to the outside world."

"What happened?"

We promised each other honesty, communication. She deserves to know just what a fucked up family she's joining.

"He's not..." I pause to admire her as she looks into my eyes, waiting patiently. She's so perfect, always listening, always supportive. More than I could ever wish for even if I did it on a million stars.

"He's not my biological father."

Sophie's eyes widen. "What?"

"Just before my sixteenth birthday, I found out my parents used a sperm donor to have me. They thought Dad was the problem. He was crushed. But then a few years later, Maddy came along. So I guess the doctors were wrong."

I stare at the calm surface of the lake. I wonder if it's hiding a deeper current. One that could take you and drag you into the darkness, drowning you without hesitation. Like the one in my gut when I talk about the past.

The one that's churning right now.

"It all suddenly made sense. Why Dad was stricter with me than Maddy. Why he always praised her and found fault with everything I did." I clear my throat as Sophie wraps her arms around my waist and holds me, resting her head against my chest. "Why I'd catch him looking at me like he hated me. The night I found out, I called Logan. I needed to get out of the house.

Away from him. Away from everyone. We stole a car. After that, things got worse. I was sent to juvie for six months, and Dad hated that I'd publicly humiliated him. I was a police officer's son; I should have known better. But I think what bothered him most was that people might find out. They might know I wasn't his, that he couldn't get Mum pregnant. His pride has always come before all else. Narcissistic bastard."

Sophie's grip on me tightens as she lets out a splintered sigh, seeped in emotion. "You didn't deserve that. God, Drew. You didn't deserve to be treated like that." She lifts her head from my chest and her eyes are rimmed with red. "You deserved a father who loved you and would put you first."

I stroke her cheek as I smile sadly. "Yeah, but not everyone gets that. At least now you know what you're getting yourself into. He's hoping one of the babies is a boy, so he gets the son he never had."

She looks at me with such hurt swirling in her eyes that I feel it in my heart. She's sharing the pain in my words as if it's her own. I knew the moment I met her—and I see it now, more than ever—she's so much more than I ever dreamed of, and I'll do whatever it takes to ensure her happiness.

"Drew," she whispers, tears pooling along her lower lashes, "it's his loss. You are incredible." She blinks and the first tear rolls down her cheek, followed by another. "I can't believe you've kept all this to yourself. What about Maddy? Does she—?"

"She knows now. It all came out. Maybe it would have been better for me to know from the start, but parents make the choices they think are the right ones at the time. I can't blame Mum for that. And I can't blame him either. He probably tried his hardest in the beginning. But I guess once Maddy was born, he saw me differently. She was his. I wasn't."

"Is this why you've been so amazing about the babies?"

A smile breaks across my face. "Our babies," I murmur, kissing her forehead. "We can find out if you want to know, about the paternity and sex, I mean. I know my father wants to know. But this is your decision and I'll support you in whatever you choose."

She gazes up at me. "Thank you. You're amazing, you know that? All this stuff with your dad, though, is that why you don't need to know? And why you have a thing about pregnancy?"

"I told you, I have a thing about Sophie Havers." I lift her chin so I can capture her lips in a kiss that makes her smile against my mouth. "And yeah, I fucking love that you're pregnant. You know how hard it makes me."

She smirks as I kiss her again. "Yeah, I know. You keep showing me."

"I love both of those babies inside you equally. I swore I'd never be like him. DNA or not, I promised myself that I'd be the kind of father I always wanted."

"Drew." Her voice comes out raspy as she grips tightly onto the back of my sweatshirt. "They're so blessed to have you as their daddy. *I'm* so blessed."

*Daddy.* My heart could burst.

"You getting soppy on me, Boss?"

"I'm getting soppy on you," she confirms, laughing gently. "But don't tell anyone I work with. They think I can handle anything."

"You can." I wrap my other hand around the back of her neck. "I know you can. But it doesn't mean you have to do it alone. We're a team, Sophie. You, me, and the babies."

"Team Havers?" She arches a brow, a smile tugging at her lips. "I'm kidding. I know you'll want the babies to have your surname."

I swipe my thumb over her lower lip. "I want all of you to have my surname. I even called your dad before we came here and asked his permission."

"You called my dad?"

"Yeah. He seems like a great guy. I can't wait to meet him properly. He gave me a long list of conditions, though."

Her mouth falls open as I drop to one knee, finally pulling the velvet box out that's been burning a hole in my pocket.

I lean forward, pressing a kiss to her bump. Her breath catches and a fresh tear slips free as she watches me.

"What were they?" she whispers.

"The first was that I understand your strength and your stubbornness, and how brilliant you are. And that I vow not to ever want to change that."

I keep my eyes fixed on hers as I press another kiss to her bump. "Done. The second was to put you and our family before all else. Again, done." I kiss her again. "In fact, everything he said to me are things I already had on my own list."

"You have a list?"

"I do. And mine's longer. I've had over four years to think about it."

"Four years?" Her voice catches on a small sob.

She's been showing her emotions more easily as the pregnancy has progressed. And as much as I love Boss-lawyer Sophie, I love her soft side too.

"Four years," I confirm as I hold her eyes, kissing her bump again.

The blood in my veins pumps around my body with enough heat in it to warm the entire roof terrace as I hold up the ring box.

"I love you, Sophie. But I think you know that already. Part of me loved you since the moment I met you, as crazy as that might sound. I knew, that's all I can say. I just knew you were it for me."

Her hand flies to her mouth. "Drew?"

She stares as I flip open the box, revealing the rock inside. Maddy told me I had to go big or go home, and the way Sophie's eyes bounce between mine and the three-carat brilliant cut diamond, I'm glad I listened.

Because my girl is speechless.

"I have a question for you." I remove the ring and toss the box over my shoulder because the cocky bastard inside me hopes I won't be needing it again.

She can't say no. I wouldn't have fallen so damn hard in love with a woman who makes my chest physically ache from just looking at her just to have her turn me down.

*Please, God.*

I look up at her, my heart laid fucking bare, because she's the only person who's ever had the power to tear it to shreds.

"Will you marry me, Ms. Havers? Because I love you so much that if I had to, I'd gladly die for you a billion times over. And I'd do it with a smile on my face."

She stares at me. And blinks. And stares.

"Sophie?"

She half sobs, half laughs, and nods.

"You've got to say it." I press my lips against her stomach, kissing her bump again. "Say it out loud. Put me out of my fucking misery and let me shout it to the world that you're going to be my wife, the mother of our babies, my whole world."

"Mr. Harper," she whispers. "I love you, too. Yes!"

The air in my lungs snags.

"Yes?"

"Yes!" She nods again, her face lighting up.

I slide the ring onto her finger and then rest my head against her body, the soft fabric stretched across her bump soaking up the wetness racing down my cheeks as I hold her to me.

"Thank you," I choke.

Her hands sink into my hair, stroking me as I just breathe her in. Breathe in every damn sensation, including the electricity thrumming through my veins as I gather myself.

Then something moves against my forehead.

I pull my head back and snap my eyes up to meet hers. "Did you feel that?"

She looks at her stomach in shock as I press my palm against it.

It's tiny, but it's there again. A tiny flutter. A rumble. A murmur.

My heart soars in my chest as I grin.

"I think the babies approve."

# Chapter 25
# Drew

"You look so damn sexy, Mama." I look at Sophie on my laptop screen, admiring the curve of her belly as we sit and chat again, just like we did last night when I arrived in New York.

"You like this, huh?" She bites her lower lip as she trails her fingertips down over the T-shirt of mine that she's taken to sleeping in now that her pajamas are getting tight and uncomfortable. She slides it up, exposing her skin.

"Fuck yeah." I lick my lips as she uncovers her stomach, which is growing more swollen by the day. "God, what I'd do to you if I were with you right now."

"I wish you were." Her eyes are hooded as she relaxes back against the pillows.

I groan and unbuckle my belt so I can slide a hand into my pants. A perk of being the boss is that I have my own private office in our New York building for when I work here.

I give my hard dick a squeeze.

"Push your panties down, let me see properly."

She does as I ask, sliding the black lace all the way down her legs and dropping it next to her on the bedsheets.

"Fuck, Boss." I angle the laptop screen with my spare hand to get the best view before I recline in my chair, my other hand wrapped around my cock as I start to jerk myself off slowly.

"If I was there, I'd have my tongue buried inside that sweet pussy."

Sophie's responding murmur has the end of my cock leaking.

"I wish this were you."

My heart jackknifes against my ribs as she holds up a pink dildo.

"I got it for when you're away. You don't mind, do you?"

I shift in my seat as my balls throb. "Course I don't fucking mind. Shit, that's hot, Sophie." I exhale in a rush, enraptured at the way she's sliding it between her lips and it's coming out shining, coated in her wetness.

"Jesus," I hiss, jerking myself faster as the tip slides inside her.

"It doesn't feel as good as the real thing," she moans, pulling it back out and circling the wet head of it over her clit. "I miss you."

"I miss you too," I groan. "You know what you need to do for me now, though?"

"What?" she purrs, almost making me come on the spot with the way her lips pout.

"You're going to touch yourself for me. Pretend it's me doing it, until I get back tomorrow and wedge this cock inside you where it belongs." I push my pants lower and slide my chair back along the floor so she can see how hard I am for her.

She licks her lips, watching my movements as I speed up. The grip on my cock turns fierce as she works the dildo all the way inside herself, then whimpers as her other hand drifts to her clit and circles.

"Imagine I'm there with you. Holding you. Kissing you. No ocean between us. Just my mouth against your ear, telling you what a good girl you are as I stuff you full of my cock."

"God," she moans, her eyes dropping to me fisting my cock as she fucks herself with her dildo.

The only thing prettier than the way it stretches her as she slides it in, is the way her pussy lips look hugging either side of my cock when she's taking that. Now that's a fucking masterpiece.

I tip my head back and groan as the head of my cock pulses.

"Tell me you're close because I'm about to come all over myself at my desk."

She bites her lower lip, arching her back, which only draws my attention back to her bump and the way it curves out above her pussy. I don't know how the hell I'm supposed to go back to work after this when all I want to do is be back home sinking myself into her all night. We're five hours behind London in New York, so I won't even be able to speak to her again until tomorrow morning because she'll be going to sleep when we hang up.

"I'm close," she whispers, the hand on her clit speeding up.

"Together then. You ready?"

She nods, her breath coming in sexy pants.

I pull my shoulders back as every muscle in my body tenses.

"Drew," she cries as she comes, her thighs trembling as her pussy clamps down onto the dildo.

The memory of how she feels clamping down onto me brings me over the edge with a rush and I only just manage to tear my shirt out of the way in time before my cum lands against my stomach in thick, white ropes.

Sophie's breathless, her cheeks flushed as she gazes at me. She slides the dildo out from inside her and my ego puffs up in my chest at the fact she doesn't whimper at its loss the way she does whenever I take my cock from inside her.

"You're beautiful." I smile at her as I grab a wad of tissues from my desk drawer and clean up.

"I miss you," she whispers, turning onto her side and tucking her arm under her head.

"I miss you too." I tuck my cock back into my pants and fix them back into place. "I'll be back tomorrow. You want to sleep at my house or yours?"

"Mine." She fails to hide the sleepiness creeping into her voice. "If that's okay? I'm going to work late and then I've got case files to read when I get home."

I fight the voice in my head that's saying she's working too hard. The voice that's worried about the babies. Because the other voice is louder. The one that loves her brilliance and her drive. The one that promised to never try and stop her doing what she loves. I'll just have to find subtler ways of looking after her instead.

"I'll give you a massage when I get back." I allow myself a leisurely sweep of her body. "See if we can get those babies moving again."

She smiles softly. "Sounds perfect."

"Get some sleep, Mama."

I smile at her sleepy face as she blows me a kiss and disconnects the call.

I close the top of my laptop and gaze out of the floor to ceiling windows that make up one long wall of my office. I pick up my phone and find the file I want, clicking play as I return my gaze to Manhattan's skyline.

The thumping of life fills the room as I lean back in my chair and listen to the heartbeat. A buzzing, excited energy fills my chest.

*Our babies.*

There's barely a knock at the door before Alicia strides in like she owns the place. It's been a year since we last slept together and I've lost count of the number of times I've told her that our casual arrangement is over. Yet she still makes snide comments when she can about our past arrangement. How I'd fuck when I was in New York, staying at her apartment with her. Then I'd fly home and only speak to her if it was regarding work in between. Until the next time I was here. And then we'd repeat the cycle. Over and over.

She comes to a stop in front of my desk, her eyes dropping over my body and back up.

"Can I get your sign off on something?"

"Sure." I nod, keeping my tone professional.

She purses her lips and opens the folder she's carrying. Then she slams a piece of paper down onto the desk like she's trying to communicate what an asshole she thinks I am with the move.

I arch an unimpressed brow at her.

"Sorry." She smiles in mock sweetness.

I ignore her stare as I scan the document before signing and handing it back to her.

"Is that all?"

"Unless you want anything else from me? Like your dick sucked? Seeing as that used to be part of my job description."

I glare at her.

Tanner told me we can't fire her because I let my dick think for me. He said she'd have a lawsuit up against us faster than she used to drop to her knees for me. He's right; she'll pull the sexual harassment at work card if we get rid of her. It doesn't matter that I met her in a bar before I realized she was a new hire of the company. I'd fucked her three times before I walked in the next morning and saw her smiling at me across the boardroom table for the morning staff meeting.

Alicia swears she didn't know who I was when we met in that bar, but I think she saw me more as her ticket to the top. Fuck the boss, get a promotion.

I was a stupid fool not to cut it off right there and then. It wasn't until I learned Sophie had moved to London last year that I ended it for good. The last time I fisted Alicia's dark hair as she choked on my cock, I was picturing golden blonde strands and pillowy lips.

I knew it was over then.

Only she doesn't seem to want to let it drop, hinting how she could ruin me if she chose to.

"It was never in your job description, and you damn well know it." I seethe.

"What were you listening to when I came in?" She changes the subject, looking at my phone on the desk and reaching for it.

I swipe it up before she gets to it.

"What's on my phone is also not part of your job description," I snap, cracking my neck in annoyance.

"It sounded like a heartbeat. Like from an ultrasound?"

"Well done, you've been watching medical dramas." I rise from my chair and shove my hands into my pockets as I stare at her. "Anything else you'd like to ask about that's not work related, and therefore none of your concern?"

"Are you having a baby with her?" Alicia's eyes widen, hurt clouding inside them. If it weren't for the fact that she's holding an axe over me should I try and fire her, then I might feel bad.

"Do you need anything else signed?" I look at the folder in her hands pointedly.

She flusters and shakes her head. "No. I don't need anything else from you." She turns to leave, then snaps her head back around. "Actually..."

My hands curl into fists in my pockets.

She spins fully so she's facing me. "I think you should know that I'm leaving. Consider this my resignation. I'll put it in writing for you as well."

"You're leaving?"

"I've received other offers. Maybe it's time I took one. I'll work my notice, of course."

"No need. I'm sure we can work something out." I keep my tone neutral, while inside, I'm fucking ecstatic.

Her eyes flash with something before she swallows and shuts it down.

"Okay."

She looks at me one last time and then strides from my office, leaving the door wide open.

I stand with one hand braced against the shower tiles. "You and those lips. They were made for swallowing my cock. *Fuck*," I murmur as I look at the photo of Sophie on my phone that I've propped up by the sink.

I continue to jerk myself off as the hot water hits my back and runs down my body.

Three hours. That's all it's been since I spoke to Sophie and came while watching her fuck herself with her dildo. Three hours that feel like three long-ass centuries. I can't even speak to her because I don't want to disturb her. She needs her sleep now that she's growing our babies inside her.

I groan as I pump faster, my eyes fixed on her lips on the screen.

I curse as the end of my cock erupts, and I imagine I'm coming inside her mouth as cum fires out and sprays over the tiles. All of the muscles in my shoulders ease, tension washing away down the shower drain along with the final spurts from my spent cock.

I rinse off, then reach out of the shower and grab a white towel to wrap around my hips. I've got another hour and a half before I need to head to JFK for my flight home.

The second I walk out into the bedroom my gut tells me something isn't right.

"Alicia! What the hell?" My step falters as I stare at her, laid out on her side on the bed in a red corset, stockings, suspenders, and high heels beneath an open trench coat.

"Surprise," she drawls, batting her lashes.

"How did you get in here?"

"Borrowed a key from the housekeeping trolley. It's no big deal." She waves an uncoordinated hand in the air which makes her wobble as she shifts into a seated position on the bed, and I sigh as I realize she's drunk.

"No big deal?" I snort out an exasperated breath. "Do your coat up," I snap, turning away from her to grab a pair of sweatpants.

She's surprisingly nimble for someone drunk. I've barely turned away before she's made it to the floor and is on her knees in front of me.

She snatches the towel away from my hips, and the next second, my dick is in her mouth and she's sucking it, red lipstick smearing over my skin.

"The fuck?" I jump back, yanking my sweatpants on so fast I almost topple over.

"Once more, for old time's sake?" she slurs, crawling across the floor toward me.

"Get the fuck up off my floor, Alicia!" I yell, incessant rage taking over me.

Her eyes pop wide and she rises to her feet shakily.

I drag a T-shirt on over my head, blood pounding in my ears.

"You used to fuck me," she whines.

"I used to do a lot of things." I glare at her.

"She doesn't have to know. I won't tell her." She sways on her feet. "Is she pretty? Is she—?"

"She's everything!" I hiss. "Fucking everything to me. So no, I'm not going to let you suck me off for 'old time's sake', despite the fact she'd probably never know. *I'd* know." I jab a finger into my chest. "I'd fuck-ing know!"

"I thought you just needed reminding how good we were. I thought..." Alicia's eyes dart side to side like she's just realized she's a lamb that's waltzed into the lion's den.

"The thought of it doesn't do a single thing for me." I gesture down at my soft dick in my sweatpants. "You know why?"

She shakes her head, eyes wide.

"Because I fucking love her! And we want to be together," I yell, making her jump. "What the hell is it that stops people understanding that? You? My father? You're the fucking same."

I stalk over to the bed, grabbing up her phone and purse before striding over and shoving them at her chest. "Sophie's going to be my wife. She's having my babies. I'd rather die than hurt her by looking at a woman that isn't her. Do you understand me?"

Some of the anger leaves my body as Alicia nods her head repeatedly, her lower lip quivering. I could lay off her more. But fuck, she's come sneaking into my room, knowing I'm in a relationship, trying to manipulate things in her favor.

*Putting my dick in her mouth.*

My anger threatens to spike again.

"Fasten your coat," I instruct again.

I march her down to the hotel lobby with one hand firmly on her elbow to steer her on her unsteady legs.

"Get in a cab. Go drink some water. And go the fuck to bed," I say in a firm voice as I lead her through the main hotel doors. "And don't ever steal a key card and sneak into my hotel room again."

A man in a dark suit with dark hair looks at us from where he's standing talking to the hotel doorman. I recognize him immediately. Griffin Parker, the billionaire owner of the hotel.

"Mr. Harper," he greets me calmly, his eyes flicking to Alicia, his mouth set in a firm line after overhearing everything.

"Mr. Parker." I meet his gaze, not needing to say anything more as unspoken understanding passes between us.

He gestures to the doorman, speaking quietly into his ear. The doorman says something into his earpiece, and less than a minute later, a dark town car pulls up in front of the hotel.

"Getting a cab at this time can be a nightmare. Please, allow my driver to escort you home." Griffin smiles politely at Alicia.

Her eyes dart to my face and she opens her mouth, but the intake of my breath through my nose seems to make her think twice about what she was going to say. Instead she pulls the belt around her coat tighter. "I appreciate not having to work my notice," she manages to utter in a steady voice. "Goodbye, Drew."

She weaves a wobbly path to the town car, nodding at the driver who closes the door behind her once she gets inside.

"She's banned from The Songbird. She won't bother you here again," Griffin clips as the car pulls away.

"Thank you." I rest my hands on my hips before cursing softly at the absurdity of it all.

Griffin's lips twitch. "Need a drink?"

"Fuck yeah."

We walk in the direction of one of the hotel's bars.

"So, what's been happening since I last saw you?" Griffin asks.

I chuckle. "You're going to need a drink first before I tell you. I know I am."

# Chapter 26
## Sophie

"WHAT ARE YOU DOING here?"

My hand curls around the edge of the door as I keep my body blocking the entrance to my apartment. It's not even eight and Henry's unplanned arrival is less than appreciated. I don't know how he got past the main security door. Someone must have let him in as they went through.

His eyes drop to my left hand, and the engagement ring sparkling on my finger.

"You don't have to marry him because you're pregnant."

Irritation bubbles in my gut and I grip the door harder. "I'm not."

His eyes lift to mine, one brow hitching as though he doesn't believe me.

"What are you doing here?" I ask again, exasperated.

"I came to talk. It's important."

The urge to tell him to get lost and come back at a sensible hour is overtaken by logic. I know him. He'll stay outside my door until I listen to him. But if I pretend to be interested in whatever crap he's come to say then he's more likely to leave after.

"Fine. Let me get dressed." I step back about to let him in when his eyes drop over the robe I threw on over Drew's T-shirt. I pull it tighter around myself, which makes Henry smirk.

"I've seen it all before, Soph." He doesn't even try to hide the languid way his eyes are raking over my bare legs.

I hold a hand up, stopping him before he steps inside.

"You know what? You can wait out there." I slam the door in his face before he can protest and curse under my breath as I head to the bedroom and pull some loungewear on.

I check my phone quickly, smiling at the text Drew sent while I was sleeping.

> **Drew: Just boarding my flight. Can't wait to get back to you, Mama. Tell those babies Daddy's on his way.**

He'll be back soon. Warmth settles in my gut, a mix of comfort and excitement. We'll get the rest of the weekend together before work gets really busy next week with trial prep.

I go back to the front door and let Henry in. His eyes drop over my loose-fitting outfit, but he says nothing as he walks inside.

"Coffee?" I offer as a force of habit, walking into the kitchen.

Henry follows me into the kitchen. "Please. You know how I like it."

I look sideways at him as I turn the machine on. His eyes are wandering around the room, studying what's changed since he was last here having morning coffee made for him by me. It's the cop in him, I guess. Always assessing.

His eyes land on the ultrasound pictures on the counter and my shoulders stiffen as he picks them up.

A small smile curls his lips as he studies them. "I want to know if mine's a boy or girl."

I ignore him for as long as possible as I make his coffee. Then I place the cup down harshly on the counter.

"I haven't decided if I want to find out yet."

His eyes meet mine, a hint of coldness held in them. "*I'm* the father. I have a right to know."

I snatch the images from him and grab my purse from the kitchen table, placing them inside. "Like I said, I haven't decided yet."

"And I suppose my son's okay with this?"

I glance up into his eyes, keeping my mouth sealed shut. I doubt Drew's told him that I know about him not being his biological father. They aren't exactly on speaking terms. But I still have to fight not to give Henry a piece of my mind about how he treated Drew growing up. How he failed as a father to him.

"I'll let you know what I decide. Tell me what you needed to talk about. You said it's important?" I lean back against the counter opposite him.

"It is." Henry sips his coffee, taking his time to drag things out because he knows the minute he's said whatever it is he came to that I'll be asking him to leave.

"Well?" I snap, impatiently.

"There's that bite." His eyes glint over the rim of his mug but I keep my expression passive so as not to encourage him.

"Okay," he concedes, placing his coffee cup down when he realizes I'm not going to play his game.

This time, I can't school my expression as he drops to one knee on the floor and produces a ring box from his jeans pocket.

"Oh, no, you don't. Get up!" I hiss.

He ignores me, flipping open the lid to reveal a large ruby ring.

"Soph."

Shock means I don't stop him when he takes my left hand and rolls his thumb over the diamond ring Drew gave me.

"Marry me instead. We were always so good together. We can be again."

He works his thumb and forefinger over my ring and begins to slide it toward my knuckle to take it off.

My eyes widen in horror, and I wrench my hand from his grasp and tuck it behind my body.

"No."

His brows flatten as a muscle in his jaw ticks.

"You know this makes sense. That's my baby you're having."

"What part of this makes sense? The part where you're a liar? The part where you're still married to someone else? The part where I don't love you?"

He doesn't even flinch as he rises to his feet, closing the box and stepping closer to me.

"You don't want to marry my son, Soph. Think about it. He's reckless, unreliable. You might think he's a good bet now, but he'll let you down, trust me."

His eyes drop down my body, coming back up to my face.

"I can give you more than he can. Remember the way you liked how I—"

"Get. Out." My voice is low and dangerous. "*Now*."

He takes another step closer, leaning down so his breath dusts my ear.

"That's my baby as well."

I tense as he flattens his palm over my bump, ice spreading through my veins as his lips graze my skin.

"I can look after you both." He slides his thumb back and forth over me as I stand, unable to move even though a voice in my head is screaming at me to shove him away.

"Or I can just look after him or her. It's your choice," he rasps in my ear.

"What?"

He smiles against my skin.

"That's my baby. If I want to, I can apply for full custody. You like going to court. You can fight me in there." His hand burns against my stomach. "I'll enjoy seeing that bite of yours again."

All the air leaves my lungs and I gasp, my whole chest on fire.

"You can't," I choke.

"Try me." Henry lowers his lips toward my neck and even though I know he's about to kiss me, I still can't move.

"What the hell is this?" Drew's deep voice breaks through the air.

Henry's hand leaves my stomach, and he steps back with a smug tilt to his lips.

"Just talking through options with Soph," he replies.

Drew strides in through the kitchen doorway.

Sickness claws at my windpipe.

"Sophie?" He's by my side in a flash, wrapping his arms around me.

"Henry was leaving," I manage to say in a calm voice that masks the explosion of dread that's overtaken my body.

Drew's eyes fall on Henry. "Get the fuck out before I throw you out. And don't ever come over when I'm not here again."

Henry holds his hands up. "We were just talking. You're both going to have to accept that I'm a part of this. Soph's having my baby."

Drew's expression turns murderous and his arms tighten around me as Henry saunters out of the room.

"You okay?"

I shake my head. My eyes are probably wild because they feel like they're about to bug out of my skull.

"He hinted that he might apply for full custody of the baby."

Drew goes rigid, but I hold him with my hands curled into the fabric of his shirt before he can storm after Henry.

"He won't get it." I search out Drew's eyes until they come back to mine. The clear blue looks so dark, like storm clouds. "The court would never grant it to him in this situation. He knows that. But the fact he's even thinking it worries me. He knows what trials do to people. The stress of taking something to court. He could steal all of those first months from us while we fight him. Those months where we should just be getting used to being a family and enjoying the babies. He wants to create that strain, push us apart. Make us lose each other."

"He's a sick fuck," Drew hisses.

I stroke the side of his face, dousing the anger that's filling every crease around his eyes. They soften a little as he looks back at me.

"He won't force us apart." He pulls me closer. "You and me, remember? We can get past anything that bastard throws at us."

"When you saw him just then, his hand on me..." I search Drew's eyes. "You didn't doubt for a second the reason he was so close."

"I trust you," Drew states simply. "And I could see in your eyes that you wanted him away from you."

"I love you." I exhale in a rush, loosening my grip on Drew's shirt. "I'm so glad you're back. I bet you didn't expect to walk into that when I gave you your own key."

"I haven't expected a lot of things that have happened in the past twenty-four hours."

The front door closes, echoing from the hallway.

"He didn't leave straight away, he was listening," I say.

Drew shrugs. "So he'll have heard us say we're not bothered by his shit and that we're in this together, no matter what. Let him hear. Let him know he doesn't have any control over us. The wedding, the babies, any of it. The sooner he accepts it, the better." He brushes my hair away from my face and kisses me. "I didn't wait four years for you to let an asshole like my father get between us. Not happening."

I slide my hands up his chest and reach up to stroke his jaw.

"He asked me to marry him just before you got here."

Drew exhales a half grunt, half laugh.

"I don't want to cause your family any more hurt. What will your mum think?"

"She's divorcing him. The papers are all being filed. She kicked him out, and this time she won't be taking him back. She doesn't blame you. She's known what he's like for a long time. She's finally doing something about it."

He does his best to ease my guilt, pressing his lips to my forehead. "She asks after you and the babies every time we speak. It might not be the usual start with a mother-in-law, but I know you'll get on great one day. She sees how much I love you. And she heard about you a lot before any of this happened. You don't need to worry about anything other than cooking those babies nicely, okay?"

"Okay," I murmur, leaning into him.

His hand drops to my bump. "I've missed you three. Want me to show you how much?"

"How much?"

"Three orgasms on my face ought to do it."

I laugh and sink my nose into his shirt, inhaling his scent.

"Sure."

# Chapter 27
# Sophie

"IT SAYS THE SIZE of a bell pepper each," Drew says, astonished.

I watch him on my phone screen as he turns the page in the baby book he's holding. I place my pen down on top of the case files on my desk and lean back in my chair.

"Nice to see you're working hard and not just calling me to talk about the babies again." A smile lifts my lips. I secretly love it that he calls me at work every day, even when it's only been a few hours since we were last together.

"Hmm?" He looks up from the page and gives me a dazzling smile. "Got to take breaks, Ms. Havers. Increases productivity in the long run." He turns his attention back to the book, his brows hitching. "It says their hearing is developing more this week." He places the book down on his desk. "Put me next to them, Mama."

"Fine." I feign a sigh, as I pick up my phone and hold it next to my bump.

"Hey, babies," Drew coos. "It's Daddy. Listen, Mummy and I love you and we can't wait to meet you. But you need to stop making Mummy want to eat the weird ice-cream flavors. I'm going to need to buy that place by her apartment with the number of visits she has me making to it."

I bite back my laugh. Drew's been going there a lot recently. It seems to be my go-to snack every evening. I think I've had every flavor on the menu, favoring the one's that Drew looks at me like I'm crazy for enjoying. Like the garlic one.

"Okay, good chat. Love you both." Drew gives a mini fist bump to my stomach and my heart somersaults in my chest at the sight of him in full business suit, sitting at his desk, surrounded by paperwork, with his clear blue eyes glittering as he fixes them on my stomach.

If I wasn't already pregnant, then I think seeing him like this would do it.

I bring the phone back to my face. "I have to go." I give him a regretful pout.

"All right, Boss. I'll see you tonight."

"Tonight," I agree.

I end the call and gather up the paperwork I need for my meeting with Chelsea. As I stand, there's a knock at the door.

"Sophie?" Jules pokes her head around it.

"What's happened?"

I close the distance between us. I know that hesitating look, and it isn't a good sign.

"Have we lost another witness?" I glance down at the brown envelope she's clutching. We've lost three testimonies from tenants in neighboring apartments of the one where Chelsea was kept against her will. They said they heard a female crying. But now they're scared. The bastard who did this has gotten to them somehow.

"No, it's not that," Jules says. "But these arrived in today's mail."

She hands me the envelope and I pull out a bundle of photographs. All are of me, taken with a long-angled lens. Outside the office getting into my car. At the deli I bought lunch from last week. The last image is the only one I give a little more attention to. It's of me leaving Dr. Melinda's clinic after a checkup. I remember that day well because it was raining so much that Drew had gone to pull the car around.

"Right," I sigh, stuffing the pictures back inside.

This isn't the first time this has happened, and it won't be the last. It's nothing more than a scare tactic used by someone connected to the defendant. Generally witnesses are targeted, with the aim of intimidating them enough that they won't want to give crucial testimonies. But occasionally, a lawyer working the prosecution falls into the firing line too. Guess today is my lucky day. If anything, it spurs me on. It means they're getting scared because they're worried I'll win.

"Did you log it?" I ask Jules.

"I did. The inspector I spoke to was really helpful. He gave me his direct number in case you wanted to call and talk to him."

I take the Post-it from Jules. "Won't be necessary, but I guess it was nice of him."

My shoulders tense as I read the name.

*DI Henry Harper.*

"You've got to be kidding me." I snort.

I crumple the paper in my hand and toss it into the trash can as she gives me a puzzled look.

"I know where to find him should I need to talk, as he so kindly offered," I say as we walk down the corridor toward the meeting room where Chelsea will be waiting.

"No worries. I'll file these." Jules takes the envelope of photographs back from me and turns down another corridor, giving me a quick wave.

"Thanks," I call as I open the door and spot Chelsea waiting for me.

"Morning." I smile at her brightly as she looks up, her hands wrapped around her usual mug of tea.

"Hi," she replies as I take a seat next to her.

She's wearing a fitted maternity top today that hugs her bump. The usual baggy sweatshirt is nowhere in sight.

"You look well," I say as I place my folders down on the coffee table.

"Oh, thank you." She smiles shyly. "I *feel* good. I told my parents who the baby's father is."

"You did?" I manage to keep the surprise from my voice. In all other conversations we've had, Chelsea hasn't indicated that she knows who the father is. I suspected it was one of the men who assaulted her, but that she didn't know which one.

"Yeah." She looks at her mug. "I was worried about it for so long. But Jake has been so supportive."

"Jake's the friend who's been going to your ultrasounds with you? The one you mentioned?"

Chelsea meets my eyes, relief shining in hers. "Yes. He's the baby's father."

"Oh. That's—"

"I know I let you think it was one of the men who…" She swallows. "But the truth is that I was worried Mum and Dad would think the truth was worse. Jake's been my friend for a long time. He was the one who insisted I hadn't run away and that something had happened when I didn't go home that day. And when I was found, I…" She fidgets with her mug, rubbing her thumbs back and forth over it. "I didn't want their hands to be the last ones to touch me."

She blinks a couple of times before clearing her throat.

"I wanted to feel normal. I wanted it to be my choice again. And Jake's always been amazing, he wasn't sure, but he could see I needed it. So we… after I got home. And he's never stopped being there for me since. I was worried that people wouldn't understand. That they'd think I was wrong to want it so soon after—"

"You are not wrong." I place my hand on her forearm. "You heal in whatever way you see fit, understand? There is no right or wrong way. Just the 'you' way, okay?"

"Thank you for saying that."

"And Jake sounds like a very special person. I'm glad you've got him helping you through this."

"He is." Her face glows. "He's amazing. And now Mum and Dad know, we've started to make plans for the baby's arrival. It feels like a whole new start for all of us."

Her eyes slide to the engagement ring on my finger.

"Are you getting married before or after the baby is born?"

I glance down at my bump. It's obvious I'm pregnant now.

"Babies." I smile. "I'm having twins. And I don't know. After, I guess. It's all been pretty fast."

"Twins?" Chelsea grins. "Wow, that sounds busy. Are they boys or girls? This one is a girl." She takes one hand from her mug and strokes her belly.

My eyes drop to my bump. "I don't know."

"Did you want a surprise? I'm not patient enough for that. I like to plan. Know what I'm up against." She giggles. It's the first time I've heard her giggle, and the sound makes warmth radiate inside my chest.

"Me too," I muse. "I always like to know what I'm handling."

I pull up to Drew's house in the new Range Rover he bought me. I've had to fight an eye roll each time I've gotten into it. Not that I don't love it, but I never pegged myself as being the kind of girl who swoons over extravagant gifts from men.

Until Drew.

They don't even need to be extravagant. It's all the late-night ice-creams he gets. The bump massage oils. The print outs of car seat research he's been doing, annotated with his comments.

It's every thoughtful thing he's done for me since I agreed that day by my car that it would be him and me. *Us*.

My phone rings in my purse as I get out of the car. I pull it out, sighing as I answer.

"Henry?"

"You okay, Soph? You sound tired."

I close the car door and lock it, heading toward the front door of the house.

"I'm fine. I've just finished work."

"That's a late one."

I don't bite. I'm well aware that it's past seven at night. I don't need Henry telling me *again* that I should give my caseload to a *man* at the practice so that I can let my clients down as I put my feet up and die of boredom for the remainder of this pregnancy.

"I was calling to check if you're okay after those photos."

"How fortunate for me that Jules called them into you, hey?" I regret the sarcasm as it leaves my lips. It's a coincidence that Henry took the call. He was just doing his job.

He doesn't pick up on it. In fact, he sounds concerned.

"I wanted you to know that you can talk to me. It can shake you up knowing you're being followed. I've seen it so many times at work. I wanted you to know that I understand it can freak you out, and I'm here to talk if you need it."

He's right. He does see it happen in his job. And he's probably got a good grasp over how unnerving it can be for witnesses. But I'm used to it. If I was easily intimidated by these assholes, then I wouldn't be able to do my job.

"Thank you," I say, meaning it. "That's nice of you to offer, but really, I'm fine."

"Good." He pauses. "How are the babies?"

Henry using the term *babies* for the first time is enough of a shock that my step falters.

"They're good. Growing," I add as I look at my bump.

"Have you thought any more about finding out if they're boys or girls? I'd just... It would be nice to know. But it's up to you."

The soft tone of his voice catches me off guard. It lacks his usual edge when he's demanding things.

"I'm still deciding. But I'll let you know when I do," I reply as I curl my fingers around my keychain and pull it free.

"Please do that. Take care, Soph."

Then he's gone.

I'm shaking my head to myself as I open the door. Drew walks up the hallway from the kitchen in dark sweatpants, a towel slung over one shoulder. He sweeps me into his arms, surrounding me with his freshly showered scent.

"Hey, Boss."

"Hey." I gaze up at him and run my fingers through his dark, damp hair. "Did you just do a workout?"

"I did, then I started on dinner." He plants a kiss on my lips. "I put your clothes on the heater in our room. Go get changed, it's almost ready."

"Thank you." I pull him to me by the front of his T-shirt and kiss him again.

"Go. Before I eat you instead." He chuckles, giving my ass a light slap.

I go upstairs, eager to stop my mind running over the events of the day. I need to switch off for a few hours. Although with the trial so close, it's easier said than done. I look outside the bedroom window, scanning the leafy suburban street for people hanging around. People with cameras, or phones pointing in the direction of the house. There's no one, just like I knew there wouldn't be. I'm not concerned by those photos. The ones at the office are a given. It's where I work. But I don't like the idea that whoever wants to rile me knows I'm visiting the clinic, and likely knows where I and Drew live.

But regardless, it's merely a spooking tactic. One I refuse to fall for.

I close the drapes, get changed, and head downstairs to where Drew's stirring something that smells incredible on the stove.

He turns to look at me over his shoulder, his eyes giving my body an appreciative sweep as he flashes his teeth at me.

"Take a seat, Boss."

I walk across the kitchen. It's all black marble and dark, dramatic walls. But it suits Drew. It's edgy and masculine, and I know he designed it and did most of the heavy lifting himself to make it so perfect. My apartment isn't too dissimilar in palette. I love rich colors. But I lack the eye for design that Drew has. I wonder what our new house will be like when we find it. How we'll decorate it with a mix of both our styles.

I take a seat at the dining table, humming happily as I sink into the velvet chair.

"I'll rub your feet for you later," Drew says as he places a steaming bowl of rice and green Thai curry in front of me.

"Before or after dessert." I smile.

He chuckles. "During, if you like? I picked you up some ice cream on my way home. Elderflower and tonic." He screws his nose up like the name of the flavor alone offends him.

I lift my glass of iced water and take a sip. The ice cream place is in the opposite direction from his office.

"Did I tell you I love you today?"

He grins. "You did. But you can tell me as much as you like. It'll never get old."

We finish dinner and Drew makes good on his promise, massaging my feet while I eat ice cream and he reads his baby book. It's so dog-eared now it looks like the spine might fall apart. I swear I fall in love with him a little more each time I watch him read it, the little fascinated expressions painting themselves over his face every couple of pages.

I cuddle up to him in bed after.

"I'd like to find out," I say as I stroke my fingertips around in figures of eight on his chest.

"Okay," he replies, tightening his arm around me as he presses a kiss to my temple. "We'll call the doctor in the morning."

I turn my head to look at his face. I don't even have to elaborate what I mean. He just gets me. "Do you have any names you like?"

"Hmm." He rubs his thumb over his lips, his dark brows flattening. "How about Sophrew or Drophie?"

I shove at his chest, laughing. "Be serious."

He chuckles, pulling me in for a kiss. "I don't know, Mama. I'll get thinking. I bought a baby name book. I'll take a look at it."

"Of course you did," I tease. "You'll be able to birth these babies yourself at this rate."

He snorts. "That's definitely your job. However, I did read we should be massaging your perineum soon. You can get special oil for it. I'll get us some."

"You're joking, right?"

He holds my chin gently, trailing his finger down over my skin so that my lips pull apart. He sinks his teeth into his lower lip with a sinful smile.

"I'll do it for you. I *want* to do it for you. It's not like I don't stretch you with my cock enough already... and my tongue."

I recognize the sparkle in his eyes.

"Relax. I've got you," he whispers.

He shifts lower in the bed, settling himself between my thighs. His groan matches my own as his tongue performs its first swipe through my flesh. "Sophie," he murmurs, taking both of my hands and placing them into his hair.

I sink my fingers into the dark strands, clutching tight as the next flick of his tongue against my clit has my back arching away from the bed. "That's so good," I breathe as he holds my lips apart, his eyes on mine as he licks me all the way from my asshole to my clit, before growling against it as he sucks.

"I want to do something for you," I say, looking down at him as he eats me out leisurely, as though this is for his pleasure and not mine.

"After I make you come," he murmurs before sliding his tongue inside me.

"Okay."

I grip onto his hair, holding him in place as he brings his tongue back to my clit and circles it in the way that's guaranteed to have me coming on his face any minute.

"At least twice," he adds.

"Uh-huh."

His eyes are on my face as he chuckles.

"Make that three times. You've got a needy little pussy here that loves to come for me."

I shake as I prove him right, coming against his mouth in a rush.

He snakes both hands up to cup my bump.

"Another," he groans, while I'm still pulsing against his tongue.

He strokes my bump and drives his face deeper into me like he can't get close enough. Then he sucks my clit in between his lips, flicking it with his tongue, and I come again, crying out his name.

This orgasm stretches into another as I pull his hair so hard I'm surprised he doesn't curse in pain. All it does is spur him on as he devours me like a dark-haired God. His mouth and tongue ravage me, full of sin, full of intense pleasure.

"Another," he grunts.

I lose count at five.

# Chapter 28
# Drew

Sophie's a beautiful, sweaty mess by the time I come up for air from between her thighs. I expect her to want to go to sleep now that I've helped relax her. But the moment my face draws level with hers, she's grabbing the back of my head and kissing me, whimpering into my mouth as her tongue sweeps over mine, drinking up the taste of herself from me.

I groan against her lips as her hand wraps around my dick and she starts working it from base to tip.

Now I know without a doubt that I was right to be jealous of Tanner and how horny pregnancy made Rachel. It's the stuff of fucking dreams. I'm going to keep getting Sophie pregnant as many times as I can, just so she'll pull at me and let out those sexy little breathy pants whenever the head of my dick rubs over her clit.

"All those orgasms not enough for you, Boss? Now, your greedy little pussy wants to be filled, huh?"

"Drew," she moans, squeezing the head of my dick and rubbing my precum over it with the pad of her thumb.

I curse against her mouth as I hitch one leg around my waist and thrust inside her. I can only get a couple of inches of friction before the bump makes it awkward. So instead, I sit back and widen my knees, wrapping my hands beneath her thighs and pulling her legs around my hips.

Her breath stutters as my cock drags over her slick skin.

"Yeah, you like that?" I hiss before I thrust my way back inside her.

She moans as I circle my cock inside her, then draw it back, covered in her wetness before burying myself to the hilt again.

"You like the way I fuck you, don't you? The way I fill you like no one else can."

"Drew," she moans, her breasts bouncing prettily as I fuck her at my chosen pace.

I look down at my cock disappearing inside her.

"I bet you'll come like this again, won't you? I can already feel you squeezing me. So needy, wanting to come around my cock all the time."

She grabs onto my wrists, her lips parting as she moans my name.

Yeah, *my* fucking name.

I dig my fingers into her ass, lifting it higher so I can push deeper, knowing I'll hit her G-spot like this.

"Don't come inside me, okay?" she pants.

I fight the pulsing in my balls as she trembles and then comes around me in a rush, her breasts quivering with each wave of her orgasm that feels like it's trying to wring all the blood out of my cock.

"Jesus," I hiss, sweat beading along my hairline. "You're killing me here. Clamping down on me as you come all over my cock, and you want me *not* to blow my load inside you right now?" I make a crazed laughing sound as I will the tingle at the base of my cock to hang fire.

Sophie writhes, riding out the rest of her orgasm, her cheeks flushed.

"I need to come, Sophie," I growl in warning, holding myself still inside her. But her pussy's still pulsing around me, draining all my reserve.

"Okay," she pants, "Okay. Pull out."

My eyes bulge in my head, and I look at her like she's mad as she wriggles up the bed separating us.

"I want it here." She looks up at me as she leans back on her elbows and points at her stomach.

I don't move for a second, blood pumping in my ears.

She reaches for my cock. The second she wraps her fingers around it, I curse, letting my eyes fall closed as the aching heaviness returns to my balls with a vengeance.

"Fuck, the way you jerk me off," I groan, dropping my head back for a moment.

She speeds up, and I open my eyes to watch her.

"I want you to come here." She gestures to her stomach again and her swollen bump.

My cock swells as she trails the fingers of her other hand over it, down the curve that leads to her pussy, and back up again to where her belly button popped out two days ago.

"You mean it?"

She squeezes my cock in answer.

My eyes spring between her bump and her soft, full lips, not quite believing I'm actually this fucking lucky.

"You want me to come all over you? Brand you with my cum? Is that what you want?" I rasp.

"Yes."

"You want my cum dripping off those tits... over that belly," I groan.

I can't believe this is happening.

"That's what I want," Sophie purrs as she cups my balls in her other hand.

"Fuck," I whisper hoarsely, reaching out to grab one breast and rub my thumb over her nipple.

Then she whispers, "I'm yours. We're all yours, *Daddy*."

*Fuckkkk.*

That one word is my final undoing, and I groan, my torso tensing as ropes of cum shoot out, splaying all over Sophie's skin.

The sound of it landing on her is as loud as our labored breathing.

"Sophie," I utter. Her name rumbles in my chest as she jerks me faster, milking every last drop from me until I'm physically shaking with the force of coming so hard.

I drag in a rough breath, running one hand down over my face as I take in the sight of her, covered in me.

Her eyes are hooded as she gazes up at me.

She's never looked more incredible. Full of babies, covered in my cum.

I slide my hand around the back of her neck, stroking her hammering pulse with my thumb, and admire her body.

She follows my gaze as I place a flattened hand against her swollen stomach and spread my fingers out.

"You're covered in me," I groan, smearing my cum, spreading it around, taking my time to paint my girl with it, until her bump is glistening.

I sink my teeth into my lower lip as I take a mental picture of her like this.

"Jesus, Sophie. I love you. I couldn't love you any more than I already do. You know that, right?"

"I love you too," she whispers, watching me as I drop my hand down to cup her between the legs.

"Seeing you covered in my cum does something to me." I grip her possessively and slip a finger inside her where she's hot and wet. "I think it does something for you too." I chuckle as I draw my finger back and suck it into my mouth.

"Maybe." She gives me a sexy smile.

"I better take care of it, then." I grin, throwing her legs around my ears. "You've got some more in there for me, haven't you, Boss?"

I spit on her swollen clit, then lower my lips and suck, chuckling at her widened eyes.

"You're a sadist," she gasps.

"You love it," I murmur, my mouth full of pussy. "Admit it."

"I love *you*," she murmurs in defeat, threading her hands through my hair. "But don't you ever need to rest?"

I answer by sliding two fingers inside her and finding her G-spot as she drops her head back to the pillow with a soft curse.

Sophie's in a sexy, black maternity dress that hugs her curves when I walk into the kitchen in the morning. She's turned the coffee machine on for me and is frowning at her phone as she sips a ginger tea.

"Okay, Mama?" I walk up behind her, cradling her bump as I kiss her neck.

She leans into my touch, her voice soft. "Boss or Mama, which is it?"

"Depends if I'm thinking about how much I love you, or about how much I want to fuck you."

She laughs as I rub her bump. "So it's love this morning then, huh?"

"I should rephrase that," I murmur against her skin. "Boss-Mama because I'm always thinking about how much I love you *and* how much I love to fuck you."

She laughs, resting her head back against my shoulder, but it's weighted with uncertainty as her attention goes back to her phone.

"Press call," I whisper against her ear, making her shiver.

"It's early; she might not be there yet."

"One way to find out." I kiss her temple.

She sighs and then taps the phone. It starts ringing and she puts it on speaker.

"This is Doctor Melinda Grace. How are you, Sophie?"

Sophie tenses and glances at me. I nod at her.

"I'm good. Everything's fine. Drew's here with me. We wondered if you could tell us the results of the tests, please. About the genders?"

"Of course, I'd be more than happy to. Would you also like to know about the DNA match?"

Sophie audibly swallows. "Yes, please."

I stroke her stomach and kiss her head again.

"Well, congratulations, you're having both. Your son was a match to Drew's sample, and your daughter was a match to the other sample that was later provided to us."

Lightness overtakes my head and I screw up my eyes. It's like a sudden burst of light has exploded inside my chest. I can't hear anything except my heartbeat and deep breathing in my ears.

*"Thank you so much."* I'm acutely aware of a distant voice saying.

I bury my face in Sophie's neck, using her as my anchor as my blood vibrates in my veins, warming my entire body and soul.

"Drew?" Sophie turns in my arms and strokes my face until I focus on her widened eyes.

"We're having a boy and a girl," I choke out, dragging in air.

"Yep." She searches my eyes.

"A boy and a girl," I repeat in awe.

She breathes out, something akin to relief settling over her face before she lights up and smiles at me.

Really fucking smiles.

"We're having a boy and a girl," she echoes.

I pull her to me, not caring that some might say men shouldn't cry. I fucking shed tears like they're G-strings at a strip club.

"I love you. You've made every dream of mine come true."

"Drew," she whispers.

I hear the tears in her voice as she clings to me.

We stay holding each other, content in silence, until I pull her lips to mine and press our damp faces together so I can kiss her.

"A boy." *Kiss.* "And a girl." *Kiss.*

She laughs against my lips as I keep kissing her, deepening it until we're both panting against each other's mouths.

I grab handfuls of her ass as she grabs my belt and starts undoing it.

"I have to leave for work," she protests against my mouth while lowering my zipper.

"I have a meeting in thirty minutes," I pant as I bunch her dress up around her waist.

She pulls my cock free a split second before I turn her around and pull her panties to the side.

Then I'm sinking inside her from behind with fast, determined thrusts, and one end goal in sight as we both moan and climb higher together.

"Come all over my cock. Let me wear you on me all day," I rasp, kissing her neck, one hand frantically rubbing her clit as the other holds her bump.

She leans forward, resting her hands on the counter so I can get a better angle, and we both hiss as I bury myself deeper.

"Drew," she cries out my name as she comes in waves around me and the pulses of her orgasm wrap around my cock like a tight glove.

I keep fucking her in deep strokes, letting her ride it out on me.

"That's so good," she whimpers.

I keep up the pace until her orgasm fades. Then the familiar heat builds in my balls. As my cock swells inside her, Sophie places her hand over the top of mine on her stomach.

I groan from deep in my chest as I start coming.

Movement ripples beneath my hand and something hard pushes out into my palm.

"The babies just moved," I choke as my orgasm continues on. I couldn't stop even if I wanted to. But fuck, I don't want to. This is every fantasy I've ever had.

The movement rolls against my palm again, drawing a fresh wave to race from my balls and spill inside her.

"Oh my God, I felt it." Sophie's voice hitches as I bury my nose into her neck and slow my thrusts to empty all of myself.

I smile against her skin as I catch my breath, every muscle in my body softening as I stroke her stomach. "Which one do you think it was?" I look over her shoulder at our entwined hands.

"I don't know." Emotion creeps into her voice as she strokes the back of my hand. "It's kind of weird, knowing they're moving in there while we're—"

"It's only weird if we make it weird. It's the most natural thing in the world. You've never looked sexier to me, you know that? I can't get enough. I'm going to be fucking you until you go into labor."

She snorts out a laugh. "We'll see about that."

I pull out of her, slipping her panties back into place before she heads to the bathroom to clean up. It's only when we're about to get into our separate cars that we speak again.

"I meant to tell you last night, I had some pictures taken of me," Sophie says as she places her purse onto the front passenger seat of her car. "It's nothing to worry about. It's happened before on other cases. But you should know in case you see anyone suspicious hanging around near the house."

"It's happened before?" I look down the gravel driveway toward the leafy street which is made up of large, individually designed houses, all set back from the road like mine. If someone were to be sneaking around, it's unlikely the neighbors would notice anything.

"It's just an intimidation tactic. I'd rather they use their energy on me than a witness." She closes the car door and looks up at me with a reassuring smile.

"You really care about your clients, don't you?" I step closer and hitch her chin higher with two fingers underneath it so I can look directly into her eyes.

Emerald glitters back at me as she speaks. "Of course. Please don't worry. I've got this."

"I know you do. And while you're busy taking care of it, I'll be busy taking care of you."

She laughs softly. "Fine. Do what you feel you need to. But I'm okay."

I smile, holding down the unease in my gut at the thought that someone… anyone… is looking at Sophie and taking pictures of her without her permission. I'll call my security installers and get them to ramp up things at my house and upgrade Sophie's apartment. She might not want me to worry, but the second she walked back into my life, I was destined to want to protect her and our babies at all costs.

"You're a flame, Ms. Havers. I'm so in awe of you, you know that?" I trace my thumb over her pouty lower lip. "Hot lawyer. Hot mama. Hot fiancée."

"Hot lawyer who's about to be late." She kisses the tip of my thumb.

I kiss her goodbye and step back.

"I love you," I call as she slides into the driver's seat.

"Love you too." She blows me a kiss, then waves as she pulls out of the driveway.

I pull my phone out and bring up the installer's number. I don't care what it costs. I'm getting it done today. When I bring Sophie back home tonight, my house is going to have security that puts a royal guard to shame.

# Chapter 29
## Sophie

"Hey, stranger, I'm beginning to forget what you look like."

"Like a woman about to tear her hair out." Halliday half groans, half laughs.

"That good?"

"Seriously, what is it with stubborn older men? Is it because they're so stuck in their way from years of pleasing only themselves?"

"Your client still doesn't want to get matched, then?"

"No," she huffs, and I can picture her rolling her eyes in the call. "He's more difficult than that European prince I worked with."

"Wow." I let out a low whistle and cradle my phone between my ear and shoulder as I gather up my purse and files I want to look over tonight.

"Yeah. But enough about him keeping me hostage over here until I can get him to cooperate. How are things with you? How are the babies?"

"A boy and girl." I grin, heading for the elevator.

She shrieks in excitement.

"Yeah." I laugh, stepping into the empty elevator and hitting the button for parking. "Listen, I might lose you for a minute. I'm in the elevator."

"You cannot leave me hanging like that!" Halliday scolds before she adds, "Call me back in thirty seconds, I'm timing you." Then she hangs up.

I lean back against the wall as the elevator starts to descend.

It's been a productive day. We're getting closer to identifying the unknown man who visited Chelsea. Another day or two and we might have a name. Chelsea sounded hopeful when I called her, but that fizzled out the moment I reminded her to be wary of anyone approaching her who mentions the case. She doesn't need to know that I've been followed; it will only scare her. But she does need to know that it's something she needs to remain cautious of.

The elevator comes to a stop, and I step out, immediately dialing Halliday.

"When did you find out?" she asks in a rush the moment it connects.

"This morning. We called the doctor." I gnaw on my bottom lip before providing the next part, "The boy is Drew's. The girl is Henry's. Biologically, I mean."

She pauses. "What did Drew say?"

My heart expands at the memory of his face this morning.

"He's beyond excited that we're having one of each."

"The man is perfect." She sighs. "Literally perfect." Her voice drops to a whisper. "Unlike the XY chromosomes who just walked in here."

"Sterling?"

"Yep. Most difficult client ever," she mutters. "I'm so sorry I have to go. I'll call you again later. We can talk more about the babies. I'm thinking Halliday is a great middle name for the girl. And something with a good energy for their first names. I'll get some ideas together."

"You do that." I laugh as we say goodbye.

I round the corner to where I parked this morning. I was running late, so I had to park further away from the elevators than usual in one of the older parts of the car park that's barely used anymore.

*What the hell?*

My heart lurches up into my throat at the sight of the brand-new Range Rover that Drew bought me.

Every window is smashed, and the ground is littered in millions of tiny sharp fragments. There are violent red streaks lancing over the bodywork, dripping inside over the internal upholstery. The sickening sight is accompanied by a pungent stench of paint that's thick in the air.

I look around at the other untouched cars. This was intended for me only. Another warning. Another threat.

"Damn it," I mutter as I call up to the office to see if Jules is still there.

The phone rings out. She'd have gone out of the main entrance because she catches the bus home. Everyone else had already left.

I tap out a quick text to Drew, then bring up a number I haven't used in months, swallowing hard as it rings.

"Soph?"

I screw my eyes shut and take a deep breath.

"Are you at work right now? I need to add something to the file Jules logged with you."

"You okay?" Concern fills his voice as I open my eyes and take another look at my car. It's no less shocking than the first time.

In fact, it's worse.

It's ruined.

Completely destroyed.

"I'm fine. But my car isn't. Can you send someone out to take a look? I haven't touched anything, but I doubt there'll be fingerprints." My eyes slide over the blood red paint before I glance around the deserted parking lot. "Tell them to buzz the office when they arrive, please. I'll wait inside for them."

Henry places his hand on my lower back as he guides me down the hallway to the main reception area of the station. He's already had harsh words with the officers who brought me here to make a statement, instead of taking it at the office. I felt sorry for them. They were only doing their job, but Henry made a point of telling them I'm pregnant and should have been taken straight home.

I made sure I was extra helpful with their questions. I'm pregnant, not ill. And the fact that whoever did this chose today, the one day I parked in the older area of the car park without CCTV, seems surprisingly convenient. They're either watching me more than I realize or they got lucky.

"Sophie." Drew rushes through the front doors and over to me the minute we walk into reception.

His blue eyes are bright beneath dark brows, knotted with tension.

"I got to your office, but you were already gone. I saw the car. Are you okay?"

I step into his arms, breathing in his scent, but not missing the way he glares at Henry's hand as it leaves my back.

"I'm fine. I'm ready to go home, though."

"My security guys haven't finished your apartment yet, so we'll stay at mine tonight, okay?"

The concern in his eyes has me agreeing easily. I don't want him stressing over this. It's a step further than I was expecting. I've never had a vehicle vandalized before. But it means we're getting closer to identifying the other man who assaulted Chelsea. Whoever it is has gotten worried. And that only makes me more determined to keep digging.

"Yeah, of course. I'm so sorry about the car."

"It doesn't matter. It's replaceable. You and the babies aren't." He fixes me with an intense look before dusting his lips over mine and lowering his voice so only I can hear. "I love you so much. I don't know what I'd do without you."

"You'll never have to find out," I say against his lips, pressing a soft kiss there.

Henry clears his throat behind me, and I turn to him over my shoulder.

"Thank you for your help when I called to report it."

"Anytime," he replies, hovering like he wants something else.

Drew's arms stiffen around me, but he says nothing as the two men make eye contact over the top of my head.

"Can I have a word, son?"

I glance up at Drew's clenched jaw and slide my arms from around his waist. "I'll wait over there." I motion toward the main entrance doors.

He looks down at me and his face softens. "I'll be quick."

"It's fine, take your time."

I pull out my phone to text Halliday, updating her about the car. Then I drop my phone back into my purse and glance over to where Henry and Drew are talking in hushed voices. Henry's eyes meet mine and then he looks away when Drew says something and shakes his head.

A few seconds later, Drew storms over, his jaw set in a tight line.

"Let's go."

He wraps an arm around me and leads me out into the car park.

My stomach sinks as he unlocks his pristine metallic blue Range Rover. I'm about to apologize again about ruining mine, even though it isn't my fault. But something about the darkened glaze that's descended in his eyes tells me that now isn't the time.

We drive back to his house in relative silence.

"Go get a shower," he says as he tosses his keys down on the entryway table as he walks into the house behind me. "I'll order us takeout, it's late."

Before I can respond, he walks off toward the kitchen. I let him go. I understand the need for personal space, even if it stings that what he wants is space from me right now.

I've been in Drew's giant shower for ten minutes, enjoying the way the warm spray is easing the tightness in my lower back, when the bathroom door opens and he walks in, still dressed in his deep gray work suit and blue tie.

I don't need to ask him if something's wrong. It's written in the tautness of his shoulders, the set of his jaw, the creasing of his brow.

I turn the water off and open the door, stepping out with a cloud of steam. I take the towel he holds out to me wordlessly and begin to dry myself.

"Sophie." His soft voice is heavy with something. And when he sighs, it makes my heart ache.

He steps toward me and takes the towel from my hands, drying me in slow, gentle strokes. A frown mars his handsome face as he works his way down my body until he's sliding the towel over my bump.

"He's right." His jaw clenches. "I let you down."

"What?" I blink as I look at him, but his eyes are following the towel as he continues stroking it over my stomach.

"My father." His eyes pinch as he says the word. "He wanted me to talk you into giving up the case. He said I needed to convince you to think about the babies."

"He has no right—"

"That's exactly what I told him," Drew says, discarding the towel and reaching for my lotion bottle. He kneels in front of me and lifts one of my feet from the floor, placing it down onto his thigh as he pops the cap off the bottle.

"I told him that it isn't just a job to you. That you care about your clients. That you have to see it through."

He squeezes lotion into his palm and then rubs it between his hands before sliding them up my calf, gently massaging my muscles as he works it into my skin.

"I told him that I'm proud of you."

"Drew," I breathe, gazing at him.

"I'm *so* damn proud of you, Sophie." He looks up at me, his blue eyes intense, before he drops them away and switches his attention to my other leg.

I fight back a moan at how good it feels to be taken care of by him as his hands expertly knead and stroke me.

"And then, do you know what he said to me?" He stands, squeezing out more lotion.

"What?"

I can't take my eyes off his face as he looks down at my stomach. He slowly reaches out and starts smoothing cream into it. Within seconds of him touching me, my stomach moves beneath his hands. Pain flashes across his face, stealing my breath as he stares, rapt at the spot where my skin pushes out.

"He said it would be my fault if you or the babies got hurt. If you were... killed."

I grab his hands, keeping them pressed against my stomach.

"He had no right to say that!" My voice trembles with anger. "None."

"But he's not wrong." He lifts his eyes to meet mine, and the torment swirling in them is gut wrenching.

"It's not going to hap—"

"You can't say that. You can't promise me that. Just like I can't promise you that the thought of it doesn't scare the shit out of me. I meant what I said about being proud of you. And I would *never* ask you to stop doing something you love. But I'm fucking terrified of losing you all."

He spreads his hands out and wraps both mine and his around my stomach.

"I love you all three of you so much."

He drops to his knees, closing his eyes as he presses his lips to my bump. I sink my hands into his hair and stroke as he presses another kiss to my skin.

"He didn't want you to tell me, did he?"

Drew rests his forehead to my skin, taking a slow breath before he stands again.

"No," he admits. "But I'll never keep secrets from you. We promised to always communicate."

"We did."

I reach up to stroke the hair at the nape of his neck where it starts to curl near his collar.

"And I'll never keep secrets from you either. If anything else happens in this case that makes me worry, then you'll be the first to know. Okay?"

His eyes rake over my face and his jaw finally softens. "Okay," he says, wrapping his arms around me.

"I'll make your suit sticky," I protest.

"I have at least twenty more." His lips curl into the first hint of a smile I've seen on him all evening.

"All right then." I smile, pressing my lotioned skin against his shirt. "You would make a hot bodyguard, though. Just so you know."

He chuckles and the sound makes my heart want to burst.

"I'd just keep you naked and underneath me all day. Then you'd not get into any trouble."

I bite my lower lip. "Doesn't sound bad at all."

He frees my lower lip with a kiss, keeping his mouth hovering over mine.

"I'd do anything for the three of you."

"I know you would. You'd set up your own body-guard business if you had to. Be a powerful leader like Mufasa."

Drew's brows lower and he looks at me, puzzled.

"I'm not the only one who hasn't forgotten our date four years ago."

"Except I wasn't *your* date, remember?"

"I know." I press a kiss to his full lips.

"You think that's why I chose Mufasa? Because he's a leader?"

"Didn't you? You said he was a powerful example."

He draws in a slow, measured breath, his next words spoken so softly that I almost miss them. "No, Mama."

"Then why?"

He places one hand over my stomach protectively.

"He's a powerful example of a *father*, Sophie. That's why I chose him."

The hurt creasing his brow tells so many stories in this moment. Of a boy who found out that his father wasn't who he thought he was. But the real heart-break being that he finally realized why he was treated differently. Why he never felt good enough. Why he wasn't loved and protected like he should have been.

Like a father should do for their child.

"Drew." My voice is a hoarse whisper as I swallow down the aching lump in my throat. "Mufasa gave his life to save Simba."

"I know. And I've never felt luckier to have three reasons to die for."

His clear blue eyes look up and into mine. But as he wipes away a rogue tear from my cheek with the pad of his thumb, there's no pain there anymore. No boy who's hurting. Just a man who's giving his entire heart away, vowing to love and protect the way he should have been.

"I love you," I whisper as another tear escapes. "I never used to cry. I think it's the hormones."

His face transforms into a beautiful smile. "You're breathtaking whether you're crying with snot running down your face, or not."

"I don't." I laugh, reaching up to touch my nose just in case.

He slides his hands down to my ass, moving me as close as we can be with my growing bump between us.

"I promise to stay safe. And never hide anything from you, even if it might worry you. I'll be honest with you, always."

His eyes shine as he lowers his lips to mine. "The same goes for me too, Mama. Always. I swear on my life."

# Chapter 30
# Drew

"I HAD BEAUFORT ON the phone this morning before you arrived."

I look up from my laptop at Tanner as we wait for the rest of the staff to join us in the conference room for our Monday morning team meeting.

"Sterling? That would have been the middle of the night in New York," I say. "He said he was happy with everything last time I was over there. The project's finished."

"He is. He couldn't sing our praises loud enough," Tanner says as he reaches for the jug of water in the center of the table and pours one.

"So what? You two just chatting about the weather?"

I look down at my phone as an email pings through from the car dealership, letting me know that Sophie's replacement has arrived. I crack my knuckles as the image of her trashed one surfaces from my memory. Nothing's happened in the few days since then. But I'm going to be damn glad once this case she's working on goes to trial and is over.

"I don't know why he was up so late. But he called to tell me he's recommended us to a business associate of his. Could lead to a big contract."

"That's great," I reply absentmindedly, drumming my fingers on the glass table.

"He also said thanks for the blow job you gave him as an added thank you for choosing us."

"Good, that's good."

Something hits me in the side of the face.

"Hey!" I snap my eyes from the rolled-up ball of paper that lands on the table and over to Tanner's face.

"You upgraded the security systems at your house and hers. It's all logged with the police. And she says she has it handled," he says, leaning back in his chair.

I arch a brow at him. "So if it happened to Rach—?"

"Yeah, I'd kill the fuckers if I got the chance." Tanner grimaces.

"Exactly." I huff out a breath and push my hands back through my hair as I lean over the table. "I bet this shit only gets worse, doesn't it?"

"The worry?" Tanner snorts. "Yeah. Sorry, Buddy. You wait until those babies are born, then you'll feel like you're barely holding on to your sanity if they so much as sneeze. Then there's the temperatures, and the viral rashes... and before you even get to that, you've got the birth and everything that can go wrong there."

He curses as his earlier paper missile smacks him right between the eyes.

"You know what, though? You'll never change a thing. You'll look back at bachelor Drew Harper and wonder how you even existed without all of them dictating your life to you every day."

"Yeah. I'm already there." I run a hand around my jaw.

And he's right. I wouldn't change a damn thing.

"That the place you're viewing tonight?" He gestures to the property listing of a large modern glass-fronted house on my laptop screen. "Nice."

"Yeah. Safe neighborhood. A straightforward commute to Sophie's office. In the catchment area for the best school for miles."

I click through the images of the house, gym and pool house, and large garden so that Tanner can see. One of the bedrooms has a vaulted ceiling. I'm already planning how we could decorate it. It'll be perfect for the nursery.

"You don't need to tell me. It's two streets away from us." He smirks.

"The one negative factor." I smirk back.

Tanner rolls his shoulders and leans his head back in the chair. "It'll be nice. The girls will like it. They can walk hang out, and you and I can run together in the mornings."

My usual sarcastic comeback about spending more time together outside of already working together every day fades from my tongue and I simply tip my head in agreement. It sounds pretty fucking nice. Suburban dad life—swapping out drinking whiskey in a bar after work with friends for having a drink at home while the kids play together. Tanner might be the only one with kids at the moment. But Sophie's over halfway through the pregnancy already, and it wouldn't surprise me if Rose and Dax followed soon, then maybe even Maddy and Logan.

"As long as you don't sulk when I whip your ass. You know I'm the faster runner."

"Yeah, whatever." Tanner chuckles. "Better hope you get the house so I can make you eat your words."

"Bring it on." I grin. "Bring it on."

"What do you think?" Nerves skate up my spine as Sophie wanders around the master bedroom and over to the wall-to-wall glass doors that lead out onto the balcony.

I managed to get the keys from the agent so we could look around by ourselves. The owner has already moved out, so the place is empty. But even without furniture, its potential is obvious.

At least, I think it is. But as Sophie turns in a slow circle, a look of deep concentration on her face as she studies the space, doubt creeps over me like a cold mist.

*If she doesn't like it, we'll keep looking. She has to really—*

"I love it." She grins, her green eyes bright with excitement. "And that room with the high ceiling would make such a cute nursery."

"You do? I'll call the agent." I stride over to her and pull my phone out of my jacket pocket.

"Whoa, Daddy." She laughs softly and places her hand over mine on my phone. "Let them sweat a bit. It'll help when we negotiate."

I smile at her and pocket my phone. She's right. It's a basic rule. Don't show your emotion. Because the second you do, all power is handed over. I'd never show my hand so early at work when talking over the terms of a deal. But wanting to buy this house for us, to have her with me every night and know that I can protect her, it's got my fingers tingling with how much I want to call the agent. She's turned me from a ruthless businessman to an emotional simp. And I don't give a shit as long as her eyes are lit up for me and no one else. The way they are right now.

"Okay." I slide my arms around her, my hands finding her ass. "How about I make *you* sweat instead?"

"It's not our house yet." She bites her lip, but her eyes are dancing with energy as she snakes her hands up around my neck and strokes my hair.

"And you weren't my date," I whisper in her ear before kissing her neck, my blood heating at her soft moan. "But that didn't stop me from telling you that you would be one day. And now you've got our babies growing in your belly. I think it's safe to assume that I can fuck you until the sound of you coming sinks into the walls of this room. Because this *will* be our house, Sophie. Just like you were always going to be my date. Just like you were always going to be the only woman I've ever said I love you to."

"You're kind of sexy when you talk like you're obsessed." A smile curves her lips.

"Like I'm obsessed?" My brow quirks. "Boss, I *am* obsessed. You saw to that the first time I met you. You might as well have made it the law—Drew Harper must be obsessed with Sophie Havers at all times."

She laughs. "Smooth, Mr. Harper. Real smooth."

I kiss her, groaning at the way her belly presses against me.

"How does that feel so good?" she moans as I kiss my way down her windpipe, unbuttoning her blouse as I go.

I open it and drag the cups of her bra down, freeing her magnificent tits. Her bra holds them up underneath like they're being presented on a platter just for me.

"Because I've spent hours studying your body." I roll one of her nipples between my finger and thumb, eliciting a sharp intake of air through her parted lips. "And I'll study it for the rest of my life searching for new ways to hear you moan my name."

I bend and draw one nipple past my lips as I tease the other between my fingers.

Sophie trembles at my touch, and I smile around her before sucking again. Her breasts have gotten bigger as the pregnancy has gone on, and it's made her already sensitive nipples as unstable as a nuclear bomb. If we had more time, I bet I could make her come just by playing with them.

"Drew." She fists my hair, squirming.

I drop to my knees and kiss my way down over her bump, stopping below her belly button where her skirt waistband sits.

"Turn around."

She looks at me through hooded lids while she strokes my hair. I lean into her touch as I slide a hand underneath her skirt.

"Turn around," I repeat as I trail a finger over the wet fabric on the front of her panties.

I hook her panties to the side and swipe my fingers over her skin, coating them in wetness. Her eyes fix on mine as I withdraw them from under her skirt and suck them clean. I have to fight to keep my eyes from closing at how sweet she tastes. It's only getting sweeter and more addictive with each passing day. I swear I'll know next time I make her pregnant before she does, just from her taste.

"You're dripping for me already, Darling," I groan, reaching up to slide her panties down her legs. "Now turn around so I can lick this greedy pussy before you come all over my fingers."

She does as I say, turning around so that her perfect round ass is level with my face.

I push her skirt up and palm her smooth skin with one hand as I unzip my pants with the other. I pull my hard dick out and give it a squeeze.

"You're soaking," I say as I stretch her between my fingers, mesmerized by the way her skin glistens with her arousal. "You really can't get enough of the way I make you come, can you?" I say, my face inches from her skin.

"Are you talking to me or my pussy?"

I blow gently, smiling as her inner thighs tremble.

"That depends." I give her a languid lick from front to back, chuckling as she curses.

"On what?" She squirms against me as I flatten my tongue against her clit and circle it slowly.

"On who's going to be the loudest for me." I move back and sink two fingers inside her and pump slowly, making the sound of her wetness echo as loudly as possible in the empty room. It's quickly outdone by Sophie's breathy pants as I find her G-spot and massage it.

"Case closed," I murmur, reaching up to hold her ass cheeks apart so that I can sink into her and eat her out in the way I've been dreaming of all day.

She cries out and her back bows as she pushes back onto my face. "God, just like that."

I reposition myself on the floor, further away from the window, dragging her with me so that she has to bend over and brace her palms against the glass.

"Wave to the neighbors," I say before I slide my tongue inside her.

Her body tenses as she snaps her head up and looks out the window over the back of the house. She curses at me before relaxing. The house isn't overlooked. I already thought of all the ways I can fuck her by this window and out on the balcony when we live here because it's so private.

*All the ways.*

My cock throbs painfully so I give it a couple of quick jerks, then hold Sophie's bump. Her bending forward like this means I can feel and stroke every incredible inch.

"You're so fucking sexy. I could come just doing this," I groan as I sink my face back into her pussy and eat her out with even more enthusiasm, my hands stroking up and down her bump, around the sides of it to her hips, and back again in a continuous show of worship.

She moans as her pussy clenches around my tongue. I lick her inside before drawing back slowly, and I'm rewarded with a rush of fresh arousal. "Jesus." I lap it up before turning my attention back to her clit again. "You going to come for me? Because I need to fill this pretty pussy."

She answers by grinding on my face.

"Fuck yeah," I hiss, pulling her back onto me. The second her orgasm starts, I feel it. Her clit swells underneath my tongue and she releases another wet gush of fluid that runs down over my face, coating my chin until it's dripping down my neck and onto my shirt.

I'm going to fucking frame this shirt.

I wait for her moans to turn into whimpers. Then I stand and feed my cock into her in one slow thrust. Her pussy's still quivering with the remnants of her orgasm as I grasp her hips and start pumping.

"Fuck, Mama. You're so wet for me."

I brace one hand next to hers on the cool glass and kiss the back of her neck. I can no longer reach her clit easily like this now that her bump has gotten bigger.

I hold her steady with one hand on her bump as I kiss the top of her spine.

"I've got you. Now rub that swollen clit for me, beautiful girl."

"Oh God, Drew," Sophie whimpers as I thrust into her, sucking and grazing her neck with my teeth at the same time.

"Come again for me," I whisper, my voice hoarse with the strain of holding back the orgasm that's been threatening me since I first had her nipples in my mouth.

"It's too much," she gasps, but her hand is still working her clit.

"You can take it. Come on," I urge. "Show me."

I suck on her neck as she comes around me with a gasp, her pussy tightening around my cock in pulsating waves.

I bury my face into her neck as I come so hard I feel like my balls might shoot out the end of my cock too. Nothing else exists in this moment except me and her and our pleasure.

"I love you," I groan like I'm in pain as heat spreads around the head of my cock inside her, spilling everywhere. "I love you so much."

"I love you too." Her voice is breathy as she places her hand over mine on her stomach.

My groan turns to soft kisses up and down the side of her neck as the blood stops rushing in my ears and my senses begin to return.

"I think... I think you should call the agent."

My cock twitches inside her as I smile against her neck.

"Yeah? You want the house?"

"I want the house," she pants, making me laugh.

I stroke her bump one final time and then pull my phone from my jacket pocket, leaving my cock nestled snuggly inside her.

I press call and kiss her neck over and over as I wait for it to connect.

"Mr. Harper? What do you think?" the agent asks.

I flex my cock inside Sophie, making her shudder.

"Take it off the market. No one else sets foot inside it."

# Chapter 31
# Drew

"I CAN'T BELIEVE WE bought a house," Sophie muses as she leans back into the couch cushions, resting her bowl of ice cream on her bump.

I turn away from the late-night news on the TV and smile at her.

"We sure did."

She's got her feet in my lap, and I stroke up and down her calves as I watch her lick the spoon.

"Do you want to keep this place? Rent it out?"

Her eyes roam around her living room. "Yeah, good idea. I'll pull some equity out of it for my share of the new place."

"Let me buy it for us."

"No." She shakes her head, the same way she did when I suggested it on the drive home. "You can fund it to begin with so we don't delay things. But I'm still paying half."

"I wonder if our daughter will be as stubborn as her mum."

She jabs me in the stomach with her foot.

I'm lucky I've received several offers for my house in the last year, even though I wasn't planning on selling. I made one call as we left the viewing, resulting in another happy couple about to get their dream home. I've got some contacts who can get the paperwork done quickly. We might even get the keys within a month.

"Oh, turn it up!" Sophie points at the TV.

I grab the remote and adjust the volume as a picture of Sophie walking into her office in a black pantsuit comes up momentarily before the camera goes back to the female news anchor.

"You look sexy in that," I murmur.

"Shh." She jabs me with her foot again and I bite down on my bottom lip.

*"The senior prosecutor on the case is Sophie Havers. She's known to her colleagues as 'Havers the Handler' due to her unrivalled success rate for winning her cases. And after today's announcement from Councilor Michael Jenkins that he's stepping down amid the charges brought against him, there's speculation that this could be one of her trickier cases as allegations of police corruption and evidence tampering have now been added to the list."*

"Bastard." I seethe as a video of Michael Jenkins being placed into the back of a cop car flashes up on screen. This morning, the press revealed him as the suspect of the previously unknown man in Sophie's case.

We listen for another minute until the anchor moves onto the next headline.

I turn the volume back down.

"He's a piece of work, all right." Sophie leans to the side and places her empty bowl down on the floor. "Apparently multiple reports made from female colleagues about him making inappropriate comments mysteriously went missing after they were filed with the police."

"You think he paid someone to lose them on purpose?"

She rubs her temples and sighs.

"I know he did. There'll be a lose thread somewhere. I just need to find it and pull. The cops will start their own internal investigation. But that could take months. Right now, I just need to prove that he was the other man involved in what happened to my client. There's DNA evidence. You know what sickens me, though?"

"What?" I ask as she drops her fingers from her temples and looks at me with tired eyes.

"It's the fact that this kind of behavior escalates. It rarely comes out of nowhere. Those missing reports were the first warning signs. But because his behavior was covered up, he went unmonitored. Then he went on to commit a bigger crime against my client."

My jaw clenches as I think about the few details of the case Sophie has been allowed to share with me. But it's enough to know those two evil pricks manipulated a young woman for their own perverse enjoyment.

"You think there's a chance it wouldn't have happened if those reports had been taken seriously in the beginning?"

"I don't know." Sophie sighs. "I can't think like that, it doesn't help my client. A crime was committed against her and that's that. The only thing I can do now is get justice for her."

I give her a lopsided smile. "You're incredible."

Her eyes soften as she looks at me. "You told me that at least ten times today."

"I'm at least twenty times behind schedule, then." I lift one of her feet, bringing it toward my mouth so I can nip her ankle playfully.

She smiles and lets out a deep breath.

"Let's go to bed—"

Her phone ringing cuts her off, and she frowns at the screen before answering.

"Chelsea? Okay...Okay, take a breath... Good... tell me." Sophie's eyes meet mine, widening as she reels off her home address.

"Everything okay?" I ask as she ends the call.

"That was my client." She swings her legs out of my lap. "She's coming here. She has something to tell me."

Sophie's intercom buzzes, and she presses a button to unlock the main door.

"You want me to make myself scarce?" I ask, walking up behind her in the hallway.

"No. At least not yet. Let her meet you so she knows there's someone else here. I don't want her to get upset if she sees you by accident."

I nod, swallowing the thick lump in my throat. This girl was kept in a filthy apartment for two days by a man who posed as her own age online so he could groom her. It makes sense she might be nervous around people she doesn't know as a result.

"Okay."

Sophie straightens her shoulders as there's a knock at the door. When she opens it a young woman and man walk in, both looking like they're on edge. The woman's eyes stay on Sophie as she fidgets out of her jacket, and a pregnant stomach extends from beneath her sweatshirt.

The guy she's with has his eyes fixed on me as I look up from her stomach. His chest expands as he looks me up and down like he's trying to figure out whether I'm a threat or not.

"This is Drew. He's my fiancée," Sophie says to the young woman.

She glances up at me. "Nice to meet you. I'm Chelsea. This is Jake." She gestures to the young man next to her. He can't be more than twenty, and he's half my width, but he's looking at me like he has no issue fighting me if he deems me dangerous.

"I'm sorry to call. I thought it was better to talk in person," she says to Sophie in a nervous voice.

"Don't apologize. Come on in and take a seat," Sophie says as she leads Chelsea into the living room. Jake follows behind her, close enough that he reaches out and rubs her arm reassuringly.

"Would you like a drink?" Sophie asks as Chelsea sits down and knots her fingers together in her lap.

"No, thank you. We won't stay. I just thought you should know what happened today."

Jake sits next to her and takes her hands in his. "It's okay, Chels," he says softly.

I watch from the doorway as he transforms from the protective guy sizing me up in the hallway to the supportive partner she needs.

Sophie catches my eye, and I can tell she's thinking the same thing.

"He was nice," Chelsea says, looking at Jake for re-assurance before she turns her attention to Sophie. Her nose scrunches up as she grimaces. "I mean... he seemed it. You can never tell."

"Who was?" Sophie urges gently.

"The man I bumped into while taking a walk around the park this afternoon. He didn't tell me his name. But you said I should tell you if anyone tries to discuss the case with me."

"You did the right thing calling. Was anyone else with you when he approached you?"

"No. I was on my own, walking my dog. I didn't see anyone else."

"Okay, can you tell me exactly what he said?"

Chelsea glances at Jake again, then swallows.

"He was making a fuss of Dylan, my dog." She takes a deep breath. "Then he said he didn't want to upset me but that he recognized me from the news and hoped that I was doing okay. He said he knew how stressful a court case can be."

"Do you feel that he was trying to make you worried about testifying?" Sophie asks.

Chelsea shakes her head. "That's just it. He was being so nice. He wasn't suggesting I should be careful. He seemed more concerned about you."

"Me?" Sophie frowns.

I bristle, my body tensing as I fold my arms and stare at Chelsea as she shuffles in her seat.

"He said he'd heard that someone wrecked my lawyer's car, and that I must understand how stress isn't good when you're pregnant. He said he was sorry I had to go through a trial, but that you didn't. That you were doing it by choice." Chelsea places a hand over her swollen stomach.

"I thought it sounded weird," Jake pipes up. "I told Chels we should call you."

"You did the right thing," Sophie says. "What he told you is correct. My car was vandalized. But it's nothing that I'm worried about. And you shouldn't be either.

He's completely out of order talking to you about the case. I'm not handing it over to anyone else, okay? I'll be right there with you in court."

"Thank you." Chelsea sniffs. "I think he was just concerned. Because he said that I should think of your baby."

"Babies," I say suddenly, making everyone look at me.

"Yeah, babies." Chelsea tries to smile as she looks at Jake. "They're having twins."

"Congratulations," Jake says, meeting my eyes.

I tip my chin at him, the blood in my veins boiling as I process Chelsea's story.

"Thanks."

Sophie's gaze slides to mine and there's a ruthless determination in her eyes as she says, "Thank you for coming to tell me. I'll deal with it."

"Okay." Chelsea stands quickly like she's eager to leave, her shoulders dropping in relief. "Thank you." She takes Jake's hand and I move out of the doorway so they can come out into the hallway.

"Do you want me to describe him?" Chelsea asks, looking at Sophie as I open the front door.

"Older? Dark hair, gray around the sides? A few inches shorter than Drew?" Sophie says.

Chelsea's eyes land on me as she assesses my height. "Yeah. Do you know who it was?"

"He's not a danger to you. And he won't be bothering you again. I'll handle him." She gives Chelsea a reassuring smile.

"I'll rip him a new asshole if he comes near her again," Jake growls, looking between Sophie and I.

"You and me both," I agree.

He tips his chin at me in solidarity for the first time since he walked through the door, then wraps an arm around Chelsea and leads her out.

"What. The. Hell?" Sophie groans as I close the door.

"Why the fuck is my father talking to your client?" I hiss.

Sophie shakes her head, chewing on her bottom lip in thought. "Your guess is as good as mine. Maybe trying to get you to talk me into handing over the case wasn't enough. He thought he'd try manipulating Chelsea into asking me to drop it by playing the pregnancy card. Use her feelings about her own baby to make her concerned about me. Asshole."

"He must have crossed a line talking to her. We could report him."

"It won't do any good. He'll just weasel his way out of it or deny it altogether. He hasn't made a threat. He saw her in a public place. No one else saw them or heard what he said."

"Fuck's sake." I slam my flattened palm against the wall.

"Drew." Sophie takes my throbbing hand in hers and kisses it.

"He can't fucking leave you alone! Does he think he can control you? Using the baby... the fact that he's..."

I screw my eyes shut and curse as my head throbs.

He's always going to make this difficult for us.

Sophie sighs. Her clear eyes search mine as I look at her. "Legally, he has the right to request access. He's going to be in our lives whether we like it or not."

I drag a hand down my face. "He won't ever stop. He wants you back."

"I don't want him. I love you," she says with a measured calmness that helps to ease the hammering in my chest. "We'll find a way to deal with it."

"Or I could make him disappear," I grit.

"I think Jake could be persuaded to help you." She offers me a small smile.

"Yeah." I blow out a breath, bringing my rage down to a simmer. "He seems like a good guy, looking out for Chelsea. Did you see the way he was looking at me?"

Sophie's smile turns into a smirk. "Couldn't miss it. You're right. I'm glad she has him and his support."

"Just like you've got mine."

I curl a hand around her hip and pull her to me. The feel of her body against mine, our babies between us calms me like nothing else. When they're here in my arms, I can protect them. My father will never understand that true, soul-consuming feeling when you love someone more than anything else. He's not capable. Because if he did love Sophie, then he'd see that the best thing he can do for her and the babies is to leave us all the fuck alone.

"You know what I'd save if the house was burning?" I press my lips to her forehead.

"You never told me." She rests her hands on my chest and leans into me.

I stroke up and down her sides, my thumbs tracing the edges of her bump.

"I'd save the law book your dad gave you. Because there's nothing in this world that means more to me than you."

"You remember me telling you that?" Her eyes shine as she looks up at me.

"Of course. If it's important to you, then it's important to me."

She gazes at me for a minute before she speaks. Her words make my stomach sink.

"I have to talk to him. Ask what the hell he thinks he's doing talking to Chelsea."

"I'm coming with you." I grit my teeth, my fingers flexing against Sophie's hips as the vivid image of slamming my fist into his face consumes me.

"Okay."

I grip the back of her head and kiss her, relieved that she isn't going to insist she goes alone. Because if I know my father, he'll try anything to get what he wants.

But I'll die before I let him hurt Sophie.

# Chapter 32
# Sophie

"HE'S COMING." DREW'S VOICE conveys disgust as he looks out of the window at the cafe we're sitting in. We figured neutral territory was the best option.

I follow his eyeline outside, my throat tightening at the sight of Henry crossing the street toward us. He's wearing one of his work suits, the same as Drew and I. This is not how I planned my week starting. I should be prepping for trial now that it's so close. But at least being dressed for a fight makes me feel better about the confrontation that's about to ensue.

"He doesn't even look worried. Asshole," Drew hisses as Henry holds the door open for a young woman who's exiting. He flashes her a charming smile as she passes, his eyes landing on her ass as she leaves.

"Typical." I snort, folding my arms over my chest.

Henry looks around the crowded space, then sees us sitting at a small table near the back. He walks over and takes a seat, nodding briefly at Drew before his gaze rakes over me.

"You're looking well, Soph. Pregnancy suits you."

Drew might as well as have steam blowing from his ears, the way that his chest expands and his eyes lock on Henry like he's deciding whether to snap his neck or strangle him.

Henry's gaze drops over my cleavage.

"Keep your fucking eyes up," Drew snaps.

An amused glint flashes in his eyes. "Nice to see you too, Son."

"Cut the shit, Henry," I say, leaning across the table before the two of them start brawling. "We didn't come here to exchange pleasantries."

He chuckles. "And here's me thinking you missed me and realized the original version is better."

Drew's chair legs screech against the floor as he pulls it closer to the table, lowering his voice to a decibel above murderous as he leans toward Henry.

"I've got no problem knocking your ass on the floor right here in front of all these people if you talk to Sophie with anything less than the respect she deserves. So why don't you try again?"

Henry's eyes narrow as he glares at Drew. Then he cricks his neck and looks at me. "Why don't you tell me what this is about? Because as wonderful as it is to see you, I'm working and I need to get back."

"My client," I say, devoid of emotion. "You approach her again and I'll have your badge."

The color drains from Henry's face, but he quickly plasters on a fake smile.

"I bumped into her. It was nothing more than a coincidence."

The skepticism in Drew's gruff exhale matches my internal eye roll.

"Don't act like we're stupid. You come near her again, whether it's under the pretense of being worried about me or not, and you'll see just how difficult things can get for you."

"Oof, there's that bite." Henry smirks, but I know I've hit a nerve by the way he's glancing around the room to make sure no one else can overhear.

I wait for his eyes to return to mine. "Are we clear?"

"Loud and clear, Handler."

The way he says my nickname makes cold goose-bumps scatter up my spine. I nod at Drew to indicate we're done, but Henry's words stop me.

"You know he'll let you down."

He doesn't look at Drew while he's bad-mouthing him. His eyes are trained on my face and reaction. I refuse to give him one.

"You'd know all about the ingredients for a happy relationship, wouldn't you?" Drew snipes before turning to me. "You ready?"

I nod and move to stand, but Henry grabs my wrist across the table. His hand makes contact for less than a second before Drew's fist closes over it.

"Touch her again and you'll lose your hand."

I look between the two men and my heart clench-es at what Drew had to endure growing up. I know their relationship has completely broken since I came along. But even before, it was never a loving par-ent-child one as it should have been.

I slide my hand onto Drew's thigh underneath the table and squeeze. He wraps my fingers inside his, stroking my pulse point with his thumb.

"He'll let you down," Henry repeats, stupidly ignor-ing the tense energy radiating around our table. "Look, I'm sorry I spoke to your client. I overstepped."

"You think?" I arch a brow.

Henry's lips purse. "But someone needs to think about the baby."

Drew's legs tenses to the point that it's like resting my hand against granite.

"You're working long hours on this case. You've been followed, threatened. You could be in real dan-ger. I just want what's best for you." Henry looks at me with what appears to be genuine concern in his eyes, but I don't buy it for one second.

"Right," I mutter.

"I just want what's best for you," he says again, not even looking at Drew as he adds, "And my son is not it."

"I'm sitting right here," Drew growls, but Henry ig-nores him.

"You know I was overlooked for promotion for years because of that joyriding stunt he pulled. I could have made it to Chief Inspector by now. You might believe in him, but he'll let you down, and you'll pay the price, just like I did."

Drew's hand tightens around mine beneath the table. "We're leaving," he hisses.

"It's not too late, Soph," Henry continues. "You've been stressed at work, not thinking clearly. It's time to stop this nonsense now and come back to me."

"You want me to forgive you?" I scoff. "You're married and have been lying to everyone."

Henry lowers his voice. "Look, I'll forgive you for sleeping with my son. We can leave this all behind us." He sneers at Drew. "It's okay, you don't have to call her stepmum when she marries me."

Drew's chair crashes to the floor as he hauls Henry to his feet by his collar. There are a few collective gasps around the room as people stare.

"Enough!" I snap at Henry, standing and grabbing my purse.

Drew's jaw clenches as they glare at one another. I wrap a hand around his bicep and he drops Henry.

Henry rubs his throat, wincing.

"I will never be coming back to you. Accept it," I say.

"Then maybe I'll be seeing you both in court. You can't ignore me and play happy families when that's my baby you're carrying."

I step closer to him, dropping my voice so the few people who are still staring at us can't hear.

"We wanted to be mature about this. But if that's how you want to play it, then I guess we *will be seeing* you in court. But mark my words. I will wipe the floor with you should you try to do anything that isn't the best possible thing for my *babies*. You know I never lose, Henry. And I won't start for you."

I turn to Drew, who's standing like a giant force of aggression, ready to unleash at the slightest thing, and I sink underneath his arm as he holds it out for me. I curl into his side, inhaling honey and smoked wood. My favorite scent in the world.

"You'll regret it," Henry says to our backs as we walk away.

# Chapter 33
# Sophie

"How are you feeling about today?"

"Great." I smile at Halliday through the phone screen as I fix another pin into my hair.

"You look like a bad-ass bitch already. Send me a picture once you get the wig and gown on."

I laugh as I grab my hairspray and mist my hair.

"I'm glad you think so. Because that's exactly what I'm going to be today. A bad-ass bitch that wins the case."

It's the final day of the trial. Both the defense and I are delivering our closing statements today. And as much as I don't want to jinx anything by being smug, there's no way the jury's going to let this guy off. The past week in court and all the evidence I've presented, and the arguments I've made, have sealed his fate. He's guilty and deserves punishment for what he's done. The judge we have isn't known for her leniency, a reputation I'm counting on her upholding when she reads out the sentencing.

"Those babies don't know how lucky they are to have such an incredible mum."

"Thank you." My hand automatically drops to my stomach.

"And an awesome Daddy. Are those irises I see?"

I look over my shoulder at the large bouquet on the counter behind me.

"They are. Drew gave them to me this morning before he left for work."

I can't help my smile. He's been incredible this week, wishing me luck, taking on all the paperwork for the new house himself, cooking for me when I'm getting home late, exhausted, but still running on the adrenaline that a day in court brings me.

"And what about...?" Even Halliday doesn't want to say his name, like it's a bad omen.

I roll my shoulders to ease the tension.

"He's been texting me every day. Apologizing about interfering with the case. I think he realized I wasn't bluffing and could report him. The fact he thought he could get away with it... He's a Detective Inspector. I don't know what the hell he was thinking."

"That's exactly why he thought he could get away with it. He probably thinks he's above the law because he's the one enforcing it."

"Yeah, well. Cops aren't above anything. You know the other guy who was named? The councilor?"

"Yeah."

"His brother is a Chief Superintendent. It's suspicious, even if the brother has supposedly checked out clean."

"I saw that. Do you wish you were prosecuting in his case too?"

I pick up my nude lipstick and put it on. "No. I know whoever gets it at work will do a good job. And it could still be a while until it goes to court."

"And you'll have two babies in your arms by then, and an Auntie Halliday coming over daily for snuggles." She beams. "Can you believe you're about to go on maternity leave?"

I look down my body, unable to see my feet. I've still got eight weeks to go, but my stomach sticks out quite far now. And I need to pee every hour. The perks of having not one but two babies squashing my bladder.

"I know. Crazy. I hope you make it back soon so we can spend some time together. Violet and Maddy gave me a gift certificate for a pregnancy massage at a spa nearby. We could make a day of it?"

"That sounds amazing. I'm coming back soon, I promise. And I'm so relieved for you that they're being cool about it. Women are the stronger sex."

"They've been amazing. I think it'll take a while before Violet and I are doing lunch or anything like that. But she's excited to be a Grandma, and Drew said that since she cut all contact with Henry, she's seemed much happier."

"That's what you need to do. Can you change your number if he's texting you every day?"

I shake my head. "I could. But he'd just get the new one somehow. Plus, I didn't want to get nasty. I was hoping we could be grown-ups about this. But I don't think that's going to happen. I could handle the daily apology texts, but this morning he sent me one telling me how I should be with him. And that he still loves me. It's suffocating."

"Restraining order?" Halliday jokes, her eyes twinkling.

Despite the situation, my lips twitch. "Maybe."

"So hear me out." She turns from the screen and picks something up. "I picked a card for you this morning." She holds up an intricately decorated card with the image of a man lying face down with multiple swords in his back.

"Gruesome."

"It symbolizes painful endings and betrayal."

"Give me the bad news, why don't you?" I laugh.

"No, this is a good thing. It's symbolic of the end of your relationship with Henry. Even though it ended months ago, it's been following you around, trying to keep you trapped in the past. This is the sign that it's all about to come to an end. The darkest hour is the one before dawn."

"Okay," I say, unconvincingly.

"Trust me." Halliday smiles serenely. "The universe has spoken. You'll be given a way out, something to bring peace and end turmoil. Don't miss that sign when you're shown it. Use it. Promise me?"

I return her smile, feeling anything but peaceful as my thoughts flash to Henry. "I promise."

"Good. Now go win another case. Love you."

She blows me a kiss and then is gone. I pick up my purse and head to the front door. As I'm closing it, my phone rings and warmth blooms in my chest at the sight of Drew's name.

"Hey."

"Hey, Boss."

"You want to put me on Bluetooth and chat while you drive to work?" he asks.

"Sure, sounds perfect."

The air in the courtroom is thick with anticipation as the jurors are led back in.

I slide my gaze over the twelve of them as they take their places. After we delivered our closing statements, the judge gave her summary, and they were invited to retire until they reached a unanimous verdict.

It took them three hours.

If he'd plead guilty, he would have been sentenced by now and enjoying His Majesty's comforts. But because he didn't, and he claims Chelsea consented to staying with him for that forty-eight-hour period, here we are.

I avoid looking at the defendant, a mousy-haired guy who looks like a regular Joe you'd see on the bus.

They don't have it stamped on their foreheads. The devils walk amongst us.

I keep my eyes on the judge as I wait for her to address the foreperson of the jury.

They have to find him guilty. *Please.*

Chelsea caught my eye yesterday as she was escorted back to the witness room by the court usher. She was offered the option of giving her evidence by video link so she didn't have to be in the room with the man who assaulted her. But she declined. She said she wanted to look him in the eye when he was made to face what he did.

I'm so proud of how strong she is.

Court cases are harrowing, but she's stayed calm the entire week, even though I know some of the accusations he threw back her way—and the lewd suggestions he made about how she was flaunting herself in her social media pictures and turned up to meet him wearing a short skirt—must have been hard to stomach.

Unlucky for him, I cut that shit right down the second it started. No matter how a woman chooses to dress, it doesn't give creeps like him the right to do anything they want.

Adrenaline pumps through my veins as the judge speaks.

"On the count of false imprisonment, have you reached a unanimous verdict?"

The foreperson of the jury, assigned to speak for them all, nods his head, his eyes set on the judge behind his thick-rimmed glasses.

"We have, Your Honor."

"And do you find the defendant guilty or not guilty?"

"Guilty."

Tingles scatter over the backs of my arms beneath my gown and I take a slow breath.

"And on the count of rape, do you find the defendant guilty or not guilty?"

"Guilty."

*Guilty.*

Euphoria races through my body like electricity through a circuit. Behind me the sounds of Chelsea's family crying fills the air.

We did it.

Another case won.

# Chapter 34
# Drew

"How's Sophie?" Mum asks.

I crane my neck, looking down the hallway toward the bedroom to check Sophie hasn't woken from her nap.

"She's... tired," I say, pushing my finger and thumb into my dry eyes and rubbing.

"Well, she doesn't have long to go now. Her body will be getting ready. Although, toward the end with you and Maddy, I couldn't sleep at all. Pregnancy insomnia."

"Oh?"

Mum must think I'm just tired because she says goodbye after telling me to take care of Sophie, and then she's gone.

I wish that's all it was. But the truth is Sophie hasn't been the same since the trial ended last week. The guy got ten years, and she blames herself that he didn't get longer. She told me she can feel deflated after a case.

Because even though she wins, it doesn't feel like a victory.

She assured me she's fine. But she's sleeping more and is quieter than usual. The mental and physical strain must catch up with her after months working on something so in depth. I wish I knew how to help her.

I told Tanner I needed some time out of the office, so I've spent the past few days at Sophie's apartment, working from the sofa and getting everything set for the completion of the house sale. We should get the keys any day. I hope it brings a smile back to my beautiful girl's face.

"Drew?" Sophie's sleepy voice floats out of her bedroom.

I abandon the baby name book I was reading and jog into her room.

"You okay, Boss?"

She yawns, her blonde hair splayed over the pillow as she pats the top of the bedding beside her.

"Come, lie with me?" Her sleepy eyes have regained some of the brightness they've been missing.

I grab the back of my T-shirt and haul it up over my head, throwing it to one side, followed by my jeans, eager at the chance to hold her close.

I climb into bed behind her, pulling her flush to my chest.

"Good sleep?" I press a kiss to her bare shoulder where the strap of her camisole has slipped free.

"Mmm," she murmurs. "Who were you talking to?"

"Mum. She called to see how you are."

"That's nice of her. Did you tell her the babies are doing acrobatics with my internal organs?"

I chuckle as I kiss her shoulder again. The babies have been really active recently. Sophie's whole stomach moves in a wave when they're fidgeting in there.

"They're just trying to work out who's the boss."

"I think the girl," Sophie muses. "She'll have her brother wrapped around her little finger."

"She'll have us all wrapped around it." I bury my face into her neck and smile against her skin as I place my hand over her bump, and it moves beneath my palm.

The two of us fall silent, concentrating on the babies' movements until they stop.

"I'm sorry I've not been myself," she whispers. "I push all my emotions aside so I can do my job. And sometimes afterward, they all hit me at once. I'll be back to normal tomorrow."

I stroke her bump, kissing along the top of her shoulder gently.

"Don't ever apologize. If you want to stay in bed, I'll tuck you in. If you want to cry, I'll dry your tears. If you need me to go out and buy a dumper truck of rum and raisin ice cream for you to swim in, I'll do it. Whatever you need."

She laughs softly, making my heart expand behind my ribs.

"I love you so much. I'd do anything for you," I confess.

She turns her head to the side until her lips graze mine.

"You know what would make me feel better?" she whispers against my mouth before she kisses me slowly, teasing me with her tongue.

My eager dick springs to life in my boxers.

"Whatever it is, consider it done," I murmur as I nip her bottom lip and deepen our kiss.

She moans into my mouth before breaking our kiss. "I want you," she says through flushed lips.

I gaze into her emerald eyes, shining with need. I know this is less about the sex right now for her and more about the connection. That need to anchor herself to the real world again and come back to it. Come back to me.

"You don't have to ask. You never have to ask."

I slide my hand down over her bump and dip it inside her panties. My fingers are instantly coated in slick arousal.

"You're wet already. What were you dreaming about?"

"Just take them off." She blinks at me. Her desperation for comfort makes her voice rasp.

It's like a hot poker through my chest seeing her like this.

"Anything you want. You just tell me," I murmur against her lips as I help her wriggle her panties past her hips before pushing them all the way down her legs so she can kick them off.

I reach back between her legs, and she arches against me with a small gasp the second my fingers brush her swollen clit.

I murmur against her neck, "I'll never get enough of you."

"Get inside me, Drew," she pants, grinding back against my cock. "Please."

I pull my boxers off and position myself further down the bed so I can slide up inside her in one smooth stroke. I bury my face into her neck and inhale the scent of her shampoo as her pussy spreads around me, welcoming me inside and gripping my dick. "Sophie," I breathe out in wonder.

From my position behind her like this, I'm being squeezed even tighter where her thighs are pressed together.

"Talk to me," she begs as her body shivers inside my arms. "I need to hear your voice. Say anything."

Where her neediness makes my heart ache, it also makes my dick swell and my balls draw up to my body, primed and loaded, knowing she needs me as much as I need her.

"Anything?" I kiss and suck her neck, rolling my hips, fucking her nice and slow.

"Something dirty... Anything," she moans, wetness encasing my dick as she clenches around it. "I love your voice."

"You know what I love?"

"What?"

I stroke her hair, gathering it up inside my fist gently as I hold her bump with my other hand.

"The way you look and feel full of our babies. You're so fucking sexy like this."

She moans as I suck harder on the delicate skin beneath her ear and stroke her bump. I pull almost all of the way out of her and then sink back in deep.

"I think I'm going to have to keep you full of our babies all the time. What do you think?"

Her response is a breathy moan.

"You okay with that?" I grit, my balls heavy with the need to spill inside her. "You okay if I keep fucking you so you're pregnant for me?"

"Drew." Her moans turn to a gasp as I trail my fingers down to rub her clit.

"That a yes?"

She shudders, a small yelp hitting at the same time her pussy works itself tighter around my dick.

"You think you can handle being full of my cum all the time?" I rub her clit in deliberate circles as she tenses inside my arms. I press my lips to her ear and growl. "Think you can handle all the times I'll make you come before I fuck you so full of me that my cum's dripping out of this perfect pussy whenever you move?"

"More," she urges in a husky voice.

I groan at the way she grinds back onto me, so greedy for a release... a distraction.

I'll give her whatever she needs.

I lower my voice to a rasp as I nip her earlobe between my teeth and continue driving into her tight, wet heat.

"I fucking love knowing you've still got a part of me inside you long after we finish. Because I push that shit deep, don't I, Mama?"

She squirms against my chest.

"I push it deep," I repeat. "Right in there. Just the way you like it. Deep inside your pretty cun—"

"Drew..."

I grin against her neck as she cries out and comes in a rush, soaking my cock with a gush.

Her hand drops to mine, still teasing her clit. She tries to ease me off her but I nudge her fingers away and slap her clit lightly. She whimpers and her pussy spasms, strangling my cock.

"Mmm," I growl. "Someone's feeling sensitive. How many do you think you've got for me?"

She trembles inside my arms and I switch the angle I'm thrusting at, picking up the pace. She needs this. It's obvious she doesn't want to think right now. And if me making her feel better by worshipping her body helps, I'll do it all day and all night.

I coax another orgasm from her easily, groaning into her neck as my dick slides in and out of her with ease, slick with her release.

"Drew?" Her tone is almost pleading.

"Yes?"

"I need you to know how much..." she pants as she pulsates around me.

"How much what?" I grit my teeth as heaviness builds in my balls and the head of my cock throbs inside her. I can feel her orgasm. Feel the way her cunt clamps around me, every muscle inside her milking my dick as she moans my name.

"How much what?" I choke, increasing my pace as her arousal runs out of her and coats my balls.

"How much I love you," she cries as the rim on the head of my cock drags over her G-spot and makes her orgasm gain momentum once more. "And I need you," she sobs. "I need you."

Her third orgasm rips through her violently, sending her shuddering and sobbing in my arms.

I bury my face into her neck, her words undoing me. My cock explodes, firing out liquid heat inside her as I bury myself to the hilt so I can mark her as deep inside as possible.

"Sophie," I groan.

I rip my hand away from her clit and grasp her throat with my wet fingers, turning her face so I can press a searing kiss against her mouth as my cock continues to fill her.

"You've got me, Darling. I swear on my life I'll never let you down."

She sobs as she kisses me back. "Promise me."

I'm painfully aware of how strong my beautiful warrior is. But her strength is only a part of her. She wears it like a shield. An armor to protect the beautiful soul inside her that is just as susceptible to heartbreak as anyone else.

Only her showing me this part of her doesn't weaken her. It makes her stronger.

It makes *us* stronger.

Because I mean every word.

"I promise." I kiss her back with a passion that makes the blood in my veins heat like liquid fire. "There's nothing in this world that would ever stop me from loving you."

Tears run down her cheeks as she kisses me back and the final surges from my dick subside until all that's left is a warm feeling of complete relaxation washing through them.

She twists her body, and my cock slips free, releasing a warm gush over the two of us as she turns to face me.

I breathe in the air that she exhales as she looks into my eyes.

"Promise me we'll always make it back to each other if we're ever apart."

Worried emerald eyes blink up at me, making my heart skip a beat. I stroke her tear-stained cheek with the pad of my thumb. I've never known her to show her vulnerability like this before. Finishing the trial has hit her hard.

Her eyes pinch at the corners as if she's scared to admit something. "I have this feeling," she whispers. "I can't explain it. But I get them in my gut, and... it sounds stupid..."

"Sophie," I murmur, resting my forehead against hers, "I waited four years for you. I'm never letting you go. We're going to be together always. You, me, and our babies, okay? Us."

She searches my eyes, uncertainty tinting hers. I'd do anything to ease the turmoil dancing inside them.

"I promise." I kiss her forehead. "You can trust me. I'll never hurt you. We'll never be apart."

# Chapter 35

# Sophie

"ARE YOU HOLDING THEM right now?" Halliday's voice squeals through the car's Bluetooth speakers.

"I am." I dangle the shiny new house keys from one finger as I glance over at Drew, who's driving.

He flashes me a bright smile before his perfect teeth sink into his lower lip.

I know that look on his face. He's as excited as I am, maybe more so. He asked if we could drop by his mum's house on the way. I think he secretly can't wait to tell her and Maddy that we've got the keys. I love how close he is with them. I guess they're the ones who loved him growing up, the way he deserved, because Henry sure as hell didn't.

But I don't want to think about him. Today is a happy day. One for celebrating.

"Oh God, you have to video call me later so you can give me a tour. And I need to know what you're using each room for. It'll help me when I'm choosing crystals for them."

Drew's lips curl into a smile as he keeps his eyes on the road. I slide my hand up around the nape of his neck and stroke his dark curls of hair.

"I will. But you can see for yourself when we have the housewarming party."

"Wouldn't miss it," she chirps.

We say goodbye, and I purposefully don't ask her about her client. She gets wound up whenever the name Sterling Beaufort is mentioned. He's proving to be her toughest client to date. She swears he wants to be alone for the rest of his life, but his daughter, who hired Halliday, insists that love is exactly what he needs in his life. Halliday is stubborn. She won't leave New York until she's successfully completed her matchmaking. Her success rate is as good as mine is.

My thoughts flick to Chelsea as I look out the car window.

"You okay, Boss?"

Drew's deep voice brings a soft smile to my face. He has this way of knowing when I'm overthinking.

"You did your best, Sophie. She knows that. She's not looking back anymore, only forward."

"Yeah, I know."

Chelsea has moved on since the trial ended. As much as anyone can, anyway. I've spoken to her, and she's sounded positive and excited to meet her daughter. Her family even sent flowers to the office for me.

*Irises.* I thought they were from Drew. But I remember telling Chelsea once that they're my favorite.

She's grateful for all that I did for her. Even if every day I question whether or not it was enough.

"This won't take long." Drew grins as he kills the engine on the driveway of his mum's house.

The first time I came here, everywhere I looked, I saw Henry. The front door knob he would have touched every day. The mugs he would have drunk from. The table he would have sat at to eat. I hated it. Hated knowing that I played a part in ruining the home he was once a part of.

But each time I've visited since, it's gotten easier. Violet's smiles when she sees me now are genuine. Drew insists she's never been happier than since she kicked Henry out. It's like she's finally living the way she wants to. And she always coos over my bump and her grandbabies, as she calls them, fussing over me, making sure I drink enough water. Now I understand where Drew gets his caring nature from.

He jumps from the car and jogs around to open my door. I slide from the seat, my bump pressing against my thighs as I step out.

"Beautiful," Drew rasps as he takes me in.

I smile as he wraps a hand around where I once had a waist and walks us to the front door.

"Did you leave your panties off like I asked you to?" he whispers in my ear as he presses the doorbell.

"Uh-huh." I bite my lower lip. "Check your jacket pocket."

His throat thickens as he slides his hand inside his jacket.

His nostrils flare. "Fuck, Sophie," he hisses. "You want me to cum in my pants?"

I snort out a giggle.

He bites the inside of his cheek as his hand slides over my ass and squeezes.

"You. Me. Our new hallway the second we get there." He stares straight ahead, his jaw tense despite the smile playing on his lips.

"Sounds good," I murmur as the door opens.

Maddy grins at us brightly, giving Drew a brief hello before she sweeps me into her arms and leads me toward the back of the house. She manages to ask me three questions about the babies, recommend a hypnobirthing show I should watch, and tell me about a book that she's seen about babies' cognitive development, all in the space of the fifteen seconds it takes us to reach the kitchen.

Violet's in there when we arrive, and she holds a hand in the air as she fiddles with a new coffee maker on the counter.

"It has decaf pods, Sophie. If I can just figure out how to make the blasted thing work."

She frowns at it, fiddling with the controls before Drew walks past me and Maddy and presses a button, making a green light illuminate on the display panel.

"Ah! Perfect. Thank you." She smiles and pats Drew on the arm.

He leans back against the counter, his lips curling as he watches his mum and sister fuss around the kitchen, making us all a drink. To anyone else, we'd look like a regular happy family.

And I guess we are, as long as no one brings up Henry.

"Look what we got for the babies." Maddy bounces on her toes, holding up two romper suits. One says 'Little Man' on it, and the other, 'Little Lady'. "They're going to look so cute," she gushes.

Violet encourages me to sit at the kitchen table and hands me a coffee. I thank her as I blow off the steam, watching Drew over the rim of the mug. His face lights up as he takes the rompers from Maddy and looks at them both.

"Thank you," I say, catching both of the women's eyes.

They both smile back at me and I relax into my seat, feeling content for the first time since the trial ended. Today's a new start. We're going to spend the night in the new house once the moving company have taken all Drew's furniture over. I'm going to leave most of mine in my apartment for when it's rented out.

"What's the news you wouldn't tell us on the phone, then?" Maddy probes.

Drew places the rompers on the table and glances at me. I nod in encouragement.

"The sale completed on the house." He grins. "We're moving in today."

"Oh, that's wonderful," Violet says.

Maddy presses her hands together in front of her chest. "Never thought I'd see the day my brother convinced a girl to live with him."

"Hey." He wrinkles his brow at her, a smile playing on his lips.

Maddy goes to say something else but stops as the sound of movement near the front door carries down the hallway.

Drew's eyes darken as he looks at his mum. "He still has a key?"

Violet's lips thin. "We're still married. I can't stop him. I'm lucky he agreed to move out. He could have insisted on staying here until the divorce is finalized."

"Mum," Drew grits, the muscles in his neck going taut, "I told you I'd buy his share of the house for you. We can get his name off it. Just give me the word."

Violet shakes her head. "I won't hear of it. You have the babies to think of and your own things to pay for."

"I've got the money," Drew presses, his eyes intent on her face. But she holds his eyes, refusing to back down.

"Me and Logan offered too," Maddy says. "She won't listen."

The front door slams and footsteps move down the hall.

Drew curses under his breath, his eyes going to the ceiling. Then he moves across the room and stands protectively by the side of my chair.

"You okay?" he whispers.

The corded muscles in his forearms flex as he curls one hand around the back of my chair.

I look up at him, my stomach knotting as the air in the room gets heavy.

I give him what I hope is a reassuring smile. His eyes pinch around the edges as he looks at me, then his attention is snapped away to Henry, who's standing in the kitchen doorway.

"Not interrupting, am I?" Henry says, a lightness in his voice that is a striking contrast to the somber expressions on everyone else's faces.

His gaze fixes straight on me and he rolls his lips as he takes in my bump. It's bigger than when he last saw me. I straighten my spine, steeling myself for whatever comment he's about to make. But instead he walks over to the new coffee machine and places a mug beneath it.

"Don't mind, do you?" he says to Violet, who sighs as she moves away from the machine.

"Fancy," he comments as he makes himself a cup.

The rest of us watch in tense silence until he turns around with the mug in his hand, smiling brightly.

"More baby shopping?" He chuckles as he looks at the rompers on the table.

Drew's fist tightens on the back of my chair as Henry moves closer to look. He inspects the rompers, then his eyes slide to meet mine.

"There's a boy and a girl?"

"There is," I reply.

He holds my gaze until the hairs on the back of my neck prick up with unease.

"You don't live here anymore," Drew says.

Henry finally breaks eye contact with me.

"Neither do you. Yet here you are," Henry counters, smiling at Drew like they're chatting about the weather.

Drew tenses next to me as Henry wanders over to a pile of mail on the counter.

"These mine?"

Violet nods.

The four of us watch as he places his mug down and leans back against the counter, crossing his legs at the ankle as he opens the first envelope slowly.

"Take them with you and leave," Drew hisses.

Henry looks up and the two of them glare at each other for a few excruciating seconds.

"Actually, Dad. Maybe you could give me a lift to work?" Maddy cuts in. "Logan was coming to get me, but he'll be in a meeting for another hour."

Henry looks at Maddy and his eyes soften. "Sure, love."

Maddy grabs her purse, giving Violet a kiss and then walking over to him, giving me and Drew an apologetic glance.

Henry gathers up the remaining mail and takes another sip of his coffee, his eyes narrowing as he looks back at me and then Drew.

He leans back against the counter again like he's in no rush to leave.

My stomach sinks.

"How's the New York project going, Son?" he asks casually, his attention zeroing in on Drew.

I'm the only one who detects the low growl in Drew's chest before he speaks.

"It's finished. I won't be going back there for a while. I'm going to spend Sophie's maternity leave with her. Now that we've got our new house keys, we need to get it ready before the babies arrive."

He arches one dark brow, a challenge in his eyes as he delivers the news. Although, I suspect Henry already knew about the house, because he doesn't so much as flinch.

Instead, he smiles, making something sour curl in my gut. He's not bothered like I thought he would be. It's unnerving how calm he is.

"Ah. That'll be why you weren't there when I called looking for you."

"You never call me at work," Drew states, suspicion lacing his tone.

"I'm glad I did though, Son. Had an interesting chat with the girl who answered the call."

Henry fixes his eyes on Drew's and the tension builds in the room until it's palpable.

*What the hell's going on?*

"Really?" Drew grits.

"You didn't tell me Alicia had left?" Henry continues to stare at Drew. "She was such a nice girl. I thought you and her were going to get married at one point. She said as much to me herself when I met her."

"Then you were both wrong, weren't you?" Drew grits.

"Pretty too," Henry continues. "Don't you think?"

The name Alicia is familiar. *Drew's ex.* The one he dated. The one he admitted he moved in with when he lived in New York.

My gut churns as though I might throw up. There's a reason Henry's bringing her up.

"Drew?" I look at him in question, but he grits his teeth and doesn't meet my eyes.

Henry chuckles, enjoying the suffocating atmosphere.

"Dad!" Maddy snaps as Violet watches him with an uneasy expression.

"You know, it's funny how rumors start in offices," Henry muses, taking another sip of coffee. "When I told the girl I spoke to I was your father and knew Alicia, she asked if I'd heard from her since the 'incident'. She hoped that Alicia wasn't embarrassed about what happened and that it wasn't the reason she left."

Drew's grip tightens on the chair so much that the wood's in danger of splintering.

"Don't," he spits. "Don't you fucking dare go there."

His reaction only seems to spur Henry on, who waves a hand dismissively in the air.

"Why? It's all innocent. I told her she must have it wrong. That you couldn't have possibly been seen waving Alicia off from your hotel. Not with wet hair like you'd just showered."

"Drew?" I utter, looking up at him as my heart begins to race in my chest, things slotting into place with each painful beat.

"It wasn't like that," he murmurs, barely meeting my eyes for a second before he's glaring back at Henry again.

"Then what was it like?" I whisper, my throat tightening and going instantly dry.

"Sophie," he whispers, finally looking at me, something heavy in his eyes that makes my heart stall in my chest.

"What was it like, Drew?" I croak as I search his eyes for the man I know. The man who would never lie to me. Who promised me it was *Us*. Communication. Honesty.

"According to the gossip circulating around the New York office, Alicia was there sucking your dick, wasn't she, Son?"

Violet and Maddy gasp.

Henry delivers the blow. But it's the lack of denial shining back at me in Drew's eyes that hits me like a sledgehammer.

All the air leaves my lungs.

"Drew?"

Sickness claws at the back of my throat until I force it back down with a thick swallow.

"That's ridiculous." Violet scoffs.

"Dad, stop," Maddy urges.

My eyes are fixed on Drew's. Fixed on the pain flashing beneath the crystal blue as he looks back at me. It's like he always knew this day was coming, but hoped if he ignored it, then it might forget us, sidestep around us, or get lost on the way.

But denial is pointless when faced with the inevitable.

"Tell us," Henry says, his voice calm despite the destruction it's unleashing. "Tell us her lips didn't touch your dick."

"Hank!" Violet snaps. "That's enough!"

Halliday's card flashes in front of my eyes. A body with swords in its back.

*Painful endings and betrayal. A way out.*

But this isn't the one I expected.

I stare at Drew, ignoring everyone else.

"Drew? Tell me—"

"I can't." His voice cracks. "I'm so sorry, Sophie. If I tell you that she didn't, then it would be a lie."

I jerk my head back as dizziness blows through it.

"What?" I grip onto the tabletop for support.

"But it wasn't like that, I swear."

Drew drops to his knees in front of me, imploring me with panicked eyes to listen to him. But all I can hear is blood whooshing in my ears.

Movement in my stomach makes my breath falter, and I rest my hand over my bump on instinct.

"What *was* it like?" I ask, my voice echoing in my ears.

Drew pushes both hands back through his hair, his eyes wild, like those of a man who is about to lose everything he cares about, knowing he can't do anything to stop it.

"She came to my room. She was dressed in lingerie. But—"

"How did her lips attach themselves to your dick?" I cry, my anger piercing the air and making my ears pop until every sound in the room is suddenly screeching in my ears.

The sound of Violet's gasp and Maddy's soft murmur of "God" drown out Henry's leisurely slurp of his coffee.

Drew watches me breaking in front of him. Because for the first time in my life, I can't hide my emotions. I can't push them down deep and get on with my job.

This is my life.

These are my babies.

The gaping, bloody hole in my chest was my heart.

"Sophie," he pleads.

I shake my head, forcing out the words, wincing as I say them, even though the situation suggests that they're true.

"You're just like him," I whisper.

Drew's eyes widen. "You don't mean that. Please. You don't fucking mean that."

My mouth parts on a muffled gasp as I stare back into his eyes.

I wish it could be any other way. I'm not sure anything has ever hurt so much. It's like a weight is crushing down on my chest, making it hard to breathe.

I take in a shuddery breath, willing myself to hold it together until I can get out of here and far away from him to think. I screw my eyes shut, tears pricking at their corners.

"I guess it's in your blood. Being a liar... a cheat."

I open my eyes in time to see Drew blink away the tears in his lower lids.

"If that's what you want to think, Soph, then I guess it is."

I choke back a sob as he looks at me with nothing but soul-wrenching loss in his eyes.

Then he whispers loud enough that only I can hear, "I'm sorry, Mama. You deserve so much better."

I sniff, forcing back my tears.

"You're right." My voice shakes as I stand from my chair and place my hand over my stomach. Drew's gaze follows it, and he makes a garbled sound in the back of his throat, like a wounded animal. "*We* do deserve better," I say, taking in a deep breath. "We all do."

I resist the compelling urge to reach out and touch him. To comfort him, the way he has done for me when I've needed it.

Because how can I?

Not now.

Not after everything.

"Drew, how could you?" Maddy says in disgust.

He hangs his head in shame, making no attempt to get up from the floor as I step around him.

Violet meets my eyes, and she looks like she's about to cry.

"I need to go," I say around the giant sob growing in the back of my throat.

I ignore the gloating look on Henry's face as Violet nods kindly and steps forward, placing a hand on my upper back and rubbing it.

I move with her, out into the hallway, unable to look back. I'm not strong enough to witness the man I love breaking. Because despite what he's just said, I can't handle seeing him in pain.

"I'll drive you where you want to go, Sophie," Violet says softly.

I don't argue as I walk on shaking legs out of the house with her.

Leaving Drew behind.

# Chapter 36
# Drew

"Have you at least called her? Begged for forgiveness?" Maddy stomps back and forth across the carpet in front of my desk.

I lean back in my chair and allow my eyes to wander, staring out of the window at London sprawled out into the distance. I can see the roof of the hotel Tanner and I did a refurbishment in. The one where Logan had his launch party months ago.

The one where I saw Sophie again for the first time in years.

I've stared at the fucking thing every day since she left one week ago. The reminder is like a knife against my throat. I wish someone would press it in deeper, slice open the artery and let me bleed out.

Something.

Anything.

Just *please*, let it stop fucking hurting like this. The pressure in my chest has been keeping me up at night, drenched in sweat and gasping for air.

I'm dying painfully every hour without her.

"Drew?" Maddy snaps.

Her eyes are wide and she folds her arms waiting for an answer.

"I'm not going to beg."

She throws her arms wide, huffing in disgust. It's the same with both her and Mum. It's in their words, their eyes, their movements. Disgust and disappointment seeps from them whenever they're near me.

I could drown in it.

"You cheated on her. After everything that's happened. It's the worst possible thing you could have done."

I press my finger and thumb into my bloodshot eyes and rub until they sting. I don't correct her. Whether I cheated or not, Sophie's gone.

Her and our babies are gone.

Maddy wrinkles her nose at all the paperwork strewn across my desk. "Why are you here, working like it never even happened? Why aren't you in LA? Camping on her doorstep until she speaks to you?"

"That's more Dax's style." My lip curls into a humorless smirk as I recall him having to grovel to get Rose back last year.

"Well, do something." Maddy stamps her foot on the spot, anger bubbling up inside her and making her look like she's about to explode. "You aren't the only one who loses if she never comes back, you know? What about Mum? What about me? They're our family too."

"Sophie made her decision the second she stepped foot on that plane and went to her sister's place in LA."

"And you're just going to take it?" Maddy flops into the seat on the opposite side of my desk and rubs a hand over her lips, her eyelids blinking rapidly. "I don't get it. You love her. Go and fix this."

"Maddy." I exhale slowly, my chest sagging beneath my shirt and tie. "There is no fixing this. I promised Sophie I'd never lie to her. Another woman had my dick in her mouth. That's the truth."

She huffs and its laced with the familiar disgust again.

"So you're a cheat like Dad? Is that it? You inherited it from him just like Sophie said?" Concentration pinches her brow as she stares at me. "You told me Sophie knew about Dad and the donor?"

Heat prickles across the back of my neck.

"I did tell her."

"Then why did she say—?"

"I don't know, she probably forgot," I bark, slamming my palm down onto the table and making it vibrate.

Maddy shakes her head and gets to her feet. Her lunch break is almost over. She's spent every one in my office since Sophie left, trying to talk me into going to LA after her. The second day she brought a plane ticket with her. But I canceled it the moment she left.

Sophie won't come home.

I know that much.

"You know I love you." She scoops up her purse from the floor. "But right now I find it hard to look at you."

My jaw clenches until pain lances up through it, making my left eye twitch.

"I hope the blow job was worth it," she mutters as she walks out of my office and slams the door.

The whiskey burns a trail down my throat before sitting heavily in my stomach. I haven't eaten properly for days, so the extra warmth it leaves low in my gut soon begins to mutate into a welcoming ache.

I sneer at the feeling and then signal to the bartender for another as I drain my glass.

I poke my finger through the keyring on the dark glass of the bar and slowly draw circles, listening to the jangling of keys as they swirl around.

It's a light sound. Joyful, hopeful.

I draw my finger back and slam my flattened palm over the top of the bundle, cursing as the metal bites into my skin.

I'm living in the house of our dreams. Alone. I spent that first night after Sophie left, alone, staring at the window in the master bedroom. The window we christened, knowing the house would be ours one day.

Because destiny said so.

I nod my thanks at the bartender and throw back the fresh whiskey in one go, screwing my eyes up as it makes them water.

Screw destiny. Destiny's a little bitch that bites you on the ass when you're distracted.

I scowl at the keys. I shouldn't be in a bar after work, drinking alone. I should be in my new house, in bed with my pregnant fiancée.

The glass swirls in front of my eyes, along with the five friends it has lined up alongside it. Or is it six?

I look away in disgust, my head spinning as I scan the half empty bar. I could be drinking my sorrows in my yard with Tanner now that we live two streets apart. The only reason he isn't here now is because he thought I was going straight home tonight. He knows a desperate bastard when he sees one. No doubt he'll be at my door at six AM again tomorrow, claiming he needs a workout buddy to keep him accountable.

The only thing being accounted for is that I haven't decided to hang myself from the balcony.

But that would be stupid. It might bring the house value down. And seeing as I made a will after asking Sophie to marry me, leaving everything I own to her, it's the last thing I want.

I already cheapened our relationship when I admitted I let Alicia wet my dick with her mouth. I'm not going to cheapen this. Sophie deserves everything and more.

More than I can offer.

"Another," I grunt at the bartender, sliding the empty glass toward him. I overestimate and it shoots off the back of the bar, smashing loudly on the floor.

"I'll pay," I grumble.

But he shoots me a warning look and shakes his head.

"Fine," I mutter, grabbing a few notes from my wallet and dropping them onto the bar. "For the drinks and the glass."

I stumble to the side as I turn, holding one hand up in apology to the guy next to me that I knock into.

He gives me a curt nod, and I stagger out of the bar and into the night air.

My eyes drop to my wallet as I'm about to fold it and put it away, but the picture inside stops me.

"Fuck." I collapse back against the wall of the bar, allowing the rough surface of the bricks to scrape through my jacket and bite into my skin as I slump against it.

I pull the image out from behind the clear plastic panel and hold it up.

Two perfect white shapes on a black background.

I clasp a hand over my mouth, dropping my chin and blinking through bleary eyes at what my future should have been.

*Our babies.*

Two little miracles that only last week would move against my hand when I spoke to them as if they recognized my voice.

Two little miracles that are now thousands of miles away in another country.

"She won't talk to me, either."

I drag my head up from my chest and squint at the voice. Blood pounds in my temples, and rage simmers through it as I lock eyes with the last person I want to see right now.

"What do you want?"

"Same as you," my father says, rolling his lips as he saunters along the sidewalk toward me, looking me up and down. "I want Soph to come back."

"Sophie," I snap. "It's fucking *Sophie*. You never wondered why I always called her Sophie? Because that's what she wanted."

My father shrugs like he couldn't give a shit.

"You're a selfish prick," I spit, but then his words from a few seconds ago register through my whiskey-induced fog. "She won't talk to you either? Have you called her?"

My father purses his lips, looking off down the street. "Course I have. Haven't you?"

I sniff and slide the picture back into my wallet, stuffing it back into my pants pocket. "It's not what she wants."

"Fuck that, Son. What about what you want? Why aren't you telling her how it's going to be?"

I stare at him. "If this is some fucked up attempt at father-son bonding, then you're decades late."

He laughs humorlessly. "It's not. But she will come home. And if you're not going to try and make it be for you, then you're making my job a hell of a lot easier. Soph's a clever girl. She knows men wander. It's life. Nothing more than some different pussy to mix things up from time to time. It doesn't mean I can't look after her and make her happy."

Hatred oozes through every cell in my body as I square up to him.

"You're fucking deluded if you think she wants anything to do with you."

Sophie might not be with me anymore. But she sure as fuck doesn't want him either.

"I've got as much chance now as you have." He glares back at me. "We're both having a baby with her. And after you sharing your adventures last week, she knows we've both followed our dicks in the past."

"Except I didn't," I hiss. "Nothing happened, except Alicia trying and failing."

"Shame." My father smiles. "If you're going to get punished for the crime, at least have the fun of committing it. And I bet Alicia knows how to suck cock. I remember those lips of hers when you introduced us." He sucks in air through his teeth as he hums. "Not a patch on Soph's, though, eh?"

The satisfying crunch of bone beneath my fist sends adrenaline coursing through my veins like I've been hooked up to an IV of it.

My father staggers back, righting himself quickly as he clutches his jaw. He works his mouth open and closed a few times before spitting a mouthful of blood out onto the floor.

"Feel better?" he growls, his eyes scanning the sidewalk for witnesses.

There aren't any. And even if there were, I doubt he'd hit me back in front of them. He wouldn't risk his job at the expense of landing a shot on me in public.

I shake my throbbing knuckles, a sour smile spreading over my face.

"Yeah, actually. That's the best I've felt in seven fucking days. Thanks, *Dad*."

He grimaces. "Good. Hold on to that feeling. Because you'll need it to get you through when Soph comes back to me."

It takes all my strength not to give the other side of his face a matching bruise.

"Despite what you think, Son, I want you to be happy."

A disbelieving laugh erupts from my chest, making him scowl.

"It's true. You could have anyone. Just not her. She was mine first."

"She's not a fucking possession," I snap, my voice bouncing off the wall behind me. "The best thing you can do for her is get as far the fuck away from here as you can. So that if she wants to come back, she can."

My father looks at me without an ounce of understanding in his gaze.

He doesn't get it. He will *never* get it.

Defeat claws its way into me, making me slam back against the wall again for support.

"You'll never leave her alone, will you?" I narrow my eyes at him. "I'll warn her to keep away forever if I have to. If that's what it takes for her to be free of you. Because I know what it's like to love someone more than anything."

I slam a fist against my burning chest.

"I know what it's like for *three* other people to matter more to you than your own life. I could have loved all of them enough for both of us," I choke out. "I do love them all. More than you'll ever understand."

I shake my head, clarity dawning on me and making sourness coat my tongue as I stare at my father. He might as well be a stranger. Because when I look into his eyes, I see nothing that I recognize.

Not one damn thing.

Especially not the love Sophie and the babies deserve.

I step forward, bringing myself toe-to-toe with him until I'm staring down my nose at him.

"I won't let you hurt her. Whatever I have to do... Whatever it takes... I swear on my life you'll never hurt her again."

Then I shoulder past him and storm a wavy path away up the street.

# Chapter 37
## Sophie

"I FELT ONE." THERE'S a delighted squeal from my four-year-old niece, Summer, as she keeps her little fingers painted with blue glittery nail polish pressed against my bump.

"Here, Sydney." She takes her younger sister's hand and squishes it against my stomach, holding it in place until Sydney's eyes widen.

"Babies," she breathes before breaking into a delighted giggle.

"Yeah, babies," I repeat with a smile.

I can't help but feel a little better with the sweet distraction they've brought since I came to stay with Holly and Jay in LA. They're completely obsessed with all things baby, pushing their dollies around in little strollers and pretending to change their nappies. They've been fascinated with touching my bump every day and feeling for movement. And I'm thinking mine and Drew's babies are going to be attention seekers, because they've put on a performance each time, making my entire stomach roll in waves as they shuffle about.

Drew. The thought of him brings a lump to my throat. I haven't spoken to him since I left over a week ago. I can't bring myself to hear his voice, because I know I'd run back to him.

I love him.

It's as simple as that.

No matter what else is happening, I can't deny that I still love him with everything I have.

I press a kiss to each of my niece's little blonde heads as they snuggle either side of me on the sofa, still feeling all over my bump.

"Girls, Auntie Sophie might not want you climbing all over her all the time," Holly says as she comes into the room and surveys the scene.

"Are you kidding? Auntie Sophie loves it." I grin at Summer and Sydney and hold them closer. "I don't get to see you two nuggets very often. I want all the cuddles."

They beam, the perfect little blend of Holly and Jay in their little faces. Where Summer is the more commanding of the two, always looking after Sydney and instructing her on how to do things, Sydney makes up for it in her stubbornness. If she doesn't want to do something, she won't.

"I wonder what these two wrigglers I'm carrying will be like."

Holly sinks into the sofa opposite me, twisting her lips as she thinks.

"If they're like their mum, then they'll come out studying a textbook and laying down laws."

I smile. "Yeah, sounds about right."

"What if they're like their daddy?" Summer gazes up at me.

My heart squeezes painfully.

"Then they'll be strong and brave," I answer truthfully.

"Will the babies have blonde hair like us?" she asks.

"I don't know." I glance up as Jay comes into the room. He walks up behind the sofa Holly's sitting on and leans over the back of it, wrapping his arms around her neck and kissing her cheek.

"Okay, Berry?" he asks her.

She strokes his arm, and I look away before the pang of missing Drew and the way he would call me *Boss* or *Mama* becomes too great.

"These babies actually have different fathers, so they might look a little different to one another," I explain to Summer and Sydney as they listen raptly. "But they have the same Daddy, who loves them more than anything else. You remember Drew, who you spoke to on the phone before? He's their daddy."

"Drew's funny." Summer grins, probably thinking about how Drew used silly voices on our last call to make them laugh.

"Drew not here," Sydney says with a serious expression.

"No." I stroke her soft curls by her neck, my mouth going dry. "No, he stayed at home so I could come and visit you by myself."

Sydney pats my hand under hers. "It okay," she says, her lower lip poking out.

The gesture is enough to make me blink rapidly to fight back a surge of emotion.

"Do you think we can hear them?" Summer's blonde hair scatters over my stomach as she presses an ear to my stomach. Sydney copies her and the two of them sit in silence for a few seconds.

"I have a recording of their heartbeats, if you want to hear? Drew took it on his phone and sent it to me after their ultrasound."

"Yay." They both sit upright and Summer jumps down from the sofa, fetches my phone from the floor next to us and then hops back up and hands it to me.

I bring up the recording and both girls clasp their hands over their mouths, their eyes wide with joy as they listen to the first *thum-dum*, followed by the second, slightly faster one.

"The first one's the girl, it's faster," Holly says.

"Yeah. That's what the doctor said."

I let the recording play again, before turning it off.

"Can we listen again?" Summer asks.

"Later." Jay grins, walking over and scooping both girls up so one is dangling beneath each sun-kissed arm. "You two have a playdate to get to."

"Are you sure you don't want to come with us?" Holly looks at me with concern.

"I'm fine honestly. You don't need to worry about me. My colleagues are prepping Councilor Jenkins' case for trial now, and there's still lots of work to do around the handling of the missing statements."

"Yeah, I know." Holly frowns. "I guess they've got a better chance with you helping them."

I give her a small smile, but there's still tension pulling at her shoulders as she stands. I know she doesn't agree with my reasons for still working on the case. She doesn't agree with a lot of things that I've told her since I arrived on her doorstep, but I know she trusts my judgment.

"I'll be fine here alone," I add, trying to reassure her.

"We'll only be a couple of hours, and you've got our numbers." She looks at my bump, even though I'm still more than a few weeks away from my due date.

"I'll be fine," I repeat. "But I love that you worry."

She lifts her matching green eyes to mine and smiles. "Okay, fine. We'll bring you back ice-cream."

"Sounds amazing."

I'm an hour into my work when the chime signaling someone is at the front gates sounds out. I close my laptop and get up from the dining table where I've been working.

Jay and Holly's security system is state of the art, and if it weren't for Drew upgrading the system at both my apartment and his house a few weeks ago, then I might have trouble working it out.

But I don't. And as a result, dread coils its way around my throat, slowly constricting like a snake around its prey as I look at the screen, displaying the main gates.

I'm thousands of miles away.

But he came.

I expected that he would, but seeing him here still sets my mind reeling, despite thinking I was prepared.

Because nothing could have readied me for the way my heart clenches seeing him again.

I stop and take a deep breath before I jab the intercom button hard enough to make my fingertip sting.

"This is private property."

"Soph." The hopeless look in his eyes shines out and up into the camera as he looks directly into it. "Please, I just want to talk."

"There are things called phones for that."

I don't miss the way his lips quirk, and I hold my tongue from making another cutting remark. He likes my 'bite', as he keeps telling me. It's more than enough reason not to give it to him.

"You're wasting your time."

"Please," he repeats.

I gnaw on my bottom lip as I study him. He's in jeans and a shirt. No luggage with him. Which means he's already checked into a hotel. There's no way of knowing what size bag he packed and how long he plans on staying if I refuse to speak to him. He could keep coming back until I do.

He continues staring straight into the camera, knowing I can see him.

"Wait there," I huff, sliding my feet into my sandals and throwing on a jacket. I slide my phone into the pocket then I walk out, pulling the front door closed behind me.

It takes me a few minutes to reach where he's waiting at the end of the long driveway.

"Wow," Henry breathes as I approach in my sundress and jacket. "Soph, you look amazing."

I fight the impulse to try and fasten my jacket around myself. The zipper won't reach so it's pointless.

His eyes perform a hungry sweep over my breasts, which I'm struggling to keep from spilling out of all my clothes this past week. They seem to have taken on a life of their own.

"Why are you here?" I sigh, looking at him through the gaps in the metal gate.

He tips his head to one side. "Can we talk without the need for a barrier. You don't think I'll do something, do you?"

I shake my head as I decide the best approach to this. "No, I don't," I finally say.

I walk to a smaller gate off to one side and place my thumb against the scanner. A deep click sounds as it unlocks and I push through, meeting Henry on the other side.

"Soph—"

"We can walk on the beach if you want to talk," I say, before he can make any more comments about how well I look.

He's obviously choosing to ignore my puffy, red-rimmed eyes and lack of makeup. Whether that's out of politeness or lack of compassion about the reason I've spent a week crying, I can't say. Although with Henry, I'd guess the second.

He nods eagerly, falling into a gentle pace beside me.

"I don't know what you're doing here," I mutter as I lead him to the end of the block and then down a small walkway that goes to the ocean.

"I came to apologize for my son's behavior. I hate that he hurt you, Soph."

I press my lips together until my jaw aches.

How can I respond to that?

"Drew can talk for himself. Why are you really here?"

I kick off my sandals as we reach the sand and bend to pick them up. I always loved walking barefoot at the beach. There's something therapeutic about it. I've spent a lot of time out here this week.

Thinking.

Planning.

Remembering.

"Okay, okay," Henry murmurs as he walks next to me with his shoes still on. "I came because I missed you. And I want you to come home with me. I love you, Soph. Always have. We could be happy, you know that. Us and the babies."

I stop and turn to face him. The breeze blows some strands of hair into my eyes, so I brush them away so I can see him properly.

He waits as I study him. I remember looking so hard for similarities between him and Drew when I first found out who they were to each other. I convinced myself there were likenesses there. But as more time has passed and I've learned about each of them, I realize that they're as different from one another as they possibly can be.

The only thing that's the same is they both claim to be in love with me.

But despite both believing that to be true, only one of them truly understands the meaning of the word.

"What would you do if you were told that one of the babies needed something? Like bone marrow?"

"What?" Henry laughs, his brow creasing up in confusion.

"If one of the babies was really sick and—"

Henry scoffs and his laugh dies, but I continue.

"What would be the first thing on your mind?" I press as he stares at me.

"Soph? What's this all about? Is one of the babies sick? Which one?"

I exhale and shake my head. "It's just hypothetical. Forget it."

I start to walk again, tilting my head toward the sun and taking a deep, shaky breath in.

"I'll do anything for you. Come home, I'll prove it," he says as he walks beside me, his eyes glued to my face.

"If I do, will you let me live my life how I choose?"

"Of course, what sort of question is that?"

"Even if that means not being with you?"

He rubs his hand along the silver stubble on his jaw as he tries to force a smile.

"You really want to be with him after what he did to you? Fuck's sake, Soph. I thought you were smarter than that. You deserve better."

"Better like you? You cheated too, Henry."

"It's not the same. I love you," he says. "It's a hell of a lot different than getting your dick serviced by your secretary just because you felt like getting off."

I take a slow breath. We're going around in circles. Henry will never be able to admit who he is or what he's done. Not without making out he's the hero of the story.

"Listen, Soph. If you come home, we can be to-gether. The divorce will be completed soon. We can get married." His eyes drop to my left hand and the engagement ring Drew gave me that I'm still wearing. "We can move. It'll be a new start. I won't let you down this time, I swear. You're safe with me."

A thousand pins prickle their way up my spine as something clicks into place.

*Safe.*

"I'm... I'm not safe." I look at him with widened eyes as images of red paint and smashed glass pierce my thoughts. I can still remember the smell of the paint, cloying in the air as I breathed it in.

"I was followed. My car was trashed. It could get worse now that Councilor Jenkins' case is going to trial. I've been helping the office with it, but—"

"You're helping them?" Henry stops walking and takes hold of my upper arms, spinning me to face him. "You're supposed to be on maternity leave."

His fingertips dig into my flesh.

"I offered to help. It makes me feel better. Like I'm doing something. And maybe we'll find out who followed me. I'd feel safer. I might..." I bite my bottom lip, my heartrate accelerating. "I might feel better about coming back."

"Baby." Henry's face softens, his eyes twinkling as he pulls me into him. I let him hold me against him, his lips skating over my temple as he inhales, smelling my hair. "You don't need to worry about that. No one's after you."

I tilt my head back and blink up at him and his arms tighten around me.

"Someone wants to hurt me," I breathe. My voice cracks as he looks at me. Then he lifts a hand and places it over my bump, stroking his thumb over it and watching its path.

My breath stalls, my lungs on pause as his hand runs over the swell of my skin setting goosebumps following in its wake.

"I'm scared, Henry," I confess with a gulp.

"Soph," he murmurs. "There's nothing to be scared of. No one's after you."

"You're wrong."

"There's no one," he repeats, spreading his fingers out over the widest part of my stomach. His thumb brushes my belly button, and he smiles as he runs the pad over the small protruding bump.

I swallow around the giant lump wedged in my throat.

"You don't know that," I croak. My tongue suddenly seems too large and thick for my mouth.

"It was me."

He says it so simply, but instinct makes me rear back. He pulls me back to him gently, wrapping one hand around the back of my neck. Then he lowers his face toward mine.

"What do you mean?" I breathe, studying his eyes as he holds his face inches from mine. So close I can taste the hint of musk in his cologne.

"You question me over what I'd do if our baby was sick. But you don't ask what I'd do for you." He gazes at me, his eyes sweeping over my face and coming to rest on my parted lips.

"That was you?"

His pupils dilate as he continues stroking my bump.

"You've no idea the lengths I'd go to for you, Soph. I wanted you to be safe. I knew they were some dangerous men you were digging into with your case. They have friends in high places. I wanted you to be careful. To be watching out for yourself."

"So you made me think someone was following me? You trashed my car?"

He smiles at me, an arrogant smugness held in it. "Did it make you more cautious? Did you get extra security? Stop walking to your car alone at night when you left work in the dark?"

"Y-yes." I search his eyes for any sign that he thinks what he's telling me is fucked up. But there's none.

He tightens his grip on the back of my neck and rests his forehead against mine.

"Then it worked. I took care of you. I've always been taking care of you. Even when you haven't seen it."

"I..." I frown at him. "You did all that for me? Just so I would be more careful?"

"Of course." His eyes pinch as his breath fans over my lips. "You question how much I love you, Soph. But the truth is no-one can love you like I can. No-one."

For once, he's telling the truth. And hearing it unfurls something low in my gut, shining a light into the darkness I've been trapped inside since my heart was tore from me one week ago.

I recognize this light.

It's *hope*.

I lick my lips, but the wetness is dried immediately by Henry's warm breath flowing over them.

"You're right. No one does it like you. It's unconventional, but... romantic."

Pride bursts in his eyes as I gaze at him.

"You've always known no one does it like me." He chuckles softly.

"You're right. You're always one step ahead." I blink at him. "Do you think you can help me look into Jenkins? Find out what happened to the missing reports?"

His hand stalls its caressing of my bump and his jaw tenses. "Stop investigating that. You're not at work anymore."

There's an undercurrent of warning in his tone.

I straighten my shoulders and place my palms against his chest, toying with his collar between my fingertips.

"I know. And maybe it's nothing more than an oversight, and they were misplaced by accident. But please?" I gaze at him through my lashes. "I'll feel better about starting maternity leave if I help my team with that one small part of the case."

He looks between my eyes, his jaw set. His nostrils flare as he takes a measured breath in.

"If I help you, will you let me take you home? Start over? Give these babies a family? I can look after you all, Soph."

I choke at his words, my lower lip trembling.

These babies must be given everything they need. Be protected and cared for. Even if this isn't the way I thought it would happen.

I'll do whatever it takes to give it to my babies.

I look back at Henry as he studies me, willing my lips to work. But I can't seem to say the words out loud. He mumbles something and turns away.

"Henry?" I cry, my grip on his shirt tightening to bring his attention back to me. "Please."

"Let me take you home, Soph." His eyes hold mine with an intensity that has my heart stalling.

I nod, managing to force the words out. "I'll come home."

His eyes crinkle at the corners, and then in a flash, his lips slant over mine. I hide my wince as they make contact.

And I let him kiss me.

# Chapter 38
# Drew

"YOU LOOK WORSE TODAY, if that's possible," Tanner quips as he walks into my office and comes to a stop in front of my desk.

I drag my eyes away from the hotel that I've been staring at again—my own instrument of self-torture.

"Can always count on you to lift my spirits."

He snorts and thrusts his hands into his pant pockets.

"How long you going to blame yourself?"

"Until I'm dead ought to do it."

He sighs and pulls the chair opposite my desk out and drops into it. "At this rate, that won't be long."

"Scatter me in that lake at Dax's estate. The one with the lilies. The fish can chew on my dust."

"You're a real depressing, self-absorbed fucker, you know that?" Tanner leans back in the chair, placing his hands on the back of his head and stretching his elbows out.

"So?" I shrug. "My father might have doused the house in petrol, Tan. But I struck the fucking match that made it burn." I grit my teeth together, rolling my neck side to side in a piss-poor attempt at dislodging any of the permanent tightness there.

"She'll come back."

*What if she doesn't?*

"All I ever wanted was to be the best father I could be." I press my thumb and finger into my eye sockets, ignoring the dry burn from eight days' worth of lack of food and sleep.

*Lack of Sophie.*

"I thought that meant being there for every morning, every bedtime story. Every cuddle, every smile, every cry. Every fucking thing." I drag my hand down my face and tip my head back to stare at the ceiling. "I thought letting her go was the right thing to do. I thought... Fuck. I don't know what the hell I thought."

"I do," Tanner says. "You were thinking like a Dad who loves his kids. Thinking of them before all else."

"She deserves better than me." I squint as I meet his eyes.

"Nah. She deserves *you*, idiot. After everything you've done, there's no way she can't see that."

"What if it's not enough?" Desperation seeps into my tone. "What if she doesn't come back? And she decides we can't leave the past behind us?"

Tanner shakes his head. "You can't think like that."

"It's all I can think like."

"You waited four years for her. You can survive until she's ready to come back."

I grunt and cast my eyes back to the window and roof of the hotel in the distance. Tanner's right. I did wait four years. But this is different. So fucking different. I know what she smells like... tastes like. I know what it feels like against my hand when our babies move inside her. I know the overwhelming sense I had that first night that she was always meant to be with me. That night, I pushed inside her and life began to grow.

Our life.

One that should be spent together. Not an ocean apart.

She's my everything. They all are.

Those first four years feel like a skip through the park in comparison to the grueling marathon I'm dragging myself around now. Alone.

"You can survive," Tanner repeats, fixing me with a look that's as much as a challenge to argue with him as it is a reassuring show of support.

"Yeah," I mutter.

His eyes drop to my phone on the desk as a text from Maddy pings on the screen.

"She coming here to give you a two-course lunch of grief again?"

"Probably." My face crumples. "I don't blame her. She saw Sophie when my father told her about Alicia. She watched her leave, just like I did."

"She doesn't understand, though. Why haven't you told her?"

"I—"

"You're getting whipped by your sister and your mum for cheating when you didn't. Fuck's sake, do you think it's penance or something? Do you enjoy punishing yourself?"

My eyes are bleary as I stare back at him.

"It's nothing I can't handle. Sophie's going through worse."

The two of us sit in silence for a few minutes as I stew. Tanner's right. In a way, I do enjoy punishing myself when I see the disappointment in her and Mum's eyes. Because it reminds me that I'm still able to feel. Even if it's the coldness of someone else's disgust digging into me.

It means that Sophie didn't take away my ability to feel.

She left that one thing.

Just one.

One thing I refuse to let go of no matter how much it burns to embrace it.

Because when she left... she took *everything* else.

I swipe up my phone, expecting Maddy to be announcing she's on her way. But the words on the screen make bile thrash its way up from my stomach.

**Maddy: You need to get to Mum's. Dad's here and something's going on.**

No further explanation is needed for me to be grabbing my jacket off the back of my chair and gritting my teeth as relay her message to Tanner.

"I'll come with you." He's on his feet a second after me, but I place a hand on his shoulder and shake my head.

"No. My father's all mine."

"Don't do anything stupid," he warns as I stride toward the door.

"Like?"

"Kill him."

I huff out a grunt. "That's too easy for him, Tan. I'd rather watch him suffer."

I tear up outside Mum's house, screeching to a halt and flying out of my Range Rover like my life depends upon it. I sprint to the wide-open front door.

There are two giant suitcases in the hallway.

"Came back for his shit, did he?" I say as Maddy rushes down the hall from the kitchen to meet me.

"Yeah, Mum called me," she says in a rush as there's loud banging from overhead. She glances at the vibrating ceiling, where the light fitting is swinging with each loud thump. "She's up there with him. Trying to talk him out of it."

"What?" I screw my face up, white rage racing through my veins. "She seriously wants him back? Now?"

"No." Maddy shakes her head, her eyes shining. "It's not that. She doesn't want him to leave because she can't bear to see him hurt you again. He's—"

Another loud bang overhead steals her attention.

"Spit it out, Sis."

She swallows and drags in an audible breath.

"He's leaving with Sophie."

The air is punched from my lungs in an instant at the same time as my head swims like it's being held deep below the surface of icy water.

"She's in LA."

"She came back." A haunted expression takes over Maddy's face. "With Dad. They landed a couple of hours ago."

Blood rushes in my ears and the walls close in until all I can focus on is my sister's eyes and the sheer devastation in them as I fight to maintain composure.

"Where. Is. She?" I growl.

She shakes her head slowly, her skin paling by the second. "I don't know. Why would she do this, Drew? I know she's mad at you... but *Dad?* After everything he's said and done. How could she?"

My heart freezes in my chest, the pain too much in this moment to allow it to beat.

"She knows what she's doing," I choke out.

My eyes move past Maddy to the staircase as my father descends with a bag. My mother is hot on his heels, pleading with him to think about other people for a change.

Maddy stares at me like I've gone mad. "What the hell? Why aren't you stopping this? Do something, Drew!"

My father walks up to me. I ball my hands into fists by my sides until my palms sting and the skin splits beneath my nails.

He looks into my eyes, a hint of regret in his gray ones. It's gone in a blink, and I question if I imagined it.

"Hank," Mum begs, "please think about this."

"I have, Violet," he says, glancing at her over his shoulder. "You won't forgive me. I have nothing here." His eyes slide to Maddy. "My kids are all grown up now. They don't need me anymore."

He looks back at me and years of buried emotions swell up until I'm practically vibrating with rage.

"I *never* needed a father who didn't know the first thing about what it takes to be a good dad," I spit.

He glares at me, his eyes hardening until the gray in them glints like cold rain on slate.

"Lucky for me I've been given a second chance then, eh? That boy Sophie's carrying might not be my blood. Same as you aren't. But I won't make the same mistakes twice." His lips lift into a smile with a hint of smugness in it that makes me think I might break my last words to Tanner and kill him right here, right now. Crush his windpipe beneath my fingers and enjoy as it gives way to a bloody pulp in my palm.

His smile grows as he clips out each word with precision. "I'll do better with my *son* this time."

Mum clutches her mouth in a sob, and Maddy sucks in a breath as I ram him against the wall so hard that a picture falls from its hook and the glass in the frame cracks right down the center. It's almost poetic that it's an old family photo taken just before my sixteenth birthday. Back when I thought I was actually related to this prick. Thank God, Maddy is nothing like him either.

He arches a brow at me, unconcerned that I have him pinned by the throat, and no one is coming to his aid. The bastard thinks he's invincible.

"I'll take care of them."

"You only know how to care about yourself," I spit.

"Sophie chose me, Son. Time to move on."

My phone vibrates in my pocket with an incoming message, but my focus is trained on my father. His eyes shine with victory like it was all a competition and Sophie and the babies are a prize to claim.

Something to own. To control.

I hold him in place and pull my phone out with one hand to glance at the screen.

"You sure she chose you?" I ask.

His eyes drop to my phone and his brow furrows as I slip it back into my pocket.

"I'm the one who brought her back, aren't I? She's at her apartment packing now."

"Running off into the sunset," I murmur, my chest warming with the knowledge that she's nearby.

"Work gave me some extended leave." His lips curl into a sneer. "I'm taking her away. Who knows if or when we'll come back."

"Good. I'm glad you're packed. It'll make you leaving faster."

He studies my face and my smirk. Then his façade begins to crack.

"I'm not going alone. Soph's coming with me."

My silence only seems to rile him, because he shoves me off him. I let him because I have him exactly where I want him now.

Packed and ready to fuck off.

"Soph's packing now," he repeats.

"You already said that."

He scowls at my flippant tone.

"She chose me. She kissed me."

My jaw hardens immediately as my eyes bore into his.

"She held onto my collar and pulled me to her. Desperate for me to kiss her." He smirks as I grind my teeth and my pulse thunders in my temple.

"Enough with the constant lies, Hank," Mum snaps.

It takes everything I have in me not to quench the thirst for his blood beneath my fist. I hold his eyes and sickness slithers through me like a virus until it's clawing at my throat.

He's not lying.

Not this time.

Sophie kissed him.

"She doesn't want you anymore," he says without a hint of empathy. "Time to move on."

"I'm not moving anywhere," I growl, ignoring the gnawing jealousy in my gut.

"We'll let you know when that babies arrive. Send you a photo if you like."

"Dad, stop," Maddy begs.

"It's okay, Sis." I pull out my phone and hold it up in the air, turning the screen so my father can read it.

His pupils blow wide. Then his brows flatten, and he reads it again.

"What's that even mean?" His lips flap as he scans my face and then looks at my phone again. Back and forth, over and over. It's almost comical.

"It means, I'll handle it from here," I say with a calm confidence.

"You'll handle it?" he splutters.

"Sophie and I will," I confirm.

The flicker of doubt in his eyes sets a rush of fireworks exploding in my chest. A mass celebration, all set off by one simple word in the text message I received a few minutes ago.

One word with infinite meaning and possibility.

The word I've been waiting to hear for days.

**Sophie: Us.**

# Chapter 39
# Sophie

I SLIDE MY KEY into the lock, my heart hammering against my ribs as I turn it. I prayed this day would come as soon as possible. But now that I'm here, dread inches its way up from my gut.

My heart's been aching for the past eight days. But since I sent that one-worded text message, it's been in my throat.

*What if I got it all wrong?*

The house feels quiet as I step into the hallway, the air still and undisturbed, confirming no-one's home. I glance through an open doorway and am greeted by piles of removal boxes, all taped shut. It's like no one cared enough to unpack what's inside. Because that would mean bringing out memories. Turning the empty space into a home.

The sight of them all piled up has me rubbing at my stinging eyes as I move toward the sweeping staircase.

I don't know what makes me climb them first. The unrelenting feeling I've had in my gut for the past eight days, I think. The one that tells me I did what I had to. That the pain was worth it. But the way my hand shakes as I grip the rail and head straight toward one room in particular, like on auto-pilot, I'm not so sure anymore.

It's too late now. Too late to question it all— the plans, all the late-night discussions before I left, the *promises*.

I slam to a halt in the doorway. A sob bubbles in the back of my throat, because now I'm faced with the evidence that maybe it was all too much. That the heartache was too great.

I question every decision now that I see what he's done.

The room with the vaulted ceiling was empty the last time I stepped foot inside it. Now it's been transformed. I don't need to look inside the other rooms in the house to know they'll be piled high with unopened boxes like downstairs.

But this room... this room is nothing like that.

I walk into the center and perform a slow three-sixty as I take it all in. The fresh white paint. The blackout drapes in a soft sage at the windows. The new, plush carpet that feels like a cloud beneath my feet.

The double changing station.

The matching glider chairs, set side-by-side by the window so that they can look out over the garden. The oversized crib. Big enough for two with a mobile hanging above it. A circle of pastel-colored ice-cream cones.

"God." I clamp my hand over my mouth, tears welling in my eyes as guilt hits me like a truck, making my stomach churn. "What did I do?" I choke as I look around again. "What the hell did I do?"

I run my hand over the edge of the crib. Inside, the two rompers that Maddy and Violet bought are laid out, like they're waiting for their owners to come and try them on. My hand drops to my stomach, and I keep it there as tightness overtakes my throat to the point of pain.

What did he endure while I wasn't here? What was he thinking on the nights alone here? I picked up the phone to call him so many times, before putting it down again. If I'd heard his voice, even just once, I know I wouldn't have been able to keep it together. It had to be that way, even if it made it all that much harder.

I'm lost in a haze, staring at the two outfits until the air in the room shifts and every cell in my body tingles. I don't have to see him to know he's there. My body knows. My gut knows. Every instinct is telling me to run to him.

But I can't make my legs work.

I curl my hands around the rail of the crib for support and lift my gaze, steeling myself for what I'll see.

But nothing could have prepared me for this moment.

Because in one meeting of eyes, the torture of everything we've done is reflected back at me in his gaze. The pain that so many conversations have led us to. The harsh truths. The plans. The choices. The promises.

All so we could have the future we desperately wanted.

He stares at me, piercing blue gluing me to the spot, suspending me like we're caught inside a glitch in time. One where only four souls exist. The four in this room.

Blood rushes in my ears, pulling me under like a punishing wave before my legs give way beneath me.

"Drew!" I gasp, choking over every letter.

His broad outline melts before me until I can't see anything through my tears.

My hands drop from the crib and I crumple as easily as a house made of cards.

"Jesus," he says. Then strength surrounds me in a rush, honey on smoked wood encasing me like a protective embrace as I'm held against something warm and solid. Something that has an internal beat hammering as wildly as my own.

"Don't cry," his voice rasps with a gravel to it that makes it sound like he's barely holding it together. "Please don't cry. You're home. You came back to me."

I press my face into his chest, sobs stealing the air from my lungs as I cling to him and shake inside his arms.

His deep voice pulls me back to reality where I've been repeating the same words over and over like a plea, "I'm so sorry. I'm so sorry."

"Sophie, I'm here. Take a breath. I'm here."

My sob morphs into a hiccup as I draw back and look at him, at the sharp cut of his jaw, the fullness of his bottom lip, the high angles of his cheekbones, the way his blue eyes are penetrating my soul as he gazes down at me.

"Tell me you forgive me for leaving." I screw my face up as more tears fall. "I've missed you so much. There wasn't a moment I didn't." I reach up to stroke his face like it isn't real and I need to touch it to reassure myself that it is.

His eyes glisten, tears gathering in each one.

"There's not a single thing to forgive." He grabs either side of my face and presses his forehead to mine. "Not one single thing."

Then his lips are on mine, kissing me like it's been the worst physical pain to have been separated. He kisses me as I sob against him, gripping him to me and sinking as deep into his arms as I can.

My chest is wracked by sobs and my tears coat the hands on my cheeks. But we keep kissing, desperately holding onto each other like if we are to let go, even for a moment, then we could be lost to one another forever.

"Jesus, Sophie." Drew scrunches his face up against mine as he dives back into another kiss that has me panting for breath.

"I left you," I gasp.

"Because that's what we decided you had to do." He kisses me again and then moves back to look deeply into my eyes. So deep that it's like he's urging me to listen to him, to understand that we planned this. We put ourselves through this willingly.

And we have to pay the price.

"I knew what we were doing. Every second for me has been the worst kind of nightmare. But I knew why we had to," he says, brushing a lock of hair away from my eyes. It comes away wet and sticks to my temple.

We stare at each other, our hearts thundering in unison. So many things to say. But one thing more important than all the others.

"I love you."

Drew's breath crackles in his throat and his face crumples. The sight makes regret pierce me deep in my core.

He swallows, his eyes holding mine. "I love you too. So damn much. It's what's kept me going these past eight years."

"Eight days," I croak.

"Felt like years." He gives me a half smile that has me hiccupping out an unattractive sniff as more tears spill from my eyes and he kisses them away.

"I'm sorry," I whisper.

"Stop." His lips glide over mine as he tilts my face up and snags my lower lip between his teeth. My breath catches as he lets my lip go, kissing me again, swiping his tongue over my parted lips. "I can't bear the sadness in your voice, Boss. Please don't blame yourself. We did this together. You and me. *Us*."

"Us," I echo.

My lower lip wobbles and I fight to maintain control. Because as much as I'm in danger of hiding in his arms, I can't. There's so much to say. So much he needs to hear. And so much I need to ask.

"Henry?"

His eyes darken, and I flinch at the pain that lances over his face.

But as fast as it appears, it's gone.

"I handled it. He's not coming back."

Lightness swarms my head and I cling to him, sucking in a deep breath.

"You played him the recording I sent you?"

Drew searches my eyes, his jaw tense before he nods. "Everything. The whole goddamn story about him following you, and him admitting to making those allegations about Councilor Jenkins go away. He didn't even sound remorseful." His brows pull together until deep lines appear above his nose. "He didn't even sound fucking *ashamed*."

"I don't think he is." I swallow. "I think all he could see was the promise of a promotion. But the sad part is, when I spoke with Jenkins' brother, he told me that Jenkins only recommended him after he'd already got one... on his own merit."

Drew sucks in a breath, making his nostrils flare. "It was all for nothing."

"We can't think like that. It doesn't help anyone. Henry did what he did. Jenkins did what he did. Those are the facts."

"And you're who figured it all out." His eyes slide from my face, down to my bump, as he cradles it. "Your mama's beautiful and smart. She's a flame. Brighter than any other."

His throat constricts, his forehead creasing as my bump comes to life, wriggling beneath his palms.

"God." Emotion clogs in his throat as he falls to his knees and presses his lips against my stomach. "I missed you both, too." He chuckles softly, sniffing as he blinks over and over, fighting back the tears that are evident in his voice. "I missed you so much. You're my world. You and your mama. Everything I ever dreamed of."

I swallow another sob as he stands and encases me in his arms again.

"Everyone thought you cheated on me. They thought you were like him." I don't manage to stifle the next sob, and it comes out as a squeak.

"But you knew the truth. That's all that matters." He looks at me with a tenderness in his eyes. "Honesty and communication. It's what we promised each other. It's how this all worked, how my father never saw it. The idea of being in an honest relationship is too alien to him. He doesn't even have one with himself."

I nod. Drew's right. Henry would never have considered that Drew told me about Alicia coming to his hotel room. That he'd be honest about every single detail.

About how she had touched him before he stopped her. I knew about it before Drew even stepped onto his plane home. He called me and woke me up to tell me. He was so distressed at the idea of being unfaithful to me. We spoke for half an hour before he calmed down and began to sound like himself again.

Hearing the fear in his voice that I'd think he was like Henry, was heartbreaking. I never doubted him for one second. Alicia called him after to apologize. Apparently Henry had encouraged her. Told her that Drew never stopped talking about her since he lived in New York, and that she just needed to push a little, show him she wanted him. He told her I was having another man's baby and she shouldn't worry about me and Drew because we weren't going to last.

The levels he was willing to go to makes me sick. But he didn't count on me and Drew. Us. He didn't count on us always communicating, always keeping that promise of honesty, above all else.

"You knew he'd bring Alicia into it and try to break us up."

Drew's brow flattens. "He wouldn't have told her those lies to encourage her for nothing. He had a goal."

"I'm sorry I said you were like him before I left. You're nothing like him." A fresh round of tears constricts my throat as they course down my cheeks. Drew wipes them away and lifts my chin so I meet his eyes.

"I knew you didn't mean it. You said it was in my blood. That was my giant sign that told me you didn't mean it. I called you *Soph* after because I was telling you I understood. We talked about it so many times. I trusted you, Sophie."

"Yes, the way I've felt being apart from you was a hell I wouldn't wish upon anyone. But we had to do this. He wasn't going to admit anything if he thought he didn't have a chance of getting you back. We had to stop it. Stop him following you. Your car..." Drew's jaw tenses as he curses. "He wasn't going to stop."

"Will he stop now?" I look into Drew's eyes, praying to see what I need to see.

That it was worth it.

That the hell we've put ourselves through—that I've put him through—was worth it.

That it worked.

Because if all I did was hurt the man I love, then I don't know how I'll live with myself.

"He's gone."

I blink twice. "Really?"

"He's gone," he states again, without emotion. "Took his bags and went to the airport. He knows your evidence will have him arrested the minute he sets foot back into the country. He's a coward, he'll not face what he did. He's not coming back."

"What about your mum and Maddy?"

"They're both hurt. He told them he'd call them, let them know he was safe, wherever he goes. But I think they're also relieved. He took a lot of pain away with him when he left."

Drew places two fingers beneath my chin and tilts it up so I have no choice but to look into his beautiful blue eyes. They're shining at me with a warmth and admiration I don't deserve.

"He kissed me."

His gaze falters for the briefest second. "It doesn't matter."

"It does." My breath comes in stuttered gasps. "He kissed me. And I let him. I didn't move away fast enough. I wanted him to believe I was coming home with him. It was the only way I thought I'd get him to admit what he'd done. I told him I was scared." My heart clenches in my chest, the back of my neck growing hot. "I told him I was scared so he'd think I needed him."

"You don't have to explain," Drew murmurs softly.

"I do!"

Even if Drew can't look at me because of this, at least I've been honest with him, like he's always been with me.

"He kissed me. For one second."

"One second?"

I look into Drew's confused eyes. "I pulled away the second his mouth touched me. I told him his cologne was setting off my nausea."

"You told him he was making you feel sick?"

I nod, swallowing down the acid burning my windpipe at the memory of his lips on mine.

"Yes, the smell of him. It worked. He gave me space the whole way home because it was already on all the clothes he'd brought with him."

"I bet he hated that," Drew grunts.

"I wouldn't know. I could barely look at him the whole flight back. I pretended I was asleep and put my eye mask on. I listened to Jenkins' case notes instead."

"You listened to case notes?"

"It calms me," I mutter.

The corners of Drew's lips twitch, and that one tiny movement has warmth blossoming in my chest. We look at each other for a few beats, soaking in the magic in the air from being back together again. Flutters in my stomach have me moving closer, pressing myself tight against him.

"You didn't know how long this would all take," I breathe.

"I'd have waited forever. It's always been you for me, Sophie. You know that."

My entire body fills with a warm tingling, but it's tinged with an ache deep in my chest.

"I had Holly and Halliday to talk to. But your mum and Maddy—"

"The less people who knew the truth, the better the chance it would work. Tanner knew. I wasn't enemy number one with everyone."

I blink back more tears at the thought of what that must have been like for him.

Drew's eyes blaze with intensity. "Don't. I was fine."

"Liar," I whisper.

His lips curl into a soft smile. "Okay, I was a hot mess without you. But I survived."

I choke around another sob as he kisses me.

"I love you, Sophie."

"I love you too."

I allow myself to sink into his healing kiss for a moment before I ask, "You only decorated this room, didn't you?"

"It's the best one." His eyes twinkle.

My smile is tinged with sadness. "Where have you been sleeping? Not in here, not on the floor, please tell me that."

"No, not here."

He takes my hand and leads me from the room, taking me to the room with the balcony.

Our room.

"I slept here." He motions to the bed. It's the only piece of furniture that's been set up in the room. "With the drapes open so I could look at the stars and wonder if you were wishing on them at night. Wishing for yourself this time, instead of someone else."

I bite my lip as I roll my engagement ring around on my finger, the memory of him proposing and me making a wish for Chelsea dancing into my mind.

"I was wishing in LA. But not for me," I confess.

"Sophie," he scolds.

I turn to him, my fingers still playing with the diamond. "I was wishing for you. Wishing that you were okay."

He pulls me into his arms, his dark brows pulling low. "I am now. Don't do this to yourself. Please." He runs his thumb over my frowning lips. "Only one thing matters now."

"What's that?"

The intensity in his eyes as he looks at me makes my knees go weak.

"That you're home. That all three of you are home."

# Chapter 40
# Drew

SOPHIE'S MOANS AND HANDS digging into my hair spur me on. My dicks throbs impatiently as I lick up another rush of wetness from between her legs.

"Jesus, you're even sweeter," I murmur as I drink her up with a deep groan.

"I need you, Drew. Please."

She pulls at my hair again, trying to coax me away from her pussy. But I'm not ready to go just yet.

I need another minute. Fuck that. I need a lifetime. I'll never get enough of her trembling like this because of my tongue.

We kissed for so long after I told her all that mattered was that she was home. That her and our babies came home to me. As we discarded our clothes, it was like the weight of the last eight days gradually shed a little more with each item.

Eight days... I'm like a bomb about to go off with how much I need her.

"I love you," I murmur before circling her swollen clit again with my tongue. "I love you so damn much."

She shudders and I glance up, but all I can see is her beautiful round belly, cocooning our babies. I plant a hand over it and rub as I spread her lips.

"Come for me first, Sophie. Just once."

"No, I want to see you," she utters around a soft cry as I suck her clit between my teeth.

I break away, my heart cracking behind my ribs at the vulnerability in her voice. My strong Boss has never been so openly needy for me. Eight days apart has been hard on her too, just as I feared it would be. But as much as it pains me to hear her begging with need for me, to the point she's almost in tears again, it also has my dick leaking so much that it's dripping onto the silk sheets.

"I'm here," I say as I climb up the bed and lie next to her, one hand immediately curling around one of her swollen breasts. Its perfect weight spills out of my palm.

"Fuck, they're bigger, Sophie." I lift it to my mouth and wrap my lips around it, kissing and sucking my way to her nipple. My eyes roll in my head the second I close around it and taste a drop of sweetness on the tip of my tongue.

"They started doing that two days ago." She arches into my mouth, moaning as I switch sides and suck another small droplet of creamy liquid past my lips.

"Jesus." I grasp my cock and give it two fierce pumps, a string of precum coming away connected to my palm as I reach between her legs and stroke her clit. "Do you think it's weird that I like the thought of drinking it?"

*I've taken it too far.* But fuck, just the thought has my dick rock hard.

"You want to drink my breast milk?"

My eyes drop to her swollen tits, and on cue, my mouth waters and my balls ache with the need to fill her.

"Yeah, I mean... When we're like this. I don't mean the way you'll feed the babies. Just..." I rub my fingers over her slippery clit and kiss my way back to her nipple. "Just a little..."

She trembles against me as I suck it and groan deeply at the new taste hitting the tip of my tongue again.

"You're so fucking sexy like this. I want it all. I want to taste and touch all of you."

I suck her nipple again then move up to kiss her lips.

"I want everything," I murmur.

"I missed you," she whimpers around my tongue as I make her mouth mine again.

"I love you," I counter, making her sob against me. "Hey," I soothe, stroking her hair. "You're home. I've got you."

I'll repeat these words for eternity if it's what she needs to hear. I've never felt so elated before in my life. Except maybe when Sophie told me she was pregnant. But this is on a level with that. This... having her here. Back in my arms where she belongs.

It's everything.

"I'm okay."

I slide a hand around to cup her throat. "The number of times I dreamed about the day you'd come home. About how it would feel to have you back in my arms where you belong. I lost fucking count, Sophie. It consumed me."

"It did?" Her green eyes shine at me as she swallows, the movement traveling down against my palm. "Show me."

It's a breathy plea. A gentle request. But I understand the meaning behind her words because it's the same need I have burning inside my chest.

*Take away the pain. Strip away the memory of how it feels to be apart. Replace it with something else. Replace it with this. How good we are together.*

I kiss her again, groaning into her mouth. Her breath hitches in response before I break away, positioning myself behind her and moving us both to lie on our sides. Her bump is so big now that we'll have to get more inventive about the ways I can take her. But all that matters now is that I do. That we feel that connection again. Creativity can come later.

I splay my fingers out across her bump as I thrust up inside her. She cries out my name, her head dropping back against my neck.

"You okay?" I kiss her temple, rolling my hips so I can move inside her the way I know feels good for her.

Her warm, wet heat hugs me tightly, clamping hard as though it's punishing me for being apart for so long. Like it never wants to let me go again.

"I'm…" She moans as I pull almost all the way out and then push back inside. "I'm better than okay. You feel so good inside me."

I curse and bury my head into the crook of her neck as I piston my hips, unable to hold back. I fuck moan after moan from her lips until I drive into her with a sharp growl that breaks into a stifled sob.

"Fuck, I love you. I love you."

"I love you too." She shudders and places her hand over mine on her bump.

A small movement beneath our palms has my kisses on her neck turning into a fevered sucks as I groan with desire.

"So fucking sexy, full of our babies. How the hell am I supposed to keep my hands off you?"

"You're not," she pants. "I never want you to. I need you."

I slide my hand between her legs and find her swollen clit. The second I touch it, she convulses in my arms.

"You like that?" I breathe against her ear.

"You know I do." She pushes back against me and grips my wrist, making sure my fingers stay on her clit. Not that I'd dream of moving them. Not when I can sense she's about to erupt into one hell of an orgasm on my cock. I can tell by the wetness running out onto my balls as she pushes herself back onto them with determined little gasps.

"That's it. It's yours. Take it. Fuck yourself on it," I growl as my whole torso clenches. "Because I've been fucking my hand every day thinking about getting back inside this magic pussy."

She stiffens in my arms, a tremble running through her body.

"Do it," I groan. "*Please* fucking do it."

"Drew!" Her cry pierces the air, and I hold her in place, anchoring her as she comes apart around me, crying and gasping, clench after clench of her body strangling me.

"That's it," I growl in her ear as I continue driving up inside her. "I've missed you, Mama. I've..." I choke as my balls draw up toward my body. "Eight days... Eight fucking days."

I screw my eyes up as I erupt, a string of I love yous intermixed with curses as I come so hard and deep inside her that I expect there'll be nothing left of my balls when I'm finished. The liquid fire floods the head of my cock, and I push it all deep, so deep.

"Drew," she moans, turning her head, fighting to meet my lips with hers.

I grab her chin as I continue emptying into her until nothing's left.

"I love you," I pant, smashing my lips to hers. "I love you, even though I don't deserve you."

"We love you." She pulls my hand over her stomach and holds it there. "So much, Daddy."

I curse softly, my eyes stinging.

She searches my eyes, her wet eyelashes sticking together as her brow knits with concern.

"Don't ever say that again," she whispers. "Promise me."

"That I don't deserve you?" I search her eyes. The emerald is dazzling. I could stare at it all my life and still be speechless when it's fixed on me like this.

"Yes. I won't hear it. *We* won't hear it." She moves my hand, stroking it over her stomach. "After everything we've been through, there's no one who deserves to be these babies' daddy more than you."

"Sophie..."

"No, Drew. You were willing to risk everything for us. Your future. Your happiness. I hated being so far away from you in LA. It was amazing to see Holly, Jay, and my nieces, but I still hated it. And I worried the entire time. We didn't know for certain that Henry would follow me and admit what he did. If he hadn't, then who knows when I'd have come home. He'd have never let us live our lives peacefully."

"I'd have moved to LA to be with you."

"Your work is here. Your life is here."

"My life is where you and the babies are."

She smiles sadly. "You'd really do anything? Just like Mufasa. He died to protect Simba."

"I know." I drop my gaze to her full lower lip before I press my mouth to it gently. "I'd do the same. If you or the babies needed something, a kidney, lung, *anything*, and I had it, I'd make the doctors take it from me."

"Bone marrow?" Her expression clouds over briefly before she smiles at me without sadness this time.

"Of course. Nothing means more to me than the three of you. You know that."

"I do." She searches my eyes. "Believe me, I do." Movement in her stomach wriggles against our hands. "They know it too."

We lock ourselves into the perfection of this moment. Just us, back together, feeling our babies.

It's perfect.

"We're okay, aren't we?" Two deep lines furrow her brow.

I press a kiss to the top of her shoulder.

"Of course we are. There was never any scenario that existed where we weren't okay. I wouldn't have allowed it."

The next word from her lips is a whisper.

"Us?"

My smile splits my face in half at the sound of the two letters that mean most to me in the world.

Then the babies move again.

"Us, Mama. Always us."

# Chapter 41

# Sophie

"YOU CAN DO THIS, Sophie," Dr. Melinda urges.

Another surge travels through me, making my whole torso contract automatically.

"You've got it, Sophie. I'm so proud of you. You can do it."

Drew's voice filters through the gas and air-induced haze as I rest my hand holding the mouthpiece on the side of the birthing pool and drop my head down to push as my contraction peaks.

"Gah!"

"That's it, Boss." Drew rubs his warm hand over the base of my spine as I bend forward in the water and bear down.

"The head's already out. Just the shoulders to go." Doctor Melinda moves in the corner of my vision, watching what's going on by using a mirror with a long handle positioned underneath the water. "They've got a head full of dark hair."

I choke out a happy cry, laced with relief as the contraction subsides.

"You're doing such a good job," Drew breathes, massaging my back.

I drop the mouthpiece on the floor beside the pool and gaze up at him. It's making me woozy, and I want to feel fully present when the babies arrive.

"Wanna swap places?" I give him a lopsided smile and rest my sweaty face against my arm on the edge of the pool.

He smiles at me, capturing me with clear blue. He's been amazing ever since my water broke last night. We'd only finished having sex thirty minutes before, and then there they were, all over the mattress, two weeks early. Doctor Melinda assured us being early is common with twins, and nothing to worry about. She was also supportive over my birth plan to have a natural water birth. I knew it might not happen with having twins. But because they're in separate sacs, I was allowed the option as long as I'm monitored continuously.

"Another one's coming." I scrunch up my face and take a deep breath in, letting it out with a deep groan as I push. I swear I sound like a cow mooing, but right now, I don't care if I grow horns and a tail; I just need these babies to get out. Because as much as I wanted a natural birth, I'm beginning to regret not taking all the drugs I could possibly have had.

"You've got it," Drew says, his voice calm and full of confidence.

I grab his hand and cry out. Something shifts between my legs and it's followed by the greatest rush of relief that strips me of my breath.

I suck back in air, desperately filling my lungs.

"Pick up your baby, Sophie."

I swallow as every sound in the room echoes around my head.

"Your baby," Doctor Melinda says again in a faraway voice.

I look at the bottom of the pool.

All my senses return to me at once like I've broken the surface of a lake and taken a huge gasp of air.

"Oh my god."

I scoop the bundle up, lifting it from the water, careful not to catch the cord that's still connecting us.

Another set of hands appears as Doctor Melinda helps me hold our baby above the surface of the water. The midwife assisting her passes over a towel, and she wraps it over the tiny body in my arms.

The little pink puckered face blinks at me twice. Then they open their mouth and cry.

It's the strangest sound I've ever heard.

Drew's warm lips graze the top of my shoulder, kissing me as he looks down.

"God." He chokes back a sob. "I can't believe it."

"Your son has a good set of lungs." Doctor Melinda smiles as she moves the towel enough to place two clamps on the cord. "And his sister isn't far behind, so we'll cut this now. Daddy, would you like to?"

I tear my gaze away from the little pink face which has stopped crying and is staring out at the world.

"Yes." Drew nods, his face paling as his expression grows serious. "I can't believe..." His eyes meet mine. "Do you trust me to do it?"

My heart could burst at the concern in his eyes as he looks at me.

"I trust you with my life." I glance inside my arms. "With *our* lives."

He clears his throat and his dark brows pull low in concentration as he listens intently to Doctor Melinda's instructions and then cuts the cord himself.

He looks at me in awe, but the minute my lips curl into a smile, another surge starts to build inside me.

"I'm about to have another," I pant.

"Okay. We're ready." Doctor Melinda takes the baby from my arms calmly and turns to Drew. "Daddy? Can you hold him?"

He looks at the baby, his eyes softening, but then I grunt as the pressure starts to increase.

"Sophie needs me." His Adam's apple bobs in his throat, and he leans closer to me in a flash. "I'm here." He kisses my forehead.

"Take the baby," I pant as I try to breathe through the contraction.

The internal struggle is clear on Drew's face as he looks from me to the towel-wrapped baby. Then he opens his arms and Doctor Melinda places our baby in his arms. He sits back on his heels at the side of the pool, a look of pure love and adoration flowing over his face.

He holds our son in his arms like he was born to do it.

It makes my head light. But at the same time as my contraction peaks and I groan.

Drew's attention comes back to me, and he adjusts the baby, nestling him in one of his strong arms. The veins protrude underneath his skin as he cradles him protectively, his long, thick fingers wrapped around him to keep him secure. Then his other hand lands on the base of my neck and his blue eyes meet mine as he places his forehead to mine.

"You've got this, Mama."

I open my eyes and look to the side of the hospital bed. Drew's reclined in the chair next to me, and one baby, wearing just a nappy, is laid out sleeping over his bare chest.

"Is he okay?" I wipe my bleary post-nap eyes and shuffle to an upright position.

Drew places a kiss to the baby's dark hair-covered head as he strokes their back with one hand.

"She's fine. Her brother woke her up, that's all. She needed a little help to drift back off."

*She.*

Tears well in my eyes as I glance at the clear plastic crib on wheels that's a little further down beside the bed. Our son is fast asleep inside it with a clean white romper on. They both have the same head of dark hair. He's the larger of the two, older by four minutes. His sister was keen to join us once he came out. Drew held him in one arm while I delivered her. And kept his other arm around me the entire time.

Being my rock.

A tiny part of me was still worried about how he'd react when he saw them both. Even though he's assured me at every turn that these are our babies and blood doesn't matter to him, a tiny part of me was still terrified. Terrified that it was too good to be true, and he'd see her differently because of her DNA.

He kisses her head again and then reaches over to hold my hand with his spare one. The look in his eyes as they meet mine can only be described as joy. Pure joy.

He didn't cry when our son was born. But he couldn't hold it in the second she appeared. Maybe it's because she looked smaller than her brother. Or that she didn't cry right away and there were a tense few seconds where Doctor Melinda had to use a sucker device to clear her airway. But whatever it was, the second he laid eyes on her and she was placed in his arms, Drew wept.

And he's kept tearing up at random moments throughout the night while we've been in the private recovery room.

"I think she likes this." He gazes down at her with a soft smile and kisses her head again. "The skin-to-skin contact, I mean. I read it helps with bonding."

Emotion bubbles up inside my throat as he kisses her again and she takes a contented breath, her back rising and falling. She looks so small in his arms. I don't think there's any danger that the two of them aren't already infatuated with one another. It's obvious seeing them together like this.

"She looks so happy there." I rest my head against the pillow and watch the two of them.

"She's perfect. They're both so perfect." He glances up at me, his blue eyes glistening as his voice wavers. "Look what you did, Mama. You're amazing."

I reach out and squeeze his hand, giving him an exhausted smile. "No. Look what *we* did."

His teeth sink into his lower lip as he blinks fast, his eyes shining. "What we did," he echoes, before looking down at our daughter sleeping happily, her cheek resting over his heart.

Her brother stirs in the crib, letting out an indignant cry at not being fed for forty minutes.

"He's working on getting your milk to come in," Drew says.

I laugh. "Wow, someone's definitely been reading their baby books."

He gives me a lop-sided smile, tiredness tinging his eyes beneath his ruffled, unbrushed hair. Yet somehow, he's never looked handsomer.

"I'll get him."

He stands, keeping our daughter nestled against his bare chest with one hand as he steps toward the crib. He places her down carefully, supporting her head and covering her with a breathable blanket. Then he picks up her brother.

"You're the noisy one, huh?" He chuckles and presses a kiss to the baby's forehead, carrying his angry, wailing little body over to me and laying him in my arms.

His eyes are glued to my breast as I take it out of my nursing bra and help the baby latch on.

"What?" I side-eye him.

"It's just amazing." He exhales, running a hand around the back of his neck. "I can't believe they're both here."

"Yeah." I smile down at the quiet little face happily latched onto my breast, a breast that looks ridiculously giant next to his tiny head.

"I couldn't love the three of you more if I tried."

I look up into Drew's glittering eyes as he leans over his legs and rests his chin on top of his clasped hands.

"I know," I breathe. "I feel the same."

He looks from our son to my face and back again.

"Marry me."

I frown. "But—"

"I know we're already engaged. But I don't want to wait any longer to call you my wife. As soon as you feel ready. The second you feel ready... Marry me. A big wedding, a small one... Whatever you want, as long as it happens."

I look into his eyes, all words leaving me. He's right. What are we waiting for? I mean, I'd like to feel good in my dress, and I don't know how long that will take but...

"That's what you want?"

"It's all I want now. You've given me everything else already." His eyes move to our daughter, then back to our son.

I follow his gaze and look at both of our babies. They still need names. Despite all the baby books Drew bought, we still haven't decided. I told him we'd know once they were born. That our guts would tell us.

Because after everything, I trust my gut again now.

But most of all, I trust him.

Who could have predicted that almost five years ago, I would have gone on a double date I wasn't supposed to be on, and met the man I was destined to be with, even though he wasn't my date? And that we'd be here today? With our beautiful babies. A family.

Us.

Simply us.

If I'd known what we would go through to get to this point then I wouldn't have thought it was possible. I'd have thought it was too much to handle.

If it weren't for Drew.

Because as much as my career might have dubbed me 'Havers the Handler', he's the one with the real strength and refusal to give in. He could have walked away so many times. But he's handled every obstacle thrown our way, still looking at me at the end of each day like it's his biggest blessing to be able to be with me. To love me.

I once thought I was handling everything. But Drew's taught me that the true gift is finding the person who wants to handle everything together.

I lift my gaze back to him and he's watching me with a soft smile on his face.

"What do you say, Ms. Havers?"

"What do I say, Mr. Harper?" I muse, my eyes falling down onto our son's cheek as I stroke it with the back of one finger. "What should I tell your daddy?" I muse before looking back up again.

Drew quirks a brow, holding his breath, waiting on my answer.

I lick my lips, a burst of warmth erupting in my chest. His eyes soften as he gazes at me.

"You want my answer?"

"I've wanted it since the day I met you."

"Then here it is... Yes."

# Chapter 42
# Drew

## *Epilogue – Six Months Later*

"I LOVE THIS ONE."

Maddy juggles our son in one arm and points at the photo of us leaving the hospital. It's taped inside the twins' baby book that Holly gave us when she and Jay visited with the girls last week. They couldn't stay for the party because Jay had filming to get back for. The picture is taken from behind as I carry the matching car seats out, one in each hand.

"Aww," a collective coo fills our kitchen as Sophie's dad holds up the book and our friends peer in to take a look. I catch Sophie's eye across the room from where Tanner and I are setting up the cake.

She smiles at me, her cheeks flushing as she reads the hunger in my eyes. Emmett and Bailey started sleeping in the nursery last week after being in with us at night. I've made sure to make the most of having Sophie all to myself. And I was enjoying the way she chose to wake me up with her lips wrapped around my dick this morning... until Emmett decided he wanted feeding.

I swear our son should have been given a name that means guzzler of milk, instead of truth, as his name symbolizes.

Bailey's infectious giggle floats across the room from where Sophie's mum is holding her in her arms as my mum presses her fingertip to her nose and makes a beep sound over and over. The delight in all of their eyes makes my heart clench. Bailey, meaning officer of justice, is our little sweet girl who always has a smile for everyone. She's so much like Sophie. Her hair started off dark when she was born, but it's turning lighter. I think she'll end up blonde like her mama.

My father, although it doesn't feel right calling him that after everything, hasn't asked after Bailey once. It makes the blood in my veins boil. If he'd wanted to be sent pictures and to see how she's doing, then Sophie and I would have sent them. We were never planning to stop him from playing some kind of role in her life. But he ruined any chance of that a long time ago. Maddy is the only one who speaks to him on occasion now. He's living in Morocco and working as a private security guard. He already has a new girlfriend.

As long as it stops him from interfering with our lives, I don't care what the hell he does.

"First six months as a daddy," Tanner comments as he passes me the two candles to put in the cake.

I survey the mound of light gray frosting on the elephant-shaped cake and opt for sticking one candle in the end of its trunk and one in its back.

"Sure is." I can't stop my grin.

"You know the party and the cake are for you and Sophie though, right? Because you survived."

I glance up at his profile. The tired lines at the corners of his eyes deepen as he smiles over at Rachel, whose legs are being tugged on by their two boys as she talks to Dax and Logan. Rose is crouching with Halliday, both talking animatedly with Ruby, whose dark hair is sticking up on the back of her head from where she was just napping on our sofa.

Her little hand reaches out to Halliday and she deposits what looks like a handful of cookie crumbs into her palm. Halliday beams at her like she's been given a great gift. I'm glad she's made it over for an extended visit. Sophie's missed her since she decided to stay in New York permanently.

I guess you never know what destiny has planned.

"Ruby still not sleeping through the night?"

"She's up at least twice every night." Tanner yawns. "I slept in her bed last night and put her in with Rach. It's the only way anyone gets any rest in our house. She's the smallest, but she runs the place."

I chuckle and Tanner narrows his eyes at me.

"Your two still sleeping through?"

"Ten hours in a row."

I grin as he grumbles.

"It's been a week. We just got lucky. But I intend to enjoy it while it lasts."

"You do that."

"Hey, one of us has to be getting a full night's sleep in the office. Why not me?" I wink at him and clap a hand on his shoulder as Sophie walks over to join us.

"Look what Chelsea just sent me." She holds out her phone and shows us both a video of a baby crawling. "She just started doing it. Isn't that cute?"

"Does she sleep through the night too?" Tanner mumbles.

Sophie bites her lower lip, her eyes sparkling. "I know... we're that couple that everyone hates with not one, but two babies that sleep. But until last week, I swear we were up every three hours, weren't we?"

I wrap my arm around her waist and kiss her temple. "We sure were."

I look at Tanner with newly acquired empathy. I love every second with the babies, day or night. But fuck me, the tiredness can be brutal. And he's been doing it a lot longer than me.

"I'm going to the bathroom and then we can do the cake, okay?" Sophie reaches up to kiss me on the lips.

My eyes fall to her perfect ass as she walks away. I chew on my lower lip for a minute as I scan the room. Everyone is occupied, busy in their own little pockets of conversations. I lower my voice and incline my head toward Tanner.

"I need to fetch a lighter. Back in a minute."

"There's one here." He holds the plastic stick up in his hand.

"Doesn't work."

He presses the trigger button and a flame bursts into life at the end of it. "Looks fine to me."

"Nope. It's useless. Goes out too easy," I call over my shoulder as I head toward the door, ignoring the sound of him clicking it off and on again, testing it.

I find Sophie coming out of the upstairs bathroom.

"You look amazing in this dress." I grab her around the waist as she steps out of the door, earning myself a surprised gasp.

"It finally fits again. Well, almost." She smiles at me and slides her arms up around my neck.

"Yeah, I can see." I drop my gaze to her full tits filling out the fabric. They're still bigger from all the breastfeeding. It just makes her even sexier. Them and the extra soft curve her lower stomach now has. She claims not to like it, but I think I'm winning her over with each kiss I press to it. It grew our babies. As far as I'm concerned it should be fucking worshipped for bringing them to us.

Just like her.

"You think they're missing us?"

"Who cares if they are?" I grab two handfuls of her ass in my palms and squeeze.

She laughs, making my already hardening dick spring to full attention.

"They'll wait a little longer."

She purses her lips before giving me a coy smile. "You think?"

I take her left hand in mine and lift it to my lips, kissing her finger above her engagement ring and wedding band.

"I know, Mrs. Harper. There's an elephant cake. Who wouldn't wait for that?"

Her laugh lights up her eyes as I pull her back inside the bathroom and lock the door.

"You know what's sweeter than cake, though?" I don't give her time to answer before I drop to my knees and push her dress up over her hips. "This beautiful pussy."

I lean forward, pressing an open-mouth kiss through the lace of her panties.

A familiar taste hits me, and I growl.

"Fuck, Sophie."

My dick leaks in my pants as I kiss her again, darting my tongue out to taste her through the already wet fabric.

"You're..." I close my eyes and kiss her again, inhaling slowly and breathing her in. I savor her before groaning against her wet skin and squeezing my dick through my clothes.

"I'm what?"

She gazes down at me as I slide my hands up her thighs and hook my fingers through her panties, pulling them down to her ankles. I lift them to my nose and inhale, my eyes rolling back in my head.

"These are mine now." I stuff them inside my pocket.

I part her lips with my fingers and give her a slow, sweeping lick which makes the end of my dick leak.

"You're..." I sink my teeth into my lower lip and shake my head with a grin as euphoria floods my veins in a sudden wave of realization.

"What?" She frowns at me.

I open my mouth to answer, then decide to wait. Instead, I sink my face into her and inhale again before I start eating her out at my own pace.

"Drew." Her hands drop into my hair and she fists it as she leans back against the sink. "What were you going to say?"

"That you're about to come on my tongue," I murmur cockily as the first rush of wetness seeps from her and I drink it up hungrily.

"Really?"

I can hear the smile in her voice. But I also hear the acceptance as she resigns herself to her fate. Because I've studied every inch of her body so well that I know it better than she does herself.

"Yeah." I grin as I push two fingers inside her and they come out coated in her juices. I slide them back inside and curse softly at the bite of her fingernails against my scalp.

"Give it to me," I urge, looking up at her as I suck on her clit and stroke her G-spot with my fingers.

Our eyes meet and her lips part on a panted moan of my name.

Her upper body jerks and her hands tighten in my hair to the point of pain as she tenses.

"Good girl, good girl," I groan. "Fuck... that's a good girl. Let go..."

Then she comes.

And I revel in the sounds her body makes as it clamps around my fingers, her wetness echoing as I finger-fuck her, never easing up on her clit as I coax her into another orgasm.

"Drew!" She cries out my name, moans it, whimpers it, fucking *sings* it.

And I lap it all up with a shit-eating grin.

Because these sounds will always be mine to hear. Mine and mine alone.

"That's it. Let it go. Soak my face. Come all over it." I dive back into her, my tongue lapping up every drop of arousal her body creates.

And it tastes sweet. Really fucking sweet.

"Oh my god, that was..." she pants, her eyes bright as I stand and unbuckle my pants.

"That was what?" I grip her chin and pull her lips to mine for a kiss as I free my aching dick.

She wraps her hand around it immediately and breaks away from me, dipping her head.

"No." I pull her back up before she can suck it.

"I thought you might want what you missed out on this morning." She jerks me off with the perfect pace and pressure until I'm hissing through clenched teeth.

I wrap a hand around her throat and hold her still.

"What I want is for you to come again. This time on my cock."

I smirk before pressing a searing kiss to her lips. Then I spin her so that she's facing the mirror above the sink.

"Watch."

I lift one of her legs and place her knee on the counter. Then I push inside her with a satisfied groan that I feel all the way down in my balls.

"Watch," I repeat as I draw back and stuff her full of my cock again.

I slap her ass cheek with one hand and reach around to grab a breast with the other. I squeeze it through her dress, relishing the way she moans as I drag the fabric down, freeing it so I can find her nipple.

"You're fucking incredible," I groan as I roll her nipple between my thumb and finger until a bead of shining white appears at the end of it. I rub it over her skin, then wait for another to replace it. The second it appears, I swipe it up and lift my fingers to my lips, sucking them with a groan.

Sophie's heavy-lidded eyes watch me and her cheeks flush. She's seen me do this a thousand times now. But she still blushes every time I suck on her breasts to taste her milk. It's completely different to the way I feel when I see her feeding the twins. I feel nothing but love and protectiveness then. But when it's just the two of us, and I know these sweet drops that escape are mine, it makes my cock hard as steel and my balls fuller than they've ever been.

*Maybe that's why...*

I pull her bra with the nursing pad inside it back up over her breast so that we don't soak her dress, then grab both of her hips and increase my pace.

"You got another one for me before I explode?"

She gazes at me in the mirror, her tits bouncing as I fuck her hard and deep from behind. Her fingertips dig into the marble countertop as I pull back and slam into her again.

"Give me another," I grit, the tendons in my neck becoming visible as I fight to keep the cum from racing out of my dick.

I reach around and swipe my thumb over her clit. That's all it takes to have her coming again, her eyes holding mine in the mirror.

"Fuck, that's it. Come all over this cock. Come all over this cock while you're full of our baby."

Her eyes widen and I smirk as I continue fucking her through her orgasm. She pants and gazes back at me. The second she has enough air in her lungs, she gasps.

"What?"

"You heard me." I slide my hand up from her clit, bunching the fabric of her dress up higher and exposing her lower stomach.

"This." I spread my hand over her skin, pulling her back against me and speeding up my thrusts as the head of my cock begins to tingle. "This is where you've been taking all my cum like such a fucking good girl. And now you're full of it... and full of our baby."

She shakes her head and her body clenches around me, drawing a deep groan from my chest.

"I'm still breastfeeding. I can't be," she pants, parting her legs wider so I can wedge myself deeper inside her.

"I've been taking you bare and coming inside you for months. We knew this could happen." My smirk grows as she blinks back at me. "Fuck, look at the way you take me." My eyes drop to the mirror where my cock is disappearing inside her. "Stuffed full," I growl. "Just the way I love you to be."

Sophie whimpers and bites her lip as she watches, then her gaze travels back up to meet mine.

"You ready to have your husband's cum running out of you for the rest of the day?"

Something flashes in her eyes and her lips twitch.

"I can handle it."

I hold her gaze as I growl out a fierce orgasm that has sweat pricking along my hairline. My grip tightens on her stomach and hip as I hold her in place, exactly where I want her while I spill inside her.

"Jesus." I screw my face up and bury it in the crook of her neck until my cock stops throbbing inside her.

Sophie reaches up to stroke my head.

"I can't be pregnant again."

There's doubt in her voice. I press kiss after kiss to the silky skin on her neck.

"You are. I can tell."

"How?"

I lift my head to meet her eyes.

"The way you taste. It's different. Sweeter... I love it." I break into a grin against her neck, kissing her again as her mouth drops open.

"No."

"Take a test."

I look at her stomach in the mirror and splay my fingers over it, imagining her with a big bump again.

"So sexy, Mama."

She looks shell-shocked as I pull out of her and straighten my clothes. I clean her up with a warm washcloth and then fetch a box from the bathroom cabinet. I rip it open and pull out one of the foil packets.

"I got a couple just in case. I wanted to be here when you took it this time."

I tear open the foil and remove the test's pink cap, then hand it to her.

"Pee on it."

Her brows knit as she takes it from me.

I avert my gaze as she uses it.

"Don't be disappointed if I'm not." She hands me back the test and I place the cap back on before putting it on the counter.

I nod, my jaw tensing as I turn back around to face her.

Will I be disappointed? Fuck yeah, I will. I meant it when I told her I wanted to keep getting her pregnant. There's something so sexy about her growing life inside her, seeing her stomach swell with it. But if I'm wrong, then I'm sure I won't be wrong for long, because I intend to keep filling her until she's full of our babies again.

She moves closer and wraps her arms around my waist.

Her eyes pinch at the corners. "Can you imagine having another so soon?"

"Yes," I answer truthfully, pulling her against me. "I can imagine us having a whole house full of kids. We can handle it. Two babies, three, ten."

She frowns and I chuckle.

"You know why? Because we'll do it together."

"I can't believe you've got me pregnant again already. I'll be back at work for a couple of months and then off on maternity leave again."

"We'll make it work. Whatever you need. I'll move work around. Mum and Maddy want to help. Tanner and Rachel are only around the corner, and your parents will come and visit." I tilt her chin up so she meets my eyes. "I love you."

Her green eyes soften. "I love you too."

"Do you want to look first?"

"No. You do it. I saw first last time."

She studies my face as I twist to look at the test.

I turn back to her with a scowl and drop my eyes to her stomach as I cup it with my palm.

"What?" Her eyes widen. "Aren't I?" She sighs and her face falls. "Oh..."

"No, you most definitely are pregnant." I grab the test and hold it up to show her.

She takes it from me and clamps her hand over her mouth, her brows shooting up her forehead as she looks at the plus sign.

"Then why do you look so angry?"

My scowl melts and I exhale and drop my head back toward the ceiling.

"Because..." I take her hand and place it against my pants. "Now I have to walk back into our kids' party with a raging fucking hard-on."

Her laugh vibrates through me warming every cell in my body.

"You think that's funny?"

"A little." Her shoulders shake as she twists her lips to stop her laugh. She wraps her hand around my aching dick and strokes up and down.

"Mrs. Harper," I growl, grabbing her wrist to halt her movements.

"Yes, Daddy Harper?" she teases.

"Call me that again," I breathe.

"You sure you can handle it?" She bites her bottom lip. Her eyes glitter as I curse out a growl in response.

"Fuck, Mama. You know how much I love you. Don't make me beg. Call me it."

I thought I was never going to have this. I watched my friends all fall in love, one by one. Even my younger sister found it before I did. But I'd wait again, a thousand times longer... a million... a fucking billion, as long as I knew I was getting Sophie at the end of it.

Sophie and the twins... and whoever is growing inside her right now.

My eyes burn as I wait for her to speak.

Holding my gaze, she places her hand over mine on her stomach.

"I love you," she whispers, "Daddy Harper."

**The (Almost) End.**
For a quick and spicy glimpse into Sophie & Drew's
future family life, enjoy the extended epilogue.

# Chapter 43
# Sophie

THE PURPLE PETALS GLISTEN in the sunlight as I fill up my glass with water. I lean back against the counter and admire them as I drink. I don't need to look at the card tucked between the leaves to know what it says.

I remember every single word.

***It's been seven years and we're sitting looking out over a lake as you feed the canine tidbits in your purse, the old balls of your past date long devoured. DH***

I put my glass down and push away from the counter, padding across the kitchen and over to the open doors that lead out onto the wooden deck of the lakeside cabin. It's become one of our favorite places to come for a getaway.

The sight that greets me is nothing short of mayhem.

Emmett and Bailey are both naked and covered from head to toe in something light brown and suspiciously sticky-looking while they run around squeal-ing at each other in delight.

"Sorry, Mama. They got into your ice cream while I was changing Evie."

Drew walks over to me with our nine-month-old daughter wrapped inside one arm and presses a kiss to my temple. She reaches out for me with little chubby arms and I take her from him, holding her against my side as I run my nose over her cheek and breathe in her baby scent.

"They don't like rum and raisin either." Drew wrin-kles his nose up as Emmett and Bailey stand with their tummies protruding toward one another and clap their sticky, coated palms together in front of their faces, staring in wonder at their dirty fingers.

I bite my lower lip as I smile. "Maybe if you stopped getting me pregnant, then I wouldn't want to eat ice-cream all the time."

His warm palm spreads over my bump as he stands behind me and kisses my hair, followed by Evie's. Hers is dark, just like Drew's.

"I told you, I can handle the questionable flavor choices." He rubs his hand over my bump and groans quietly. "Because I love it when you're like this. You know what it does to me."

"I know that once this baby's born, you need a vasectomy before you touch me again," I tease. "Or you might have me pregnant again before I leave the hospital."

He chuckles into my neck before trailing his lips up to my ear. "You say that like it's a bad thing."

I lean back against him and sigh happily as Evie grows heavier in my arms. Her name means life. And the moment she arrived, she made ours fuller.... and even busier. I thought I was going to pass out when I found out I was pregnant again when she was only three months old.

Drew seems to be serious about his promise of keeping me full of babies all the time. But I can't pretend I don't love it. And I've still been able to work. Violet has been amazing, helping out when Drew's at work. She's at our house most days so that I can get a few hours work done from home or sneak a quick visit into the office. I haven't been a lead prosecutor on any big cases for a while. But I don't miss it like I thought I would. And there's plenty of time for that when the kids are a little older.

Right now, I'm handling our wild, noisy life just fine.

"She's ready for a nap," I say, looking down at Evie's heavy lids. Her long dark eyelashes flutter against the tops of her round cheeks as she rests her head against my shoulder. "I'll go put her down. Can you get those two in the bath tub?"

"Sure thing, Boss." Drew kisses me, then he runs over and scoops Bailey up under one arm and Emmett under the other. They erupt into peals of laughter as he flies them around the deck like airplanes.

"You were right. Seven years and here we are." I turn Drew's card from my flowers around between my fingers as I sit, snuggled into his side on the decking sofa with just a small firepit and a sky full of stars providing the light. We're enjoying the few hours peace we'll get while all the children are asleep. Emmett and Bailey will sleep until morning, but Evie will likely wake for a feed around midnight.

Drew strokes his hand up and down my arm, his other stretched across the back of the cushions.

"Told you I'd be your date." His lips stretch into a smug smile as his eyes roam over my body, coming to rest on my stomach. "I should have told you I'd have you full of our babies all the time as well. It would have been more accurate."

I poke him in the ribs, making him chuckle.

"Yeah, because that's a great chat-up line when you've just met."

He shrugs. "Would have worked for me if you'd said it."

"Oh yeah?"

"Yeah." His dark brows lower over his eyes as his gaze intensifies to smoldering while he strokes my swollen skin. "You telling me you were going to be full of my babies all the time would have been the best fucking chat-up line."

He gets up from the seat, and then he's on his knees on the floor, pushing my dress up over my bump.

"Best fucking line," he murmurs as he hooks my panties to the side and swipes his tongue over my hot flesh.

"Drew."

I sink my fingers into his hair and push his face down so that he licks me deeper. I tilt my head back and moan as wetness builds between my legs and runs out onto his tongue.

"Jesus, so fucking sweet," he mutters as he peels my panties down my thighs. "Tastes like it's made just for me. Another reason why you're so perfect like this."

His hands cup my belly, and I ride his face with a deep moan. I thought I was horny during my first pregnancy, but it only seems to be getting worse with each one. Drew says Tanner used to have to go home at lunchtime sometimes because Rachel would call him.

Drew's not even made it into the office until lunchtime on two separate occasions because I was practically shaking with the need to come multiple times until I could function.

I've never been so grateful to Violet for offering to take the kids to the park before so I could get on with some work. Except the only work I was doing was working myself up and down Drew's dick as I rode him.

"Just like that." I twist my fingers in his hair as he sucks on my clit.

He strokes my bump as I grind against his face.

"Good girl. You ready to come for me?"

I whimper out a response as he sinks two fingers inside me, curling them against my G-spot. Then I come in a rush against his mouth.

He dives into me, licking and sucking as I pant, and my thighs tremble around his ears.

"Oh God." I clamp down on my lower lip as my orgasm rips through me, sending wave after wave washing through me.

I whimper and push against his mouth.

"One's never enough for you, is it, Boss?"

He grins and rises to his knees, grabbing the back of his T-shirt and dragging it over his head before pushing down his sweatpants.

I can't stop my tongue from darting out to lick my lips at the sight of his cock. He eyes me hungrily as he fists it, squeezing as he gets to the tip, until a fat drop of precum collects on the crown.

His mouth lifts into a sinful smile as he positions his cock perfectly so that the silky bead of liquid drips onto my clit. He hisses through his teeth, holding the base and tapping the head against my sensitive clit as he caresses my bump with his other hand. I jerk as he slaps it against me a little rougher, setting a tremor of desire surging through me.

"You ready to take my cock now?" He looks at me, arching a single dark brow.

"Yes." I writhe against the sofa cushions, trying to get closer so that he'll push forward. I'm so turned on I swear I'll come again the second I feel him inside me.

He rubs the fat head against my clit, smearing more of his arousal over it. The sensation has me gasping out loud.

"Drew. Please!"

"So needy for my cock, aren't you? Is it my cum you want? Is that it? You're so fucking greedy for it, Sophie."

Then he slams inside me without warning, forcing the air from my lungs as I cry out.

"Feels like it's made just for me," he growls as he fucks me without mercy, his hands now gripping onto my hips and pulling me ruthlessly down onto him.

"So greedy for my cum, aren't you?" His jaw ticks, his nostrils flaring as he stares at where I'm stretching to take him.

"I said, so fucking greedy for my cum, aren't you?" His eyes snap back to mine, glinting in the moonlight as he slaps my ass cheek.

I whimper out a moan and nod my head.

His lips curl into a satisfied smile as he continues fucking me with deep thrusts, setting a punishing rhythm that has our skin slapping together and echoing in the open night air.

No one can see us here. No one can hear us.

It's just me and him.

Us.

"Drew!"

My orgasm takes me by surprise, grabbing me by the throat and wringing the air from my lungs. I blink up at him, capturing the dark flash in his eyes as he sinks his teeth into his bottom lip.

"That's it, Mama. Come all over my cock."

He watches me, desire burning in his eyes as I soak his cock and cry out his name.

"So beautiful," he rasps.

He thrusts inside me a few more times, groaning as my body clenches around him.

"I'm going to fill you. Come so deep inside you. Just how you like it."

My chest rises and falls with fast breaths, my heart racing as he places both hands onto my pregnant belly and smiles.

"You ready?"

"Yes," I cry out in desperation.

He thrusts deeper, giving me everything. The intensity in his eyes is hot enough to brand me. I gaze back as he swells inside me.

"This is for you, Mrs. Harper." He grins, his eyes flashing wickedly. "Think you can handle it?"

"You know I can handle you, Mr. Harper," I tease.

He drops his forehead to mine, coming apart with a deep growl.

"I know, Darling," he utters as he empties inside me. "Because you're a flame. My bright, beautiful flame."

**The End.**

**Ready for the final book in The Men Series?
Get your copy of Playing with Mr. Grant here:
https://mybook.to/playingwithmrgrant**

# Elle's Books

Handling Mr. Harper is Book 9 in 'The Men Series', a collection of interconnected standalone stories. They can be read in any order, however, for full enjoyment of the overlapping characters, the suggested reading order is:

Meeting Mr. Anderson – Holly and Jay
Discovering Mr. X – Rachel and Tanner
Drawn to Mr. King – Megan and Jaxon
Captured by Mr. Wild – Daisy and Blake
Pleasing Mr. Parker – Maria and Griffin
Trapped with Mr. Walker – Harley and Reed
Time with Mr. Silver – Rose and Dax
Resisting Mr. Rich – Maddy and Logan
Handling Mr. Harper – Sophie and Drew
Playing with Mr. Grant – Coming Soon
(Also available by Elle, Forget-me-nots and Fireworks, Shona and Trent's story, a novella length prequel to The Men Series)

**Get all of Elle's books here: http://author.to/elle nicoll**

# About Elle

Elle Nicoll is an ex long-haul flight attendant and mum of two from the UK.

After fourteen years of having her head in the clouds whilst working at 38,000ft, she is now usually found with her head between the pages of a book reading or furiously typing and making notes on another new idea for a book boyfriend who is sweet-talking her. Elle finds it funny that she's frequently told she looks too sweet and innocent to write a steamy book, but she never wants to stop. Writing stories about people, passion, and love, what better thing is there?

Because,

Love Always Wins

xxx

To keep up to date with the latest news and releases, find Elle in the following places, and sign up for her newsletter below;

https://landing.mailerlite.com/webforms/landing/m7a1n0

Facebook Reader Group – Love always Wins – https://www.facebook.com/groups/686742179258218

## Website – https://www.ellenicollauthor.com

http://author.to/ellenicoll

facebook.com/ellenicollauthor

instagram.com/ellenicollauthor

bookbub.com/authors/elle-nicoll

pinterest.com/ellenicollauthor

tiktok.com/@authorellenicoll

goodreads.com/author/show/21415735.Elle_Nicoll

# Acknowledgements

I will start as I always do, with the lady who gave me the courage to go on this journey...
TL Swan,
You gave me the courage to follow a dream... thank you.
Sara, my PA, for always checking up on me when I'm deep in my writing cave.
My beta readers; Sara, Rita, and Kelly. Thank you for devouring Drew and Sophie's story and for all of the messages and chats we had about them.
Zee, my wonderful editor for sending me back assignments that earned me a discount off the next book for getting correct! Haha!
Thank you to Abi and Sherri for the gorgeous covers.
Thank you to my ARC, street team, and to Shauna and Becca, and the team at The Author Agency; I couldn't do this without you all!
I am so, so grateful to everyone who has shared my books.

Finally, to you, the reader. Thank you for picking up my book! May reading continue to bring you the wonderful escape we all need some days.
If you enjoyed Handling Mr. Harper then please leave a review on Amazon and share it with your book besties. It helps indie authors so much.
Until the next book...
**Elle x**

www.ingramcontent.com/pod-product-compliance
Lightning Source LLC
Chambersburg PA
CBHW050603170726
48283CB00001B/82